ANCIENT REUNION

Book One:
Raven

SUE PATERSON

Interior formatting by Rachel Bostwick

ISBN: 979-8-9872345-0-1

DEDICATION

To my Native Family worldwide
Thank you for your strength, wisdom
and unconditional love

TRADITIONAL PUEBLO BLESSING

Hold on to what is good,
even if it is a handful of earth.
Hold on to what you believe,
even when it is a tree that stands by itself.
Hold on to what you must do,
even when it is a long way from here.
Hold on to life,
even when it is easier letting go.
Hold on to my hand,
even if someday
I'll be gone away from you.

Author Unknown

1683 AD - North Fork Río de los Pinos, in the foothills of the Rocky Mountains

Raven sat crouched and huddled under the rock ledge. Her stomach rumbled at the distant memory of dinner.

Was it only yesterday that I stood in my village and welcomed the new day?

Was it only yesterday I looked up and saw Strong Eagle step out of the trees, a smile on his face and desire in his eyes?

Where is he now? Did he get away?

Was it only yesterday I sat with my mother and sisters in the circle of women, bright sun shining down as I sewed beads on my wedding dress, listening to village gossip?

Oh Mother, what happened?

How I long for the warmth of the sun now...

ONE

Raven opened her eyes as the first hint of daylight danced shadows on the leather walls of the teepee. Smiling, she adjusted her hip against the unexpected warmth of Chitto, her little brother. He had been crawling in with her as the nights grew colder. Close by; soft snoring sounds assured her that her sisters slept. Nearby her mother stirred, and as Aiyani did every morning, reached over, touching the empty spot where her husband used to lay. She tucked the fur around Chitto, then crept out of her sleeping hide and unlaced the door.

Morning dew caressed her face as she walked barefoot to the edge of the village, toes leaving soft imprints in the dirt. Raising her arms to the east, Raven stretched her fingers to the sky, and reached for the golden light that trickled through the treetops. Eyes closed, imagining rainbow light as it gathered from the mountaintops, streams, and new sunlight, she turned in each direction and with each breath, felt the rainbow energy flow into her crown. Like a river, it coursed through her body, deepening as it settled into her womb. Raven paused, greeting the new life that grew inside her, wondering how it would feel to be a mother. With her next breath, energy moved through her hips and legs, the bottoms of her feet and into the Earth, like roots of a tree, pushing down, winding around rocks, and dropping into deep, crystalline waters. Raven whispered a prayer of gratitude for the ancestors who held the sacred space that allowed her to walk on the Earth this day. She wiggled her toes, sensing the energy of the earth as it flowed back up through her body, caressing the new life in her belly, then smiled as it rose through her heart and crown, through her fingertips, and back to the heavens and to the new day. Coming full circle, she held her hands to the sky and scooped up the warmth in the palms of her hands, and held them first to her crown, her belly, and heart whispering: "Part of earth and all of life."

Raven opened her eyes and looked to the path leading out of the village, hoping to see her father standing there. But not today. Lusio left with traders months ago to guide them across the mountains. They were a peaceful tribe, sustaining themselves with fishing and hunting. Afternoons were spent gathering berries, roots, and herbs in the nearby forest, which they offered to traders who brought brightly colored beads and trinkets to barter. But traders had come less often, and there were rumors of hostile tribes and renegade soldiers. And today, a feeling of uneasiness puzzled Raven.

Sensing motion in the trees, she looked up as Strong Eagle came into view. Tall and sinewy, clad only in a loincloth, his black hair hung loosely around his shoulders. Bow and arrow in hand, to her he was strength and gentleness all in one. Eyes locked in a gaze; Raven felt a warmth flow through her that made her eager for the evening. Strong Eagle turned to a shout in the woods, then smiled back at Raven, waved and disappeared into the trees.

As the village came alive around her, Raven turned to the river, listening as the water from the mountain's snowmelt lapped at the riverbank. The tall, marshy grass growing along the water made a soft whistling sound with the breeze's rise and fall, carrying the sweet scent of the grass. A rocky cliff filled with crevices and overhangs stood across the river, protecting the village from the west. Where the river narrowed, Strong Eagle built a secret bridge with fallen logs. They would meet there just before sunset.

Sounds of chatter drew Raven down the river path to the bathing hole, where she joined other women and children from the village. Dropping her dress on the ground, she waded in, immersing herself until only her hair floated. Popping out of the water, the sun sparkling on her face, she met her mother's questioning eyes.

"Raven, you're getting rounder and softer by the day," Aiyani said as she rubbed yucca root into Aponi's hair. "Too much flatbread?"

Her sisters giggled into their hands. "Too much of something." Morning Dove looked down as Raven tossed her hair over her shoulder, glaring up at them. She had seen their heads bobbing in and out of the grass, spying on her and Strong Eagle.

Aiyani, aware of her growing belly, had been watching Raven. She knew her daughter would marry Strong Eagle, but the gossip worried her.

Chatter filled the air as the women and girls drifted back to the village, gathering around the community fire. Aiyani filled the large black kettle with fresh water and herbs, then glanced up as Running Elk passed by, almost tripping as he glanced over at Morning Dove, who watched him out of the corner of her eye. At Aiyani's glare, Morning Dove looked down, but not before Aiyani saw the smile between them.

"Running Elk," Aiyani called. The sharpness in her voice made him stop in his tracks. "Help me with this." Running Elk lifted the kettle and slid it onto the fire, grinning. Unable to resist his infectious smile, she shooed him away, chuckling as she gathered a bundle of cut grass and joined Raven, who sat under the large oak, a basket of beads on the ground next to her, and a white leather hide in her lap. Raven looked up and smiled as her mother sat down, tucking her feet under her fringed leather dress. "That's beautiful, Raven." Aiyani reached down, running her fingers over the soft leather. A vibrant beaded sun was emerging under Raven's fingers.

"Last night, I dreamt of my wedding dress. I saw a sun with red, orange, and yellow beads here." She lay her hand over her chest. "It celebrates my favorite time of day. Each morning the birth of the sun brings many chances for joy and love."

"You amaze me." Aiyani gazed down at the dress, in awe of her daughter's beadwork, sought after by traders and other villagers. "When will it be done? Should I plan a wedding feast?"

Raven pulled a red bead snug, revealing a ray of the sun. "Yes, soon."

Looking up, they smiled as Aiyani's youngest daughter Aponi appeared, a doll made from corn silk tucked under her arm. "What are you doing, Mama?"

"Making a new belt." Aiyani smoothed the long strands of damp grass over her lap, counting out twenty-one strands.

"Why do you do that? Count them?"

"The grass that grows along the rivers brings sweetness to us." Aiyani held out the grass as Aponi bent over to smell it. "Braided this way, we honor our journey in this life."

"Journey?" Aiyani looked over and met Raven's eyes. They smiled at the memory of a similar conversation they had when Raven was a young girl.

"It's an old tradition passed on from our ancestors." Aiyani held the grass up for Aponi to see. "You take twenty-one strands, knot it together at one end, then divide that into three bundles of seven strands each."

Aponi watched her mother. "Can I try?"

"Watch me make this belt, and then I will show you how." Aponi grinned, settling in next to her mother.

"Why seven, Mama?" She asked, gently touching the grass.

"The first seven strands represent the seven generations behind us, our ancestors, sometimes as much as two hundred years ago. It represents what our grandmothers and grandfathers have woven into our spirits, bodies, and minds. Who we are and what we are is because of them, so we remember and honor them in this way."

"Ohhhh." Aponi's eyes got big. "What about these?" She pointed to the middle bunch.

"This bundle represents the seven sacred teachings. Do you remember what they are?"

"No." Aponi giggled, her small hands covering her mouth.

"I know." Morning Dove turned from the group of friends she was talking to. "Love, Respect, Honesty, Courage, Wisdom, Truth and Humility."

"But what does that mean, Mama?" Aponi asked, puzzled.

Aiyani paused. "Our ancestors gave us these seven teachings to feed our souls and to help us be better people. The most important one for you to know right now is Love. It's limitless, like the stars, and leads to Respect, or how we treat others. Do we honor who they are - their feelings, wishes, and traditions, even if they differ from us? By not judging, being polite, and listening, we show everyone respect."

"Like when the traders come?" Morning Dove asked, joining her mother and sisters. She pulled out a bunch of grass and counted out twenty-one strands.

"Yes." Aiyani tugged on the braid. "They come from a different time and place. We can show them respect, be their friends, and still be who we are."

"Traders haven't been through in some time." Raven paused and looked up at her mother. "It's been at least six moons since we saw Andre and Jacqo... just after Papa left." She looked over and smiled at Morning Dove, who blushed at the mention of Jacqo.

Aiyani glanced towards the path leading out of the village with a distant look.

"Are you worried, Mama?" Raven asked. "About the rumors of soldiers?"

"Who knows what will come?" Aiyani looked into Raven's eyes. "Each moment is a lifetime. If my last moment is looking into the beautiful faces of my daughters, it would be a blessing."

"But Mama." Aponi squirmed, touching the grass, bringing her mother's attention back to the task at hand. "What about the last bunch?"

"Oh." Aiyani picked up the last seven strands of grass, bringing her attention back to Aponi.

"The last bunch represents the next seven generations. My children, your children, and so on..."

"My children?" A grin crept out of the edge of Aponi's mouth.

"Yes." Aiyani laughed. "One day, you'll have children, and they'll have children of their own. That is what these seven strands represent. It is important because everything we do to Mother Earth today will one day affect them. We live in a way that the Earth will nurture future generations, just as it does us now." Aponi watched as Aiyani picked up the grass and began braiding the three bundles.

"Woven together in this way," Aiyani said, "the braids represent where we came from, who we are now, and where we are going. You can wear the braids as belts or let it dry and burn it in a ceremony, breathing in the sacred messages of our ancestors."

Aponi pulled out some grass from the basket, counting out twenty-one strands, then reached up and whispered in her mother's ear.

"A new belt for your doll – that's a wonderful idea Aponi." Aiyani looked around at her daughters, quietly crafting, surrounded by the sounds of laughter and chatter amongst the tribe.

Suddenly Chitto, Aiyani's youngest child, ran up to them. He held his pudgy fists stretched out in front of him, eyes sparkling with excitement.

"Pick a hand, Mother."

Aiyani's eyes lit up in surprise, hand over her mouth. "What's this, Chitto?"

"It's a surprise! Pick one!" His body squirmed in anticipation.

Raven watched as her mother chose Chitto's right hand. He opened it and in the palm was a silver rock, flecked with mica, which shot out beads of light as the sunlight hit it.

"Oh, Chitto, that's beautiful. Is it for me?" She took it out of his hand.

"Yes, for you, mother." He grinned, face smudged with dirt, hair in his eyes.

"But Chitto, what's in the other hand?" Aiyani raised her eyebrows.

He opened his left palm, which was empty, and bellowed out a laugh. "You chose well Mother."

"Well, I have you, don't I?" She pulled him into a hug, tickling him.

Chitto shrieked with laughter, then wiggled out of her grasp and ran towards his group of friends who were busily attaching a cornhusk to a tree. Laying her hand over her belly, Raven watched the whole interaction with amusement. *I can't wait to tell Mama about the baby.*

The day had been peaceful. In the late afternoon, the air balmy and the sun waning, the community came together and sat around the fire, each holding a steaming bowl of buffalo stew. Young girls brought around baskets of hot flatbread. Raven smiled up at her young friend in thanks, watching as Chitto and his friends threw pretend arrows made from sticks at the cornhusk they attached to the tree, dreaming of the day they would be old enough to have their own bow and arrows. Her gaze drifted across the fire, where Strong Eagle was in earnest conversation with his father, Lone Elk. Feeling her gaze, they both looked up at her and smiled. Blushing, she smiled back. Soon it would be time to meet Strong Eagle at the bridge. Raven left the circle to prepare for her lover. As she returned from the bathing hole, she stopped at a tall lavender bush in full bloom and plucked off several blossoms. Rubbing them between her fingers, she brushed her hands through her hair and along the back of her neck.

Strong Eagle smiled as she parted the grass and stepped through. Hand in hand, they fell naturally in step with each other as they crossed the bridge. Raven, smiling at the eagerness in his eyes, put her foot into his cupped hands, then grabbed outcroppings of stone, boosting herself up and over the top onto a large flat rock, hidden under an overhang. Strong Eagle scrambled up after her.

Raven pulled her dress over her head, then turned to see Strong Eagle toss his loincloth on the ground. "You're so beautiful." He pulled her close, and kneeling together, they lay on the large flat stone, still warm from the afternoon sun, making love with an urgency neither of them understood. Strong Eagle cradled Raven in his arms, his breath warm on her neck. Together they lay, watching the sun go down over the village.

Raven took his hands in hers, placing them on her belly. "Strong Eagle."

"Did I not please you, my love?" He tickled her, then leaned in to nuzzle her neck.

Giggling, she said: "I want you to see something."

Concern flickered in his eyes and he propped himself up on one elbow. She sat up, took his hand again, and placed it on the bulge in her belly. His eyes grew big.

"A child? You carry my child?" Sitting upright, he pulled his hands away with a jerk.

"Yes. I hope our baby has your eyes. They are so beautiful." Raven searched his face. "Does this trouble you?"

"No!" He gathered her in an embrace, running his fingers through her hair. "No, I am pleased. She will be lovely like you. And strong." Tears filled his eyes. "Oh, Raven. A child."

The distant howl of a coyote filled the air as night fell around them. "It's Running Elk's first night to guard the village." Strong Eagle squeezed her shoulder. "I must check on him."

"Are you worried?"

"It's been too long since traders came through." He stood, reaching for his loincloth. "Last time Andre and Jacqo came through, they warned us of rogue soldiers that deserted from the Spanish Army in the south. My father and the rest of the council decided to post guards at the entrances of the village."

"He's so young."

"I know, but he insisted, eager to show his manhood." He leaned down and kissed her, lingering. "Better go."

Strong Eagle stopped midway across the bridge and pointed to a shooting star, which sped across the night sky. "Our star." Pulling Raven close, he stroked her belly. "A child, Raven. I'm so happy." Outside of her teepee, he hugged her. "Soon, we will be together every night." He kissed the top of her head, then cupped her face in his hands. "I spoke with father tonight at the fire. He said we could share his teepee until ours is complete."

Raven's eyes glistened. "My heart is full of joy." She stood and watched as he jogged down the path. The last thing she remembered was lying snug in soft blankets and furs made of hides, dreaming about her wedding day.

She woke to the sound of Strong Eagle's voice. "Raven, get out!" he yelled. "Go to the rocks! I'll find you."

Startled awake, breath frozen and heart pounding, chaos erupted around her. Men shouted as the clang of weapons exploded in the air. Women screamed and children cried.

"My family." Hands shaking, she shoved her feet into her moccasins and pushed open the flap of the teepee, and sprung out into the dark just as Aiyani ran out of the trees and fell to the ground, an arrow in her back.

"Mama!"

"Run, Raven," Aiyani gasped, blood coming out of her mouth. "Run."

At the sound of footsteps, Raven jumped behind a tree. Barked scratched her face as she peeked around and saw a strange man staggering in her direction, eyes wild, a hatchet held high over his head. Willing her feet to move, she turned, parted the grass, and fled.

TWO

It was the crickets that reminded Raven she was still alive. Huddled in the rock crevice all night, she drifted in and out of exhausted, uneasy sleep. Limbs heavy, her body didn't want to move, but the bulge in her belly pressed into her back. She needed to pee. Her legs trembled as she stretched her body into the morning sun. Running her fingers through her thick, black hair, now tangled with grass and sticks, the memory of the chaos from the night before returned.

"Strong Eagle?" She called out. *Why didn't he come?*

Mind racing, Raven curled her toes against her moccasins and climbed down, collapsing as she hit the ground. Body shaking, she pulled herself up. At the bridge, she leaned in, listening. Dread filled her at the silence from the normally vibrant sounds of her tribe. Hidden in the grass, she walked toward the village.

"Argh." Icy water filled her moccasins. She looked down as her feet sunk into the mud along the riverbank. Pulling them free, she reached down and snatched the laces as her moccasins disappeared. Raven tied the wet shoes to her grass belt with a sigh of relief, letting her fingers linger for a second. It was the one her mother had woven and given to her yesterday.

"Mama..."

Paralyzed with fear, the need to know drove her forward. Grass enfolding each step, Raven listened for any signs of life. The moccasins came loose, falling at her feet with a wet thud, tripping her. Cocooned in the soft grass, she stared at the sky.

Get up. You must get up.

As she retied the moccasins to her belt, her fingers brushed against a small lump in the secret pocket underneath. Reaching in, she pulled out the small, gray stone her mother had given her as a child and traced the etchings that formed a picture of a face.

"That's you, Raven... hair a mess and berries on your face." Her mother laughed. "Always up to something." In a quiet moment next to the fire that evening, Aiyani placed the talisman in the palm of her hand and curled her fingers over it. "It never lies. Carry this with you always."

And she had. Her fingers tightened around the stone, the memory of her mother's voice overwhelming. Tears clouded her vision as she put one foot in front of the other and kept going. Parting the last bit of grass, Raven stepped into the village. The smell of death, mingled with odors of blood and excrement, hit her. Leaning over, she retched, her world forever changed.

Like a ghost she moved along the path, pausing at the teepee of Strong Eagle and his father, Lone Elk. Reaching to untie the door, she jerked her hand back as if it were fiery hot.

"Is this a dream?" Raven inched along until she reached the center of the village. Dazed, she stared at the red and orange embers still glowing in the firepit, then looked around, paling at the scene. Women lay scattered on the ground, skirts bunched around their waist. Bloodied children lay nearby, the tortured cry of death on their faces. Her breath caught as she looked at the young girl who held out the basket of bread to her yesterday, now huddled against the firepit.

Hand clasped over her mouth, she silenced a cry as she looked towards the woods. Chitto lay in the dirt next to a tree, the same one he shot practice arrows at earlier, cornhusk still attached to the trunk. He was still as if asleep; the pretend arrow clutched in his hand. Knees weak, she closed her eyes in horror, tears squeezing out as they ran down her cheeks. This had been not just a destruction of her village, but of her people. Tears squeezed out of her eyes, running down her cheeks. She took a step towards the woman nearest her.

"Nooooo." The arm of her sister, Morning Dove, distinct with the yellow beaded bracelet Raven made for her, was sticking out from underneath another woman's body. Grief ran through her like a river threatening to overflow its banks.

Suddenly, the hair on the back of her neck prickled. Speaking in a language she didn't understand, men's voices grew louder as they walked out of the woods and towards the firepit. Stepping back into the shadows, she watched as they rustled through the food cache, indifferent to the bodies lying on the ground, laughing as they shoved food into their mouths. The sound of chewing fueled icy shards of rage in her. A scream built, threatening to explode. She grabbed a long stick off the ground and took a step forward. Stick raised, she heard Aiyani's voice. "No! Run, Raven. Get away."

In a haze, her head filled with the men's laughter, Raven turned and ran towards the teepees. Vision blurred by tears, she tripped, crying out as she fell next to her dead mother.

Hands shaking, she stroked Aiyani's hair. "Oh, Mother, I'm sorry." Panicked as the voices grew close, she pushed herself up and ducked behind Strong Eagle and Lone Elk's teepee, unlacing the back flap. Inside, she grabbed a pottery cup and bowl, hastily tying them to her belt. Spinning in circles, she tried to think. On impulse, she picked up a white owl feather off the family altar, pulled out several strands of her hair, and wound it around the shaft. Blowing into the feather, she placed it on Strong Eagle's sleeping hide, where he laid his head. Staring longingly at the space they would have shared after they married, Raven bent down and picked up his sleeping fur, wrapping it around her shoulders. "If you live, I will wait for you."

She froze at the crunch of footsteps, which stopped at the teepee in which she stood. One man swore as he fumbled with the front flap. Grabbing the bundle in the corner, Raven stepped out of the back, quickly lacing it up. As she heard them enter, she turned one last time to glance at the village she loved, then disappeared into the grass.

Raven's heart pounded as she fled from the village. Just around the first bend, she halted at the sound of rustling bushes and footsteps behind her. Breathless, she stepped behind a tree, pressing into it. The whizz of urine followed by a loud sigh made her shudder with rage. Inching around the tree, she watched the back of the soldier as he returned to the village. Stepping out onto the trail, the bundle she carried caught on a branch, pulling it back like a slingshot. It snapped against the tree when it came loose. The footsteps paused. The soldier stood listening and then turned, looking over his shoulder. Above her, a family of birds squabbled, making the branches sway as pinecones fell and rolled onto the path. The soldier shrugged and continued walking. Trembling with relief, Raven stayed near the trees as she went south along the river.

Gradually, the sun rose further in the sky and the voices grew dimmer until all she heard was the rush of the river. Brown velvety cattails on long green stalks hung out over the trail, reaching for the sun. She touched the soft, downy head of the cattail. It had been just a day ago that her mother collected a basketful of them, excited about their strong medicine. Raven rubbed the powder with her fingers and put some on her tongue. Grimacing at the bitterness, she spat it out, pushed them aside so she could pass, and then stopped. Pulling out several strands of hair, she wrapped them around the branch. A few steps ahead, she tied more strands on another.

I'm wasting my time... Strong Eagle would have died fighting for his village. Minutes later, she spotted mud formed by water pooling under a bush. Pulling her moccasin off, she stepped in it, leaving her footprint.

I must not give up. If Strong Eagle lives, he will find me - I will protect my child. I must go. But where?

THREE

Sharp needles burned his eyes as he opened them in a squint. Closing them against the scorching afternoon heat, Strong Eagle licked his lips, but his tongue felt only dry cracked skin. Distorted images drifted through his mind as he floated in and out of consciousness.

How long have I been here?

"Raven?" He whispered, throat raw and parched.

Coolness allowed him to open his eyes as the clouds drifted over the sun. Looking around, he saw only mesquite and juniper bushes. On a large rock a few inches away, a lizard sat, silent but alert. A yellow, black-bellied chickadee flew down, buzzed around Strong Eagle's head, then perched itself next to the lizard. He stared at the creatures, their shapes blurry. The quiet was deafening.

"Oooh." Lifting his arm, he winced as he touched a large bump on his head, then looked at a jagged tear from elbow to wrist, covered with dried blood. His broken bow lay just out of reach, with arrows scattered around it.

Must get up... He tried to bend his legs, but something heavy lay across them. "So hot." He tried bending his legs again and gave up, everything blurring in the scorching sun.

"Raven." His mind wandered to the day he knew he would love her forever.

Hidden in tall grass near the river, knife cool in his hand as he carves the soft wood, an eagle emerging. Sounds of chatter. Bending the grass, looking out... Raven and her sister Morning Dove, laughing as they go to the river for water, the sloshing of almost empty jugs hanging carelessly off their shoulders. Passing, just inches away. Ten years old and hypnotized as she walks, her long, black, shiny hair brushing her hips. Face reddening, hot and cold running through his body, reaching down and touching that new sensation. The girls walk around the bend and out of sight. Years later, sitting in the same grass carving arrow, watching Raven sew yellow and orange beads on a dress, a bright sun emerging on white leather. She looks up, her smile a promise. A ten-year-old love, now a forever friendship.

Fragmented memories of the night before ran through his mind. *A baby? My baby?*

The silky touch of her hair on his lips and the faint smell of lavender as he kissed the top of her head, tears of joy meeting on their cheeks as they said good night. Then feeling uneasy, needed to hurry, check on Running Elk. In his teepee gathering his bow and arrows the soft hoot of an owl caught his attention. Standing, he listened. The sound came again – not an owl, it was Running Elks voice, a call of danger, a cry for help. Suddenly, the clang of knives on hatchets, shouting, and screaming exploded around him.

"Raven, get out," he yelled as he ran towards the chaos. Soldiers came out of the darkness with crossbow arrows and hatchets flying. Spinning around, plunging his knife into the belly of a soldier, the man falling dead at his feet. Then up and running to the entrance of the village.

He pushed again against the weight on his legs, but overcome with weakness, let go, his mind drifting into a haze. "I will die here." Eyes closed in the heat; his world went blank.

Each step heavy, Raven stopped every few minutes and looked back. *What if I had just stayed hidden in the rocks? Did anyone else survive?* Every time she took a step back, needing to know. But each time, she was flooded with the sound of the men chewing... swallowing... the bloodied hatchet held over the soldier's head, wild look in his eyes. Stomach clenched in fear, she continued, moving further away from the village.

FOUR

Dust skittered around the brothers' feet as they stepped off the final descent of the mountain trail and turned to the narrow dirt path leading to the Native village. Andre brushed the steep rocky cliff with his calloused hand, looking down at the deep ravine of juniper and mesquite on the other side. Jacqo, the slighter of the two, led a mule piled high with gear. Hungry and tired, their heads ached after drinking the last of their fermented corn beer the night before.

"Watch your step," Andre said as the mule stepped dangerously close to the drop off into the ravine.

Jacqo looked back, his hat falling to his shoulders, and tugged on Willie's lead, pulling him closer to the rocks.

"Should be there soon, midday at the latest." Andre tilted his wide-brimmed hat back and looked up at the sky, then kicked a stone away with the toe of his boot. "Hungry... haven't seen anyone in weeks."

"It'll be good to see friends." Jacqo's stomach grumbled at the thought of the big pot over the fire, always full of stew.

I hope she's there... Jacqo recalled the sweet young woman he met a few months before on their last trip. Eyes downcast, he could picture her smile as she glanced up, flirting with him next to the fire.

Morning Dove... Has she married?

Sweat trickled down his back under a blue chambray shirt. Itchy, he couldn't wait to bathe in the river and get some food in his belly. The past ten years of being voyageurs had taken its toll. They traversed mountains, traded with natives, and paddled canoes for the fur traders. Just survived. He tugged on Willie's lead, urging the mule forward.

"I've been thinking." Andre stopped and wet his kerchief from the half-empty waterskin, wiping the sweat off his brow.

"Oh?" Jacqo looked up at his brother as Willie snorted in displeasure at the abrupt stop.

"There's land out east," Andre began. "Last time we were out that way, I talked to a guy, a French Huguenot who remembered seeing the flyers Father printed and distributed around town, you know, about the rebellion?"

Jacqo looked up from the mule with curious eyes. In sharp contrast to his brother, he wore leather knee-high moccasins and pantaloons that buttoned just above them. His long brown hair hung midway down his back in a braid.

"It was good to hear about our people, our history." Andre hooked the waterskin back on his belt. "Said he was sick of the trails but especially tired of politics with the Coureur des Bois. He wanted to settle." Andre scratched his face through his long beard, streaked with golden strands from the sun. "It might be nice to be around our people. I'm going on twenty-seven. We're young enough to start over, have something to call our own."

"I don't know." Jacqo wiped the sweat off his face with his shirtsleeve. "I mean, back when we had no food, it was good of the Coureur de Bois to take us on." He smiled at the memory. "Runners of the Woods... we mighta died, if not for them. They taught us well - well enough to take off on our own. But the Natives have been good to us." He looked down, not wanting to meet Andre's eyes. "I don't know if I see myself settling down yet. I miss Mother and Father every day but going there won't bring 'em back."

"You're becoming more Native than French." Andre reached out to put his hand on his brother's shoulder, surprised when he pulled back. "I don't know, Jacqo... you're still young, only nineteen. I'm tired." He took his hat off and wiped his balding head. "We could have land for free and a home among our people. Settling down feels good." Jacqo studied his brother's face for a moment, then tugged on Willie's lead and kept walking.

"Jacqo, look at this." Andre stopped, pointing at the ground, trampled with footprints. "It's not the footprints of the moccasins the Indians wear." Without making a sound, Jacqo took the musket off the mule and snugged it into a leather sling over his shoulder, then led Willie into a brushy cove nearby, tying him to a branch. Thorns on the mesquite bush snagged his pants. He untangled himself, then stooped down and retied his moccasins. Reaching over, Jacqo traced a footprint with his finger and looked up at his brother in concern.

Andre, chiseled face brown and leathery from years on the trail, pulled the bladder sack of water off the mule, knocking the extra rope loose. He picked it up, recoiled it, and handed it to his brother. Walking toe to heel in silence, their blue eyes, locked in alarm, became darker as years of silent communication between the two kicked in. Andre broke the stare and raised his fingers to his mouth, whistling a bird call that would let the tribe know friends were here. They waited for a return call, but none came.

The air was hot and still, filled with a growing stench with each step. Andre whistled again. No response. Backs to the rocks, they edged around the bend, then stopped in shock. Bodies of Indians and soldiers lay on the ground, weapons scattered where they had fallen. Hands gripping their knives, they stepped around the bodies.

A yellow, black-bellied chickadee flew up from the ravine and fluttered around them, buzzing Jacqo's head. "What the hell?" He brushed the bird away, then watched as it flew back down into the ravine, landing on a rock. Many of their Indian friends believed chickadees were a bringer of messages. He looked again. Near the rock, under a large juniper branch, lay the body of their friend, Strong Eagle.

Jacqo jabbed his brother in the back and pointed. Nodding in agreement, they slid down the ravine towards

28

their friend, feet catching on juniper branches which slowed their fall. Strong Eagle lay motionless. Jacqo bent over his friend and shook his shoulders.

"Strong Eagle, wake up! It's Jacqo."

Seeing his burnt face and lips, Jacqo reached up, taking the waterskin from Andre. He dribbled water onto Strong Eagle's lips, so dry it ran down his chin and into the folds of his neck, then groaned as Andre wrested the large branch off his legs.

Jacqo shook his shoulders again. "Strong Eagle! Wake up!" Untying the handkerchief around his neck, he soaked it with water, then wiped Strong Eagle's forehead. He trickled more water on his lips, swollen shut. They opened just enough to let drops of water pass. Strong Eagle groaned again, then coughed as the water reached his parched throat. He opened his eyes, seeing doubles and triples of Jacqo's face. Startled, he lifted his arm to defend himself, but it fell to the ground.

"Calme-toi," Jacqo cooled Strong Eagle's face with the wet handkerchief.

Strong Eagle opened his eyes again. "Jacqo?"

"Oui, mon ami, oui," Jacqo murmured, smoothing Strong Eagle's hair out of his eyes.

On the rock where the chickadee landed, the small lizard pulsed his body, watching them with intense eyes.

Andre lifted Strong Eagle's legs, bending them and checking for injuries. He noted the jagged cut on Strong

Eagle's left arm, which had dried and crusted over. "Good to go."

Jacqo unrolled the rope, dropping one end near Andre, then climbed up the ravine.

Andre looped and tied the rope around his waist, then bent over and in one motion, picked up Strong Eagle and hoisted him over his shoulder. Bracing his boots in the dirt, Andre wrapped his arms around his friend, whose hands dangled limply down his back, and trudged up the ravine while Jacqo pulled.

At the top, they returned to the shady cove and lay Strong Eagle in the soft grass near Willie. Andre removed his handkerchief, doused it with water, and laid it around Strong Eagle's neck. Reaching over, he poured water on Jacqo's, who laid it over his friend's forehead. Strong Eagle groaned again as Jacqo drizzled more water into his mouth.

In trips past, not only had Strong Eagle traded the finest bows, arrows, and wood carvings, but welcomed them with food and drink. The brothers always left with plentiful rations for the trip ahead. Strong Eagle's father, Lone Elk, was the tribal chief, but he was aging. They watched over time as Strong Eagle prepared to take over. He was not only their friend, rare in these parts but a good ally. They would save him if they could.

Andre knelt on the ground next to Strong Eagle. "Toss me a blanket. Who knows how long he was out there in that hot sun. Don't want him to get chilled."

Jacqo pulled out a tattered brown blanket from a knapsack on Willie and tossed it down. "We should check out the village." He stroked Willie's thick mane as the mule's lips quivered, then retied his lead to a stronger branch.

Andre nodded, standing. He leaned the water pouch up against Strong Eagle's hip where he could reach it. "Right, let's go." They stepped out onto the path. "Doesn't feel good." He brushed the toe of his boot over footprints in the dirt.

FIVE

Strong Eagle opened his eyes and followed the mule's snorts as he pulled on the rope. Staring at the blurred shape of the strange animal, he wondered - *Am I dead?*

Drifting back into a restless sleep, he saw his mother's face. "If only you had lived..." Strong Eagle had never known her, but Lone Elk and the tribe told him of her kindness and beauty. Yet every time he saw a woman hug her child, yearning flooded him. The tribe had been good to him and Lone Elk after his mother died giving birth. "I just wish..."

Her touch was feather soft as she stroked his cheeks, brushing hair out of his eyes. "I'm here now, son." He reached out to touch her but felt only empty space.

Warm breath touched his other cheek. He heard Lone Elk's voice in his ear. "Wake up, son. It's not your time."

"Father? I don't understand."

"Son, listen to me," Lone Elk whispered urgently. "It's up to you now." Strong Eagle knew he needed to listen, to wake. But this was a feeling that he craved his entire life.

He felt the softness of his mother's lips as she kissed his forehead. "I'm so proud of you," she said softly. "Now, open your eyes and go find her. She waits for you."

"Don't go," he mumbled, hot tears burning in his eyes. "Don't..."

Shivering, he opened his eyes and looked up. At the shady cove entrance, the same yellow chickadee he had seen earlier sat on a branch. Squeezing his eyes shut against tears, he willed his parents to return. But he knew they were gone. Strong Eagle looked again. The branch, now empty, gently bounced up and down.

A bird... I'm sure it was there. Usually brown - seen some yellow ones. Traders said the yellow ones are from the north.

"Traders?" Feeling the pressure of something against his hip, he reached down. "Water." Hand trembling, he pulled it up and tilted it into his mouth. Most of it ran down his chin, but he managed a few sips, soothing his parched throat.

Jacqo and Andre - they're real.

"Jacqo?" He called out. "Andre?" All he heard was Willie snorting and pawing the dirt.

SIX

Andre tied his handkerchief over his nose and mouth against the stench. A buzzard swept in low. With their backs to the rocks and hands gripping their knives, they crept around the last bend. Bodies and weapons littered the ground. Andre held his finger to his mouth, nodding his head forward. Silently they inched to the entrance, passing under the old oak where Lone Elk always sat, greeting newcomers. The log was empty. A few more steps in, they stopped in their tracks.

"Oh my God," Jacqo gasped, hand over his mouth, holding back vomit that wanted to spew out. "Oh my God, Oh my God..."

Bodies of women and children, carelessly used and bloodied, were piled on top of each other. A large black cooking pot hung over the firepit, scorched and smoking over the glow of embers. Too late, they heard the rustle of branches above them. A man dropped from the tree, tackling Jacqo. They hit the ground hard. Jacqo's knife skittered out of reach, and his musket fell off his shoulder.

"Jacqo!" Andre scrambled after his brother. His hands brushed the attacker's coarse linen shirt, but he couldn't get a grip on it. He didn't hear the second man sneak up behind him. A few seconds later, pinned under his attacker's knee, Andre looked over helplessly as Jacqo and the other man rolled in a death grip towards the fire pit. Andre looked up and stared into the black eyes of his attacker, grinning at him with a toothless smile, spittle running down his scrubby whiskered chin. With one hand, he pushed back Andre's head, baring his throat. In his other hand was a silver blade, raised high and glittering in the sun. With a smirk, the attacker brought down his arm.

I will die a failure. It was my job to protect Jacqo, Andre thought as he stared death in the face.

A loud bang exploded behind them. Andre's breath burst out as the soldier fell on him. He pushed the man off and jumped up, chest heaving. Strong Eagle stood at the entrance, musket nestled against his shoulder, barrel smoking.

"Andre!" Jacqo yelled.

Turning to his brother's voice, Andre saw the flash of a blade. He pulled his knife from the sheath at his belt and jumped on Jacqo's attacker. Grabbing the soldier's long, greasy black hair, he yanked the man's head back and with one swipe, cut his throat. Blood sprayed in a large arc, soaking Jacqo's shirt and covering his face.

Andre kicked the soldier aside. "Saloperie!" He spat at the soldier. Taking Jacqo's hand, he helped him up, then turned and spat on the soldier again. "Trash."

"Andre, who, what?" Jacqo wiped the blood out of his eyes.

"Those deserters we heard about," Andre said. "They wear the uniform of the Spanish army." The brothers spun to a sound behind them. Strong Eagle stood; eyes glazed as he stared at the destruction. Swooning, his hand fell open, and the musket fell to the ground with a thud. Andre and Jacqo ran to their friend, catching him. Then, for the second time that day, Andre flung Strong Eagle over his shoulder.

"There's a place over by the teepees." Jacqo led as Andre stepped around the bodies of the dead soldiers.

He lay Strong Eagle on a grassy space, sheltered by a teepee on either side. "He'll be okay here. Let's see what else is out there, or who." Andre stepped on the path and glanced over. His breath caught at the sight of the body of a woman, face down on the ground. Jaw tightening, he knelt next to her and pulled a crossbow arrow out of her back. Swallowing hard, he turned her over. "It's Aiyani."

Jacqo stood watching as emotion flooded his brother's face, a face generally void of expression. They knew Aiyani's husband, Lusio, had left with traders and not returned the last time they were through. He also remembered how Andre's eyes followed her.

"She was trying to get away." Andre sat motionless for a moment, then picked her up and carried her over near the fire pit. He lay her on the ground and sat next to her with his face in his hands. "Nothing left Jacqo. Nothing."

Jacqo rested his hand on Andre's shoulder, then offered his brother a hand. "Need to get this done." They searched the rest of the village, a short while later returning to the firepit. "Can't believe it." Face pale, Jacqo took a long drink of water. "I'll get Willie."

"Grab the spades," Andre said, looking over at Aiyani's body. "I'll start digging."

Minutes later, Jacqo coaxed the scared animal into the village. Willie dug his hooves into the dirt and threw his head up, violently jerking the rope. "Calme toi," Jacqo whispered, nudging the mule around the fire pit. Willie snorted as Jacqo led him into the shade near the teepees, tying him to a tree. He took a waterskin off Willie, then stooped and placed it next to Strong Eagle, sighing in relief at the easy rise and fall of his friend's chest. His stomach growled. An empty belly always reminded him of his boyhood in France...

Mother's pretty face, cloaked with soft brown curls, hands trembling as she put dinner on the table. Father, clothes stained with ink, just in from the printing press. Dinner, our favorite time. But something is wrong. There's sadness in mother's eyes and father, so quiet, never smiles anymore. "What's a revolution, Papa?" His gentle soul, a lover of poetry and music, didn't understand. His parents arrest that night, then begging in the streets with Andre – pushing and shoving in a fight for scraps of bread. Knocking on their Aunt Elsie's door and seeing her shake her head no. Hours later, lying in a doorway, waking to a gentle hand on his shoulder and seeing her face. "You boys can work for food and passage." She took them to the dock where a large ship waited. Over time, life toughened Jacqo, and his gentle soul retreated inward.

Jacqo shook his head and brushed his hair back with his hands, pushing the memories away. It had been morning since they had eaten. Nausea rippled through him as he looked at the dried blood on his hands and shirt. Legs heavy with fatigue, he walked through the camp, now eerily quiet. He chose the two teepees near to where Strong Eagle lay, cleaned them up, and made a small fire pit in between for cooking.

"We need to get the bodies covered before dark," Andre said as Jacqo walked up. Buzzards circled overhead, and a coyote howled in the distance. "They're close."

"We should keep the fires burning." Jacqo said, handing Andre a waterskin. "It'll keep them away for now."

"I'll see to it." Andre took a long drink, then silently, the men went back to work.

Jacqo gathered blankets and hides from ransacked teepees to cover the bodies while Andre picked up the spade. He scored off a rectangular area and started digging the mass grave. He went to the dead one by one, straightened their clothing and closed their eyes, then carried the bodies to lie side by side near the gravesite. As he made his way around the large fire pit, Andre gasped as he came to a tree deep in the shade, a corn husk tied to it. "No." He knelt next to Chitto. "Oh, Aiyani. Your boy." Emotion overwhelmed him as he picked up Chitto. Tears blurring his vision, he pushed back hidden desires of a life with Aiyani, his love for her children, his guilt at wishing Lusio gone. Gently, he carried Chitto over and lay him next to Aiyani. Reaching for a blanket to cover them, Andre became overwhelmed with the memory of the last time he saw his parents.

A knock on the door just after dinner. Andre's mother pushing the brothers behind a curtain as their father puts his fork down and stands. Men entering, shouting, then shackling his parent's arms and marching them out the door. Mother, turning and looking at her sons. Silence, her tear-filled eyes say, as she holds her arm up against the weight of the shackles, placing a finger to her mouth. Hidden in shadows, he follows, watching in horror as they take his parents to the village square. Up on the gallows, ropes around their necks. His last memory was his mother's shoe dropping as her feet dangled. At that moment, all innocence and trust in life left him.

Andre's stomach clenched in a hard knot. He stepped into the juniper brush and vomited green bile onto the berry-laden branches, using his shirtsleeve to wipe the foul-tasting liquid off his mouth. He watched as Jacqo pulled a dress over a woman's legs. His brother's soft heart worried him. Since childhood, he tried to protect him, shielding him from this harsh world. But the world was proving to be harsher than even Andre could stomach. Shoulders hung in defeat, he watched as Jacqo rolled a dead woman off another body. Picking her up, he glanced over and met his brother's eyes. Volumes were spoken in that brief, silent gaze. Over time, they became like one person, walking in perfect sync over mountains and across rivers. They had been pieces of a puzzle that fit together perfectly.

Jacqo broke the gaze first. Something out of the corner of his eye caught his attention. Arms sagging from the weight of the dead woman, he looked at the girl on the ground. A bracelet of bright yellow and white beads adorned her wrist.

Those beads... that bracelet.

His eyes followed the arm to the face, covered with dirt and blood. Her eyes were open. Watching him.

The taste in his mouth still sour from the vomit, Andre felt the hair on the back of his neck prickle. "Everything okay over there?"

"Just seeing things, I guess." Jacqo stood, carrying the dead woman over to the gravesite. "It's Lomasi. She was Morning Dove's friend." He lay her next to an older woman, face drawn and pale in death. "This was her grandmother, Macawi. She always gave me an extra bowl of stew." He stood, scratched his head, returned to the other woman, and knelt at her side. Reaching down to close her eyes, as he had done with countless others, he jumped back as she raised her arm, trying to brush his hand away. The yellow beaded bracelet broke as her arm fell to the ground, beads glimmering in the sunlight as they scattered.

"Morning Dove?" Tears streaked through the dirt on his face as he lifted her and stood. She looked up at Jacqo, looked around, looked at Jacqo again, and fainted. "She's alive, Andre. Get the water."

Andre scrambled for his waterskin. Empty. He threw it on the ground and ran to the teepees, digging through the supplies piled on Willie, pulling out their extra. The mule protested with loud snorts and swung his head around, nipping at Andre. He jerked his arm back, then looked at Strong Eagle, who stirred and moaned in his sleep. Grabbing his handkerchief off the ground, he wet it as he ran towards Jacqo.

"Hurry, Andre."

"Over here." Andre ran ahead and into the teepee. Grabbing a sleeping fur, he smoothed it out on the ground. Jacqo followed, laying Morning Dove on the fur. Andre squatted on her other side, sponging her face with the wet handkerchief. Her eyes opened and filled with fear. She tried to scream, but only scratchy sounds came out of her throat.

Jacqo sat back, hands raised and palms open. "It's okay, Morning Dove. It's okay."

"Jacqo?" She turned her head. "Andre?"

"Oui," Jacqo spread a blanket over her and offered her the waterskin. She took a few sips, then, hands shaking, dropped the waterskin on the ground and closed her eyes.

SEVEN

Feet heavy and dragging with each step, sweat ran down her back under the heavy fur. Raven looked up at the sun and sighed. It was just past midday. "So hot." She followed a narrow path to the river, dropped her things on the ground, and lay on her belly at the riverbank, splashing her face. Nearby a fish jumped, reminding her it had been hours since she had eaten. Suddenly, there was a rustling in the bushes. Heart racing and ready to run, she sighed deeply as a lone rabbit darted across the path. Unclenching her hands, she stepped back onto the trail, looking in the direction of her village, an agonizing need to tend to the dead.

Mama...

"I can't." Even though the voices no longer filled the air, they lived in her head. "What if they saw me and are waiting, for just the right moment?"

Turning to the south, she gazed at the mountains in the distance. Her father's childhood home lay somewhere in those mountains. Memories of him telling her stories of running up and down the mesas, feet bare in the hot sand, calmed her somehow.

Maybe I can find them. Perhaps I will find my father.

She fell into a rhythm with the water, which lapped at the riverbank. A giant green bullfrog croaked, jumping across her path. Days ago, she might have said: "Greetings, Brother Frog. What have you come to teach me today?" And she would have hopped like a frog to see if the message was in the motion, as she knew messages came in many ways. But today, thoughts and words were frozen. Stomach rumbling, she reached for the frog, just missing as it jumped into the grass.

"Oh... Owww." A sharp stone pierced the bottom of her moccasins. Legs buckling, Raven fell on the pack she took from Strong Eagle's teepee. Crawling off the path and under the shade of an old oak, she curled up around the soft hide, letting the sounds of the river numb the men's voices in her head, and the images of her family lying dead on the ground. Hands on her belly, Raven wondered for the first time what it would be like to give birth. Drifting into a dream, she could hear Morning Dove and Aponi's footsteps, running to fetch water for the birth and hot stones from the fire to relieve the ache in her back. Mother's face calm as she held her hand, letting her know all would be well. Strong Eagle on the other side, smiling as he eagerly waited to welcome his daughter into the world. She floated in her dream, not wanting to wake.

The hot afternoon sun beat in her face, eyes stinging as sweat streamed into them. Rolling over, she squeezed her fingers over the talisman in her hand and held it to her nose, wishing for the slightest scent of her mother, but that was long gone. The next breath was filled with the dirt she lay on. Raven rose and went to the river, letting the icy water soothe her throat. She sat on the riverbank and gazed at the ripples, imagining she was a ripple herself – an extension of the energy of the water flowing through her veins. In a daze of hunger and exhaustion, she stood and took a step down the slippery bank, ready to be one with the ripples, allowing the river to take her grief.

Aiyani's voice filled her. "No, Raven. You are stronger than that." Shaken, she fell back onto the riverbank and lay looking up into the trees. Above her sat the chickadee, its melodic voice floating into the air. Just as the ripples of the river called her, she let the chickadee's song fill her heart. Tucking the talisman into her pocket, she sat up.

EIGHT

"It'll be dark soon." Andre stepped out of the teepee and looked at his brother. "They'll need water and food when they wake."

Jacqo nodded as he gathered up empty waterskins.

"I'll cover the bodies," Andre said, picking up the spade. "You clean up, get water and find food. I'll come back and get the fire going."

Jacqo slung the waterskins over his shoulder and headed towards the river. Stopping by Willie, the mule snorted as he rifled through their belongings. He pulled out the pouch of yucca root they traded for in the last village, then with clothes rolled in a fishing net, he looked up at the darkening sky and hurried down the path to the bathing hole.

Never want to see these again. He thought, kicking the grimy clothes into the bushes. Goosebumps covered his skin as he sunk in the icy water. Lathering his body with the yucca root, he watched the dirt and blood reflected on the surface as he rinsed, then dunked his entire head under, shaking it back and forth as the river carried away images of the day.

The clean pantaloons and linen shirt felt crisp and cool on his body. He fastened a woven belt around his hips and secured his knife into the attached sheath. Balanced on one foot, he pulled on a knee-high moccasin, the leather lace breaking as he pulled it tight. "Damn." He stood and stared at the lace, then looked at the bottom of the other moccasin, noticing several small holes. "Need new ones soon." He shrugged and tied a knot in the lace.

Kneeling on the riverbank, Jacqo filled the last of the waterskins, then glanced over, pleased to see two large rainbow trout wedged in the net. He gathered his things and with a string of fish in hand, headed back.

Andre looked up from a robust fire as Jacqo entered the camp. "I'll be back." He walked with a quick step, then stopped and looked up at the sky, now turning crimson.

Jacqo took the knife out of his belt and looked at it. They needed to eat, but with so much death today, he couldn't bring himself to gut the trout. Taking a deep breath, he allowed a necessary but cold feeling of disengagement to come over him, then holding the fish steady on the grass, in one motion, slit the bellies, then lay them on a hot rock over the fire. The smell of the trout cooking permeated the air.

Andre walked back into camp, hair wet and slicked back. "Have they awakened?"

"Morning Dove drank some water, then went back to sleep." Jacqo turned back to the fire, flipping the fish with his knife. "We should move Strong Eagle into the teepee before it gets any later."

While the fish cooked, Jacqo laid a second fur inside the teepee. Strong Eagle roused, but too weak to stand on his own, leaned on the brothers as they helped him. Blank stare in his eyes, Strong Eagle looked up from the fur before he closed them and returned to sleep. Night fell as Andre and Jacqo sat near the fire, eating. "I'll take first watch," Andre said. "Fires are going steady. We'll be safe tonight, but one of us should be awake. You get some sleep."

Jacqo nodded and grabbed his sleeping gear. Bedroll laid out next to the fire, he crawled in.

NINE

Poking his head into the teepee, Andre paused. Strong Eagle was curled in his sleeping fur, but sensing he was awake, whispered his name. After no response Andre shrugged and stepped outside. "Guess you'll make it known when you're ready," he muttered as he walked to the center of the village. Out of the cover of trees, he saw grass shimmering in the light, surprised a moon half full could be so bright. Circling the area, he added more wood to the fires and looked up. Shooting stars streaked through the night like diamonds. Several treks back, he stood in this very spot with Strong Eagle.

"Each star... ancestor." Over time, they learned each other's language.

Maybe they're gathering now, saying goodbye, telling of their new journeys, and encouraging me not to give up on mine.

Andre studied the sky. "Aiyani, which star are you?"

Sensing a presence, he turned as Strong Eagle stepped out of the shadows. Andre walked over and offered him his arm. Together they walked as Strong Eagle took in the decimation of his village. Tears glistened in his eyes as reality set in.

"Ancestors." He leaned into Andre. "They help us be strong." The men gazed at the stars, now streaming through the sky like arrows, and watched as another one, brighter than the rest, streaked across the sky.

Strong Eagle stood in Andre's steady grasp under the night sky. A shiver ran through him and rubbing his arms, he pulled away and staggered towards the fire. Andre stepped in between his friend and the fire just as Strong Eagle fell on the ground.

"Cold?" Andre hugged his arms around himself.

Strong Eagle nodded. His deerskin leggings and tunic were warm, but he felt cold inside and was dizzy every time he stood.

"Stay here." Andre pointed to the ground. Strong Eagle sat with his arms wrapped around his knees, cushioning his head. He looked up, nodded, then lay his head back down.

Andre went back to the teepees, throwing wood on each fire as he went. At camp, he found Jacqo tucked inside his bedroll, snoring. Opening the flap to the teepee, he watched as Morning Dove tossed and turned, moaning and calling out in her sleep. Her skin felt warm earlier. *She needs water and food, perhaps more.*

A few villages back, Jacqo insisted on trading a knife for a basket of medicines and salves. "It's our last one," Andre protested, but Jacqo insisted.

He may have been right. Morning Dove may need them now.

Fetching a blanket and waterskin, he took it out to Strong Eagle, who now lay on the ground, watching the sky with a vacant look in his eyes. Andre lay the blanket over him, then handed him the waterskin. Strong Eagle sat up on one arm, took a long drink of water, and then lay back down.

Unsure if he should stay or go, Andre sat on a rock nearby, staring into the fire. A sense of unrest had been growing within him. Jacqo changed over the last year. He wore moccasins now, his hair long and in a braid. The flirtation between Jacqo and Morning Dove on their last trip through was obvious.

Where will that lead? What if she dies?

Joints hurting, he felt fatigue and weariness move through his body. The joy he once felt traversing the land with Jacqo had been missing for a while. He tried to talk to him about this being their last journey, but only met resistance.

Would Jacqo come? Could I leave him if he didn't?

Satisfied that Strong Eagle was safe, Andre walked back to camp. Not wanting to wake Jacqo, he draped a blanket over his shoulders and sat on the ground near the fire with his back to a tree.

I'll just rest my eyes... He pulled his hat down over his face.

TEN

Strong Eagle felt the cool ground under his back as he lay and watched stars streak across the night sky. Tracing the beadwork Raven had sewn on the front of his tunic, he could see her hair as it tumbled past her shoulders, her long slender fingers creating a colorful design of a hand holding the moon. A burst of stars shot across the sky. "Oh, Raven, are you seeing these? Where are you?"

Raven woke throughout the night, head swarming with sounds of the strange men's laughter and images of dead bodies on the ground. Unable to bear it, she squeezed her eyes tight and returned to a night of restless, numbing sleep. She woke again to the sight of shooting stars against the pitch-black sky.

This is the day of my birth and I enter my sixteenth summer. Shooting stars always come on this day.

Awake, she gazed at the stars and reminisced about happier times, snuggled up with her family. Some women in the village whispered that shooting stars were ancestors being released from hell, now pardoned of their evils. But to her, stars were magical – shiny bits of light that made her feel happy.

"What is hell, father?" She asked one night as he wrapped a soft blanket made of rabbit fur around her. "The storytellers said..."

"Don't listen to them, Raven." Lusio hugged her close. "It's just gossip. How could anything so beautiful be bad?" He pointed to a star that streaked across the sky. "I'm sure our ancestors are around, but who knows what another's journey is?"

Across the fire, she saw her mother smile, then wink at her father. "But what about the stars? What do they mean?" Raven persisted.

"That," Lusio said, squeezing her shoulder, "is a secret between you and the star. It's magic, and to tell someone would spoil it."

"Ohhh..." She looked up and grinned.

"I know! Let's see if we can hold our breath until we see another one. Then we will make a wish. Ready?"

Together they took a deep breath in. Lusio puffed out his cheeks dramatically, eyes twinkling. Raven tried hard to hold it, but giggles escaped along with her breath.

Ancient Reunion

What did I wish for that night?

As a young man, Strong Eagle loved sitting near Raven and her family as they watched the stars. "Your special time, Raven," Lusio said. "The stars come on your day of birth to celebrate your walk on this earth."

"But the stories, papa," she would argue. "I don't want bad things to happen."

"Don't listen to them Raven. Trust your heart, it always knows." He wrapped his arm around her as she snuggled into his shoulder. Strong Eagle would watch Raven falling asleep as her parents gazed into each other's eyes across the fire.

Over time, Strong Eagle built a friendship with Lusio. While his birth father, Lone Elk, carried the more traditional and conservative beliefs of northern tribes, Raven's father was different. Many years ago, born in a southern tribe, he had been a guide for traders, navigating mountains and rivers. When he came to their village, he brought the lighter, heart-centered quality of the Zuni, often bridging the gap of superstition and judgment, which caused conflict. As Raven and Strong Eagle began their courtship, the family embraced and welcomed him. Joy filled him at the memory.

I have loved you ever since, wanted what they had, with you.

A star shot from behind the tree line and across the sky.

"Father, where are you?" He wondered, then snugged the blanket around him and closed his eyes. He didn't notice the lizard as it crawled into the warmth of his shoulder.

ELEVEN

Jacqo bolted awake. In a dream, his mother was calling for him. He rubbed his eyes and looked around. The sky was black with night, and the light from the dying fire reflected on Andre, who sat against a tree, hat over his eyes. Sounds of a woman crying made him sit upright.

Morning Dove!

Shivering in the cold mountain air, he pulled a candle out of his pack. Candle lit, the fire flared as he threw wood on it. Holding it up for light in the teepee, he looked at the small fire pit in the center. *Should have made a fire last night.*

Gathering dry brush, soon a small fire blazed in the teepee. Puzzled that Strong Eagle's sleeping fur was empty, he turned his attention to Morning Dove, who tossed and turned, a sheen of sweat on her face. Kneeling next to her, he lay his hand on her forehead. Hot. Her breath was coming in gasps. Lifting the waterskin, he dribbled water into her mouth, flinching as she coughed and sprayed droplets of water into his face. "I don't know how to help you."

TWELVE

Raven opened her eyes as dawn sparkled through the trees. Birds chirped morning greetings, but she sighed and closed her eyes, too weary to stand and greet the day. Reaching under the grass belt Aiyani had woven for her, she pulled out the talisman from her pocket. With the stone in her right hand, she put her left hand over her heart. "Mama, I feel your hand on mine."

Aiyani's voice floated through Raven's mind. "When you feel lost, the stone will connect you to the earth and your inner wisdom. The answer will always be there." Comforted by the memory of her mother's voice and touch, Raven lay drifting in and out of sleep.

"Mama, I need help." Voice husky, her dry throat reminded her of the need to drink. A sudden rustle in the brush startled her awake. Remaining still, out of the corner of her eye she saw a grown fox marching her young down the trail and into the grass, scolding them with short growls and yips.

Sighing in relief, Raven stood and stretched into the sun, unaware of the yellow chickadee who sat high on the branch above her. Across the trail, she picked a bunch of soft, fuzzy ear-shaped leaves growing in a sunny spot, then nearby, she found an area free of scrubby brush and squatted to pee, using the leaves to clean herself.

Gathering her things, Raven stepped out onto the trail. Once again, her heart yearned to return as her eyes lingered back toward her village. But sounds and images of the soldiers continued to flood her mind. Filled with fear, she turned, looking to the mountains and to the river which flowed south. Pushing on, she limped. The cut on the bottom of her foot hurt.

Strong Eagle woke with muddled dreams drifting through his mind. Pangs in his stomach reminded him he was alive. And hungry. He pulled himself up and strode back into camp, nodding good morning to Andre. A lizard stopped, frozen in motion on the rock nearby, chest pulsing and eyes intent, watching. Strong Eagle felt a chill go down his back and looked over, expecting to see his father. But the space was empty.

"Grub." Andre squatted next to the fire, fish sizzling on the hot rock. Next to it was a rabbit roasting on a spit made from a long green stick, juices spattering as they fell into the fire. He flipped the trout onto a slab of wood and handed it to Strong Eagle.

Strong Eagle piled greens and berries from a nearby basket onto the fish, and sat on the ground, cross-legged, eating in silence. Gazing into the fire, he looked down and traced the lines on the dish, picturing the hands of the woman who crafted the clay, a bittersweet smile on his face. He could hear the laughter and chatter of the group as she put her unique marks on it before putting it into the fire to harden.

Belly full, Strong Eagle set his dish aside and stood. He searched the vacant teepees, lingering in each one as he gathered pottery they could use. Retrieving the scorched cooking pot from the community fire, he took it to the river and used mesquite branches to scrub it clean. Filled with fresh water, he carried it back to camp, the cool water splashing his legs. Setting the pot on the fire, he went to nearby trees and stripped pine needles off long branches, then gathered elderberries, tossing them into the water for tea.

Jacqo, eyes bright with tears of worry, came out of the teepee. "Morning Dove is sick."

Strong Eagle followed Jacqo into the teepee. He looked around at what used to be his home. His jaw tensed when he saw the family altar upended against one wall. Shaking his head in disbelief, he anchored the flap to the front and back of the teepee, allowing light and fresh air to enter. Morning Dove lay drenched in sweat, eyes closed, moaning. Jacqo stood nearby, wringing his hands. They looked up as Andre ducked under the doorway.

Kneeling next to Morning Dove, Strong Eagle leaned in and began to sniff. He stopped midway down her body. "There." He reached for his knife, but the sheath at his hip was empty. Looking up in frustration, he nodded thanks as Andre handed him his. Strong Eagle cut along the sleeve and shoulder of Morning Dove's dress. Easing the material back, he exposed her chest and rib cage. Just under her left breast was a red and festering wound. Andre watched as Jacqo stood motionless.

"Jacqo, the medicines!" Andre looked over at his brother. Jacqo's eyes wavered, but he didn't hear.

"Jacqo! Get the medicines!"

This time, Jacqo heard him. He ran out of the teepee to the mule and dug into their supplies, throwing blankets and tools on the ground until he pulled out the pouch with the potions and salves. Running back to the teepee, he passed Andre at the fire, filling a large ceramic bowl with tea. Strong Eagle dabbed around the wound. A bulge just below her rib cage puffed out like a blister. Strong Eagle took the knife and cut her skin, releasing large amounts of foul-smelling liquid. Bloody pus oozed out as he pressed. Reaching up, he took the bowl of pine tea mixture from Andre and poured it over the wound, using the handkerchief to wipe away the drainage. Strong Eagle looked up at Andre. "Help?"

Andre squatted and held Morning Dove's shoulder and hip as Strong Eagle rolled her onto her side, looking for other cuts and wounds. He sighed in relief at the unbroken skin on her back and gently lay her down. Cutting the rest of her dress down each side, he covered her with the blanket, then reached under to remove the soiled clothing. Then, as he did on her back, he uncovered small pieces of blanket and looked for other wounds on her front side but found none. Jacqo handed the pouch of medicines to Strong Eagle, who took them out and looked at them one by one. The third tin held a bright orange salve. He smelled it and nodded in approval. Removing the handkerchief, he scooped out salve with his finger and spread it over the wound. Andre wet a clean handkerchief and handed it to Strong Eagle. Picking up the tea, Strong Eagle wet Morning Dove's lips with it, then drizzled it into her mouth. Swallowing small sips, most of the liquid ran down her chin. With her breathing less difficult, Morning Dove settled into a restless sleep. Jacqo, face wrinkled with worry, sat next to her and looked at Strong Eagle.

Getting a fresh bowl of tea from the kettle, Strong Eagle brought it in and handed it to Jacqo. "Drink." He nodded towards Morning Dove. Jacqo looked at Strong Eagle for a long moment, and then took the bowl. Hands shaking, he flinched as it spilled onto his hand.

THIRTEEN

Raven continued south along the river. Without stopping, she pulled her hair into a braid, sighing as the air dried the sweat on her arms and neck. "How long have I been walking? Two days?"

Mama is dead. Dada is gone. Strong Eagle didn't come...

Smoothing her hands over her belly, the grass belt came loose, making it easier to breathe.

Soon it will be obvious. If I come upon a village, they might think I am a witch, alone and with child. I need food and shelter. I'm alone. I have never been alone before.

Exhausted and lost in thought, Raven didn't notice the sharp bend of the trail and stumbled on a root and tripped. The pack fell to the ground, the hide coming loose, its contents spilling out. Mouth watering at the sight of pemmican, dried berries and corn, drool ran down her chin as she shoved bits of food in her mouth, wiping her face with the back of her hand. Raw hunger satisfied, under the cover of a large, leafy mountain willow, she sat on a round patch of grass pressed down from a sleeping animal. Putting another piece of pemmican in her mouth, she chewed slowly, her stomach settling with the comfort of food.

Raven settled in to examine the rest of the pack. There were simple tools needed to hunt, fish, and make camp. Among them were several stone lances, a scraping knife, a rock mallet, a snare, flint, and a straightening stone. Closing her eyes, she could see the hands of elders, teaching her and other young women how to use each tool. She patted her belly. "I am grateful. I can take care of you now."

Underneath the tools, folded in woven grass mats, were long pieces of sinew. One had a metal hook on it, which sparkled as she held it up to the light. Strong Eagle had shown her how to use it. She lay down, snuggled into his fur, and drifted with memories...

Crawling along the riverbank, laughing. Strong Eagle snaps a sharp stick and digs for slugs. "Aha." He smiles, pulling one from a nest. "Hold this." Hands tingling at our brief touch, I hold the string taut as he threads the slug on the hook, tying the other end to a long willow branch. His hands brush mine again and he holds my gaze for a moment. The water splashing as he drops the hook into the river. Then, sitting with our backs to a tree, we wait. His hand on mine... he leans in. Our first kiss...

The silver hook, hot from being in the sun, burned her fingers. She dropped it back onto the grass mat, then went over to the river and put her hands in the icy water. Rolling up the mat, she smiled at the memory of Lone Elk as he negotiated with a trader for the fishing hooks. A heated exchange, Lone Elks arms folded, body stiff, and turned away from the trader to show determination, but always watching out of the corner of his eye. There was no better negotiator than Strong Eagle's father.

I wonder what happened to him. He would have stayed inside the village to protect the women and children.

Talisman secured in her pocket, she repacked the bundle and continued south along the river. Hours later, arms and shoulders aching from the heavy pack, she stopped and slipped out of her moccasins. Raven sat on the riverbank and dangled her feet, sighing in relief. Taking the knife out of the pack, she cut enough leather off the hide to replace the bottoms of her moccasins and pulling off the old soles, tossed them aside. Then using the sharpened end of a bone from the pack, poked holes in the hide. Each time reality sunk in a little more, like holes were being poked into her heart. Taking out the sinew tucked in the grass mats, Raven ran her fingers over the coarse cord.

Whose hands packed this?

With a heavy heart, she laced the new soles to the moccasins.

What will happen to me?

Lifting her foot out of the water, she looked at her heel. The cold water cleansed the cut, but it remained red and sore. Pulling damp grass by the root, she squeezed the mud onto the bottom of her feet, then smoothed the grass into the bottom of her moccasins. "Ah, better." Standing, she gathered her things and continued, ducking as the chickadee swept in low over her head. Raven stopped for a moment, studying the bird.

"Hello, sister. I keep seeing you. Are you my family now?" The chickadee fluttered her wings and flew up on a branch, watching as Raven continued down the trail.

FOURTEEN

Strong Eagle looked down as Andre took his left arm, tracing the wound from elbow to wrist, now red and oozing pus. He handed him the yucca root, clean cloth and salve, pointing to the river. Strong Eagle looked at Andre, took the supplies, then turned and walked away. As he sat on the riverbank, flashes of the massacre washed over him, just like the tree limb which twisted and turned with the current, out of control.

The hoot of an owl... Running Elk in trouble. Weapons clanging... must tell Raven to get away. In the village, knife out, swinging wildly, plunging it into a soldier's belly, watching him fall, then tripping on another. Through the brush and running under cover of trees through, then through stalks of corn. Reaching the entrance to the village. Men fighting... Running Elk... Oh no... Running Elk overwhelmed by soldiers, terror on his face but fighting like a warrior. Firing off arrows. Soldiers falling... too late... didn't see the one in the shadows. Falling together on the ground, pinned down, reaching up, gouging the soldiers' eye - horrified as one eye dangles out of its socket. Push him off. Another soldier, ax held high, striking out - pain, arm gushing with blood. Circling the soldier in a bear hug, plunging the knife into his back and losing balance and falling. Then darkness.

Strong Eagle shook his head to clear the images and knelt on the riverbank. He hung his arm into the icy water, wincing as the wound on his arm opened in the fast current, watching the blood and pus wash away. The warm rock felt good as he sat, the sun warming him. Pulling the lid off the tin of salve, he smoothed some over his arm, then wrapped the clean strip of cloth over it. He lingered for a moment, hoping the heat would melt the chill inside him. Shivering, he stood.

I need to find my father.

Andre stoked the fire, then walked out to Willie, who snorted and pawed the ground. Blankets and packs lay in disarray, hanging off the mule. He removed everything, organizing it in piles on the grass, then led Willie along the river, the breeze ruffling his hair. They met Strong Eagle, his arm wrapped in a clean cloth and two large catfish hanging from a string. Andre opened his mouth to speak, then stopped at the hardness in Strong Eagle's face. He tied Willie to a branch where the mule could graze and drink, then headed back. It was going to be a long day.

FIFTEEN

Raven's arms ached from the weight of the bundle. Coming around a bend in the trail, shoulders scrunched to relieve the pressure, she pushed an overhanging branch aside. On the other side, a small pond formed inside a circle of rocks, the river rushing downstream on the other side. Thirsty and hot, she put the talisman in her pocket then then peeled off her deerskin dress, stuck to her skin with sweat. Laying it over a rock, she placed her moccasins and bundle next to it - all she had left from all she had ever known.

Goosebumps covered her skin as she stepped into the icy water, which sparkled like crystals in the sun and cast shards of light onto the surface of the pond, mimicking the movement of the tiny fish that swam just below. Immersed, Raven felt the grit and grime of the last few days wash away. The cold water cleansed her being's outer surface, but didn't touch the memories burnt deep in her soul. She floated, hair spread out in the ripples that formed with each movement, watching the sun drift to the west.

Reaching for a branch, she stepped out of the pool, pulling herself over the slippery rocks. Refreshed, a tiny spark of hope pierced her heart. Naked in the sun, for the first time since the massacre, she opened herself to the light as it entered her fingers and crown, then traveled through her body to the earth. Imagining deep roots sprouting out of her toes and soles of her feet, she said:

> *"I, Raven, greet you, Father Sky and Mother Earth.*
> *Thank you for the coolness of this water,*
> *The heat of the sun and the beauty all around me.*
> *And I, Raven, ask for your help.*
> *Please show me the way.*
> *Aho."*

SIXTEEN

Strong Eagle stood at the community fire. Sadness ran through him as he gazed at the empty log where Lone Elk sat, always aware of who entered and left the village. Flashes of memories threatening to paralyze, he walked out onto the path where much of the fighting had taken place. Legs shaky, he knelt by Running Elk's body, tunic stained with dried blood, eyes staring up at him. Gently closing his friend's eyes, he picked up the body. Sharp pain in his arm made him look down at the cloth covering his wound, now stained with bright red blood. Ignoring it, he cradled Running Elk against his shoulder. At the gravesite, he lay the young warrior next to his family. "You fought a good fight, brother." Strong Eagle's voice broke as he lay an arrow over Running Elk's chest. The sound of a spade rhythmically removing mounds of dirt seemed so far away. He looked over to see Andre now waist-deep in the grave.

How is it I survived? It should be me lying here, not Running Elk.

Andre stood and wiped the sweat off his brow with his shirtsleeve, then met Strong Eagle's gaze. Above them, buzzards circled closer. The smell of decaying bodies in the summer heat was sharp. Jacqo came down the path, spade and fresh water in hand.

"Morning Dove?" Strong Eagle asked.

"Asleep," Jacqo tilted his head, laying it on his hands, eyes closed.

Strong Eagle nodded, face softening.

Jacqo handed a waterskin to Andre, who tipped his head back and drank, then offered the rest to Strong Eagle.

Passing under the large oak, Strong Eagle returned to the entrance of the village. Bodies of soldiers, dark-haired men he had never seen, lay scattered. His body felt hot and cold as anger began to surge through him like a raging fire. He rolled one body after another off into the ravine. Anger turned to fury. He pushed and kicked the bodies, harder and harder, until his breath came in gasps, arms weak. Shoving the last body over the edge, he watched it roll down the steep hill, clothes catching in the brush, then he spat at the ravine full of dead soldiers. Energy spent, legs trembling, he sat on the ground, face in his hands.

Must not be weak... I need to find my father.

Sweat poured down his back as he walked towards the village center. He had seen everyone in the tribe except for Raven, Lone Elk, and Aponi. Exhausted but determined, he circled into the wooded area behind the fire pit, then froze at the sound of whimpering coming from the trees. Remaining still, he listened. Silence.

I'm imagining things...

But the whimpers came again. Stepping around a pile of dead leaves, his foot brushed against something hard. He bent down and felt along the ground, gasping at the sight of his father's knife, distinct with a handle carved from the antler of an elk. Heart racing, he inched forward. Between two trees lay Lone Elk's body, face down with an arrow in his back. A small arm reached out from underneath his father.

Over time, Lone Elk stayed close to camp, letting the younger men hunt and defend. If there were an attack, he would take as many women and children as he could into the shelter of the trees. The small arm under Lone Elk's body moved. He knelt and removed the arrow from his father's back and turned him over. Underneath, Strong Eagle saw large brown eyes looking up at him.

"Aponi." He wiped the dirt away from her eyes and smoothed the hair off her face.

"Strong Eagle?" she held her hand out, small fingers clasping his hair.

"Yes." Pulling her close to him, he nestled her into his shoulder as he stood. She fell limp against him.

Jacqo came down the trail, carrying a plate of cooked fish and berries, reaching Andre just as Strong Eagle came around the fire pit. Stunned, both brothers stood rooted in place, then jumped into action, getting to Strong Eagle at the same time.

"Aponi." Strong Eagle held the young girl, blood now saturating the cloth binding the wound on his arm. Aponi lay with her head on Strong Eagle's shoulders, listless. Andre opened his arms, taking Aponi from him as Strong Eagle, legs shaking, knelt on the ground.

Jacqo set the food on a rock, then brought a waterskin over, squatted down, and put his hand on her back. "She's breathing, barely." He pulled Aponi's head away from Andre's shoulder, then wet her lips with droplets of water. Groaning, she turned her head away.

Andre looked at Strong Eagle's arm, cloth now bright red with dripping blood. Catching Jacqo's eye, he motioned towards Strong Eagle, then walked to the shade of the tree.

Jacqo went to his friend, unwrapped his arm and emptying a skin, washed the wound. Grabbing a nearby blanket, he ripped off a corner and bound Strong Eagle's arm. Tearing more cloth off the blanket, Jacqo made a sling and cradling Strong Eagle's arm in it, tied it around his neck. They both looked over as Andre, cradling Aponi in his arms, sat on the ground with his back to a tree. Jacqo reached for the food and gently touched his friend's shoulder. "Eat, drink."

Strong Eagle, paling at the odors of food and death mingling in the air, held up his hands in protest to food but took a drink of water. He then stood and walked away, back to the woods, to his father.

Each step heavy, feet shuffling, he willed his legs to carry him. He sat on the ground and cradled Lone Elk in his lap, tracing his fingers along the blood staining the front of his shirt. Looking into his father's eyes one last time before closing them, he remembered their last conversation at the fire.

"Traders said there are rogue soldiers attacking villages... we must be ready." Lone Elk looked at his son, then dipped cornbread into his soup.

"We have put lookouts at each entrance." Strong Eagle met his father's eyes. "Running Elk offered to take the first watch - he is already there. Dustu is watching the path to the river.

"They are young."

"Yes, I know, father. This worries me as well. But they are proud to have their own bow and arrows. They insisted."

Lone Elk smiled at the solemn look on his son's face. "What else worries you?"

"I wish to marry Raven. Will you bless us? Accept her as your daughter, as my wife?"

Lone Elk had seen the two together and noticed Raven's thickening belly. His face relaxed with relief. "Yes, son, she will be a good wife and mother to your children. You are welcome to bring her to our teepee until you have your own."

"My heart is full, Father..."

Lone Elk's voice still echoing in his mind, he sat on the ground and held him. Strong Eagle knew the body no longer housed his father's spirit, but as he held him in his arms, everything became real. Chills ran through him as reality rushed upon him like an ice storm, penetrating the numbness. He looked up and saw Jacqo standing nearby. The men's eyes met with complete understanding. Together, they picked up Lone Elk and carried him to the grave. Andre lay down his shovel, picked up the waterskin, and walked over.

Strong Eagle knelt, covering his father, then stood and looked blankly at the brothers.

"Sorry, friend," Andre said, offering him the waterskin. "Drink. It's hot out here."

Strong Eagle stared at Andre, then turned and walked towards the teepees.

"Should I go with him?" Jacqo asked, watching Strong Eagle walk away.

"No, he just needs time." The brothers stood surveying the mass grave. "Should be big enough." Andre glanced over by the large tree. "Aponi?"

"Resting," Jacqo said. "I found her rabbit skin blanket in their teepee. She drank, then lay down on the blanket and went to sleep."

"Morning Dove?"

"Asleep, and breathing easier." Jacqo looked again in the direction of the teepees, a worried look on his face. "Hopefully, Strong Eagle is there now."

Andre nodded and looked at Jacqo. "Good. She needs her tribe."

Jacqo's eyes flickered with hurt before glancing away.

"Jacqo, I know you like Morning Dove, but..."

"Better get this done." Jacqo picked up the spade.

SEVENTEEN

Strong Eagle stepped into his teepee and sighed in relief. Morning Dove was asleep, breathing deep and natural. Fresh anger surged through him at the sight of the brightly colored feathers and beads that decorated Lone Elk's ceremonial robe discarded against the wall like trash. Reaching down for the robe, something caught his eye. On the ground, wedged under the hide where he slept, was the white owl feather they kept on the altar in memory of Strong Eagle's mother. He picked it up, noticing that the shaft felt different. Outside in the sunlight, his heart skipped a beat when he saw the shiny black hair wrapped around the feather.

Raven...

Her essence flowed through him as he stroked the softness of the shiny strands of hair, hope filling him for the first time. Tucking the feather under his sleeping hide, he took his father's robe and went to each teepee, finding personal objects for each of the dead. He gathered arrows to place next to the warriors, toys for the children, jewelry for the women, and bowls to fill with food so that they might have nourishment in their next journey.

Strong Eagle walked past Raven's teepee several times, both drawn and repelled. Now he stepped in, breathing in the scent of herbs and medicines that Aiyani stored in the back. Spotting what he was looking for, he picked up Aponi's doll, smiling sadly as he remembered her bright eyes and eager face, crumbs of cornbread and honey on her chin as she offered her doll a piece. He looked at the doll now, with stains of honey on her lips. Arms full of everything he gathered, on the way to the village center, he stopped and squatted next to Aponi, tucking the doll in her arms. She woke briefly, hugged her arms around it, and returned to sleep.

Strong Eagle wrapped his father in the robe as the sun drifted west, tucking in the feathers that fluttered as if to take flight in the breeze. As was their tradition, he lay his father's arms, stiffening in death, with hands crossing his torso. Strong Eagle picked up Lone Elk's knife, tracing the patterns on the handle. Opening his fathers right hand, he placed the knife there, then closed his father's fingers over it. Strong Eagle heard something fall and looked down. The knife had fallen out of his father's hand and lay at his feet. Placing it back into Lone Elk's hand, he heard his father whisper. "It's yours now, son. Carry it with honor."

Tears flooded Strong Eagle's eyes as he touched the coolness of the antler, knowing it was just yesterday his father held it. He looked up at the cloudless sky as salty sweat poured down his face, burning his eyes as it mixed with his tears.

"Father, I am honored."

He placed the knife in the empty sheath that hung from his belt, then removed and untied the medicine bag from around his neck. It held a collection of sage, sweetgrass, feathers, and locks of his mother's hair. Pulling several strands of his own, gray strands from his father and combining it with his mother's, he wound all of it together around his finger and into a small circle. Placing the hair in the medicine bag, he tied it shut, and leaned down, tucking it inside his father's robe. Then, Strong Eagle placed Lone Elk's cup and bowl next to his right shoulder and filled them with water and bits of dried meat and berries.

"Journey well, father. We will meet again."

Strong Eagle turned to the remaining bodies and, one by one, placed families together. He lay Aiyani into the grave, cradling Chitto against her shoulder. At the sound of footsteps, he looked up to see Andre, eyes bright with tears. He knew Andre and Raven's mother had become friends.

But was there more?

The last time the brothers came through, Strong Eagle noticed Andre, Aiyani, and Chitto gathering herbs together on a nearby plateau. Andre gazed at Aiyani, watching her go about her work. At the evening fire, Chitto sat on the ground and leaned against Andre's leg. Lusio, Aiyani's husband, had been gone for months. Strong Eagle had seen the yearning in the family's eyes watching for him, but the nights were cold. Back then, it seemed too soon. And now, too late.

He looked down at Chitto, who in life, always had a grin on his face, much like Lusio. Yearning for the day they would have their own bows and arrows, which would show what splendid warriors they had become, all the young boys of the tribe spent their days throwing make-believe arrows at the cornhusk on the tree. Strong Eagle knew Chitto had hidden in the tall grass, watching him as he fashioned new arrows out of sticks, wanting to be like him. He took the finest arrow out of his pack and tucked it into the fold of Chitto's right arm, then placed a shiny, sparkly rock in his left hand. The rock and the arrow would guide him on his next journey.

EIGHTEEN

Raven dressed and gathered her things. Refreshed from bathing in the cold water, she set out, continuing along the river trail, jumping as a rabbit darted across the path in front of her. She watched it veer off onto a separate trail bordering a stream that branched off the river. Curious, she pushed scrubby mesquite branches away and followed it. After a few quick twists and turns, the path opened into a grassy clearing. Chokecherry bushes bordered the north, and a short distance up the hill, rock ledges and overhangs were in the west. She pulled the talisman out of her pocket and held it over her heart, which skipped a beat.

There may be a cave up there - I can pick chokecherries, fish, and catch rabbits to stock up for my journey. But a journey to where?

She looked at the trail behind her, then turned to the mountains in the south.

The mountains call me, but I must cross them before winter. But what if no one is there?

Raven hiked up the short hill behind the clearing and found a large rock overhang with a small cave underneath. She stood on the ledge, looking out. The opening would welcome the morning sun and give her shelter. It was big enough to have a fire but would hide the smoke and keep animals out.

From here, I can see the river, the clearing, and the trail. I feel safe here. I'm tired.

She gathered bunches of dried grass and binding them together with a small piece of sinew, used it to sweep out the cave. In the corner, there were droppings and chewed bones.

Will it return, looking for its bed? She wondered as she swept the rubbish off the ledge.

Raven created a fire pit just inside the cave entrance. Gathering twigs and wood, she placed them in the center. Looking uneasily at the oncoming darkness, she took out the flint and scraping knife, put them over the dry grass, and rubbed until there was a spark and soon, a fire. Warmer now, she gathered more wood and built up the fire to last the night, then rolled out Strong Eagle's sleeping fur and crawled in. For the first time in days, she slept deep and unafraid.

As the sun set on the third day since the massacre, Andre and Jacqo laid all the bodies to rest in the grave. Strong Eagle came off the river path and stopped, looking at the brothers. Andre leaned on the spade as Jacqo turned, greeting Strong Eagle. "It's done."

Strong Eagle nodded his thanks. "Tomorrow, when the sun leaves the sky, we will honor and say goodbye."

The brothers nodded in agreement. Exhausted, the men separated. Jacqo used the remaining daylight to wash up in the river as Andre scooped up Aponi and carried her back to the teepee, laying her on the sleeping fur next to Morning Dove. As he stood watching the sisters sleep, a restlessness filled him. Even in his exhaustion, he needed to move. Lost in their thoughts, the brothers nodded as they passed each other. Andre heard Willie snort and went over to untie him, leading the mule to the water to drink. As darkness claimed the night, Andre headed to the bathing hole to cleanse the day off him.

Strong Eagle circled the village, gathering up remaining weapons scattered on the ground and piled them near the central fire pit. He could still hear the hushed sounds of gossip and the laughter of children. Expecting to see Lone Elk sitting on the log, he reached down and touched the knife in the sheath at his side. "Guide me, father."

Standing at the cold, empty firepit, he looked at the weapons they gathered. Bows and arrows beyond repair went into the pit to burn. He set aside three intact bows and six arrows. On the next heap were hatchets and knives, black with crusted blood. They needed more arrows. Turning to the gravesite, Strong Eagle picked up a large round sandstone and placed it in the Center, then untying the pouch of cornmeal from his belt, took a pinch in his fingers. Blowing a prayer into the cornmeal, he held it to the sky, touched his heart, then sprinkled it on the stone. Then, beginning in the east, he lay smaller red rocks between the center and the edge of the Sacred Circle and repeated this in the north, west, and south. Stepping back, it pleased him to see the spokes of the Sacred Circle forming.

NINETEEN

Dawn crept in on the fourth day. Blue sky shimmered as the early morning sun peeked through the trees. Birds sang, buzzards circled, and coyotes howled in the distance. Raven lay sleeping, wrapped in Strong Eagle's fur. In the old village, the dead lay next to each other in the mass grave. Wrapped in blankets and furs, each had a bowl for sustenance and something familiar, an arrow for the warriors, toys for the children, and jewelry for the women to help guide them on their next journey.

Morning Dove's first sensation was the wet, soiled fur underneath her. She tried to sit but cried out in pain, collapsing back onto the ground. Wincing, she forced herself to turn on her side, off the wet fur. A small fire in the center of the teepee warmed her face. Nearby, her sister Aponi lay fast asleep, arms tucked around her doll.

What happened? This is not my teepee... I have soiled myself... I have pain...

She listened for the laughter and chatter which usually filled the air in the mornings, but it took a few minutes to realize that it was missing. "Mother? Chitto?" she called out.

"Aponi, are you awake?" Her sister didn't stir. Only silence greeted her.

The flap opened, and Jacqo ducked under the door, a fresh sleeping fur draped over one arm and a steaming cup of tea in the other.

"Jacqo?" she asked, surprised to see him. "Mother? Raven?"

He stood without speaking. The sadness in his eyes frightened her.

"Jacqo?" Voice husky, tears filled her eyes. He set the tea down and looked up, relieved to see Strong Eagle step under the flap.

"You're awake," Strong Eagle knelt by her side.

"What happened?" She searched his eyes.

"Let's get you a dry fur." He pulled her forward, hands on her hip and shoulder.

"Ohhhh!" She cried, grabbing his arm, tears of pain and fear in her eyes.

Jacqo pulled the wet fur out and lay down a dry one. Strong Eagle rolled her on her back and covered her with a blanket, then wiped her tears. Morning Dove's eyes followed Jacqo as he stood, gathered the soiled fur, and left the teepee. Strong Eagle picked up the cup, fragrant with the scent of pine and honey, and nodded in understanding. "Jacqo found you lying underneath Lomasi. They shot her with an arrow, and when she fell on you, it pierced you here." He touched her side. "What do you remember?"

Morning Dove closed her eyes. "I was putting elderberries and sage into the cooking pot, then filled it with water to heat overnight. In the morning, we would add honey for sweet tea. I turned and smiled at mother." Large tears welled up in her eyes. "She... she smiled back at me."

Strong Eagle reached down and took her hand.

"Strange men came out of nowhere." She continued, voice choking. "They screamed as they charged the camp with knives and hatchets over their head. Mother yelled at me to follow her." Her lips trembled as she continued. "I ran after her but tripped and fell. When I woke, someone was lying on top of me. I couldn't move. Lomasi?" She sobbed, tears running down her face. "Oh, Strong Eagle, my mother is dead?"

He held her as she wept. Aponi nestled into Strong Eagle's embrace, clutching her arm around his back.

"I want to see them." Morning Dove looked up, eyes red and voice raspy.

Strong Eagle nodded, nudging Aponi off his lap. He got up, leaned over, and helped Morning Dove to sit, then stand. Her legs buckled as she leaned against him. Strong Eagle lowered her and called to Jacqo, whom he knew would be just outside.

Jacqo came in, and together the men helped Morning Dove stand. Holding her between them, they moved out into the daylight. Morning Dove blinked at the bright light and leaned on Jacqo's shoulder.

"Aponi, get the blanket," Strong Eagle clasped arms with Jacqo behind Morning Dove's back.

Aponi ran into the teepee, grabbed the blanket, and brought it to Strong Eagle. He ripped a strip off with his teeth, then lay the blanket around Morning Dove's shoulders. As Jacqo supported her, Strong Eagle undid the belt around her dress and looked at her wound. Satisfied, he wrapped the strip of cloth he had torn off the blanket around her torso, binding the wound.

Strong Eagle looked down at his bandaged arm, the sling Jacqo made hanging loose around his neck, then up to Jacqo. "Carry?"

"Yes," Jacqo lifted Morning Dove into his arms.

Strong Eagle took Aponi's hand as they headed down the path towards the gravesite. Andre dropped a large rock on top of a growing pile and looked up as the others approached. Strong Eagle nodded towards the grave, then walked over and knelt on the ground, looking up as Jacqo set Morning Dove down, squatting next to her. Aponi stopped a few feet away, holding her doll close. Andre held out his hand. She took it, then nestled in close to his leg.

Strong Eagle leaned over and removed the blanket from Aiyani and Chitto. Aiyani's eyes were closed as if she were sleeping; Chitto snuggled into her arms, head on her shoulder.

Morning Dove stared at them. "Mother? Chitto?" Reaching down, she shook Aiyani's arm. "Wake up. It's time to wake up." Her hand jerked back at the coldness of her mother's skin.

Strong Eagle leaned in close and said: "Their Spirits are on another journey now."

"Noooo..." Morning Dove turned away from him and buried her face into Jacqo's shoulder.

Strong Eagle looked up as Aponi stepped towards the grave. She kissed her doll on the cheek, brushed her fingers over each eye as if to close them, then bent over and lay the doll next to Chitto. Aponi looked up at Andre. Her wide dark eyes spoke not only of the loss before them, but of wisdom rare for a child so young. He held out his arms and lifted her into a hug.

Strong Eagle covered Aiyani and Chitto, then turned to Morning Dove.

"You can rest now, but first you must eat and drink."

"Yes," she brushed tears from her eyes.

Jacqo carried her over to a grassy spot under a large shade tree, sitting down so she could lay her head on his leg. Andre and Aponi followed.

Strong Eagle walked back to the camp and returned with blankets draped over his arm. In one hand, he carried a bowl of hot tea, and in the other, a flat rock with the fish Jacqo had been cooking when they heard Morning Dove wake. On top of the fish, he piled fresh berries.

Jacqo reached up and took the steaming tea from Strong Eagle. Pulling Morning Dove up into a sitting position, he held the bowl to her mouth. Hesitant at first, once the taste of fresh pine and honey met her tongue, she drank. Strong Eagle lay the blankets on the ground next to them. "Eat," he said to the sisters, pointing to the food. Aponi took a handful of berries and put them in her mouth one at a time. As the juice of the berries woke her appetite, she reached out and took fish off the plate, eating. Strong Eagle held up the plate of food for Morning Dove. She turned her head in protest.

"You must eat and drink." He squatted and supported her as he pushed her shoulders forward with his arm.

"No." She jerked away, clutching her side in pain. But as the smell of the fresh food reached her nose, her mouth watered. Tentatively, she took a few berries and put them in her mouth. Juice burst from each berry, dribbling out of the side of her mouth and running down her chin.

Jacqo dabbed it with his handkerchief. "Cest bon, Morning Dove."

Encouraged, she took a piece of fish, pulling the meat off the bones with her teeth. Andre spread the blankets under the shade of the tree. With food in their bellies, the sisters soon lay on the fur together, eyes closed.

TWENTY

Raven squinted against the morning light as it shined into the cave. Mica in the rocks sparkled, creating streams of light that danced shadows on the walls. Mesmerized, she drifted in a jumble of beauty and loneliness, longing to remain snugged in Strong Eagle's fur, curled up in the cave's safety as her dreams danced with the light and shadow. But chilly in the morning air and only embers left in the fire, she crawled out and stood, adding more twigs and grass to the fire, rubbing her arms against the cold as flames came to life.

Rested for the first time in days, Raven took stock of her surroundings. Near the cave, she found a stick and dug a latrine, then returned. She looked longingly at the sleeping fur on the ground, but then her hands came to rest on her growing belly, reminding her she needed to take care of her baby.

"I need to take care of my baby."

Sleeping fur rolled up, tools organized, Raven stood on the ledge of her cave. Filled by the warmth of the new day, she raised her arms to the sun rising over the river.

*"Grandfather, Grandmother,
I give thanks for this day.
I thank you for my life,
I thank you for my death.
I welcome all you bring me this day.
Help me to honor my mother and father in all that I do.
Aho."*

Eyes closed, she imagined Strong Eagle in the trees by the river, smiling as he watched her morning ritual. Disappointment filled her as she opened her eyes. She put her hands over her heart, filling them with love, then raised her cupped palms and blew the energy out into the universe. "May this love find you wherever you are."

Raven explored the inside of the cave. Along the back wall was a ledge big enough to sit on. The rock was cool under her as she sat and opened the bundle of food, eating a small amount of pemmican and berries. Satisfied, with the bundle wrapped up and placed back on the ledge, she gathered grass still damp from the morning dew and relined the bottom of her moccasins. Ready for the day, relieved that the pain in her foot was less, she gathered large stones and wood nearby, layering them in the firepit in a circle, making a smoking pit to keep the embers hot, ready to cook any fish she might catch. Pleased, with the bundle of tools in hand, she climbed down the rocks.

In the clearing, she chose two long sticks. With the first, about as tall as herself, she took the straightening stone, a round stone with a hole in the center, and slid it up and down the stick, grinding off knots until the wood was smooth. Then, securing a sharp stone lance to the end with sinew, she held it up.

A spear Strong Eagle would be proud of.

"I wish you were here now," she said, reflecting on the days spent along the river, learning how to make simple tools and weapons, and how to use them. She practiced throwing the spear and was confident she could use it for hunting and to protect herself.

She took the second stick and the piece of sinew with the silver hook on it and walked down to the river. Setting her items aside, Raven disrobed. Careful of the slippery and sharp rocks, she stepped into the cold water and washed. Refreshed and back on the grassy bank, she sat for a moment, enjoying the heat of the day as it dried her. Naked, she ran her hands over her breasts and belly, notably fuller.

Three or four moons. I need to be across the mountains by the seventh moon...

"Will there be a village that will accept me?" Standing by the water, she looked up at the snow-capped mountains to the south, then turned and looked to the path leading back to the old village.

Journey or no journey... hunter or no... live or die? I don't know. I have always had someone tell me what to do. I must decide.

"Today, I will feed myself and my child." The sound of her voice quieted the doubts that constantly ran through her mind. Slipping into her buckskin dress, Raven returned to the task at hand.

With the second stick, she tied the sinew with the hook on it to the narrow end of the long willow branch, then crawling along the riverbank, found a nest of slugs. Carefully plucking one out, she placed it on the hook, just as Strong Eagle taught her. With the stick anchored in the elbow of a small tree, she dropped the hook into the water. Keeping an eye on it, she used her spear to cut wet grass and wove mats to hold the fish for smoking. Soon, there was a tug on the line. Raven jumped up and ran over, grabbing the stick just before it fell into the water. Pulling out the sinew, she was pleased to see a giant catfish on the hook, drops of water sparkling in the sunlight as it flapped in the air. Removing the fish from the hook, she cut it's head off with her stone lance.

"I am sorry for your sacrifice, brother catfish. I must eat."

Soon there were several fish caught, cleaned, and gutted. Wrapped in the wet mats, she took them back to the cave and placed them in the rock pit to smoke. With the smell of fish cooking in the air, Raven returned to the clearing. A cottontail rabbit was in the snare she fashioned and set out earlier.

She sat for a moment, touching the soft fur and feeling the rapid heartbeat of the frightened animal. "I'm sorry, brother rabbit. I am a hunter now." Raven felt numb as the blood spurt from the rabbit's throat, and closed her eyes at the act of violence. Above her she heard the chattering of birds and looked up to see the chickadee. It seemed to stare straight into her heart as it wove a melody into her. "Thank you, sister."

Strengthened, she gutted the animal, saving the stomach and intestines that could be used as pouches to carry herbs and other small items once washed and dried. Setting them aside, Raven cut off the hide, careful to keep it intact, then wrapped the meat in another grass mat.

Up in the cave, she placed the mat in the smoking pit with the fish. Mouthwatering from the smell of food cooking, she pulled pemmican and berries out of her pack and slowly ate as she sat on the ledge, overlooking her new world.

TWENTY-ONE

Strong Eagle caught Jacqo's eye, nodded toward the river, and walked away. Jacqo watched his friend's back as he disappeared around the bend, wondering what the coming days would bring. Throughout the day, clouds wove patterns through the blue sky as the sun moved across the horizon from east to west. The sisters slept. Spades shoveling dirt, filling in the empty spaces along the Sacred Circle, was the only sound as the brothers prepared the gravesite for the ceremony at sunset. The yellow chickadee sat high in a tree, swaying gently as the breeze caught the branch. Below, soaking in the heat of the day on a large rock, the lizard sat pulsing, watching.

Later, as the sun moved behind the trees and the sky turned into a display of purple and gray swirls, Strong Eagle stood in the shadows, observing the others sitting under the tree. Andre leaned against the trunk, hat pulled down over his face, while Jacqo and Aponi were drawing pictures with a stick in the dirt. Her giggle was the first sign of joy the village had heard in days. Morning Dove sat with her knees pulled up to her chest, fur behind her back, and stared at the colors dancing in the sky.

Cloaked with a beaded ceremonial robe, face blackened with ash and the long white owl feather woven in his hair, Strong Eagle stepped out of the shadows. He walked to the gravesite, now filled with dirt, and stood at the place where his father lay.

Morning Dove tried to get up, but legs shaky, she dropped back onto the ground. Jacqo took her hand and helped her stand, holding his arm around her waist. Steadier, she smiled up at him and lay her head on his shoulder as they walked to the gravesite. Even in her weakness, he marveled at the grace she displayed in the simple act of sitting on the ground. He looked over and smiled as Aponi snuggled close to her sister. Uncertain where to be, Jacqo sat on the ground a few feet away. Andre brought a blanket and covered the sisters before going over and sitting on a rock.

Strong Eagle untied a long eagle-bone whistle from his belt, then raised his arms, the leather fringe from his robe dancing with each movement. Facing the west, he put the whistle, long eagle feathers dangling from the end to his mouth. The whistle's high piercing sounds filled the air, which shimmered in the setting sun as the treetops blew softly in the evening breeze. He faced each direction, inviting the eagle's spirit to come, to give wings to the spirits ready to soar to their new journey. Tucking the whistle into his belt, he pulled out his rattle, a short thick stick carved with suns and moons. Deer hooves hung on the end of the stick, tied with leather throngs so that as he shook the rattle in a soft steady rhythm, the heartbeat of the earth echoed in the sound. His voice filled the air as he sang:

"Heya Heya Heya Heya Heya Heya Heya Ho...
Heya Heya Heya Heya Ho... oh oh."

Chanting to the sound of the slow, steady rhythm of the rattle, Strong Eagle stepped to the left, tracing a large circle in a reverse spiral around the grave. Jacqo, mesmerized by the sounds, lay on the ground, hands under his head. He went into a dream as the moon rose, surrounded by stars in the black sky. It felt as if the heartbeat of the earth become his own.

As Strong Eagle chanted and stepped, the air grew quiet, a stillness deep as a well. The soft voice of Morning Dove joined Strong Eagles, creating a perfect harmony as energy gathered, spiraling from the earth to the heavens.

Jacqo listened to Morning Dove's voice. He loved the sweetness of her. It was the same sweetness he remembered in his mother's face. Aponi's voice joined her sisters with an earnestness like the energetic thread that holds everything together. Cool night air lay on his face as calm settled deep within him. Contentment filled him he hadn't felt since their life had been uprooted in France. The steady sound of the rattle and Strong Eagle's voice resonated within his body yet sounded far away as they chanted:

"Heya Heya Heya Heya Heya Heya Heya Ho...
Heya Heya Heya Heya Ho... oh oh."

Andre sat a distance away from the ceremony. Eyes closing in a combination of fatigue and emotion, he drifted into a trance held by the ancient chant of his friends. Envisioning the village as it had been the last time he and Jacqo came through, he could hear the chatter and the laughter of children, sitting around the fire with each other, sharing stories and food. He couldn't deny his eagerness to see Aiyani when they visited and secretly hoped her husband had not returned. Drawn to the beauty in her face, he was fascinated with her dedication to healing with herbs and plants. Her simple beauty was complex and intriguing, yet uncomplicated. Sitting on the rock now, he could feel his heart break open.

Startled to feel something brush against his cheek, Andre opened his eyes. Keeping them in a soft squint, he looked over at Strong Eagle as he chanted and danced in the spiral formation he was creating over the gravesite. The air was growing misty around him. Andre saw faint shadows of figures all around Strong Eagle. Feeling a gentle touch on his shoulder, Andre looked up. The faces of his parents smiled down at him. Love in his mother's eyes penetrated time and space as she reached down and caressed his cheek. Stunned, he watched his parents walk towards the spiral. Aiyani stood, holding her hands out to them, then looked over and smiled at Andre. He softly wept into his handkerchief. He wept for the boy who had been forced to become a man as he watched his parents hang. And he wept for the woman whose love he would never realize.

Sounds of the rattle and soft chanting came to a stop as Strong Eagle reached the center of the grave. He pulled the eagle-bone whistle from his belt, and the piercing sounds of the eagle filled the air once again. The wind rose and gently blew leaves in the treetops, and as the night deepened, the mist cleared. Stars sparkled in the black sky as the moon rose in the distance. Strong Eagle tucked the whistle back into his belt and untied a pouch of cornmeal by the light of the fire. Adding to the cornmeal he offered yesterday, he took pinches in his fingers, gave a breath of thanks to the corn, then offered it to each direction until a circle sparkled in the center of the spiral. The moonlight shone down on him, reflecting the white owl feather in his hair. Reaching up, he touched it, drawing strength from Raven's hair wound around the shaft of the feather. He felt the love of his ancestors and spirits as they began their ascent upwards, onward to their next journey.

Strong Eagle began retracing his steps. He held the pouch in his hand, and little by little, left pinches of cornmeal along the way as he wove his way out of the spiral, towards the new life waiting for them.

Raven watched the sun disappearing over the trees and into the river. She tossed some wood on the fire and crawled into Strong Eagle's sleeping fur. Soon, she fell into a dream. Her sisters were singing with Strong Eagle as he danced. Waking briefly, it was as if she were back in the village, surrounded by the people she loved. But as exhaustion claimed her, she fell into a sleep filled with the songs of her village.

Strong Eagle knelt at the riverbank, washing the black charcoal from his face. He stared at the water dripping off his hands as it reflected in the moonlight. each drop a universe unto itself. This was a new beginning he hadn't asked for. Restlessness filled him as he walked to the bathing hole, dropped his clothing on the bank, and shuddering, stepped into the icy water. Long hair fanned around him, he floated, the white feather in his hair sparkling on the water. Gazing at the sky, he watched stars form a big dipper, then morph into a bear as the clouds cleared.

Are you looking at these same stars, Raven? I miss watching them with you. I miss you.

The moon drifted east. Shivering, he stood and brushed wet hair out of his eyes. Reaching back to touch the feather, he felt a panic colder than the water surge through him. It was gone. He looked around and saw it lodged against the outer circle of rocks. Frantic, he turned and tripped, falling forward into the water, creating a wave. The feather swept up on the rock towards the fast-running river. He stretched, reaching. The feather danced as the water pushed it toward the edge. He stretched harder, his fingers taut and painful. Finally touching the feather, he grasped it and held it close, tears of relief dropping into the water.

"I was careless... I could have lost it, lost her, again."

Cold, he stepped out of the water, wrapped his robe around his shoulders, and carefully tucked the feather into his belt before walking back to camp. Warmer in buckskin pants and shirt, he laced up moccasins lined with rabbit fur. The wound on his arm felt raw under the leather shirt. Ducking into the teepee, he opened the tin of salve, scooped some out with his finger and spread it on his arm. After binding it with a clean strip of cloth, grateful the others hadn't returned, with a pouch filled with jerky and dried berries tied to his belt, he grabbed a sleeping fur, blanket and waterskin. Following the river's path, he parted the grass with his hands and stepped through to the bridge.

On the large flat outcrop where he and Raven had last been together, Strong Eagle spread his sleeping fur. Taking the feather out of his belt, he braided it into his hair. Wrapped in the blanket against the night chill, he looked up at the stars and wondered if one of them was his father, watching over him. "I wish you were here, father." He snugged the blanket tighter. "My thoughts are like a flock of sparrows, fighting for the last crumb." Unable to remain still, he knelt on the fur, held his long arms to the sky, and cried:

> *"Great Spirit, whose voice I hear in the wind,*
> *Whose breath gives life to the world... Hear me!*
> *I come to you as one of your children.*
> *I am small and weak...*
> *I cry for a vision...*
> *I need your help."*

The prayers calmed his restlessness as exhaustion overcame him. Curled into a ball with the fur blanket tucked around him, he drifted into a restless, dream-riddled sleep. A young wolf wove its way in and out of his dreams, showing him rivers and mountains, revealing brilliant sunrises of blue and purple skies. Raven, standing on a ledge, arms stretched out to the new day, the wolf sitting on its haunches at her side. Gradually his body relaxed, long legs stretched with one knee over the other. Then, for the first time since the massacre, Strong Eagle slipped into a deep, restful sleep.

TWENTY-TWO

The sun shone brightly into the cave. Raven squeezed her eyes against the light, pulling the hide over her face, reaching for a dream that had woven itself through her sleep. On the fringe of sleep and waking, she felt movement next to her hip. "Chitto." She reached down, tousling her little brother's hair. "You're too old to climb in bed with your sister."

Suddenly, fully awake, a realization hit her. It wasn't hair. In one movement, she jumped up and backed into the corner of the cave, spear held high. Looking down, she saw the fuzzy, gray ball of a wolf pup, sharply pointed ears poking out of the fur. It looked up at her forlornly. Breath caught in her throat, she felt as if her heart might stop. For one second, she was back in her village, little Chitto still alive, snuggling against the chilly morning.

The wolf cub whimpered, bringing her attention back to him. Sitting on his haunches, his eyes tentatively watched her. He had big feet.

Raven looked uneasily at the cave entrance, expecting to see the bared fangs of the pup's mother. Listening for sounds outside the cave, she heard nothing.

Wolves travel in packs.

Confused why this cub was alone, she climbed down, holding out dried rabbit meat to entice the wolf pup away from the cave. He followed, trying to nip the meat out of her hand. She busied herself in the clearing, pondering what to do. But he followed her everywhere. "Go!" she yelled, chasing him away with her spear. He ran away, but time and time again, she would turn around to see him sitting, blue eyes silently watching her.

"You can't stay! I can't defend myself against an entire pack!"

But the cub wouldn't leave her. They sat on the ledge of her cave, the pup content to sit nearby, ready for a toss of jerky.

"Hungry little guy?" She touched the downy fur on his back. "Where is your mother?" She let her eyes wander around the perimeter of the clearing below and looked up as buzzards flew high above the rocks.

TWENTY-THREE

Strong Eagle woke to the soft light of daybreak. Brushing a small lizard off his shoulder, he watched it skitter a short distance away. It stopped, turned, and stared at him with its beady eyes and chest pulsing. Strong Eagle touched his shoulder where the lizard slept and recalled the dream. Raven, standing on a ledge, reaching out, a wolf at her side. Pondering what the message might be, he watched as the lizard disappeared into a crevice.

Turning, he eyed a large rock several feet away, with a young tree full of green buds growing through a crack in the rock. He stood and took aim, smiling with satisfaction as the rock darkened with moisture. The chickadee flew out of the new buds. Scolding him, the bird circled and landed on the tip of a mesquite branch. For a few seconds, their eyes locked, then he watched the bird fly away, south along the river path. He continued staring long after she was gone.

"Raven, where are you?"

Hunger pangs reminded him of the pouch of jerky and berries hanging off his belt. He opened it and took out a piece of buffalo jerky, the tangy juices filling his mouth as he chewed. Sleeping fur rolled up and tucked away, Strong Eagle sat on the edge of the rock. His eyes drifted to the river path leading south.

Is it possible?

Eager to tell the group how the spirit of the chickadee showed him the way, he jumped down off the rock, crossed the river, and headed back to camp. But Andre and Jacqo were still asleep. He peeked inside the teepee at the sleeping sisters. Strapping bow and arrows on his back, he took fresh food and a waterskin. Careful not to wake anyone, Strong Eagle stepped through the camp and back onto the path to the rocks and across the bridge. He didn't see Aponi peeking out as he left.

Aponi crawled out of her sleeping fur. "Strong Eagle?" Puzzled where he went, she stayed on the path, but forgot about Strong Eagle at the sight of Willie. The mule brayed softly in greeting. Aponi smiled and walked over, touching his velvet nose. Willie nuzzled her face and pawed on the ground with his hooves, just missing her bare feet. Giggling, she jumped back, then reached out and gave his head a scratch before continuing along the river. A giant orange butterfly darted around her, landing on a large rock just ahead. Climbing to the top, she sighed in disappointment as it flew off, laughing in delight a few seconds later when it

118

returned. Sitting on her knees, she remained still and slowly held her arm out. The butterfly returned and landed on her outstretched hand, tickling her skin. Tangled braids fell in her face as she pulled her arm in close and studied the bright oranges and reds dotted with specks of white. Touching the softness of the black wingtips, her breath caused the butterfly's antenna to flicker. Spreading its wings, it flew away to the sound of her laughter echoing over the water.

Andre watched from a distance. Half-awake, he saw Aponi slip out of the camp and follow Strong Eagle. Concerned, he followed. Now he stood fascinated, watching as tendrils of rainbow light streamed out of her fingertips, calling the butterfly to her.

Does she know of her magic?

Aiyani - she's just like her, the same timeless wisdom in her face, thoughtfulness in her eyes. A pang of what could have been washed through him. With the chaos of the last few days, he had forgotten about the doll. A couple of villages back, an old woman offered dolls in trade for colored beads. He thought of Aponi as the woman held out the doll in her wrinkled hands. On impulse, he gave her the last of their beads in trade. The doll had long, braided corn silk hair and wore a belted dress made of rabbit fur. She had big eyes and a happy smile painted on her face. Seeing Aponi sitting safely on the rock, he backtracked to Willie. The mule looked up and nickered. Andre found the doll in the bottom of a cloth bag on the ground. Touched when she laid her doll next to

Chitto's body, he wanted to give this to her now. Turning, he walked back to Aponi, the doll tucked under his arm.

Andre came around the bend just in time to see Aponi jump off the rock and run towards the riverbank, hand stretched out to another butterfly, flittering just out of reach. In a flash, he saw the steep embankment, the fast current of the water, and Aponi as she lost her balance and fell, tumbling over the edge. Dropping the doll, he ran. Reaching the edge, he saw the back of her dress as her head went under the churning current. Andre jumped. The current swept around his body, soaking his clothing, the weight threatening to pull him under. Kicking his legs up, he reached her in three long strides. He grabbed the back of her dress and pulled her head above water. Coughing and sputtering, she scratched at his face. With one arm wrapped tightly around her waist, he used his other to grab an overhanging branch. Pushing his leg up onto the rocky bank, he pulled them onto dry ground. Both shivering, he hugged her to him, stooped to pick up the doll and walked back to camp.

Andre set Aponi next to the fire and went into her teepee. Finding her clothes, he pulled out a deerskin dress. Back at the fire, he handed it to her. Shyly, hair tangled and dripping with water, she took it and went into the teepee where Morning Dove slept.

Andre put on dry clothes. Draping his wet pants and shirt on a branch near the fire to dry, he looked up as she came out. Wiggling his finger, he called her over. Head down, she shuffled towards him, bare feet dragging on the ground. Brown eyes filled with tears as she looked up at him.

Smiling, he brushed the hair out of her face and patted the ground next to him. She sat while he smoothed and braided her hair with his fingers. He pulled out the cloth doll from behind him and lay it in her arms. Looking at the doll, then up at him, the glitter of tears turned to joy. It pleased him to see her cheeks rise in a smile. Doll tucked in her arms, she leaned her head against his knee. He wondered what she was thinking and feeling, what she remembered. Reaching over, he grabbed his pouch of dried berries next to his bedroll and held them out to her. After offering one to her new doll, she took a handful and put the rest in her mouth, chewing slowly.

Across the fire, Jacqo came out of the woods, adjusting his pants. He looked at the wet clothes on the branch. "What happened?" Aponi and Andre looked at each other, then up at him.

"Our little friend was chasing a butterfly and fell in the river." Andre nudged Aponi.

Nodding, Jacqo turned and put wood on the fire. As it blazed up, he set a kettle of water on it, adding wild raspberries and blackberry leaves left from the day before. Jacqo stretched and, after smoothing his long hair back, he tied it with a strip of leather.

TWENTY-FOUR

Raven busied herself in the clearing, chasing the wolf pup off only to look over her shoulder to see him a moment later, sitting and watching her. Rustling sounds in the brush made her freeze. The wolf pup stood with hair raised along the ridgeline of his back. She looked again and relaxed. Two deer stood grazing along the chokecherry bushes, pursing their lips as they reached up, sucking off the ripe berries. The wolf pup came over and stood by her side. Sighing, she reached into her pouch and pulled out dried meat, comforted by his soft moist tongue as he nuzzled it out of her hand.

There is life all around me and life within me, she thought. "Yet nothing feels real..."

Her tribe had been travelers, ready to pack up and go with short notice – to follow the game or get distance from hostile tribes. But someone was always nearby. They lifted each other, held one another. She looked over at the wolf pup, intense blue eyes watching her every move. Loneliness plagued her. Used to being with the people of her village day and night, she longed for the sound of a human voice, a touch, a smile.

"Could anyone have survived?" She looked down at Little Wolf. "Will they find me? Should I go back?" She watched as the deer left the clearing, pushing through the brush as they went to the river to drink. Raven took a step toward the path leading back to her village, impulsively retracing her steps. The pup stood back for a moment, then followed.

"I need to know..."

She made it to the fork in the path and stood looking at the pool where, after three days of walking, she bathed. The pup sat down next to her, his downy fur brushing against her leg.

I don't know what to do. Despondent, she turned back, tears running down her face. Pulling the talisman from her pocket, Raven prayed.

"Please help me, Mother. I am a hunter now. But I cannot kill this little wolf, and he won't leave. I am afraid." She clutched the stone tight in her hand. "This world is too much. I am alone. I need help."

Raven didn't hear the humming sound coming from a nearby tree, nor did she see the chickadee fly down, fluttering just above her. The wolf pup watched her for another second, then disappeared into the brush and back to the clearing. Following him, Raven carved out a notch in a nearby tree, marking the time since she found the cave. She already had three rabbits and six fish in either the smoking pit or food cache.

"Tomorrow, I'll decide what to do." And with heavy steps, Raven returned to the cave.

TWENTY-FIVE

Morning Dove pulled the fur up around her shoulders against the chill of early morning. She looked over, saw the fire had gone out, and Aponi's empty sleeping fur. Rolling over, she winced. Her belly hurt, and the sleeping fur under her was wet.

I have soiled myself again.

Reaching down, she felt a sticky fluid and raised it to her nose. Blood.

My first moon time.

The flap opened, and Jacqo stepped through, a cup of tea in his hand. Seeing her awake, he set the cup next to her, then put wood in the firepit, and soon a small fire was blazing. He knelt and supported her back as she sat up. Morning Dove held her side as they stood and stepped out of the teepee. Looking down, he saw the stain on the back of her dress. Their eyes caught as he looked up in understanding. She blushed. Jacqo just shrugged and picked up the tin of salve.

Morning Dove stopped at her family's teepee. Jacqo opened the flap and tied it to the side, letting in daylight. Legs shaking, she stooped and looked through her things.

Finding a clean dress, she put it over her arm, then went over and pulled out a basket from the corner, supplies Aiyani gathered for her first moon time. Tears blurred her vision as she went through the basket and took what she needed. Leaning into Jacqo, they followed the twists and turns of the river path, passing Willie, who looked up with strands of grass hanging out of the corner of his mouth, big eyes inquisitive. She stopped and stared with her mouth open in surprise.

Jacqo laughed. "This is Willie, our mule."

"Willie? Mule?" She reached out and ran her fingers over Willie's coarse hair, jerking it back as the mule tried to nuzzle her hand. She looked up at Jacqo and repeated, "Willie?"

"Yes." He chuckled as he reached into a pack, pulling out the last of their yucca root and a clean blanket. As they walked away, she turned and looked back at the mule. Once she had seen wild horses from a distance, but never this close. "Mule," she said under her breath as she turned and looked again. Jacqo caught her arm as she stumbled.

Passing the rock where Aponi sat earlier, Morning Dove's legs buckled. Piling the blanket and yucca root in her arms, Jacqo picked her up and carried her to the bathing hole, a circle of stones set off the river, protected from the rushing current.

Morning Dove stood and held onto Jacqo's shoulder as he leaned down, unlaced his moccasins, and rolled his pants above his knees. Setting their things on a flat rock, he stashed the yucca root in his belt, dropped the blanket near water's edge, and together they waded into the bathing hole. Morning Dove blushed and turned away as he pulled her soiled dress over her head, removing the cloth which covered her wound. He tossed them on the bank, then helped her down into the water.

Grimacing as the cold water hit the wound on her side, she dipped under the surface of the water and felt the blood from her first moon wash away, along with the grime and grit of the last few days. Jacqo took the yucca root out of his belt, rubbing a handful into her hair until white suds formed. She reached up, taking handfuls of the soap and washed her body, and then dunking her head, she rinsed her hair, creating small, white foamy crests, which quickly fell apart with each motion.

Jacqo stood and watched, struck by the exquisite mix of fragility and strength. Emerging a few moments later, drops of water sparkled on her face as the sun warmed her.

She's so beautiful. As she stood, he held her steady with one hand and with the other reached for the blanket, draping it around her. She leaned against the rock as Jacqo lifted the blanket and applied salve to her wound, then picking up the clean strip of cloth, wound it around her torso as Strong Eagle had done. His hands lingered for a few seconds, breath caught at the dampness of her hair and the softness of her skin. Their eyes met. Morning Dove broke the gaze and shook out her dress, shrugging into it as the blanket fell to the ground.

A tingling in her belly at his touch, Morning Dove watched Jacqo out of the corner of her eye. Back turned, he ran his hands through his hair. She reached for the leather thong packed with soft grass and pulled it up under her dress, surprised at how comforting the grass felt against her. Pulling her dress down, she sat on the rock, the sun warm on her back. As she sat, she heard her mother's voice:

"With your first blood, you leave childhood and become a woman. This is a blessing and a powerful time." Aiyani lifted Morning Dove's chin with her finger and looked into her eyes. "You should not engage with a man during this time."

"Why?" Morning Dove pushed her chin against her mother's fingers, embarrassed.

"Fluids in your body, like all water on earth, move with cycles of the moon which waxes and wanes. As your body connects with the moon, the energy can overwhelm a man." Aiyani paused, laying one hand on each cheek. "During this time, you and any other woman on her moon time will remain in a lodge, away from others. Free from daily responsibilities, you can rest and reflect on these new sensations."

"How many days?" She was already worried about what she would miss.

"Three or four, depending on how long you bleed. You may have pain here," Aiyani held her hand to her belly. "But the first moon brings strength and confidence that will stay with you for the rest of your life."

Morning Dove could feel her mother's arms hugging her. Eager and scared, she thought her mother would be here like she had been with Raven and other girls in the tribe. Her shoulders drooped as loneliness settled on her like a dark cloud.

I will return to the teepee and stay there for three days. I will do my best.

Stepping off the warm rock, she looked up into Jacqo's soft gaze. Hand in hand, they walked back to camp. She went into her family teepee, lay a fur on the ground, then gathered wood and brush stacked near the door, placing it into the fire pit. Jacqo lit a stick in the campfire and brought it to her. Hands touching, they stood for a moment and looked into each other's eyes, then reaching over, she untied the flap and let it close.

Morning Dove turned and stoked the fire, watching it grow into a small blaze, then opened the back flap of the teepee, grateful to breathe fresh air. As she stared into Jacqo's eyes, it had been hard to breathe. Longing for her mother, to talk to about such things, she pulled Aiyani's basket with herbs and plants out of the corner and sat next to the fire, holding it in her lap. Beads of sweat forming on her forehead, she backed away, welcoming the coolness from the open flap. At the height of summer, she only needed heat from the fire at night, but the soft glow comforted her for now.

Gazing into the fire, she watched shapes and images appear and disappear as wood dislodged and shifted with the heat, reflecting the changes she felt in her body. Deep in the fire's belly, a small blue flame created a cavern, then transformed into the shape of an eye.

Jacqo's eyes...

Touching the place on her back where his hand lingered, her belly fluttered. *Is this what it is to be a woman? To feel this way when a man touches you?*

The blue flame caught on the wood above, slowly creating a larger space. Blue shifted to amber and then orange, casting a light on her mother's medicine basket next to her. "Mama, I have dreamt of this day, of sharing stories, learning about becoming a woman. Who will teach me now? Raven? Is it possible she lives?"

The flames shifted, and she saw her father's face in the fire.

What will he think if he returns and finds the camp abandoned?

Will we leave? Where will we go?

Will Andre and Jacqo come?

The flap opened, and her sister's face peeked in.

"Come in, Aponi." She put the basket aside and patted the fur next to her.

Aponi stepped in, carrying a plate of roasted rabbit and roots smothered with freshly picked raspberries and wild greens. Her mouth watered as she took the plate and placed it between them. Shyly, Aponi sat down next to her.

"Share with me. I am happy for your company."

Aponi, with her new doll tucked under her arm, took a rabbit leg off the plate and pulled the meat off the bone with her teeth. Chewing, she looked up at Morning Dove and held out her new doll.

"Ohhh! She's pretty!" Morning Dove, with a mouth full of berries, wiped the drool off her chin. "Where did she come from?" Softly, she touched the purple and red corn silk hair.

"Andre." Aponi hung her head as she pulled the doll close.

Morning Dove saw a tear run down the side of Aponi's face. "What's wrong?" Pulling Aponi's chin up like their mother used to do, she looked into her sister's eyes.

"I was chasing a butterfly," Aponi's voice caught. "It was pretty... I fell into the river." Tears turned to sobs. "I was scared... Andre saved me."

Morning Dove wrapped her arm around Aponi, pulling her close. "You went alone. I'm sorry I wasn't with you." She kissed the top of her head. "Promise you won't go off by yourself again?"

Aponi nodded, wiping her eyes with her fist.

"You were chasing a butterfly?" Morning Dove asked, feeling her sister's soft hair as she rested her chin on the top of her head. "Were you on the path?"

"No... I sat on a rock, and the butterfly was on my arm, then it flew away. I wanted to see it again, so I jumped down and ran after it."

"Ohhh... What color was it?"

"Orange and red, with black around its wings." Aponi looked up, eyes glistening with unshed tears. "It was really big, and I touched it, and it was soft..."

"It sounds pretty. So pretty, you might have forgotten to stay on the path?"

"I tripped. I wasn't looking, and the river was so cold. I couldn't breathe."

"Promise you'll come and get me next time? We always go together, remember?"

"Okay."

"Andre saved you?"

"Mmm... hmmm." She looked up at Morning Dove. "He brought me back to the camp and braided my hair. And gave me this." She brushed the cheek of the doll with her fingers.

"Does she have a name?" Morning Dove smiled down at her sister.

Aponi shook her head, rubbing the tears out of her eyes. "I want to call her Chitto, but that's for boys."

"How about Etu? It's like the sun. He would like that, don't you think?"

"Etu." Aponi leaned down and whispered to her doll. "Yes, she likes it." She smiled up at her sister.

"I have an idea." Holding her side, Morning Dove slowly stood and went over to Chitto's things, pulling out the leather pouch he used to carry arrows. "Perfect fit!" She draped the strap over Aponi's shoulder. "Etu can ride in here. What do you think? We can tuck her in, and your arms will be free."

Aponi nestled the doll in the pouch and snuggled it under her arm, softly caressing it. "I miss Chitto."

"I do too," Tears clouded Morning Dove's vision. Picking up one of his pretend arrows, she placed it in the bag. "We will put his arrow in here, to watch over Etu. He can be her warrior spirit."

Aponi put her ear to her doll's mouth, then looked up. "She's happy. Thank you." The sisters hugged good night.

TWENTY-SIX

Jacqo sat near the fire, brooding. He looked up as the flap to the moon lodge opened, hoping for a glimpse of Morning Dove. But only Aponi stepped out, closing the flap behind her. She set the plate down and stood for a moment by the fire, twisting a braid around her finger. Andre came into camp and looked at Jacqo, eyebrows raised.

Jacqo shrugged again and layout his bedroll, then walked off into the trees. Squatting, Andre stoked the fire. He looked up as Aponi came out of her teepee, sleeping fur and blanket bunched up in her arms so that her eyes just peeked over the top. A smile lighting his eyes, he took her sleeping fur and lay it on the ground near the fire between his and Jacqo's bedrolls. Relief softened the tension in her face as she lay her blanket on the fur, tucked her doll in, and then crawled in herself. Andre went to his things, removed and shook out his poncho, then came over and covered her with it. Kneeling, he brushed her face. "Good night, Aponi." As he stood, she reached out and grabbed the bottom of his pants. Jacqo returned and came over, peering over Andre's shoulder, winking at Aponi.

"Etu." Her small hands held out the doll, anticipation in her eyes.

Andre reached down and brushed the doll's head lightly.

"Good night, Etu," the brothers said.

Aponi snuggled in with her doll, and within seconds, her eyes were closed.

Jacqo lay on top of his bedroll, hands behind his head, staring into the trees, while Andre sat near the fire. "Seen Strong Eagle today?"

"Nope. It must have been around this morning. Weapons are all sorted and stacked up. And he made a Sacred Circle over the gravesite with rocks."

"Hmm..." Andre was quiet for a moment. "Last I saw was when he walked out of camp this morning when Aponi ran after him." Standing, he untied his bedroll and gave Jacqo a hard stare.

Where will we go from here? Jacqo is drawn to Morning Dove.

He looked over at Aponi, now sound asleep, the fire reflecting off her face.

She's a special one, so much like Aiyani - could I leave her? Would they come with me? Be homesteaders? Settle in a new place? He walked over and poked at the fire, throwing on a piece of wood, then watched as it flamed up, reflecting his thoughts.

So much has happened... But it would be a fresh start for all of us.

Just as darkness fell, Strong Eagle walked into the camp carrying two large trout. He nodded in greeting to the brothers.

"Hello, Strong Eagle." Andre nodded towards the fish. "Great catch,"

Strong Eagle knelt next to the fire, taking the knife out of his sheath, neatly cut the heads off, and began scaling the fish. "Morning Dove?" he looked up at Andre.

"Moon time," Andre motioned towards her family teepee.

"Ah," Strong Eagle glanced over at Aponi, sleeping soundly, then put the fish on a flat rock over the fire. Sizzling, the flames sparked and sputtered as juices dripped into the fire. Strong Eagle used his knife's tip to flip the fish and then a few minutes later slid it onto a brown handcrafted plate. Jacqo stood and gathered up remaining roots, greens, and berries and brought them over. He poured cups of tea for all of them, holding his cup up in salute.

"Dawaa'e," Strong Eagle said, acknowledging Jacqo with a nod as he accepted a cup of tea.

"You're welcome," Jacqo sat on the ground next to Strong Eagle. Andre joined them, and together the men sat around the fire eating in silence.

Jacqo let out a belch, then walked into the woods. Back a few moments later, he sat down heavily and lay on top of his blanket. Andre pulled off his boots and crawled into his bedroll. Strong Eagle scraped the plates with a pine bough as the brothers fell asleep, then gathered them into a pile to wash in the morning. Restless, he stood, looking around, then turned and wandered out to the gravesite.

With the oncoming darkness, Raven's fear grew. She chased the wolf pup out of the cave.

"You can't stay! I can't defend myself against an entire pack!" As the night sky grew black, she built up the fire, nervously watching the opening of the cave, convinced his mother would come for him. He sat on the rock ledge and howled.

Tears that bubbled from a deep spring of grief ran down her face, sorrow that had not dared escape as it might never stop. Talisman held tightly in her hand, she prayed.

"Please help me, mother." Drawing strength from the talisman, she lay back down on the fur, watching the entrance of the cave as she waited for her mother's answer.

TWENTY-SEVEN

Morning Dove peeked out the back as nightfall descended. After closing the flap, she gathered up piles of dead leaves, twigs, and wood in the basket by the door. Adding it to the fire, the flames low and steady, she sat cross-legged on the fur and pulled her mother's medicine basket in front of her. Placing bundled herbs, roots and plants around her in a circle, the purple flowers in the dried lavender caught her eye, followed by the sweet, heady smell as she held it to her nose and inhaled deeply. It reminded her of the day she picked this very lavender with her mother.

It seemed a lifetime ago but had only been days since they hiked up to the rocky plateau, birds singing in the early morning sun and tall grass brushing against their legs. Scrubby plants grew in between the rocks, each with spiky stems covered with bunches of purple flowers that reached for the sun. She watched as her mother stood, waiting until she felt called to a particular plant.

"Why do you do that, mother?" She leaned in to smell the fragrant bush, impatient to pick the flowers.

"It's always important to ask permission before you take something, be it a flower, a rock, or even a leaf off a tree.

Everything and everyone has a unique energy and doesn't always want to be touched or picked at."

"Oh," Morning Dove stepped closer. "How do you know what the answer is?"

"As you deepen your relationship with each plant, they will talk to you. Take, for instance, this one," Aiyani walked over to stand in front of a large lavender bush and reached out, gently caressing the branch. "Perhaps it has something to teach or has received just the right amount of sun and water to give us the best medicine." She lifted a handful of the long spiky branches, gently tracing the woody stem. "See how thick and rough the stem is?"

"Yes," Morning Dove touched it gingerly, not wanting to offend but still unsure how her mother knew this.

"She's an old woman, yet still produces much beauty and wisdom..." Aiyani trailed off as she pinched a small flower off the bush and rubbed it between her fingers. "Whew! She lifts my spirits!" She pointed to the bush. "Try it, Morning Dove. You'll see."

Those were her favorite days, gathering plants and making medicine with her mother. She wanted to be a healer, like Aiyani.

"I miss you, mother. Who will teach me now?"

She gazed into the fire and inhaled the lavender again, trying to bring back the joy they felt that day on the plateau, wanting to wrap it around her like a cloak. But the memories were bittersweet. It would take time. Placing the lavender next to the fire, she turned to the rest of the plants, sorting them. Setting bundles of sage and cedar next to the lavender, she took out a small bunch of dried Mugwort and put it in her cooking pot with water for tea. The other plants went into the basket, set aside for later.

TWENTY-EIGHT

As night fell, Strong Eagle sat near the gravesite, holding his father's chanupa. Lone Elk had been the chief and pipe carrier

for the tribe. Now it was in his hands, loaded with prayers woven within the tobacco that filled the bowl, gently held in with a ball of sage.

"I'm not ready, father," he whispered. "I know tribes have warred and stolen, had disagreements and fights. But the pure hatred of these men, I don't understand the bad spirits." His hands brushed over the long cedar stem, the vessel for prayers to be transformed into smoke and carried to the heavens. "Help me, father."

He stood with the pipe cradled in his arms. "I'm not ready..." Head bowed, he knelt on the ground. "I can't sleep here. My body betrays me with hunger pangs, with the desire to live." He bent forward, so his forehead touched the ground. "I feel the bad spirits in me now... like I have become one of them. I don't know how to take the next step." Strong Eagle put the pipe back into its leather bag and placed it on the center stone. "I don't deserve this. I'm sorry, father... I have failed." Then, following the light of the moon, he parted the tall grass leading across the river and to the rocks.

Raven lay on the fur. The wolf howled. She listened for his mother's howl in the distance, but it didn't come. Eventually, her eyes tired of watching the cave entrance and gave into sleep. Dreams of happier times wove in and out. She woke in the darkness, the warmth of Little Wolf nestled in a ball next to her. Reaching down, she stroked his fur. "Somehow, it will be okay, Little Wolf. Somehow..." Raven fell back asleep with the pup snuggled at her side. She dreamt of Strong Eagle, that he was alive and reaching out to her.

"Raven, Raven – where are you? I can't find you."

"I'm here... waiting for you," she mumbled in her sleep.

Strong Eagle tossed and turned on the cold, hard rocky ledge. Somewhere in the distance, a wolf howled. He reached up and touched the feather in his hair, then snugged the blanket around him as the night air grew chilly. As he fell into a restless sleep, he dreamt a snake was coiled around his foot. He stood frozen. Any movement would demand action.

"It's bad luck to kill a snake," he heard his father say. "If you kill one, a thousand more will come for you."

146

He looked down. The snake rattled its tail as he stared into the beady eyes, mesmerized by the quickening rhythm of the rattling tail. He couldn't contain the need to strike out, to hurt someone or something. Slowly he lowered his hand, reaching for his knife.

"The bad spirits want to control you," his father whispered in one ear. "Make you powerless, do things you'll regret."

"You are better than that," his mother said in his other, softly kissing him on the cheek. "Let it go…"

Tears began to fall. Grief and rage poured out in large drops, falling on the snake, dissolving it. As he slept, he felt the strength of his father and the love of his mother holding him.

TWENTY-NINE

Morning Dove sprinkled dried sage and cedar onto the rocks around the fire, watching it dance and sparkle. Taking the owl wing out of the medicine basket, she fanned the smoke towards her and swept the feather over her body, feeling the protection and purification that owl medicine and these plants brought.

Next, she took the cup of simmering Mugwort tea and sipped it, adding a spike of lavender to the sage and cedar, which continued to sparkle on the rocks. Relaxed from drinking the tea, she gazed at the herbs which continued to sparkle on the rocks, and then leaning into the fire, she used her arms to draw the sweet scent to her, swirling it around with her hands.

"Oy ya tee hee, oy ya tee hee." Humming the ancient chant, she threw more lavender and cedar buds on the fire. Chanting and sipping the tea, the colors became even more vibrant shades of red and gold, creating another cavern, dark and inviting. She picked up a handful of Mugwort and threw it into the cavern, using the owl wing to pull the smoke towards her, inhaling. Her body felt relaxed yet tingly, and the pain in her side was gone. Suddenly, bursts of energy surged through her like fire.

"Now I understand." The energy continued to build.

"Oy ya tee hee... Oy ya tee hee..."

She stood, feeling tall and strong. Dancing, her feet shuffled in a circle.

"Ancient ones, grandmothers, sisters, come to me... Teach me."

In the fire, blue flames sparked out of the dark cavern, like hands opening, welcoming her. She threw more lavender into the fire, giddy with the joy at the sweetness.

"Mama..."

The wood shifted. She danced. As the roots in the bottom of her feet deepened into the earth, serpent-like energy entered her. It pulsed up her legs, circling in her womb like red flames. Childhood fell away as the earth's energy filled her with its ancient wisdom of what it is to be a woman. The energy rising into her belly in orange and yellow swirls, her heart opened with visions of green and pink flowers bursting. Her voice filled with new clarity as the energy turned blue and moved into her throat. Shifting to purple as it filled her head, visions floated through so fast she couldn't catch them as they erupted out of her crown with white light, bursting out to the stars, becoming the grandmothers, the ancient ones.

Spiraling down, she fell to her knees by the fire on the earth, face dripping with sweat. Hair plastered to her face, she curled into a fetal position and gazed into the cavern. It appeared smaller and rounder now as the wood settled. She could feel her heartbeat pound as she threw more herbs onto the fire. A spark lit up within her as the log transformed into the face of an old woman with wrinkled skin and scraggly red hair. Dark and intense eyes looked into Morning Dove's heart, whispering: "One hand, one heart... energy strong, yet always soft," the woman whispered. Morning Dove's eyes became heavy and soon closed. Drifting into sleep, Morning Dove felt Aiyani curl up next to her. At that moment, she knew her mother would always be with her.

Strong Eagle woke, kicking his leg. He could still feel the snake wrapped around his ankle. Unable to see in the dark, he grabbed his things and jumped down off the rocks. Bow and arrows strapped to his back, knife in the sheath at his hip, he went across the bridge and towards the river path. Clouds cleared, and moonlight filled the sky, lighting his way.

He sat on the riverbank under the waning moon, water sparkling in the light.

We would all be dead if Andre and Jacqo hadn't come along. Resentment filled him at the thought. *I was ready to die... It would have been easier. I don't deserve to live.*

His mind drifted back to his dream. Lone Elk was with him in an instant. He felt his spirit flow through him, gentling him as only his father had been able to do in life. The energy of spirits passed, and spirits to come filled him and gave him strength. Looking up at the light filling the sky with a new day, he knew the answers would come when he was ready.

THIRTY

Willie snorted and pawed at the bare ground. He lapped at the runoff of river water that created a small pool, yearning for the weight of a pack on his back, a job to do.

Aponi woke to the sounds of squirrels scampering in the tree above her as pinecones dropped randomly to the ground near her head. She giggled, dodging them. Looking over, she grinned at the sounds of snoring from Andre's bedroll. "Let's go see Willie," she whispered to Etu and slipped out of her fur. Tiptoeing, she crept out of the camp and down the path towards the river.

Willie gentled as Aponi walked towards him. He loved the soft touch of her fingers as they scratched his head and the exchange of heat in their breath when she kissed his nose.

Jacqo lay in his bedroll, tossing back and forth. Out of the corner of his eye, he saw Aponi leave the camp, her doll tucked snuggly in the bag she wore across her shoulder. Andre didn't stir. Quietly, Jacqo got up and pulled on his moccasins. Feet pushing into the fallen pine needles with each step, he watched Aponi go around the bend to greet Willie and smiled as she went across the path, pulling bunches of wet grass. Returning, she fed it to the mule, round lips quivering as he stuck out his tongue, pulling blades of grass into his mouth. Aponi giggled as his whiskers tickled her hand. On the ground nearby, Andre's pack had come loose, his belongings scattered. A cross lay on the ground.

"Bonjour, Aponi." She jerked around, mouth open in surprise. He winked at the sheepish look on her face as he walked over, leaned down and picked up the cross. His calloused fingers traced the edges, a faint memory of seeing it in his mother's jewelry box. The Huguenot Cross, a symbol of the French Protestant Church, the reason his parents were executed. It was distinct with four silver flower petals, each rounded on the edges with an open space between each petal. Hanging from the bottom on a gold ring was a dove pendant. His mind drifted back, one-minute, eating dinner and the next, loud banging on the door. The fear in his mother's eyes as she pushed him and Andre behind a curtain. "Reste silencieux. The last Jacqo saw of his parents was his father's stiff back as they led him out along with his mother. Andre told him to stay put and followed their parents. When he returned, his eyes were red, and his face ashen. "Take what you can carry. We can't stay here."

His stomach grumbled as he remembered the wandering days, filled with hunger, challenged by bullies for every morsel. Shunned by family and friends, at ages eight and sixteen, they were alone on the streets. Then on the ship, rats crawling over their feet as they tried to sleep, bellies aching with hunger. Ten years passed since they stepped foot on American soil, but now, standing here holding the cross, it seemed like yesterday.

Soon after arriving, rather than work as indentured servants, they ran away and found fur traders willing to take them on. They worked hard, traversed mountains, rowed boats, and carried packs, eventually learning the territory. After a few years, they set out on their own, becoming respected guides and traders. Most of the tribes they came across readily accepted the likable young men.

Bit by bit they pieced together their history. Memories of helping his father in the print shop, making fliers supporting French Protestants, and denouncing Catholics. Jacqo could still see the bold print, the black ink stains on his hands. Men coming in the dead of night to pick up stacks of fliers to tack up around the village. A few years after leaving, they met some French Huguenots who had also fled.

"You're lucky ya'll got out." The man rolled tobacco in a paper, then put it in his mouth and lit it, giving Jacqo a hard look. "Too bad about your parents, but that happens. Sorry, kid."

Jacqo put the cross back into Andre's bag and closed it. Gathering the rest of their belongings, he piled them on top of Willie and tied it all down with the one rope they had left.

Willie, grass hanging out of the side of his mouth, looked up at him as he came over and untied his lead from the tree. Jacqo handed Aponi the lead and grinned as her eyes got big with the responsibility. Pleased, she squared her shoulders, patted Etu, then tugged on Willie, leading them down the path.

Andre opened his eyes, slowly waking.

Got to get a plan together. Strong Eagle's never here, and Jacqo wants to be with Morning Dove... someone needs to look out for Aponi. She would have drowned yesterday if I hadn't...

He lifted his head and looked over. Her bedroll was empty. "Oh, not again."

At that moment, Aponi entered the camp leading Willie, Jacqo patting the mule's rear to keep him moving. Andre sat up in his bedroll, scratching his head.

"Aponi has a new friend," Jacqo smiled at her, then turned to Andre. "I gathered our stuff and brought it back." He undid the rope and took their packs off Willie. "It's probably time to sort through and figure things out."

Andre's face relaxed. Standing, he rolled up his sleeping gear. "I was thinking we head back to the last village we were at. They know us and will help. But we need a plan. Any idea what Strong Eagle wants to do?"

"No. Ahhh, look here." Jacqo set their packs inside the teepee, then knelt and pulled a bowl and a pouch of cornmeal out of a bag. "Thought we ate all our food." Opening it, he peered inside, then shrugged, dumping it in the bowl. At the fire, he added water and leftover raspberries, then stirred them into a batter. Grabbing a can of lard from the teepee, he scooped some out, putting it on the flat rock over the fire, then poured rounds of batter into the lard as it melted. The cakes bubbled up, and using his knife, he flipped them over. Andre added dried meat, and together the trio sat and ate. Aponi offered Etu a bite and then went over to Willie, holding a piece of cake in her palm. He gently licked it clean. Picking up his lead, she looked at Jacqo for permission, pointing towards the village.

He nodded his head. Leading Willie, she walked the path to the village center.

Strong Eagle stood in the trees and watched Aponi as she stood by the gravesite, holding Willie's rope loosely in her hand. Feet bare and dirty, her face was smudged with berries from breakfast. The air shimmered around her as the yellow-bellied chickadee swooped in low. She looked up and smiled at the bird as it flew into the nearest tree, perching on a low branch.

Strong Eagle stood, mesmerized. *Just like Raven as a young girl.*

Willie had his nose stuck in a patch of grass but at the sound of Aponi's voice, he lifted his head. She pointed at the graves and said to the mule: "My mama is sleeping here with Chitto." She looked into Willies big round eyes and whispered. "I don't think they are going to wake up." Holding Etu extra close, Aponi leaned into the crook of Willie's long neck. He nickered as she rubbed her face into his fur, then flicked his tail, sensing someone nearby. Aponi looked over and saw Strong Eagle in the trees.

"Strong Eagle." She looked up and smiled.

The struggle of bad spirits warred inside, threatening to return and control him. She was a reminder of what life had been, her smile an invitation to connect with all they had lost. He took a step towards her.

"Strong Eagle?"

Each step felt heavy as he walked towards her. He took another and then another until he was near enough to take her small hand in his. Her skin was soft in his weathered hands. Reaching out, he stroked the mule's neck. "Hello, Willie."

The mule's lips quivered as he exhaled loudly and bent his neck back down to the grass.

"Are Mama and Chitto going to wake up, Strong Eagle?" Aponi stared up at him with unblinking eyes.

Strong Eagle took a deep breath and felt the Spirit of his father move through him. Bad spirits melted away as he looked into the innocence of Aponi's eyes.

"No, Aponi, their bodies sleep here, but their spirits fly." His voice caught.

"Like the chickadee?" Aponi pointed to the bird resting on the branch of a nearby tree.

Strong Eagle looked up, surprised she knew the bird was there. "Yes."

I have not been here for her, he thought, brushing crumbs off her face. Grateful to Andre and Jacqo for all they had done, he knew it was his job. Squatting on one knee, he pulled her into his shoulder. "It's just us now."

"Will Andre and Jacqo go away too?" She asked, stroking Etu's hair.

"I hope not."

"Where's Raven?"

Strong Eagle's breath caught in his throat. "I don't know."

They were quiet for a moment.

"I see you made a new friend." He scratched Willie on the nose.

"Yes, we go everywhere together." She giggled as she brushed her face against his whiskers. "It tickles when I put my face near his."

"Let me try." He put his cheek next to Willies whiskers, then laughed. "You're right, Aponi."

Willie pawed his foot in the dirt, ready to move.

Strong Eagle looked at the gravesite. They filled most of the empty spots in with dirt and red stones, clearly marking the Sacred Circle. He walked over to the center stone, picking up the pouch which held the pipe, then turned to Aponi. "Want to go fishing?"

"Okay." She held onto Willie's lead with one hand and taking Strong Eagles with the other, together they turned and walked back towards camp.

THIRTY-ONE

Raven ran her hand over Little Wolf's belly as they lay in the sleeping hide, the sun now bringing warmth into the cave. Her dream felt real, as if Strong Eagle were still alive. She nudged Little Wolf out of the way and reached into her pocket, pulling out her talisman. Laying her hands over her heart, she closed her eyes and prayed.

"Please Great Spirit, if he lives, help him find me."

She wasn't sure she believed in prayers anymore, but it was all she knew to do. Little Wolf rolled and peeked up at her from the fur.

"Good morning, Little Wolf." She looked up at the entrance, still expecting to look over and see his mother standing there. "What happened to your family?" she asked, stroking the soft baby fur around his neck and shoulders. "I had a family not long ago, and they were killed." He nuzzled her hand. Chuckling, she crawled out the fur and got some jerky out of the food cache, tossing it to him.

As she completed her morning chores, Raven noticed Little Wolf wandering around the rocks restlessly. Earlier, a large robin flew back and forth from the clearing to the rocky ledge above her, carrying grass in its beak. Buzzards circled over the rocks.

"What's up there, Little Wolf?" She reached out to scratch his neck. "Shall we see?"

Raven led, navigating rock ledge to rock ledge, Little Wolf close on her heels. Pulling herself up on a narrow ridge, she looked up. High in the corner there was a large nest. Using stone out-crops as a ladder, she climbed up and peeked in. There were several speckled blue eggs. Tipping the nest, she took three eggs, leaving some so the mother would not be upset when she returned. Carefully, she placed them in the grass pouch she had woven.

Little Wolf whimpered from the other side of the ledge. Looking down to the drop off on the other side of the narrow ridge, she saw the body of a wolf, its large paws extended out as if running, gray and white fur around its neck, matted with blood. Sadness filled her as she jumped into the small clearing. "Oh, Little Wolf, is this your mother? I'm so sorry." She reached for him.

He growled at her and sat close to the dead body.

Raven left, scrambling down the rocks. Back in the cave, she put the eggs in her food cache, then gathered tools and a bit of meat. Returning, Little Wolf was still next to the body, whimpering. With the meat in her hand, she sat on the other side of the big wolf with her back to the pup, motionless. Soon Little Wolf came to her and nuzzled her hand. Opening her palm with the meat in it, the pup ate, licking her scent.

"We are both orphans now." She laid her hand softly on his back. "I will be your new mother."

Little Wolf wandered away. Unsure how he would react to what she was about to do, Raven wasted no time. She skinned the hide, saving the internal organs, then stripped tendons off the muscles and limbs to make new sinew with. She noticed the stomach had little food in it.

"You were hungry. Were you sick?" She looked at the blood matted around the neck. "What did this?" Raven looked around uneasily. "I'm sorry, Mother Wolf. I will take care of your pup." She rested her hand on the coarse hair covering the wolf's large gray and white head, then gently closed the wolf's eyes.

After taking what she could use, Raven discarded the rest of the body parts, throwing them off the ledge, watching as buzzards swooped in. Wrapping everything else into the large hide, she carried it back to the cave, tossing the bundle from ledge to ledge then climbing down. After scraping the hide, she staked it out in the sun to dry then took the internal organs down to the river. Washing them at the riverbank, she was careful not to tear them, as they would dry into flexible pouches that she could use to carry water in.

Walking back through the clearing, she hummed softly, harmonizing with the joyful songs from the birds in the trees. Deeper tones of sadness and grief wove into the harmony. Nearing the cave, she hoped to see Little Wolf waiting for her, but the ledge was empty. The hope she had just minutes ago diminished as she went into the cave, now dark and cold from the dying fire. She stoked the fire and soon a blaze lit up the cave, shadows reflecting on the walls. "Little Wolf?" She called, looking out into the night.

THIRTY-TWO

Morning Dove stretched, waking. Still relaxed from the Mugwort, she got up and opened the back flap. The fresh air felt good as she stepped out into the trees. Changing the grass in her thong, she was happy to see her bleeding was slowing. "Maybe tomorrow I can come out."

Back inside she sat next to the fire, sipping tea brewed with mint and lavender, the scent filling the teepee.

Something is different today. I feel stronger, taller somehow.

Vague memories of visions throughout the night floated through her mind. Reaching down, she felt the scabbed-over wound on her side. The pain was almost gone. She spent the day going through the family things left in the teepee. Things that had been of little importance a few days ago now seemed treasures.

Picking up Chitto's shirt and leggings he wore for dancing and ceremonies, she pressed it against her face, feeling the soft leather, breathing in the mingled scent of dirt and sweat. The shirt, decorated with beaded designs of colorful birds, was fringed on the arms so when he danced, they shook and sparkled. Not long ago, under the full moon, the tribe gathered...

Fire glowed brightly against the night sky as the drumming started. Children danced around the fire, heads bending and bobbing up and down, each footstep a connection to the earth. Women formed a middle line around the circle and danced counterclockwise to the children, holding hands, raising and lowering their arms in time with each step sideways. Their voices accompanied the beat of the drums as they celebrated the lives they birthed, now dancing in front of them. Behind them the men formed the outer circle, holding their community safe and whole. The steady shake of a rattle joined the drums. Chanting softly, the men joined voices with the women, giving thanks to the earth and celebrating Creator and Coyote for birthing them into these mountains. The dancing went on for hours as the fire keeper patiently sat by the fire, watchful, adding wood as needed to keep it blazing.

Morning Dove remembered the day she could leave the children's circle and join the women. She and her friend Lomasi would catch each other's eye and break out into giggles, bringing stern looks from their mothers. Strong Eagle said Lomasi's body covered hers, saving her life in the massacre.

Who will be my friend now? I wish she were here, sharing womanhood with me... I miss Chitto's laughter spreading through the trees as he ran with his friends...

Sighing, she folded up his ceremonial garb and set it aside. "One day I will have a boy and name him Chitto. I will give him this... and tell him our stories."

Scooting over, she came to Raven's basket full of beads. Jealous, she stood back and watched her sister's natural beauty and talent unfold. Morning Dove looked through the basket of beads, carefully sorted and tucked inside pouches by color and size. Underneath lay the wedding dress she had been making. Pulling it out, she held it up. The leather had been bleached into a soft snowy white. Light coming in from the open back flap made the beaded sun on the chest sparkle with rays of red, orange and yellow like the sunrise. With fringe on the bottom neckline and along the arms, she could picture it on Raven, grace and beauty coming alive with each movement. "Will I ever see you again, Raven? I hope so... I will save it for you." Folding up the dress, Morning Dove tucked it into the basket and covered it with the beads.

Next, she looked through Aiyani's things, surprised with the simplicity of what was there. Picking up a piece of clothing, she held it to her nose, inhaling the scent of her mother, always fresh with whatever herbs and plants she picked that day. She looked up at the branches and leaves of plants which still hung on sinew strung across the teepee as her mother's voice filled her.

"Some things need to dry slowly," Aiyani said. "That way they keep the strongest medicine." Their teepee always smelled like flowers, reminding her that even after death, her mother would always be nearby. As she folded up her mother's things, she set them aside. "Keep? Burn? What is the right thing to do?" She pulled out a grass belt woven by her mother and a necklace Raven beaded for her. Maybe someday Aponi would like to have a memory of their mother.

She already set aside the few items belonging to Lusio. "What if he returns and we're not here?" Morning Dove added a waterskin and a pouch of pemmican and berries to the pile, just in case.

The rest of the day seemed to drag. Bored, when she heard footsteps pass by, she wanted to peek out and say hello. Aponi brought her food but never stayed long. Relieved to see evening approach, she built up the fire. Tomorrow, perhaps she would come out of the teepee... a woman.

Would Jacqo be waiting?

THIRTY-THREE

Raven banked the fire for the night, then pulled out the rabbit skin blanket she made. Wrapping it around her shoulders to ward off the chill, she sat on the ledge watching the sunset. Wolves howled in the distance. "He has found his pack."

Looking into the night she listened for the sound of Little Wolf's paws, coming up the rocks. As the night deepened, loneliness washed over her. Tears began to fall and little by little, turned into sobs. Keening sounds became howls, reaching out to the wolves in the distance, or to anyone or anything that might hear her, that might acknowledge her existence. Ignoring the moon and stars this night, tucked into Strong Eagle's sleeping fur, she let the fire die as she cried for her family, for her lover and for Little Wolf, allowing the limitlessness of night to take it, gradually relieving her of the weight she carried since the massacre. Drifting into a deeper sleep, Raven dreamt of her mother and of the chickadee. Steps light as a feather, her mother no longer walked with a limp. Raven had never seen her mother without dragging her left foot. Standing in the shadows of the dream, she watched as her mother shapeshifted into the chickadee and flew up to the nearest branch, only to become still and, seeing through her dream state, looked directly into Raven's heart.

Morning Dove lay on the fur, feeling peaceful for the first time since the massacre. All she needed to do was think of her mother, and it was like she was right there. Aiyani would continue to teach her, but in a different way. Drifting off to sleep, she wondered what the future would bring. Morning Dove dreamt of a new place, one she had never seen before. In front of her was a tall pine, and on the lowest branch was the chickadee. It looked at her, singing a melody sweet yet strong. She followed the sound into the roots of the tree, inside the earth. There on a scrubby path stood Aiyani, waiting.

"Follow this path." Her mother smiled at her.

"Come with me," Morning Dove begged.

"No, my darling, this is your journey now." Aiyani faded from the dream.

Feet bare, as she walked the warmth of the dirt filled her legs with each step, pulling her forward. Hearing voices, she followed the twists and turns of the trail, coming upon a circle of women sitting under a willow. Drawn to the old woman sitting with her back to a tree, she watched her, talking excitedly, and waving her arms. It reminded her of the old woman's face in the fire. Eyes shifting around the circle, they stopped at a young woman, long black hair covering her face, bent down, sewing beads on a leather shirt. The young woman's belly was large and round with child. Sensing a presence, she looked up.

"Raven! It's you!"

Raven had tears in her eyes but smiled and called to her sister. "Follow the chickadee."

THIRTY-FOUR

SPLAT!

Raven woke with a start. The sound of something hitting the floor of the cave startled her. Barely light, eyes crusted with tears, she searched for the sound. At the entrance of the cave sat Little Wolf. Fur dripping and red tongue hanging out of his mouth, his blue eyes were full of anticipation. On the ledge, a large fish flapped wildly, its rainbow colors reflecting into beams of light as the sun caught each movement.

"You came back! Oh, Little Wolf, you came back." Raven crawled out of the sleeping fur and walked over to the entrance. "And you have been fishing. We will have breakfast. Thank you!" New tears rolled down her cheeks, making trails where the old ones dried. Little Wolf nuzzled her, somehow knowing he had done something good, but perplexed what to do with this wild, wiggling creature.

Raven noticed a slight pain in her back as she stood and stretched, her belly now the size of a large, round fruit. But, feeling happy, she ignored the pain, laughing as she went over to the fire pit and stirred the ashes. She gathered twigs, dry grass and wood, making a mound in the pit, then with two flicks of the scraping knife on the flint, a small fire blazed. Adding wood to make it hot, she placed the flat stone on top to heat.

"I will take care of the fish, Little Wolf." She picked up a stone lance and the fish by the tail, taking both to the outer ledge. "You caught it, now I'll show you what to do."

Setting the fish on a rock, she held up her knife. "Watch your nose pup." Nudging him away with her knee, with one motion, she neatly cut the head off the fish and threw it off the edge, down into the rocks for the buzzards. Little Wolf sat on his haunches and watched. The fish gutted, cleaned and scraped, Raven laid it out on the flat rock she put over the fire. There was a faint pop and sizzle as the fish cooked.

"Oh, I know!" She took out the three robin's eggs from the food cache. One at a time, she cracked them open and put the egg on the flat rock with the fish, tossing the shells to Little Wolf which he caught midair, chomped, and swallowed in one bite.

They sat on the ledge sharing food as the morning sun came into full view.

THIRTY-FIVE

Strong Eagle sat on a rock near the riverbank and watched as light filled the sky, his thoughts reflected in the changing colors. Picking up a long skinny stick nearby to use as a pole, he attached his fishing line and dropped it into the river.

We need to gather food... prepare for our journey. Andre wants to go west...

As the sun rose, he secured the pole between two rocks, then gathered shorter sticks and sat fashioning new arrows with his knife.

I am grateful to Andre and Jacqo... they are good men... good friends. But I need to find Raven.

Startled out of his thoughts by a tug on the line, he jumped up and pulled it out of the river. A large catfish dangled at the end, its tail flinging drops of water into the air. He rapped it on the head, strung the fish on a piece of sinew and dropped the line back in, and then froze. The hair on the back of his neck prickled at the sound of soft whimpering, like a baby's cry.

Puma!

Crouching behind a tree, he looked around. A big tawny cat walked down the path towards the camp. Reaching down, he felt the surrounding ground until his hand closed on a rock, then picked it up, stood and threw it. Surprised, the puma turned and ran off into the woods. He grabbed the fish and with knife in hand, sprinted up the path to the camp and looked around. Bedrolls were empty and Willie was gone. "Andre? Jacqo?" he called, laying his bow and arrow near the fire.

"Raven?" Morning Dove called out.

"Follow the chickadee," Raven said.

Fuzzy with sleep, Morning Dove slowly woke and realized she had been dreaming. "Follow the chickadee? What does that mean?"

She emptied the last of the water into the pot and tossed in a handful of raspberry leaf. With the kettle on the fire, she went over and pulled out a tin of honey from a nearby basket. Scooping it out with her finger, she drizzled it into the tea, then licked her finger clean. "Mmm..." As the tea brewed, she pulled up her dress and looked at her wound. Pink skin emerged under the scab and it itched more than hurt. She mulled over her dream while sipping her tea. "Chickadee..."

As light flickered on the walls of the teepee, Morning Dove stuck her head out of the back flap. The sun was creeping into the treetops as the crispy morning air touched her face. Stepping out into the wooded area, she removed the thong and squatted. *No blood.*

With lightness in her step, she came inside and put on a clean dress. Pulling out the grass belt she saved out of Aiyani's things, she could feel her mother's deft but soft touch as she tied it around her. Combing her hair with her fingers, Morning Dove made one long braid and pulled it over her shoulder. Hot tea in hand, she opened the front flap and stepped out.

Strong Eagle knelt near the fire. The smell of fish cooking drifted out around him. Turning at the sound of her footsteps, he smiled in welcome, then gestured to the fire as he reached in and flipped the fish with his knife.

She stood sipping her tea. "It's so quiet. Where is everyone? Why are there no birds singing?" She looked down and saw his bow fully loaded on the ground next to him.

"Puma." He pulled the fish off the fire, then looked up and met her stare.

Morning Dove's eyes grew big, and she gasped. They looked up as Aponi and Willie came into the camp followed by Andre, a worried look on his face.

"Mountain Lion... tracks." He pointed towards the village.

Strong Eagle nodded. "Saw it by the river."

Morning Dove glanced up at the men, then hugged Aponi protectively. "You smell good." She nestled her nose into her sister's hair, making Aponi giggle. "How's Etu this morning?"

"Hungry!" Aponi grinned at Morning Dove, then sat next to Strong Eagle at the fire.

Morning Dove looked around. "Jacqo?"

"He's checking the rest of the camp." Andre tied Willie securely to a tree. Returning to the fire, he placed the basket of berries he and Aponi picked on the ground between them. Aponi reached in and took a handful, offering one to Etu.

Chilled, Morning Dove rubbed her arms, went into the teepee and put on her moccasins, tying them at the ankles. Wrapping a blanket around her shoulders, she stepped out of the teepee just in time to see Jacqo pass by her moon lodge, a surprised look on his face at the open flap. He peeked inside, then stood, eyes searching the camp. Their eyes met.

Jacqo grinned. Morning Dove blushed as he walked over and reached out and stroked her face. Lightly cupping her chin, he took her hand and led her to the fire.

Watching the interaction, Strong Eagle exchanged a knowing look with Andre, then looked down, thoughtfully chewing. The group sat quietly eating as Willie nickered softly and pawed the ground. "Everyone stays close today." Andre looked at Aponi, who blushed at the attention and looked down. Andre chuckled, reached over and tousled her hair. She giggled, snuggling in close to him.

"Will it come into camp?" Morning Dove asked, scooting over to sit next to Strong Eagle.

"Nah. Mostly they attack if you're moving." He looked around at the group. "Sometimes they attack randomly. Take one of us with you if you leave camp, even to the river to wash."

"Ok." Morning Dove sat down close to Strong Eagle. "I had a dream. Raven was in a circle of women. She was sewing beads onto leather and her stomach was large with child. She looked at me and smiled but had tears in her eyes."

He gave her a puzzled look.

Morning Dove hesitated, then continued. "She told me to follow the chickadee."

"I have seen that chickadee twice. Yellow bellied?"

"Yes," Morning Dove said.

"The last time I saw it was by the rocks. It hovered for a minute, then flew south along the river." His face tightened with worry.

"Do you think those men took her?" Morning Dove asked.

Strong Eagle's eyes darkened. "I don't know. But I must find her."

"Ma always said when you see something three times, it's a sign," she said. "You saw it two times, and I saw it in a dream. That's three. I hope she's okay."

"I saw it the day we found you." Jacqo joined them. "It was like she guided us to where you lay."

"It flew south... We need to go south." Strong Eagle tossed his scraps into the fire.

Andre interrupted. "Might be best to retrace our steps west. The last village we were at was friendly."

"We need to go south," Strong Eagle repeated. He stood and walked away.

Jacqo watched as Andre's expression changed to worry. "This will not be easy," Andre looked at his brother, then followed. He found him sitting on the large rock overlooking the gravesite. "Strong Eagle." he approached tentatively.

Strong Eagle gave him a hard look then turned away.

"We know the trail west. The last village was friendly and they will help us."

"I was shown the trail south." Strong Eagle looked at Andre. "Raven is there."

"Do you think she lives?"

"Yes," Strong Eagle showed him the feather with her hair wrapped around it. "We need to go south."

Andre looked at Strong Eagle, arms crossed. After years of trading with the Natives, he knew when an argument was futile, and this was one of those times. "It's south then," he said. "At the base of the mountain there is a trail that leads east. There's land to settle on..." But Strong Eagle had already walked away. *Maybe I can convince them... and if Raven lives, we'll know by then.*

Jacqo passed as Strong Eagle stepped into the first teepee. He walked over to Andre. "Well?"

"Damn stubborn Indians. Looks like we're going south." Andre shook his head. "Got to hand it to him. Just like Lone Elk, he knows how to get what he wants."

Jacqo grinned in relief. "When will we leave?"

"Soon. We can go south to the split, then head east. Otherwise, we'll end up going over the mountains and could run into snow."

"We can sort through our things tonight and get ready." Jacqo ran his fingers through his hair. "Morning Dove wants to gather herbs and dig up some fresh yucca root up on the plateau. Aponi wants to come."

"Take your musket. And be careful." Andre sat back down on the rock, twisting the long hair in his beard around his finger.

THIRTY-SIX

Strong Eagle spent the day going through the teepees, gathering food and weapons they would take with them. Each teepee had an emergency cache with food and supplies. The attackers raided the main food cache and eaten or destroyed almost everything. But with the supplies he gathered from the teepees, there was enough.

Wait. One food cache was missing, the one from his teepee. His heart filled with hope.

He turned to the sound of footsteps, smiling at Morning Dove and Jacqo. "We need to go through the rest of the teepees to gather clothing and personal belongings of the dead and put it all in the fire pit." Looking at Morning Dove, he added: "Set aside Lusio and Raven's things. We will save them. And if there is anything you want to keep..." he trailed off, looking away.

"I know," Morning Dove said. "I have already gone through their things." Turning to Jacqo she asked, "Will you help me?" Strong Eagle watched them walk away, shoulders touching, heads bent. He couldn't hear the words they spoke but thought... *They are good together.*

Suddenly sounds of commotion came from the camp. He ran around the bend just in time to see Willie run through the grass and ran towards the river.

"Aponi untied him," Andre gasped, out of breath. "Something spooked him, and he ran." Andre fell in stride with Strong Eagle. They stopped at the edge of camp, but Willie was nowhere in sight.

"Get your musket, then follow this way." Strong Eagle pointed at the rough path on the outskirts of the village. "I'll follow his tracks."

Back in camp, Jacqo had Aponi and Morning Dove secure in the teepee. He handed Andre his musket and with his in hand they took off at a sprint.

Strong Eagle followed the winding path. It widened after a few turns but remained rough and full of brush. He saw Willies hair caught on a mesquite bush, then heard loud braying up ahead. Running, he found Willie caught in an outcropping of juniper, his lead tangled in the branches. The mule brayed, pushed and pulled, kicking his hind legs up - just getting himself more tangled in the brush.

Sweat dripping off their faces, the brothers ran up behind Strong Eagle. Jacqo handed Andre his musket, then Strong Eagle and Jacqo slowly crept up on either side of the mule. Strong Eagle reached in and untangled the lead while Jacqo spoke in a soft voice, firmly but gently squeezing his neck. "Calme toi Willie... Calme toi."

As the mule calmed, Strong Eagle handed Andre the lead behind him and slowly the brothers backed him out of the tangled brush. Strong Eagle turned to follow, then looked down. In the dirt was a dried footprint. He would recognize it anywhere.

Raven.

THIRTY-SEVEN

Filled with wondering, Raven walked back towards her village once again. Unsure of the whereabouts of the assailants, she never went far and always returned to her new home, her new existence. But today the path South slowly opened, and with spear in hand, she walked toward the mountains, following the deer trail along the river. A little way down the trail two large yucca bushes appeared, the red flowers dried on the ground, leaving the long-pointed stems, seeds, fiber and roots. Using the lance on her spear, she cut the sharp pointed stalks and dug surface roots.

Back at the cave, taking the long stems, she stripped the fibrous plant into threads and wove them into a pack and a basket to carry water. The pack was the right size and looped easily over her shoulders but was scratchy. Leaning the pack against a rock, she laid a large rabbit skin over the back and wove it around the edges with a small sharp bone and yucca fiber. Loading it with tools, she looped over her shoulders. The pup looked up at her.

"What do you think, Little Wolf?" Loading it with tools, she looped the pack over her shoulders. "Maybe I can make one for you." Tossing him a piece of jerky, which he snapped out of the air, she picked up the water basket and ran her fingers over the tight weave, examining it for holes. Then she looked at her food cache, the pile of furs and sleeping pack. *Plenty for the journey... but I need something to carry it on.*

"Let's go see if the basket holds water, Little Wolf." She climbed down the rocks, the pup at her heels. The chickadee swooped down from a tree and flew a circle around Raven before flying back into the branches. "Good morning, sister. How are you this morning?" Raven looked over and laughed at Little Wolf, who was nose deep in the chokecherry bushes, dirt flying out behind him as he dug.

At the river she dipped the basket in the water, then set it on the bank as she splashed her face. A rustling in the bush made the hair on the back of her neck prickle, but she turned just as Little Wolf come bounding through and jumped into the river. Laughing at her fear, she stood and with basket in hand, they headed to the clearing.

Raven found long skinny pieces of wood to make a travois big enough to carry what wouldn't fit in her pack. Nostalgia washed through her at the memory of the last time her tribe had moved...

"Time to go," Lone Elk announced at breakfast. "We leave before the sun hits the center of the sky." Everyone looked up, and the scramble began. Families hurried to their teepees and in an hours' time belongings were packed, teepees were down and hides wrapped around poles. Travois loaded together, they headed out, following the trail of deer and buffalo. They helped each other along the way, shared food, and when a water source was near the young boys ran and filled water pouches so everyone could drink. At the end of the fourth day, they found the place by the river, surrounded by large rocks, forest and open land for growing summer crops...

Raven wiped tears off her cheeks as the pictures and sounds of her family and friends flowed through her mind. Reaching into her pocket for the small stone, she took a deep breath and remembered her purpose. With the long skinny pieces of wood, she fashioned a small travois, Laying out the long poles so they narrowed at one end, she used shorter branches to connect the larger poles, just as they had done in their village. She held up the narrow end around her waist and smiled. "I can manage this."

Little Wolf's ears perked up as something moved through the bushes. Reaching for her spear, as her hand closed over empty space, she realized it was still up in the cave. Stepping behind a tree, she peeked around. The deer returned and were peacefully nibbling on the grass.

"How can I kill these creatures?" Little Wolf, now calm, nudged his nose into her hand.

In her tribe the men would return from hunting parties, deer hoisted over their shoulders, buffalo carried in on travois. The women received the kill and were skilled in harvesting the entire animal. They cut up meat, tanned and cured hides, then set aside bones to dry. Veins and tendons were stripped for sinew and organs for pouches. They wasted nothing.

Raven leaned the travois against a tree, then picked up the basket of water. A small trickle came out near the top, but otherwise the basket held. Nodding in satisfaction, she picked up the basket to take up to the cave, stopping at the tree and marking another notch. The travois was ready, and she had plenty of dried fish and rabbit. Soon the moon would be full and it would be time to go.

THIRTY-EIGHT

Strong Eagle paced around the camp. He checked Willie's lead, which was tied to a tree near Andre's sleeping roll. "Tomorrow we prepare." He looked around at everyone. "And we will leave the next day." Andre looked at Strong Eagle, then glanced at his brother. "Haven't seen the puma, but it could come any time."

The sisters stood in the teepee's door. Morning Dove's eyes met Jacqos. Smiling shyly, she looked down and stepped inside, but Aponi stood her ground with her blanket and doll in her arms. Strong Eagle walked over and knelt next to her. "You have to sleep in her tonight Aponi." She stifled a giggle when he squeezed her shoulder and made a funny face. "Good night." He closed the flap.

Aponi poked her head back out. "Strong Eagle, will you stay with us tonight?"

"I'll be close by."

"Ok." Aponi smiled at Strong Eagle, then disappeared into the teepee.

"I'll check the rest of the village." Strong Eagle turned to walk away.

"Going to the rocks?" Andre asked.

"No." Strong Eagle stared blankly at Andre for a moment, then left.

As the sun set, Strong Eagle walked the perimeter of the camp. Not seeing any fresh tracks, he went and sat on the large rock overlooking the gravesite. The Sacred Circle represented their journey in life and honored the new journeys for the bodies that lay buried below. He looked up as a star shot across the sky.

"I will find you Raven."

Raven sat on the ledge to her cave with Little Wolf at her side, the fire burning steadily behind them. In the distance a large half-moon rose as she watched stars fill the sky, their light rippling across the fast-moving river. It hadn't been that long ago that she sat on different rocks with Strong Eagle, wishing upon the stars.

What happened to those wishes?

Are they lost?

The sky became black around her, lit only by stars. Picking up a couple of pieces of wood, she fed the fire. "When the moon is full, we must go."

Night came, and Raven was happy to have Little Wolf nestled snug at her side. Her thoughts wandered as she drifted into sleep, vivid dreams weaving throughout the night. In one dream she was laughing as her daughter, now a

192

young girl, sat with legs astride a large brown animal, her hands gripped in the hair that grew atop its long, graceful neck. Her child had flowers in her hair and a feeling of happiness filled the air. Even this tall, beautiful animal seemed to smile. The sun shined brightly overhead, and a celebration was occurring. Her daughter was in the middle of it, long black hair flowing in the breeze around her hips, brown eyes twinkling. Raven's heart filled with joy.

Her dream flowed to a passage through the mountains and valleys. The sun marked the path, making the leaves in the trees sparkle with green hues. An occasional leaf fell and brushed her shoulder before gently floating to the ground, unattached to where it landed. She journeyed onward, feeling carried by unseen forces.

The dream shifted back to the celebration. Gazing at her beautiful daughter, Raven felt hands touch her shoulder. She looked down at his strong brown arms as he hugged her, nuzzling her neck. The scar from hand to elbow reminded her of the trials they had been through.

"She's so lovely." His voice was husky with pride. "Just like her mother."

Together they watched the celebration unfold. Taking her hand, he led her away.

THIRTY-NINE

Strong Eagle woke as dawn came. Unable to sleep, he returned to the rocks. Stretching, he stood and jumped off the rock ledge. Across the river, the soft cry of the puma rose above the swishing of the grass as he pushed it aside. Silently, he took the bow from his back and loaded an arrow. Arm raised and poised to shoot, he stepped onto the path.

Arrow pulled back, staring into the amber eyes of the puma, he froze as the cat's eyes shifted to brown, becoming Lone Elk's eyes – clear, curious and as always, able to see right through him. The black line that traced the tawny face from the cat's eyes, curving gracefully around its mouth, moved slightly as the puma growled.

"Son, the puma sees into the darkness. It eats what is aching in your soul so that doors to the light can open..."

Andre and Aponi appeared on the path coming from the river, Aponi's gasp startling Strong Eagle back into the present. Andre pulled Aponi off the path, but at the sound of her gasp the puma turned and sprung into the trees just as Strong Eagle released the bow. The arrow flew through the air, landing where the big cat stood only seconds ago. But the cat had been too fast. *Or I was too slow.*

Aponi stared with her mouth open, eyes big, squirming to get down. "No." Andre tightened his hold as they walked back to camp. Strong Eagle could see the tension in Andre's shoulders and sweat on the back of his neck. In camp Andre set Aponi down and walked over to Jacqo, who was tucking their bedrolls under the ropes on the travois. "Mountain Lion on the path."

Jacqo reached over and pulled his musket close, then looked over at Morning Dove. Aponi was holding her arms out wide, telling her about the big cat. She looked up at Strong Eagle and the brothers, worry on her face.

Raven woke. The dream felt real. It was as if Strong Eagle were still alive. She could still feel his arms around her. Laying with her eyes closed, she willed it to be true, but a short time later woke to the sound of growling. Little Wolf stood at the entrance of the cave; teeth bared. Raven reached for her spear and stood, joining the pup at the entrance of the cave. The bushes at the edge of the clearing rustled as whatever had been there ran away.

Or whomever...

Torn between the comfort of her dream and the fear that filled her, Raven sat on the ground, the feeling of heaviness overwhelming. She looked at the stacks of rabbit skins and the food cache, which was overflowing. The wolf skin was bundled and tied, and in the clearing her travois was ready. Nothing else was needed. Raven looked up at the moon setting over the river in the pre-dawn. It would be full soon.

FORTY

Strong Eagle stood in front of the community fire pit. New arrows were bound, and the hatchets and knives had been cleaned of the dry, crusted blood. He turned to see Morning Dove and Jacqo come out of her family teepee.

"Done?" All the other teepees had been taken down. They would take two with them, using the poles as a travois. But she insisted on leaving their teepee intact with Lusio's things, as well as food and water.

"He's coming back. I know it." She looked at Strong Eagle, determined. "We need to leave a sign so he can find us."

"No, he's a good tracker. If he returns, he'll find us."

"Strong Eagle, what if..." But he had already turned to walk back to the camp. Jacqo tilted her chin up with his finger and she smiled. Together they walked back to the camp in silence. Above them, the yellow-bellied chickadee flew higher into the tree.

Raven and Little Wolf climbed down the rock to the clearing. Spear in hand, she walked around the perimeter, shaking the bushes with her spear to make noise. They followed the trail out to the bathing hole, then back in, not seeing any signs of animals or people. She knelt around a fresh track and held her hand around it. "It was big. What was it Little Wolf? Was it your family looking for you?" He sat on his haunches, looking at her with curiosity. "You're not worried. Is it gone?" She found tracks down by the river, then more leading north on the trail. After a little way, they turned and walked south to the yucca bushes, then back to the clearing. "I'm glad you're with me, Little Wolf." He nuzzled her hand, then pulled a piece of jerky out of her bag, tossing it to him. He caught it, then scrambled up the rocks after her.

Up in the cave, she cut out new moccasins from the wolf hide and sewed them together. As her hands wove the sinew through the holes she poked with the sharp point of a bone, she wished she had beads to decorate them with. "I was going to marry Strong Eagle." She touched Little Wolf, who sat on the edge of the rocks near the cave. "I made a beautiful dress. It had a sun over my heart to remind me to always be open to the warmth of the sun and what each day can bring." She set the completed moccasin down and looked up, meeting the pups gaze. "I'm sorry about your mother." He lay his head on his paws, watching her. Raven looked out over the clearing. "Think we'll stay here today, little pup. We don't know what's out there."

FORTY-ONE

Morning Dove paused at the entrance of their family teepee. Aponi squirmed down from Andre and grabbed onto the back of her sister's dress as she opened the door. Together they stepped in. Aponi watched as Morning Dove pulled down the last of the herbs that Aiyani hung to dry. Smells of lavender and sage filled the space as they crushed and sprinkled the flowers around the teepee. Going over to the pile of Lusio's things, she pulled out extra jerky from the leather bag that hung from her belt and tucked it into his things.

"Is Papa coming?" Aponi asked.

"Yes, and he'll be hungry." Aponi quietly watched as Morning Dove folded and unfolded her father's belongings. Finally, tucked away in the corner with a fresh waterskin leaning against the wall of the teepee, she took a handful of blossoms from the floor nearby and sprinkled them over his things.

"Why are you doing that?"

"Blessing his journey." Morning Dove smiled at her sister. "Wherever he is, we need to connect him to this moment and this place so he can find us. Maybe he'll sense our love and it will give him hope." Sighing, she stood and took Aponi's hand.

The girls stepped out of the teepee just as Strong Eagle came from the community fire pit carrying arrows, hatchets and knives. Morning Dove closed the flap, tying it. "I know Dada is coming," she said, meeting his hard stare. Strong Eagle turned and started back to camp, the sisters falling in step behind him. Jacqo looked up from the fire and smiled, then turned to his brother.

"Ready?"

"Ready as we'll ever be," Andre snugged the last rope down on the travois. "We'll leave room in case Aponi gets tired." He sighed. "I hope this isn't a mistake."

Strong Eagle stood silently observing the brothers, and then turned and walked into the darkness.

Jacqo shrugged as he looked at Andre's worried face. "Going to go clean up, be right back." Andre nodded absently as he watched his brother leave. He tied Willie securely to a tree nearby, then turned and looked at the girls as they braided each other's hair. Stirring the fire, he wished he could see their future in the flames.

FORTY-TWO

Raven stepped into the icy water as Little Wolf splashed nearby. She sighed in relief from the heat of the summer day. Her earlier worries about the footprints she had seen drifted away as she watched Little Wolf. She laughed as he lost his grip on a small wiggly fish, looking puzzled as it swam away. Still small enough to curl up in a ball next to her when they slept, she teased: "Will you still share my bed when you're grown?"

Bare feet on the ground, her hair dripped down her back and legs as she stood and dried in the morning sun. Stroking the taut skin of her belly, she traced the bulge, bigger now. "What will be your name?" Raven mused, turning to walk back towards the cave.

In one bound Little Wolf leapt out of the water and was at her side, drenching her with water as he shook.

"I just got dry." She laughed, smoothing her hair into a long braid. Crossing the path back to the clearing, Raven stood and stared in the direction of her village. Disappointment filled her. "The moon is almost full." She rested her hand on Little Wolf's head. "I don't think anyone is coming." She looked at the path going south and the mountains in the distance.

Why? What is there? It's safe here... I have shelter and food. What if I run into more attackers? But who will help me with the baby? Should I go back? I feel like I am dreaming...

Little Wolf looked up at her, then nuzzled her hand. Shoulders slumped, she ran her fingers through the hair on his back.

"No, Little Wolf." Her shoulders slumped. "It's not a dream."

They climbed up the rocks to the cave. At the top they stood looking out over the clearing and river beyond. Little Wolf looked up. Above them, an overhanging branch bounced as the chickadee sat, chirping.

"Hello sister," Raven held her hand above her eyes so she could see better. "You have a pretty yellow belly. What news do you bring today?"

The chickadee flew down and circled her three times, then flew north out of the clearing. Raven watched the bird fly away. The chickadee stirred something in her. She took out the talisman her mother had given her, holding it over her heart. "What is the message?"

Jacqo walked into the camp from the river path. "Where is everyone?"

204

"Saying goodbye." Andre put on his hat on, then together they walked towards the village. As they neared the clearing they stopped, struck by the beauty of their friends. Dressed in buckskin pants and shirt, Strong Eagle wore a headband decorated with brightly colored beads, which sparkled in the afternoon sun. Hanging neatly down the back of his long black hair was the white feather. The girls wore beaded bracelets and held baskets of brightly colored flowers and green leaves. The trio walked to the center stone of the gravesite. Strong Eagle took the pouch holding the sacred pipe off his shoulder and held it to the heavens. As he prayed, the girls tossed handfuls of flowers in the spokes of the Sacred Circle, tracing the wheel in a spiral.

Jacqo was mesmerized as he watched the flowers and ferns mingle in the air with each toss before falling randomly to the ground. He looked at Aponi's small fingers as they opened, releasing petals, then at the larger delicate hands of Morning Dove, her slender arms reaching out, scattering beauty and life... honoring her family and friends that lay below her feet.

"The Sacred Circle is a map of their life." Andre pointed at the center stone. "Standing in

The center, one can see the journey of their life and all possibilities. Each direction holds special wisdom which can guide you in which direction to go. For instance, when you seek a vision, one might stand in the east, where the sun rises, and ask to be shown what is ahead for you, or what your first step should be." Andre looked at Jacqo, then back at their friends.

His heart filled watching them. *So like Aiyani... so beautiful. Was I wrong to want another man's woman? To still want her?*

Jacqo looked up at his brother, then back at their friends.

Voice loud and resilient, Strong Eagle held the pipe up to his chest:

> *"We will take your prayers and*
> *remember you...*
> *with each footstep and*
> *with each breath.*
> *We will honor you with our*
> *lives and with our love.*
> *Watch over us... Show us the way.*
> *Aho."*

The trio wove their way in a reversed spiral out of the Sacred Circle, then turned and stood for a moment with arms around each other. Nearby on the large rock, warming under the hot sun, a lizard sat watching, its body pulsing, eyes intense.

Jacqo looked up and pointed. The yellow-bellied chickadee hovered over the family, then flew through the trees going south. In the firepit, red and orange embers remained hot from the fire that burned the belongings of the dead. One teepee remained with food, water and clothing should Lusio return.

At Strong Eagle's nod, they turned and walked away towards the brothers and to their new life. Morning Dove's eyes glittered with tears as they met Jacqos. Holding out his arms, she melted into them, tears falling on his shoulder. Andre scooped up Aponi. Strong Eagle watched as the group headed towards the camp, and called out: "We leave at first light." Jacqo raised his hand in acknowledgement. Strong Eagle walked over and sat on the empty log where his father used to sit.

"How I long to hear your voice, Father, to see the truth in your eyes. Help me." His fingers touched the knife handle carved of the antler of an elk. "Thank you, father. I will follow in your footsteps... I'll do my best." Strong Eagle walked back through the camp and knowing he wouldn't sleep there, left and returned to the rocks... their special place.

A child Raven... we created life here. Will I ever see you again?

Raven crawled into the sleeping hide and pulled the sleeping fur around her, Little Wolf curled at her side. She reached down and ran her fingers along the soft, downy fur of his spine. For a moment she let her thoughts drift to Chitto and to her sisters. "I'd give anything to see you again..." she whispered. Sensing her sadness, Little Wolf looked up at her, nuzzled her hand, then stretched out alongside her. Comforted, Raven closed her eyes and slept.

FORTY-THREE

Strong Eagle pulled on his pack and patted the sheath at his hip which held his father's knife. He looked around the camp one last time, then at the group standing around Willie and the travois.

Aponi dropped the mules lead and walked over to him, tracing the thick scar that was forming on his arm, then looked up at him.

Kneeling, he stroked her face. "It'll be okay. Stay with Andre and Jacqo. They will protect you." He hugged her, then stood. "I'll go first and scout out the trail," he said. "If the travois is too long for the curves on the trail, put it aside. We'll come back for it." The brothers nodded in agreement.

Morning Dove nervously repacked her bag and checked that Raven's bundle on the travois was secure, then stood watching the dwindling fire. Aponi murmured soothingly to Willie, kissed him on the nose, then came over and took Morning Dove's hand. Strong Eagle knelt in front of them. "It'll be okay. Stay with Andre and Jacqo. They will protect you." He hugged them, then stood. Nodding at the brothers, he left, following the path south.

Andre rechecked the travois, securing the harness on Willie, who pawed the ground. One teepee provided the base for the travois and the other one was rolled and put on top. Everyone carried a supply of jerky and berries plus a waterskin.

"He didn't even look back." Jacqo looked up at Andre, then threw dirt on the fire, putting it out. "I thought they would take one last walk around the village, you know, memories."

"That's not their way. They believe doing that would keep the spirits of the dead trapped. It's sort of like a snake shedding its skin. Snake doesn't look back to see how the old skin is doing... just moves forward with the natural flow of new life. It's an act of faith. Of respect."

"Hmmm..." Jacqo shook his head as he put on his hat. Shrugging on his pack, he checked his musket then secured it in the strap hanging from his shoulder. "Let's go."

Andre led with Aponi, who held Willie's lead in her hand, the travois creaking as it dragged along the dirt path. Morning Dove stopped and looked with longing at the village behind her. Jacqo stood with her for a moment, then took her hand and led her out of camp.

Near the firepit, on top of a rock, sat the lizard, its chest pulsing with life, eyes a mixture of sadness and joy as he watched them leave. A mist settled over the rock as a shape swirled up in the center, revealing a man wrapped in a ceremonial robe, long gray braid down his back. Lone Elk stood, swirled back into the mist, and was gone.

Strong Eagle could hardly hold back from running. With eagerness in each step, he followed the path, stopping briefly where Willie had gotten tangled, and looked at the footprint. Filled with hope, he kept going, sprinting.

No signs of the puma... but it could be anywhere... come out of nowhere...

A cottontail branch brushed against him and snagged his shirt. Reaching down, he brushed it away, then noticed the long strands of black hair wrapped around the tip. Heart beating faster, his steps quickened as fear and hope battled for a place in his heart. A bit later he found another footprint tucked under branches on the side of the path, and then more hair.

Only her footprints...

Morning Dove walked behind the travois, watching her sister sleep. Andre picked up Aponi and nestled her in among sleeping furs on the travois, then took Willies lead. Jacqo's stare burned into her back. She glanced over her shoulder.

Jacqo's face reddened at her smile. Spellbound, he had been watching the curve of her hips with each graceful step, the flip of her braid when it got too hot. Beads of sweat dotted the back of her neck. He wondered if they would taste salty.

Suddenly Willie reared, preparing to bolt as something darted out of the brush. Aponi woke and sat up, rubbing her eyes. Jacqo pulled his musket up as Andre turned, knife in hand. They chuckled as a large jack rabbit ran across the path. Sighing in relief, Jacqo gentled Willie while Andre jostled the bushes to see what else might be there. Everything secure, he lifted Aponi and set her on Willie's back. She stroked his neck and lay her face against his coarse hair. He nickered softly as the group continued.

Raven leaned her travois up against the tree and tightened the laces. Nearby Little Wolf lay watching her, and as she walked towards the rocks, he jumped up and was at her side. Together they climbed up to the cave. Raven tossed Little Wolf scraps of meat as she made a paste of chokecherries and water and smeared it over the fish that was cooking on the fire. As the afternoon waned, they sat on the ledge together.

"Soon we will leave this place, Little Wolf." She reached in and pulled out the talisman, which grew warm in her hand as she gazed at the first stars of the night, sparkling over the river. "I wonder which stars belong to our mothers?"

Late afternoon, the group found Strong Eagle kneeling under a tree. He had a small fire going and several large trout cooking. Nearby run off from the river created a small pool. Morning Dove and Aponi ran, splashing water on their faces, then at each other. Their laughter filled the air. Standing next to Willie, the brothers grinned at their playfulness. Later, bellies full, the girls snuggled in their sleeping furs on the ground near the fire, soon fast asleep.

"I'll keep watch." Strong Eagle grabbed a waterskin and sat down on a nearby rock. The brothers stretched out under a tree, hats over their faces.

Strong Eagle woke to Andre's gentle shaking. Eyes open, he saw Andre's finger held up to his mouth, then tensed at the familiar soft cry of the Puma. He reached for his knife, a surge of fire running through him, his heart beating fast. "Are you stalking me?"

The sound softened and then disappeared. The two men sat back-to-back guarding the camp as the others slept. Feeling the support of his friend, little by little, Strong Eagle felt his body relax. It was as if he was doing a dance with the puma. A fight to get his power back. The power he lost the night of the massacre. His heart sunk at the memory of those who died, whom he didn't save.

The sound of his father's voice drifted through his head. "The Spirit of Puma stalks in the dark and eats away the bad things that would consume you, the things that distract you from the light, which is always there. But only one wins the battle. Which will you feed? The light or the dark?"

FORTY-FOUR

Strong Eagle left just as the sun rose through a low-lying fog. Determined to find Raven, he ignored a gnawing sense of foreboding, the memory of the puma. Sweat mingled with the cool mist of the fog as he jogged, feet barely touching the ground.

"Can't see." Jacqo tightened the lead on Willie. "He won't see the puma if it's around." Morning Dove tucked their sleeping furs on the travois, then helped Aponi adjust the pack as she pulled the grass braid over her shoulders.

"He's not listening," Andre picked up his hat off the ground, shook it out and put it on his head. "Only one thing on his mind."

Jacqo nodded. "Want to ride, Aponi?" he patted Willie's back.

Aponi shook her head no and took Morning Dove's hand.

"Stay close then." Jacqo looked up, meeting Morning Dove's eyes, who blushed.

"Let's go," Andre called out.

Raven woke early and sat on the ledge in the morning sun. "You're growing." She ran her hand over his course coat. "Something feels different today," she mused, scratching his neck. "Come on, little guy, let's go to the river and wash." Slipping into her moccasins, she grabbed her spear, and they climbed down the rocks. At the river Little Wolf splashed as he chased fish in the water while Raven bathed. Immersed in the cold water, Raven didn't see the sky grow dark.

Morning Dove trudged along behind the travois. Looking up, she watched as the sky darkened and turned to night. "The sun is dying." Grabbing Aponi, they ran under a tree for shelter and covered their eyes. Nearby Willie pulled at his lead, braying and pawing the ground. Andre tied him to a tree near the girls as Jacqo stood by. Strong Eagle bound into the camp holding a cloth over his head. He squatted next to the girls.

Raven panicked. Slipping, she dug her toes into the muddy bank and hoisted herself out. "Run, Little Wolf! Back to the cave! The sun is dying!" She pulled her dress over her head as she ran, bare feet skimming the grass in the clearing, still wet from the fog. "My moccasins." She looked back at them lying in the grass, then climbed barefoot over the rocks and up to the cave.

Raven crawled into her sleeping hide and covered her eyes. Pulling out her talisman, she held it to her belly. "Oh little one, please be okay. I ran as fast as I could." Stories from childhood filled her head...

"The moon spends her entire life chasing the sun," the storyteller began. "And the sun runs and runs in circles every day shining his light then hiding it fearful the moon will catch and kill him, putting him into darkness forever. His whole life purpose is to be a brilliant light for the world." The storyteller paused, then whispered ominously. "He mustn't get caught." Children and adults alike crowded closer, hands over their mouths, oohs and aahs slipping out between their fingers.

"One day the sun was a little relaxed and a little less watchful," the storyteller continued. "The moon crept up and ever so slowly embraced him until just the edge of the sun was covered. Then, little by little, she took possession of him. By the time the sun realized he was caught, the moon had him in a full embrace. His light was gone.

"Ooooohhh Nooo," the villagers moaned. "What happened to the sun? To the light?"

The storyteller held her finger up in warning. "Ever so slowly... I mean very, very slowly the moon, after enjoying a full embrace with the sun, gently crept across his face. And you know what happened?"

"What?" The villagers covered their mouths, fingers separating them just enough to allow words like "tell us," and "will the sun light the world again" to escape.

"Well..." the storyteller's eyes twinkled as the crowd held its breath. "As the moon moved across the sun, his light slowly emerged from the other side, reborn and as brilliant as ever." The crowd went wild with cheering, happy to know the sun would shine again.

"But hear me!" The storyteller admonished. "Creator made the sun and moon as sacred beings. You are not to watch this!" She pointed her finger and made eye contact with each person in the crowd, "It is an embrace, an intimate moment between the sun and moon. If you watch, it can affect your mind or body, especially if you are with child. It can put a spell on you." She shook her head sadly.

"What can we do?" Moans and cries filled the air.

"A special ceremony can remove the spell, but it still changes you..." The storyteller paused, brushing her fingers over the birthmark on her cheek. "It can bring bad dreams. You must stay inside and not get caught when the sun dies. This is the way to honor nature." A sigh was heard among the crowd. The sun would live to light the

world another day, and the moon would still show herself
and her mysteries each night.

The storyteller made a strong impression on Raven, but her
father had a different view. His people came from a southern
tribe. A guide for traders when he came to their village, he
fell in love with her mother and stayed. Laying huddled in
the fur, she wondered why he hadn't returned.

His voice ran through her head. "Don't listen to them,
Raven. Once in a while the moon catches the sun, they
embrace, and the sun is reborn. It simply acknowledges our
own nature. Nothing bad will happen if you watch. It just
reminds us to remember that the sacred lies within, just as
with the sun and moon. That is easy to forget if you are
looking somewhere else."

"Oh Papa, where are you?" She cried, face hidden in
the fur. "Have I harmed my child?" She rubbed the twinge in
her low back. "I will do a ceremony for my baby to protect
her

Strong Eagle peeked out over the cloth as the darkness
passed.

"Is everything okay?" Andre asked.

"It is bad luck to see the sun die," Strong Eagle said, eyes downcast. "I'm sorry. I hope nothing bad happens to you." He looked up as the sun broke through a cloud and lit up the day. Birds and squirrels chattered again.

Strong Eagle avoided eye contact with Andre but went over to the girls. "Okay?" He asked, kneeling next to them. They nodded. Eager to continue, he stood. "I'll keep going."

After he left, Jacqo looked at Andre, confused. "What was that about?"

"I don't know, you've seen them when the moon casts a shadow on the sun. They think it's bad luck to watch it." Andre shrugged. "Who knows? Maybe he's right."

Scratching his head, Jacqo said: "Ready?"

"Let's go," Andre called to the sisters. Aponi sat on Willie as Andre took the lead. Behind the travois Morning Dove walked, occasionally looking over her shoulder at Jacqo. His face lit up when their eyes met, and butterflies stirred in her belly. Each step took them away from loss and towards hope. Towards the future. She looked at Aponi astride Willie and wondered what their future held.

At least we have each other...

Raven woke to a sound outside. Crawling out of the sleeping hide, she peeked out, relieved to see the sun in full brilliance. On the ledge sat Little Wolf, watching her. "I was worried. I thought you ran away when the sun died. But look! It shines once again!" She smiled at him, gathering ash from the fire and red roots from her basket. Smashing them into a pulp, she added water from the skin until a thin paste formed. Using her fingers and a thick stick, she painted the sun and the moon on the wall of the cave. Underneath she painted a woman and her child holding their arms up to the sky and prayed:

> *"Spirits of the Sun and Moon I greet you.*
> *Please look upon me and my unborn child*
> *with blessings and grace.*
> *Aho."*

FORTY-FIVE

Filled with renewed hope and a sense of urgency, Raven gathered and organized the smoked fish and meat in the cache, stacking it near the door of the cave. Running her fingers over the soft fur in the bundle of rabbit skins, she smiled over at Little Wolf who sat watching her in anticipation. "It's time." Reaching into the small leather pouch on her belt, she pulled out a chunk of jerky and tossed it to him. "It's you and me, little guy. Tomorrow we leave to find my father's people."

Little Wolf sat gazing at her.

"I feel as if I see lifetimes in your eyes. It's as if my family is here with me." She fell silent for a moment. "I miss them. Do you miss your mother, Little Wolf? Where is the rest of your pack?"

Raven spread the sleeping fur out on the ground for the last time and crawled in as daylight dimmed from the sky. Too restless to sleep, she got up and joined Little Wolf on the ledge. She sat with her legs dangled over the side and together they watched the sunset.

Andre led Willie around the bend and spotted Strong Eagle kneeling next to a small fire on the riverbank. Four fish lay on a flat rock over the fire, steaming as the skin blackened. He looked up at the group and smiled. Everyone gathered around the fire, eating in silence. Morning Dove pulled the sleeping fur and hide off the travois, then looked over and smiled at Willie, who was grazing near the river. Spreading the fur on the ground, she sat down and patted a spot next to her. Aponi came over and lay down and soon their eyes were closed and breath soft. Jacqo watched as the sisters prepared for sleep, loving the sweetness in them, how they cared for each other. He looked over at Andre, torn.

Will I have to choose? Can I?

Raven pulled her legs up on the ledge and as she stood, felt the twinge in her back again. Stretching into the night, she pulled her talisman out of her pocket and held it next to her heart. Eyes closed, she prayed to her mother...

"I'm worried, Mama... I am alone. I am afraid I have harmed my baby. Please help me." Somewhere in the distance a pack of wolves howled. Little Wolf sat straight up, ears perked, listening. He looked at Raven, then pointed his nose to the sky, letting out a single howl. Raven shivered as the pack of wolves howled in return.

"Is that your family, Little Wolf, calling you?" Raven went into her cave and snugged into the sleeping fur, relieved when Little Wolf came and lay next to her.

Strong Eagle paced restlessly around the camp. He was eager to keep going, but not knowing where the puma was made it dangerous. As darkness settled over them, a pack of wolves howled in the distance. He stopped and listened, remembering his father's words: "Wolves are like family, son. Much like us, they mate for life and keep their family in packs. And they will fight to the death to protect each other, especially their young."

At that moment, the howl of a single wolf came, calling out to the larger pack. Somehow it comforted him. He lay near the fire and slipped into a dream... a dream where Raven stood, holding her arms out, waiting for him.

FORTY-SIX

Strong Eagle woke to the soft wetness of fog on his face. Sitting up, he looked over as Andre stirred the fire and Jacqo tightened the rope on the travois. Morning Dove and Aponi, hand in hand, came out of the grass nearby.

A dream... Raven... Strong Eagle shook his head, clearing his thoughts.

"Wondering when you were going to wake up." Andre brought a slab of wood with steaming fish to Strong Eagle, who nodded in thanks, shoving the food in his mouth. Eager to go, he took a long drink from his waterskin and pulled his bow and arrows on his back. Buckskin pants and shirt tucked into his pack, with only a loincloth and moccasins on, he shivered as goosebumps covered his skin.

"Wolves around." Andre gave Strong Eagle a hard look.

"I heard them." Strong Eagle put his hand on his knife. "Puma?"

"No, but that doesn't mean anything."

Strong Eagle went over and squatted next to the girls, wrapping his arms around them.

"Are you going to find Raven?" Morning Dove asked as Aponi looked at him with round, curious eyes.

"I hope so." He hugged them. "Stay close to Andre and Jacqo, okay?"

"And Willie." Aponi folded her arms over her chest.

Strong Eagle's face softened at her voice, and he smiled. "Yes. And Willie."

"Follow in a little while." Strong Eagle looked at Andre and Jacqo.

The brothers watched Strong Eagle's back as it disappeared in the fog. "Be careful," Andre called out.

Raven woke, surprised to see the pup pacing back and forth on the rock ledge outside the cave. "What is it, Little Wolf?" she called, pulling a piece of jerky out of her pocket. He turned at the sound of her voice and caught the jerky as she tossed it. Crawling out of the sleeping fur, she rolled it up and put it on the stacks of rabbit fur she had along the wall, and then stepped outside. "You're restless today. Is something out there?" Little Wolf looked up and nuzzled her pocket. She pulled another piece of jerky out. "You're supposed to be the hunter. You're a wolf!" Laughing, she picked up her spear and together they climbed down the rocks and into the clearing. "I don't think anyone is coming, Little Wolf." She put another notch on the tree, and then pulled the travois closer. "Let's go wash and then we'll pack up." She looked around nervously. "Wish I knew what was out there." Spear in hand, she looked for new tracks as they walked to the river.

Rather than jumping in and splashing as usual, Little Wolf sat on the riverbank, much more subdued than usual. Puzzled, Raven finished quickly and climbed out. "Let's go." She slipped her dress over her head. But Little Wolf took off running down the path leading out of the clearing. "Little Wolf, where are you going?"

Maintaining a slow, steady jog, Strong Eagle stopped at the rustling of bushes just ahead. Reaching for his knife, he chuckled as a young wolf poked its head out, teeth bared.

"You're just a baby." The wolf growled again, looking behind Strong Eagle.

Too late, Strong Eagle turned and saw the puma crouched in the tree. It jumped, knocking him to the ground. The leather throng holding his bow and arrows clenched tight around his neck as the puma's powerful jaws clamped around the bow. He heard it snap and for the second time, prepared to die.

"Raven, I'm sorry," he whispered.

Suddenly, there was a jolt and he felt the puma go slack, it's last breath hot on his neck. Rolling, he pushed the animal off him and sat up, gasping for breath. Shrugging off the broken bow, he looked over and saw the big cat, it's lifeless body lying next to him. Sensing a presence, he turned his head and he saw her. An arm's reach away stood Raven, mouth hanging open in surprise as she looked at the dead puma.

Stunned, he stared at her. "Raven?"

Startled at the sound of his voice, Raven looked from the puma to Strong Eagle, her eyes big. "Strong Eagle!" Running towards him, she stopped as Little Wolf leapt between them, teeth bared.

"Little Wolf! No!"

Andre came running around the bend, musket raised, aimed squarely at Little Wolf.

"No!" Raven stepped in front of the pup.

"Andre, stop!" Strong Eagle shouted, jumping up. He reached Andre just as the musket fired, pushing the gun up. Everyone stood in stunned silence at the loud blast. The smell of gunpowder filled the air.

"Little Wolf." Raven called. He growled and ran into the bushes. Turning to Strong Eagle, her voice trailed off. "Is it really you?"

"Raven?" And then she was in his arms. "Oh, Raven..." Tears met on their cheeks. He pulled his face away and gazed at her, caressing her cheek, then pulled away. "Look." He put his hands on her shoulders, turning her so she could see the path behind them.

"Morning Dove? Aponi?" Raven gasped as her sisters came around the bend. "Is this real?" She turned back to Strong Eagle.

"Yes, go to them." Just as Raven reached her sisters, collapsing in a pile of shrieks and tears, Willie came around the bend. Dust flew as he snorted and brayed, the travois teetering and then coming loose, falling on it's side. The sisters gasped and jumped out of the way.

Jacqo ran behind, arms waving as he tried to grab Willie's rope, but the mule was too fast. Strong Eagle sprung forward trying to land on it, but missed. The mule was determined. Willie ran down the trail, the brothers close behind.

Raven looked up at Strong Eagle with a confused look on her face.

"That's Willie. Their mule." He smiled at her, taking her hand and pulled her close.

"Andre? Jacqo?" Raven asked.

"They saved us, Raven." Tears filled his eyes. "If not for them, we'd all be dead."

Raven stood looking at him, then reached up and stroked his face. "I can't believe you're here."

He looked over at the pup who sat on his haunches peeking out of the grass. "Who's this?"

"Little Wolf," Raven pulled jerky out of her pouch, tossing it to him. "His mother died, and I adopted him." Aponi walked towards the pup.

"No!" Strong Eagle stepped out to stop her.

"It's okay." Raven put her hand on his arm, holding him back.

Aponi looked up and smiled at Strong Eagle, then reached out, letting Little Wolf smell her fingers. He took the jerky she offered, then licked her hand. Giggling, she sat on the ground next to him. Strong Eagle watched, shaking his head.

Jacqo and Andre came back into the circle, leading a reluctant Willie by the rope. "Damn mule."

Morning Dove looked up at Jacqo and blushed, then glanced over at Raven. The sister's eyes met and Raven smiled in understanding.

Strong Eagle came over and took her hand, helping her stand. "You're real." He touched her face, raising his eyebrows. "And you killed the puma? You saved me?"

"Always... I will always save you." Raven hesitated as a fleeting look of hardness flashed in Strong Eagle's eyes. "What is it?" She leaned in, cupping his face in her hands.

"It's just... it's just that..." Then he lay his forehead against hers. "The only thing that is important is that I found you."

EPILOGUE:

A lone figure approached the narrow path leading into the old village. He walked with a limp, his left foot dragging slightly behind him. Raising his hands to his mouth, he made the familiar bird call announcing his arrival. Silence. Alarmed, he continued. To his left he looked down into the ravine. Several dead bodies of Spanish soldiers lay, eye sockets empty and mouths open in death. Lusio quickened his step. He entered the village and stood under the big oak.

To Be Continued....

AUTHOR'S NOTE

Seven years ago, with a filing cabinet full of stories and satisfied just to see words flowing onto paper, I wasn't looking for a new project. Then one day, my mentor put out a series of photos of dried tears which had been photographed under a microscope, each picture showing tears from different emotions. (Rose-Lynne Fisher: Topography of Tears.) Drawn first to one, then another, the minute I picked them up, the entire novel flashed before me. These pictures had something to say. After the writing, I turned over the images and smiled at the titles. "Timeless Reunion" and "Grief." It all made sense. They gifted me with a story. Now it was my job to write it down. The characters stepped into my dreams, informing me of what they wanted us to know. Jacqo would wake me at night with advice. "It's hot out there, don't ya think a man needs a hat?" And so they got hats. I listened and wrote, then listened some more.

Authors agonize over editing. No exception to this, I shied away from the publishing world. Then I remembered something I learned over the years with native and indigenous teachers. The Art of Deliberate Imperfection, (Kaushik Patowary, August 2017), speaks about creating slight mistakes on purpose, such as a stray white thread on a black background or a missing comma, which allows a pathway for spirit to move in and out of the piece of art, taking the energy to where it is needed, regardless of or perhaps even because of those little mistakes. So I forgave myself for being an imperfect writer and hit the publish button. Just an excuse for lousy editing? Maybe. But it brought peace of mind and gave me the courage to let these characters out into the world where they wanted to be.

Thank you for reading. For more information, you can find me on my Facebook page: **Sue Paterson – Writer.**

ACKNOWLEDGEMENTS

Thea Constantine – From our early days of writing at Beaterville Café to the present, you make writing fun, inspirational and honest. Thank you for the prompt which birthed this story.

Christi Krug – A fellow writer in our critique group once said: "Stick with Christi, and you'll be a better writer." And it's true. From Wildfire Writing to fifteen years of mentorship, your ability to see the positive and inspire, peppered with honest critique, is priceless.

To my fellow writers in critique groups: you took me on as a novice writer, listened to my stories, and shared yours with me. I wouldn't have had the courage to do this if not for you. Thank you to GC Troop, Connie, Jan-Marie, Chuck, Morry, Patty, Vicki and Bryan. If you're reading this, please know you made a difference in my writing and my life.

Viktoriya: Your eagerness to read my pages kept me writing. I still have your sticky notes from the first draft, which helped to shape the story. Thank you.

Katherine Custard and Paul LeRoq – Had it not been for your editing, support, critique, and encouragement, this story may still be filed away. Thank you for your encouragement.

Healers I have worked with, including Richard, Barret Eagle Bear, Ashera, Vilma and many more. You will recognize some of the words on these pages. Thank you making the world a better place to be in.

Larry - my husband, best friend, historian and fellow journeyer. It's been an adventure, hasn't it? Charley and Phillip – my sons. Thank you for walking this life with me and teaching me to be a better human.

Finally, to all the animals that surround me every day, convincing me that all will be better if I just step outside for a moment and walk barefoot in the grass.

www.ingramcontent.com/pod-product-compliance
Lightning Source LLC
Chambersburg PA
CBHW061246310726
48971CB00007B/2244

Her days of peace and bead-crafting fell to a murderous end. Will her quest for safety across rugged terrain claim this desperate girl's last breath?

1683. Sixteen-year-old Raven is living the life of her dreams. Pregnant with her first baby and set to marry her childhood sweetheart, the young Pueblo artist relishes her quiet village community. But her solitude shatters when deserting Spanish soldiers invade and brutally massacre her entire tribe.

Believing she's the only survivor, Raven embarks on an arduous journey through the mountains in a risky search for her father's people. But the mother-to-be only finds unforgiving elements and crippling grief threatening to send her to a merciless grave.

With an innocent unborn life on the line, can Raven survive an unimaginable tragedy?

Raven is the powerful first book in the Ancient Reunion historical fiction series. If you like resilient female characters, Early American backdrops, and well-researched tribal customs, then you'll love Sue Paterson's tale of perseverance.

Buy Raven to embrace the human spirit today!

Sue Paterson is a writer, nurse, and farmer. She and her husband live in the Northwest with llamas, chickens, ducks, cats, and dogs.

"To all the women who need a reminder that being yourself is beautiful."

One

BELLA

Nobody was allowed to see me cry, which meant I had to read *Phantom of the Opera* in the solitary confinement of the bookstore's storage room. The author broke my heart when he killed the phantom, and that still didn't compare to the heroine's choice of eloping with her costar. The costar jerk promised to take her away from the opera house. Who would run away with a guy from her childhood when the Phantom was right there?

Yes, Phantom was the villain of the opera house, but it didn't mean he wasn't sexy.

"Bella, I'm here to throw you over my shoulder and trap you in a dungeon until we fall in love," I spoke to my reflection in the small, round mirror that hung on the back of the storage room's door in my best, deep man's voice.

Alas, my life wasn't a novel, and Folklore Falls didn't offer storybook romances with dark and brooding men.

Not unless you were my best friend. Loxley and Gideon were about to pop out their first baby after a whirlwind romance, which was followed by a year of engagement and another year married. I'd picked up a few trade secrets on the lying front and claimed my only tearful breakdown was at their precious wedding.

And I cried—sure. But it wasn't because of the *beauty* of it all—I wasn't that sappy. I cried because of the curse.

A muffled jingle snapped my attention to the present. The bell on the bookstore's front door chimed, so I slapped the pages of the gothic novel shut and hopped off the stool. I slipped between the maze of stacked books in the storage room and emerged to see a familiar face.

"Speak of the devil," I muttered.

Gideon knocked into a stack of precariously balanced bodice-rippers, and the tower toppled into a pile of novels. I rolled my eyes, but he didn't so much as apologize. The wild look in his eyes told me he didn't have the headspace to worry about the mess he'd just created in my shop.

"Loxley is in labor," he said, raking his hand through his hair. Sweat shined on his forehead like a beacon of desperation. "She won't let me take her to the hospital. You're the only one she listens to when she gets stubborn like this."

"Fine," I said, as I marched past him and pushed through the door. "But I need to be back this evening for an appointment with a client." Gideon knew I referred to my customers with a more formal title because they came to me with problems that I helped them solve through books. Literary therapy, of sorts.

"Thank you," he breathed.

I only shrugged and doubled back to grab one of my favorite romance books. The worn pages felt like a home I could hold in my hands. I snuck a sniff of the well-loved book before tucking it under my arm.

"What do you need a book for?"

"Labor is longer than you think," I said.

"We're taking her to the hospital. Now." Gideon jabbed his finger at his feet as if his sheer determination could save the day.

"We'll see," I said. "Good thing I've read plenty of romances with midwives."

"You're going to convince her, right?"

I shrugged again, my signature move meaning *whatever*.

"Right?" His voice pitched higher in desperation.

"Right. And I'll meet a tall, dark villain and fall madly in love." I spun around and twisted the key in the bookstore's lock.

"Shoot," he cursed. "What in the world are you talking about?"

A coming autumn breeze tossed my hair into my face. I plucked the dyed strands of black sticking to my lipstick, ruining the perfect shade of purple. Folklore Falls's trees had turned red and brown. Leaves covered the parking lot, and orange pumpkins lined the front of the shops in town.

"The curse," I mumbled. "I'm talking about the curse of being unlovable. Not that you'd understand." Of course, the stupid curse was so much deeper and darker than growing into a lonely old cat lady, but I avoided thinking too much about it, because if I did, I'd have to admit it scared me.

Leaves speckled the dirt parking lot with color as the wind picked up and stripped the trees of Sherwood Forest bare. The moody weather suited me. Thick clouds threatened rain. A distant sheet of gray hung over the hills that housed our town's famous waterfall.

Even hurrying, Gideon walked with a stick up his butt, and I couldn't help but smirk. The dude was perfect for my best friend—a rule-following grump with a soft spot so squishy he reminded me of a donut. His budding dad-bod helped the visual. It was cute, a word of which I hoped never to describe a man I dated.

He yanked the car door open and dropped into the driver's seat with a wave at me to get my butt in gear. A stick-free butt, to be clear. I took a giant, achingly sluggish step and moved my arms in slow motion to get a rise out of him. Loxley had warned me this would happen. The strings that held Gideon together were wound so tight I was convinced he'd unravel like an old Raggedy Andy in a high-powered washing machine.

Before I shut the car door, Gideon shifted the car in reverse and squealed out of the parking lot. We passed the town's bed and break-fast, Bones's tavern, and an eternity of trees. Sherwood Forest's exces-sive shedding decorated the small highway on the short drive to Loxley and Gideon's house. As the quaint patio came into view, I spied a round woman in a green robe. Loxley gave zero craps what others thought of her, especially now that she didn't have a life of crime to hide.

Gideon dove out of the car and released a shriek at the sight of a puddle beneath his wife's feet. I climbed over the center console and settled into the backseat as Loxely waddled to the car under Gideon's paranoid supervision. Now I regretted moving slowly. At least this whole labor and delivery drama offered me a non-fictional escape from thoughts of the curse. A curse that made itself known every year around my birthday.

"It's okay. It's okay," she repeated, as she eased into the passenger seat. Auburn locks tumbled down her shoulders as the hair claw that normally tamed her mane couldn't compete with luscious pregnancy growth. The over-production of hair reminded me of Folklore Falls in the spring when I hated this town the most. Bright colors and singing birds made me sick.

I laid my hand on her shoulder and leaned forward. "How're you doing?"

"I'm telling Gideon it's okay," she said with a nod of her chin at the frantic man stuffing their packed labor and delivery bag into the trunk.

I rolled my eyes. "Well, duh. But in all seriousness, how much does it hurt on a scale of seeing someone dog-ear a book's pages to a book's original cover being replaced by its movie poster?"

Freckles smashed together as she wrinkled her nose and cringed. "Definitely the latter." Her voice came out tight, and I assumed another contraction had rippled through her.

"So, no convincing your husband to let you stay home as long as possible?" I repeated the plan she'd told me yesterday.

"I hate hospitals," she groaned. "But when a bucket of water drops between your legs, you get a little freaked."

I raised my arms in surrender. "Hey, you don't have to tell me. I can't even think about blood much less see it." I took a deep breath and silently chided myself for mentioning what made me dizzy.

She nodded and exhaled.

When Gideon scrambled into his seat, he slammed his foot against the gas pedal and left their little house in the dust. The hospital was a good twenty-five-minute drive down the highway, and despite Gideon's newfound lead foot, it felt like we crawled.

"Breathe," I said.

Loxley gasped and groaned, and I hated how helpless I was stuck in the backseat. We stared at her like an animal in a zoo with our jaws hanging open. I pushed Gideon's face forward and demanded he focus on the road.

"Remember that time I fell off the trellis at Jensen Resort and had to go to urgent care for a broken wrist?" Loxley asked. "That's when I got caught and charged with community service."

"What about it?" I tilted my head and let black hair fall into my face—a style I'd grown used to with the thick, overgrown bangs.

"I don't know." She paused and released a tiny squeal, then breathed again. "Help me focus on something else—" Another gasp interrupted her. "Anything!"

"Breathe," I instructed, as I scooted as far forward as the seatbelt allowed. I unclipped the claw in her hair and gathered the loose strands in it for a tighter hold to keep the hair from her face. "In and out. Imagine this is an archery competition or a bet over darts. Exhale just before you loose the arrow."

Dang, I'm good. Loxley controlled her breathing, and she relaxed enough to look out the window and watch as we passed the apple orchards. Bright red fruit hung from the trees, ripe and ready to be plucked. I wondered if I'd have to see blood. Logically, it didn't bother me. Physically, I couldn't help but faint. It was a drag, really, considering I had to strategically imagine another substance whenever an author explained violence in detail.

Loxley waved her hands. "It's not working."

"Okay, um…" I glanced around for ideas, and my gaze landed on the book in my lap. "Did you know that this author has an actual collection of corsets that she pays male models to rip off her for these cover shoots?" I leaned against her seat and stretched my arm out to show her the book.

"Nope." She shook her head. "A hot man got me into this position. Nix talking about steamy Fabio models."

Hot? *Debatable*. Gideon was more like a warm cinnamon roll than the men I preferred, who growled when they spoke and had a jawline that could slice my cheek open during an aggressive and passionate kissing session. Of course, those men were fictional and only dangerous in the form of papercuts.

"Still five minutes," he glanced at the map on his phone.

"Bella, tell me some gossip. Something I don't know," Loxley begged. She dipped forward, and her hand shot out. It gripped Gideon's arm like a vice and yanked, causing him to wrench the steering wheel and swerve the car.

"Holy—" I cut off my swear, realizing it wouldn't help. "Okay." *Something she doesn't know?* "So, I know we're best friends, and we tell each other everything, but I have a secret. It's not illegal, so Gideon can keep his panties untwisted. But it's worse, actually. I'm… I'm cursed."

It worked. Loxley slowly exhaled as she glanced back. Her green eyes bore right through me like my skin was as see-through as the black lace and mesh tops I always wore. Dark clothes matched the style of the gothic romances I loved to read. Mirroring them tricked my brain into believing love could be a part of my life, too. In fact, my life depended on it.

"Wait—" Loxley rocked forward as Gideon stopped too fast at a red light. We both shot him glares that could laser his head right off his shoulders if I had a bit of magic. But the magic in my family line was long buried, only resurfacing with the curse itself. "Why do you look freaked out?" she asked me. "I've literally never seen you scared of anything. And you talk about curses and angry spirits and haunted houses all the ti—" Her words rose into a scream. With flailing hands, she prodded me to answer.

The car lurched to a halt along the curb outside the hospital entrance. Though we were out of Folklore Falls and into what I'd consider a big city since it had not two gas stations, but three, the hospital wasn't big enough to have one of those fancy overhangs that looked like a grand hotel roundabout. Instead, the building looked as old as my family's mansion and about the same size—massive for a house, tiny for a place that saves lives. I knew this hospital better than I could quote *Phantom of the Opera*, but it still unsettled me every time I saw it. A gurgle in my stomach reminded me that bitter coffee and sniffing books didn't cut it as a nutritious breakfast.

I hated this place as much as Loxley did, but not for the same reasons. Of course, it wasn't all bad times here. The quaint hospital had a spooky abandoned wing that I loved to explore and ghost-hunt in as a kid as much as it pissed my mom off.

Cool air rushed into the car as Gideon kicked his door open and leaped out like a rocket taking off. I wanted to take off in the opposite direction. This hospital brought back too many memories, and those memories were like a stack of books—one life scene after another that all culminated to one thing: Bella Marie Villeneuve was an unlovable problem.

A repetitive banging on the car window knocked me from my thoughts. Gideon's fist bounced against the glass before Loxley screamed, and he went white as the ghosts I'd pretend to go hunting at the mansion when I really just wanted answers. As he waved for me to get out and help, his arm went limp. I scrambled for the handle and shoved the door open. I watched in horror, as his knees buckled under him and his body tilted forward. Dark eyes rolled back into his head, and he folded like a Raggedy Andy who'd just dropped the doll on top of her mama's giant pregnant belly.

A gasp squeezed in my throat, and I lunged forward to wrap my arms around his squishy middle. Before he could smash his wife and unborn child, I used all the strength I'd gathered from a childhood of climbing the abandoned wing to yank him back. Concrete connected with the bones in my butt, and I yelped as Gideon went entirely unconscious on top of me.

A nurse arrived from the sliding doors and helped Loxley into a wheelchair while another attended to Gideon. I stood and ignored the ache in my butt.

"Everything is ruined," Loxley said. The nurse continued to push her toward the hospital, and I knew I'd need to be her advocate. "I had a birth plan. My-my husband was supposed to distract me." With

another scream-turned-growl, Loxley begged for Gideon. "We practiced together. He had a story saved that he knew would distract me."

The sliding doors rolled open, and we arrived in the lobby, a place I
knew all too well. I released a slow breath, as if I was the one pushing
a human out of my body. Birth was magical and intense, and I admired
the courage Loxley had. I needed a bit of that because I'd never spoken
about the curse aloud before, much less told anyone.

But it was the perfect distraction. And with my birthday coming
soon, it was time I acknowledged it.

"I can help," I said, as I glanced back to see Gideon, conscious
now, but in a wheelchair himself.

Loxley waved for me to hold her hand. "It hurts so bad," she
breathed and squeezed my fingers.

I gnawed on my lip. If I didn't speak about my family curse, it was
easier to pretend it was all fictional and that I wasn't silly for believing
in dark fairies with witchy tendencies, the way my mother had
convinced me.

"He doesn't look so good," Loxley groaned. "You're up, tell me
about the curse." I followed as the nurse pushed her toward the
elevator.

"So," I began, "you know how Folklore Falls claims to have once
had an opening to the fairy realm?" Of course she knew. Loxley ran a
whole museum dedicated to the lore of our beloved town. What she
didn't know was that my ancestors founded the town. The bones in my
hand nearly snapped as she squeezed so hard, I started sweating.
"Okay, um, yeah. Not all fairies are nice, right? They manipulate and
make bargains and deal in curses. And, well, the Villenueves, my
family, were idiots and made a deal like a hundred years ago or something." I waved my free hand, the one that wouldn't need a cast after
all of this.

The elevator dinged to the second floor where labor and delivery
were combined with a small pediatrics section.

"The story goes," I continued, "that my great-great-and-change-
grandmother wanted money, so she went to the town witch, who was
actually a fairy. She made a deal that she would work for the witch

until she turned thirty-five to get rich, but, supposedly, she fell in love with the witch's son. When the witch found out it was just my grandma trying to con money out of her son, the witch cursed her, and every woman in her family after, with seven years bad luck if she couldn't get someone to fall in love with her before her thirty-fifth birthday."

Loxley gasped, and I assumed it had to do with the birth, but she was looking at me. If anybody else would believe this crazy story, it was her. It felt good to be heard on this, to admit this family burden dropped on my shoulders.

Pain twisted Loxley's face, and I hurried to finish with my heart pounding as if the storm was inside me. "So, Great-gram was a crappy, greedy chick, and she was gold-digging and didn't actually love the guy at all."

Medical staff directed the us into a cramped curtained area in labor and delivery where a doctor would check her. Colorful moons and stars decorated the curtain that surrounded us.

I dragged a chair closer to the bed so I could continue holding her hand. "When the fairy discovered Gram just wanted a sugar daddy, they didn't just screw her over, they cursed her lineage, too."

Auburn hair flipped into my mouth as Loxley shook her head. I ignored it and welcomed the end to my confession. I wanted to forget about my rude, old great–times-three-grandmother as easily as they say women forget the pain of childbirth so that they'll bear more. It was her fault I was unlovable. At least, I preferred to blame her.

I shuddered.

"What was the curse?"

I snapped back to the present to see my best friend looking up at me. Though I maintained a rare smile, for her sake, I frowned on the inside. The curse… the reason I hated my birthday.

"It's dumb. My mom says its not real and she's probably right." I shrugged, trying to believe it but Loxley only blinked at me and waited for the answer. "If I can't get someone to fall in love with me before I turn thirty-five, I'll bring seven years' of bad luck to me and everyone I know."

A familiar laugh echoed. Of course she'd arrive now, just after her minions did all the work. My mother wasn't one to get her hands dirty.

As if on cue, a nurse pulled the curtain back to wheel Gideon into the area, and I got full view of my mother's disapproving eyebrow arch.

She folded her arms. "I thought that was your voice."

The nurse helping Gideon, returned with another medical professional in tow. Supposedly all the rooms were full which meant Loxley wouldn't get a private one. Except that all changed when they jumped at the command of the hospital's chief executive officer. Also known as my mom—the one person I didn't want to be left alone with.

The medical professionals hurried to wheel Loxley's bed and Gideon's chair out of the curtained area and into the hall to find a room.

"Nice to see you, Isabelle," she said with an arch to her penciled eyebrow.

Before I could say anything, she marched after her crew of medical professionals all following in Loxley's wake.

I wiped the sweat from my face, successfully smudging black eyeliner across the heel of my palm.

"Oh," Mom paused and spun around. "It's a good thing you believe that hideous old building keeps the so-called curse at bay."

I frowned. "Why is that?"

"Because you had the story wrong. It's not thirty-five. Bad luck begins when a Villenueve turns twenty-five, and I seem to remember *somebody* has a birthday next month."

Two

BRETT

A possession must have compelled my parents to buy this stupid, old house. Whatever it was, I'd hunt it down and squeeze the life out of it, because this hunk of junk had become a thorn in my side.

You wouldn't know a good thing if it bit you in the face, Brett. My mother's words echoed in my head. Childhood in this spooky building left me with zero trust that she'd made the right choice. That was the game in the Jensen family: lies, blackmail, and dinner parties for political purposes only.

And right up until her last breath, my mother pinned me between guilt and a promise. *Fix our family's house and the town. Make us proud.*

I flicked the flashlight to the infamous stained-glass window high above the overhang. The glass was cut, painted, and shaped into a wilting rose. The stem hung precariously drooped with two petals suspended in mid-air over a pile on the ground. I never understood why this window had become a staple, a monument to the town of Folklore Falls.

I shook my head and stomped up the steps. It took several tries of rattling the key in the lock to get the door to budge. It'd only been a couple years since we'd left Folklore Falls and this house empty while

I traveled and my parents built a life in New York, but the house felt devoid of life long before we'd left.

When I finally shoved it open, it creaked, and I grunted a laugh at the irony of it all. As much as I hated this house, its haunted style was a perfect representation of the Jensen family. I stepped inside with a sigh and instant regret for coming back here, but I'd made a promise.

Folklore Falls didn't come with good memories for me, so I came up with the idiotic plan to recreate my experience. At least, it was the best plan I could come up with after getting stuck with this destructive inheritance. Mom was gone, Dad was busy, and my brother had dragged his family to some small island he'd bought.

That left me to deal with the Jensen estate.

"I should have just flown coach," I mumbled to nobody. I'd always ridden first class in an airplane and didn't intend to explore anything beneath it now. But the flight arriving at a reasonable hour was full, so I had to accept the midnight time. I'd landed at the airport outside Folklore Falls after three in the morning and wanted to collapse. That was before I'd decided to rip the bandage off, chug two black coffees, and stay at the house my mother had wanted me to love.

Moonlight shone through the hallways that led in opposite directions from the entryway. I wandered down one, angling the flashlight toward the long row of framed photographs. The dim glow cast enough light to see my parents' frowning faces in the family portrait on the left. I stalked toward it to get a glimpse of my mother before she got sick. Even then, healthy and beautiful, she never smiled, not real smiles anyway. Not like the one smile I remembered when we first moved to Folklore Falls just after my seventh birthday.

I reached for the light switch, but nothing happened. The generator would have to do until I tore the house down, no point in restarting the power bill now.

Autumn wind drafted through the house and sent the door banging against the frame. I cursed at myself for leaving it open. My footsteps echoed, joining in the howling wind.

The chill of mid-September left goosebumps on my bare arms. The howling reminded me of the ghost stories my brother would tell me when we were children. He never stopped trying to scare me, even when we grew up. But adulthood brought real spooks, like blackmail and broken hearts.

But when I reached the front door, it was already shut. "What the hell?" I muttered and flicked the flashlight's beam down the opposite hall, searching for the source of the noise. Rhythmic banging continued from somewhere inside the old mansion.

I trudged through the entryway and past the grand staircase to search my father's old office. It was quiet and dark, so I moved into the open space and shoved through the double doors that led into the massive ballroom—an antiquated space, really, since we didn't often host 'balls.'

After ensuring the sound didn't come from the ballroom, I let the heavy oak door fall shut and squinted up at the glow of the moon glinting off the chandelier in front of the twisting staircase. Another gust of wind sent the banging echoing louder, and I snapped my head toward the source of the sound, clearer now with the increased volume.

The stained-glass window in the arch over the huge front doors was open. The frame banged against the wall, eighteen feet above my head. The old window must have had a faulty latch.

"Just my luck," I said with a sigh. If I left it rattling and hitting the wall, the stained-glass image would likely break. Even though I intended to bulldoze this house down and rebuild with my new image and new life in Folklore Falls, I couldn't let this piece of art get destroyed—it'd wreck my chances of garnering votes before my campaign got off the ground. I had to play by their game, get people in Folklore Falls to like me so I could give the town the update they didn't know they needed.

Once I removed the stained-glass window and bulldozed the house, I'd give it to that lame little museum ran by the thief girl, Loxley or whatever her name was. She could preserve all the silly lore in the Falls's supposed history while I tore everything outdated down and rebuilt the town.

"Out with the old, in with the new," I repeated, as I stalked across the side yard toward the little house that sheltered the help we used to employ. Raindrops had started pattering the ground, and I hated to get my hair wet since the thickness always curled and twisted with humidity.

After locating and dragging a ladder back to the main house, I secured it against the inside wall and stomped up each rung. I'd extended it to its full height to reach the window, but I still had to balance on the highest step and stretch myself to reach the edge of the frame.

"Come on," I grunted, reaching as far as I could. The bottom of the window brushed against my fingertips. I snagged it and pushed the window until I heard it connect with the frame. The latch still hung, unattached from the lock on the window's frame. All I needed to do was flick it over and drop the pin through the loop. But since I couldn't reach, I didn't bother.

Nothing but the sound of my strained breath filled the house now. Though I was used to a house full of tutors, employees, advisors, and plenty of other wealthy families that my parents rubbed elbows with, the quiet soothed me now.

Relief lasted only a moment before the wind blasted against the glass. A rippling crack sounded, and I craned my neck to see a crack grow and snake around one of the petal's in the window's image. It formed the perfect shape of the rose's falling petal and snapped out of the glass as though cut with a surgeon's precision. The tiny piece of glass slipped from the place it'd remained for a hundred years and fell to its death. I watched as the petal disappeared into the darkness below.

Silence, then the glass shattered against the marble floors in the entry.

I flicked my eyes back to the window, a faint glow of light streaming in through the hole. It illuminated something on the wall across from it. The entryway's ceilings were not as tall as the rest of the house, but I never considered why.

I squinted to make out a keyhole on the wall opposite the window. I trailed my eyes along the smooth wall until noticing a slit in the wooden panels.

"Is that... a door?" I whispered. It made no sense. Who would put a door way up here—and with a lock? It was already impossible to get to.

Another gust of wind flung the window open again. I shouted a curse at the awful autumn weather for toying with me. Angry now, I thrust my arm up and over the frame, then hauled myself up with pure upper body strength. I must have looked ridiculous half-hanging out the window, certainly not the well-behaved boy my mother had raised. But nobody was around to witness it except the ghosts of my past.

Rain wet my face as I grunted and held myself there, with my feet brushing against the top of the ladder. It was reckless, exactly what'd I'd always been advised against. The Jensens were a calculated people, precise in our decisions and never impulsive.

But the window was old, and I didn't give a crap about the cold, so I rattled the rusty screws from the wall and pull the whole window from the frame. I'd take a wet entryway and the howling wind over the banging. I set to work, pinching the loose screws and twisting them out of the wall on the top. Once those were removed, I eased back down to the rung and balanced firmly on the ladder. I gripped the frame with my left hand and set to work unscrewing the bottom screws with my right.

The storm picked up, whipping the air in every direction. Another blast of wind shoved the front doors open as if the house had a mind of its own. The change in air pressure blew the window the opposite way now with a force I couldn't have predicted. The sharp edge of the thin frame smashed my fingers between the window and the wall.

I gasped at the crushing blow. It wasn't until I managed to pry the window open again that I began to feel dizzy. Blood beaded where the sharp edge of the glass cut through my flesh. I swallowed a scream at the sight of my crushed fingers as my mother's voice filled my head again. *Well-behaved boys never scream.*

Three

BELLA

Heat snaked up my neck and burned my cheeks. Frustration with my mother's flippant response combined with memories of the bad luck our family suffered left me hot and clammy. I tugged at the tight, black choker necklace, pulling it away from my sizzling skin.

"Twenty-five?" I said to my mom's back. Her red hair swayed as she shook her head at my silliness. *Curses aren't real*, she'd always say. Mom marched from the hospital's lobby and disappeared around the corner behind administration. Back there, she'd hide inside her office and deal with the behind-the-scenes work it took to run a hospital.

The smell of disinfectant sent me back to childhood when I'd first heard about the curse from Grandma Villenueve. She'd lost her eyebrows one night, waking up to a face as smooth as a baby's bottom. When she'd dragged me along with her to a checkup with the doctor, I spent an hour in the waiting room listening to story after story of bad luck in our family. Bad luck brought about by my mother and the fact that nobody fell in love with her before her twenty-fifth birthday.

Sally, the receptionist, smiled at me from behind the lobby's desk. She mouthed a 'hello, Bella' while answering a phone call.

What was it Grandma had said? The closer it got to my mother's twenty-fifth birthday, the worse the luck grew—a warning from the fairy witches that the next seven years would be living hell for the Villenueves and anyone who came in contact with them.

I tried to return Sally's smile, but it quickly twisted into a frown when a spot of red dripped from her nose. Sally dabbed at her nose and looked at her hand with pursed brows and a slight gasp. I snapped my gaze away, but it was too late. My head spun, and the heat in my neck doubled in temperature.

I stared at the empty hall on the right, taking slow breaths to avoid the impending faint. The figure of a man zombie-walked across the end of the hall, and I snapped out of my daze. My vision focused to make out Gideon. A nurse hurried after him.

"Sir? Sir, you need to sit down!" she called.

Gideon grunted something about retrieving a snack for his wife, then disappeared down the maze of hallways. I snorted until it dawned on me. Was Loxley's sudden labor from my bad luck? And Gideon's dramatic bought of unconsciousness?

"Okay, WWCDD?" I mumbled. What Would Christine Daae Do? The heroine of *Phantom of the Opera* was naive and rarely made her own decisions—but in the end, she planned to sacrifice herself to save the opera house. If she could agree to marry the Phantom to stop others from getting hurt, I could suffer dating a lame Folklore Falls guy for the fate of our family.

But who? The town was full of elderly couples and families, and I couldn't stand the tourists and elite vacationers who flooded our hiking trails and waterfall beaches in the summer. The few eligible bachelors were childhood buddies that I'd friendzoned a decade ago.

I blocked my view of Sally and her bloody nose and made my way to the waiting room. I'd be safe from fainting in there.

Speaking of eligible bachelors, the tavern's owner, Bones sat in the corner nursing a possible head wound. With his face in his hands, I didn't dare linger looking for an injury, but Katrina caught sight of me. I spun on my heel, resigning to the fact that I'd have to sit outside and wait for news on Loxley. The risk of running into blood was too high, hence my reason for escaping to the abandoned wing of the hospital when I was a child.

"Hey, Bella!" the barmaid and Bones's only employee said. She stopped rubbing little circles over his back to wave at me.

I forced a smile and avoided looking at Bones. Like crying, I'd hid my issues with blood. If people thought I fainted over every little thing, they'd stop coming to me with their problems, and I'd lose my favorite part of running the bookstore—recommending stories to help the townsfolk.

Katrina hiccupped. "Oop! Excuse me. We're a little hungover." She laughed. "I was worried Bones got dehydrated with all that puking."

Bones groaned, and I wrinkled my nose. At least the thought of vomit didn't make me dizzy.

"I don't get hangovers," Bones said, rubbing his eyes.

"You didn't," Katrina corrected. "But something changed. and you need to accept it so we can get fluids and feel better."

"Absolutely not." He shook his head, then groaned and squeezed his eyes shut. I dared to look at him, knowing he didn't have an open wound now. "I'm known for how well I handle my alcohol."

Wait. Just last night, I'd stopped by the tavern for a late-night drink. Bones was totally sober when I'd left after midnight. And he was right, everyone in Folklore Falls knew Bones could drink them under the table, then rise and shine for a sunrise hike to the waterfall the next morning.

It couldn't be my curse? Could it?

Suddenly, I was seven again, sitting in the same seat Katrina and Bones occupied now. I was looking up at Grandma V. while she waggled a finger at me.

Everyone you come in contact with after the curse begins will suffer a string of bad luck for as many years as you've been alive now.

"Can we leave now?" Bones asked Katrina. He looked at her with starry eyes as always, and as always, she didn't notice. She was busy thumbing a pamphlet about safe drinking. "It's just a headache."

Not just a headache. Bad luck. *My* bad luck.

Heat burned behind my ears.

"Ouch!" Katrina squealed. The pamphlet dropped to the floor as she gawked at beading blood on the tip of her thumb. She stuck it into her mouth and sucked to stop the papercut from gushing.

I swallowed, trying to ground myself before my light head lifted right off my shoulders and spun around like a helicopter. I swayed. *I have to get out of here.*

Besides, I didn't have time to waste. I needed to find a guy to fall in love with me before the curse continued doling out papercuts and nosebleeds.

I turned and leaned against the frame of the waiting room door before shoving off and heading for the sliding doors.

"Bye, Bella!" Sally called.

I didn't drop my hand from my forehead to wave back.

My head spun, and my neck burned. I loved black, except when it came in the form of spots that dotted my vision.

"Fresh air," I said. I'd sit on the curb in the autumn air until I felt better. Then, I'd brainstorm who might be able to help me break the Villenueve curse. It hurt my heart to consider tricking an innocent man into falling for me. Despite my tough exterior, I prided myself on being as kind as Christine Daae herself.

None of the Folklore Falls dudes deserved to be used, and I couldn't stomach the thought of spending enough time with a vacationer to get him to love me. If only a fictional man could save me now.

The elevator dinged, and a doctor exited, speaking to an intern that followed him, talking about working with the phlebotomist to get better at drawing blood.

Blood. No, fresh air and books. *Think about fresh air and books.* And breaking the curse before my birthday—AKA Halloween.

I was stuck, and time was running out.

I stumbled toward the sliding doors. Fresh air was just a step away —no fainting today. I forced one foot in front of the other, determined not to go down like Gideon.

When the automatic doors rolled open, I nearly collided with the hulking figure storming through from the other side.

I knew his face, but my dizzy brain didn't register who it was before my eyes flicked to the horror in front of me. The huge man came to a halt to stop from running me over. He held his hand cupped to his chest, wrapped in bloodied bandages—right at my line of sight…

My gaze flicked to his face where I recognized the angular jaw, dark eyes, and intensive stare. *Think about how hot he is, not the blood. Crap, why'd I say blood?*

My neck was on fire, and my knees buckled without my consent. Before my favorite color darkened my vision, I saw the guy's uninjured hand shoot out to catch me.

So much for hiding my fainting.

Four

BRETT

Bella was a wisp, light as a feather in my arm. So, I crouched low enough to lift her with my good hand and carry her through the sliding doors with my arm secured around her waist. A well-behaved man shouldn't carry a lady like a football, but with one mangled hand, I didn't have a choice.

The weight of her limp body didn't bother me, I'd dealt with drunk chicks before, but I didn't have time to help damsels in distress today. Except, this was *Bella Villenueve.* If it'd been anyone else, would I have caught her?

The spikes on her black belt dug into my forearm. I glanced down and spied dark letters tattooed down the back of her neck. I hadn't been this close to Bella since high school graduation, but the tattoo didn't come as a surprise.

The blonde at the administration desk gasped and leaped from her chair, leaving it spinning behind her. Her southern belle blue eyes darted from the dried blood on my hand to the limp body in my other arm.

"Oh my," she said, hand to her chest. Instead of calling a code over the intercom, as a professional should, she squealed for someone by the

23

name of Ms. Villenueve but didn't direct it toward Bella. "I've called her mama to come help both of you."

I frowned. This was why I avoided the hospital and spent the early morning hours bandaging my fingers myself. I'd had some medical training, and I didn't trust the incompetent people in and around this pathetic little town. The blonde only proved me right—Folklore Falls needed to learn civilized behavior. Lucky for them, I had the resources to turn this town around, though the campaign would have to be fast and furious with the elections quickly approaching.

"You're the guy who just announced he's running for mayor of the Falls, right?" she said, as she backed up and grabbed for a phone on the desk.

I nodded.

"I read the news on Facebook when it's slow around here," she said, phone to her ear but still speaking to me. She twirled her blonde hair around one finger and grinned, gaze dropping to my bicep. "I don't care what they say about you. You'd have my vote if I lived in the—oh, yes, we have a man with an injured hand in the lobby."

In the Falls. My brain finished her sentence with the slang outsiders called my hometown. What were people saying about me?

It'd only been moments, but the weight in my arms was too much combined with the lingering pain in my hand. I'd lost enough blood to join the unconscious girl in the dark, and I didn't need that black mark on my reputation just as I'd arrived to transform Folklore Falls. If nothing else, news traveled fast, even from the hospital on the edge of the town's borders.

I knelt in front of the desk and carefully rolled Bella face up as I eased her to the floor. Thick black makeup coated her eyelids and curled up at the ends like a villain's mustache. Once upon a time, in my schoolboy days, I'd teased her friends. I'd like to think I'd matured a little since then. Her lashes flickered, and when her eyes blinked open, I held her gaze.

Bella gasped and launched herself upward, nearly colliding into my forehead. I leaned out of the way just in time. The light scent of vanilla and pumpkin drifted from her hair, masking the unbecoming sting of hospital-grade disinfectant. Her sleek, dark hair was rolled into two thick buns placed behind her ears—a style I'd never seen before. After palming her forehead, she took a shaky breath and twisted her neck to gape at me.

"I'm sorry—" her apology cut short, and her eyebrows pinched. Espresso eyes raked over me, and I frowned. I felt naked, like she'd stripped me of the reputation I carefully curated and knew what I really thought of this place. "Brett?"

The distaste in her tone sparked a memory—one I'd buried deep and hoped to change after coming here. She was one of the many lifers I'd attended school with. During the brief and scattered years that my mother had fired all my tutors and couldn't get another one to work for her, I went to public school.

I shuddered.

"Bella!" the blonde squealed with delight, as she returned. "Are you okay? I was so worried. I called for your ma, but she's in a meeting."

"I'm fine. I think I just need to go home and wait for a call from my friend," Bella said, as she rolled to her knees, then used the counter to pull herself up. "She's in labor. Will you keep me updated on her and her baby?"

"Of course," the blonde said. "But you're in no state to drive, Bell. Want me to put a call out for a pickup?"

"No!" Bella shouted at a volume nobody with an inch of manners should speak. It matched plenty of memories I'd had of her where she told kids in our class terrifying stories or simply glared at me until I'd look away. It fascinated me once upon a time but embarrassed my mother whenever I'd spoken of Bella. *We don't fraternize with people like her.* Except now, all grown up, 'people like her' were the town's favorite, the girl everybody knew from the hole-in-the-wall bookshop.

"Already on it," the blonde ignored her. "Everybody in the Falls loves you. I bet one post on the town's page will have a hundred folk offering a pickup."

I glanced between them. I didn't know what a pickup was, but it sounded like Bella needed help moving something. My brain worked in overtime, piecing the puzzle together. Everybody *did* love her, and if townsfolk caught wind of me giving her aid, it'd be the first of many curated moments to change their minds about me.

"Do you need a truck?" I intercepted.

Both of them looked at me, and the blonde gasped. "I forgot!" She waved at my hand. "A doctor will be right down, but you should take a seat." She scurried toward an open door with the sign over it that said Waiting Room. "You're just so…" she giggled, "tough, so it slipped my mind that you're injured. Was it a raccoon attack? I read on the town's page that there's a feral one roaming the Falls. I spend too much time on that page, but it's just so entertaining. Bella knows. She has a whole thread on there, right, Bell?" She leaned closer to me and covered her mouth like it was a secret. "Personally, I don't get why she's Ms. Popular. She only posts about books. But you, Mr. Future Mayor, have started to take over the town's page with your whole fancy campaign."

A snort came from behind us. I twisted to see Bella's black hair swishing as she unrolled the two low buns and let the locks fall free down her back. It covered sight of the tattooed words down her spine, visible through the mesh top. She marched for the doors, and the smell of vanilla pumpkins faded.

Ms. Popular, huh? Now that the useless hospital administration had shared her gossip, more memories flooded me. Everybody in Folklore Falls frequented Bella's little shop, even vacationers and families whose status matched my own.

"Uh, Bella!" The blonde hurried after her. "I really don't think you should drive."

Bella waved her off. With every step of her big black boots, my opportunity was dwindling. And with a gossip like the blonde here to witness it, my good deed would surely make the top of the town's social media page.

I could hear my campaign manager now, or was it my mother's voice again?

You wouldn't know a good thing if it bit you in the face. That was exactly why I'd hired the best manager in politics to head my campaign as Folklore Falls's mayor. Maybe I was learning from my manager already, because this opportunity was too good to pass up.

"I'll just wait outside, Sally." Bella tossed the reassurance over her shoulder.

"What if you pass out again and hit your head on the concrete? Ms. Villenueve will kill me if I let you walk out of here without some assistance."

"I'll drive you," I said. My voice came out deeper than I expected. I'd been ignoring the pain pulsing in my hand. I didn't have the energy to lighten my tone as my manager had instructed to make me more 'likable.'

Bella ignored me, stomping through the doors that opened for her like she was a queen.

"Bella," I jogged after her. I didn't have extra time today, not with the demolition crew coming this afternoon, but a good deed with the town's favorite bookstore owner was worth the PR. "Let me drive you. It's my fault for causing you to faint in the first place."

She side-eyed me, avoiding looking for too long, and then laughed. It was an odd reaction, but I didn't spend a lot of time around chicks who wore boots instead of heels and permanently branded their spines with blocky letters.

"Not your fault," she said. Her gaze fluttered over my hand, and she paused in front of the sliding doors, then dropped her hands to her knees. A key dangled at the side of her face, hanging from an earring. It was an odd choice for jewelry and didn't match the black studs lining her other ear.

"Are you okay?" I asked, tilting my neck to try to meet her eyes. I really didn't have time to waste, but everybody knew Bella, and one positive interaction could catapult me into the town's good graces. Hell, it might even save time, which I desperately needed since my manager only gave me two days to get settled before the campaigning began.

Bella blinked rapidly, and it sent her eyelashes fluttering in an innocent way that didn't match the tiny spikes on her black bracelet and jagged choker necklace. Memories of schoolyard days slowly filtered back. I'd pushed thoughts of public school out long ago as per my mother's request to forget that embarrassing bout. Even at ten years old, Bella dressed like a widow at her husband's funeral and scowled at everything except cats. Though the scowl never worked, every kid within a hundred miles of Folklore Falls wanted to be Bella Villenueve's best friend.

She straightened but swayed ever-so-slightly. "You should get your hand looked at."

I shrugged and inspected the dark blood and scabs forming around the wound. "I cleaned and bandaged it. Probably better than the backwoods doctors in this—" I bit back the word 'dump' and remembered my manager's advice. *Every interaction has to be a positive one.*

But it didn't matter. Bella was already through the sliding doors, in the purgatory between inside and outside where two sets of motion-sensing exits created a cubicle of nothingness. I needed to regroup and pretend that I loved backwoods doctors. I hurried after her, squeezing through the first set of doors before they squished me.

"It's no trouble," I called after her. "Let me give you a lift."

"Look." She halted just as the second set of doors slid open. A blast of cool air rushed in, sending stray leaves to coat the carpet of purgatory. When she spun around, the toe of her heavy boot landed on my foot. "Oh, son of a beast!" Bella danced back. "I'm sorry. See? This is it. This is the curse. You have to get away from me." She was barely talking to me, which was good, since I hadn't a clue what she was saying. I suspected it could be a literary reference coming from her.

"I didn't even feel it," I said. This was quickly becoming more trouble than it was worth. I glanced over my shoulder to see if the gossipy blonde was still witnessing my good deed.

Bella raked pointed black fingernails through her hair and groaned. "Honestly, you're probably a murderer knowing my luck. So, I'm better off not getting into your car."

"You know me from Sherwood Forest Elementary and Folklore Falls High?" Why did I want her to remember that version of me? I didn't even want it saved in my memory bank. I was a nuisance, a wild child, I was never a *well-behaved boy.*

"Well, yeah," she scoffed. "Everybody knows the Beast—uh, Brett Jensen." She curled her bottom lip under and gnawed on it while turning faux innocent eyes up at me. They were huge and dark and all-encompassing. I could get lost in her gaze and never find my way out—creepy.

I shuddered.

The doors rolled shut since we'd stopped moving. Without the fresh air, I could smell hints of vanilla and pumpkin again. I used to hate pumpkin. Halloween wasn't so bad, but it meant Thanksgiving was coming, then Christmas and New Years soon after. Each holiday came with a double dose of Little-Boy-Brett-Disappoints-His-Family-Once-Again.

"Wait, did you call me… a beast?" My brain finally caught up with her comment. That couldn't be good for my campaign.

Bella shrugged, but her forced smile told me all I needed to know. "I didn't mean to say that. This is just bad luck after bad luck, and I need to stop it before it gets worse." Her rambling didn't make sense, but it came to a sudden stop.

The naked feeling crept back as she stared up at me. She wasn't a short girl, and certainly not small in those thick-soled boots—why couldn't I get my mind off the dang boots—but I was taller than average. Maybe that was all 'beast' meant. I could only hope.

Bella's stare bore right through me, and her lips, painted a dark shade of purple, curled up. Her mouth split into a faint smile, revealing teeth whiter and straighter than most folks' in the Falls.

"Okay," she said, as she rolled her shoulders back. With her posture straighter, and the skin tight black clothes stretching over curves, her shapely figure became more prominent. She arched an eyebrow in a Wednesday Addams expression that sent me right back to my first boyhood crush on the character in a show I certainly wasn't allowed to watch. But I never listened.

"Okay?" I tried to gather my thoughts. Whether it was the reminder of Wednesday, or the loss of blood from my injury, I couldn't think straight.

"Okay, you can drive me home." Bella spun around and nearly

smacked into the glass on the sliding doors. The exit didn't live up to its name. No sliding occurred, and she glanced back at me, eyes wide.

She stomped her feet twice, then tapped the glass. Nothing happened. The doors remained sealed shut.

"Son of a beast," she said. "Er, sorry." With another shrug, she slipped past me. "It's a spooky nickname, but I like spooky." She paused and waved her hand over her outfit as if presenting herself. "Obviously."

My eyes slipped to the black leggings hugging her hips as she faced away from me and tried the doors closer to the inside of the hospital.

They didn't budge, and by the look on the blonde receptionist's face, this had happened before.

We were trapped, and my opportunity to look good on Folklore Falls's social media site came to a screeching halt.

Now I didn't get the medical care I needed nor the reputation boost for my campaign. And the morning was quickly slipping away. I knew I shouldn't have wasted time coming into the hospital when I had a crew coming to tear down the house.

I cursed under my breath, but it was Bella who said the actual words.

She banged the glass with her fist. "Stupid freaking curse!"

Five

BELLA

Trapped inside a stuffy hellhole with the hottest jerkhole in town meant I couldn't decide if my luck had turned good or bad. I bit my lip and swallowed another mention of the curse.

I'd decided the second I accidentally said his old nickname out loud that he was the perfect patsy for my plan. Since Brett was a giant grumpy bully, I could make him fall for me without an ounce of guilt. Plus, his Phantom-adjacent attitude gave me all the feels. I could enjoy a few dates with him, break the curse, and run back to my fictional guys without a scratch.

If I could get him to fall for me. And mentioning I was bad luck definitely wouldn't help.

"What are you talking about?" Brett repeated, impatient now. His tone had flipped a switch, becoming gruff and irritable when the doors wouldn't open.

My brain raked over everything I knew about Brett Jensen. Bully. Rich as hell. Family used to run the resort that almost put everyone in town out of business. Never worked a day in his life. Loved luxury gym clothes apparently.

I didn't even know the brand he wore made menswear. I arched an eyebrow at the gray fabric clinging to his thighs. Though he was known for his anger, punching other guys in high school and such, that never stopped me from fantasizing about him. Now, with him right in front of me, a potential, temporary boyfriend to help me break the curse meant I couldn't stop the fantasies from creeping in.

I must have been staring. Two peaks gave his brows a pointed look and I snapped my attention from his muscular legs.

"Nothing. I'm just…" I glanced around. "Missing my… leg… day." That was what gym rats called it, right? I was terrible at this. Lots of people liked me, but it always stopped there—general friendliness. I was likable, but to get someone to fall in *love* with me was a whole other feat.

Brett pursed his lips, his disbelief apparent.

"The curse of hanging out with people who don't care about gains, right?" I forced a laugh.

He cocked his head like a confused Doberman, dangerous, an attack dog, but still a dog. "Isn't your friend having a baby?"

Dang. I was bad at this. I could give anyone in town advice and be a listening ear during their struggles, but when it came to my own life, it barely existed beyond the pages of a book. I knew everything about Katrina and Bones and Sally, even my mom. And multiply that knowledge by ten when it came to my fictional friends. But myself? I didn't know who I was beyond the girl who loved books. Maybe that was a good thing. I could draw on all kinds of characters' personalities to play the role of the perfect girl for Brett the Beast Jensen. Easy peasy lemon squeezy.

"So." I took a step closer to him, eager to change the subject. The thought of labor and delivery didn't exactly spark attraction. What could I say to get him to ask me out? "Do you need someone to show you around the Falls?"

The Doberman expression returned. "I grew up here."

Okay, I wasn't normally *this* awkward. It had to be the bad luck. Brett lifted his hand and examined bandaging and dried blood. I wrinkled my nose and darted my eyes to the leaves blowing around the parking lot.

Thank goodness the curse, door malfunction, and Brett's pants had distracted me from the injury at hand—literally.

The door malfunction definitely came from the curse. Maybe speaking it aloud set it in motion, or maybe it was as Grandma V. had said, the closer it got to my twenty-fifth birthday, the worse the luck would be. It was a warning, she'd claimed, like a reminder that we were the Villenueve women: cursed, unlovable gold-diggers.

Brett seethed.

"Does it hurt?" I asked and instantly regretted it. Thoughts of the scabs forming around the base of his fingers left me light-headed. Before I bashed my head against the glass I crouched and took a deep breath.

"Pain is weakness leaving the body."

My eyes rolled so far into the back of my head, I thought they might stay there forever. The stupid gym-poster quote completed my picture of Brett—spoiled, shallow, and vain.

I sat with my back against the glass on the outside-facing doors and twirled a leaf in between my thumb and middle finger. Brett paced, cupping his injured hand.

This was the Brett I remembered—an angry bully who played pranks and grew into a pretentious prick with a jawline to match. And I loved it. But hated him. If only he were fictional so I could swoon over his gruff voice and scary expressions.

A sigh escaped him as he scrubbed his good hand over his face. "I don't have time for this," he mumbled.

"You and I both," I said.

He shot me a pinched glare. "I have a demolition crew coming in —" he paused to glance at the screen on his Apple watch. He tapped the screen and groaned something about backwoods WIFI running on manure. "Two hours."

"Demolition crew?" I looked up and brushed away my bangs from snagging in my eyelashes.

"I'm rebuilding the Jensen Estate."

Before he finished calling it by that blasphemous name, I was on my feet and pointing a finger in his face. "That house was built by the Villenueve family. *My* family."

He eyed my finger, then gave me a skeptical look. "And your point? My family fixed it up years ago. It was abandoned."

I hated that he was right. When Grandma V. died, my mother left it behind. She didn't care that it was our history. She had the money to forget it and buy a new house closer to the hospital outside Folklore Falls. But money couldn't buy good luck.

"That's because of the curse," I said, firm in my belief that my mother ran from there not for proximity convenience to cut down on her commute, but because deep down, she knew Grandma V. was right. The house reminded Mom that the Villenueve women were unlovable. And I was pretty confident my existence did the same, considering I'd never, in my almost twenty-five years of life, had a real boyfriend. That was, unless I counted the time I casually dated Bones for two years to help him make Katrina jealous, and my mom happy.

"What the hell are you talking about?" Brett coughed and cleared his throat. His voice lightened. "I mean, would you mind explaining?"

This new, saccarine-sounding tone came out forced, like every word he spoke could cause an accident in his pants. His attitude flipped quicker than a page when I was speed-reading.

"About this curse?" he prodded, impatient. "Is this a prank?" He lifted his angular chin toward the doors that wouldn't slide, and I frowned.

"Weren't you the king of pranks?" I folded my arms.

"So, it is? I really don't have time—"

I stepped into his space, careful to avoid sight of his hand. "Too busy planning to tear down a Folklore Falls monument, huh? Just what I'd expect from the Beast."

"Excuse me?" he huffed.

"Don't act like you didn't know everybody called you that."

A curl escaped the prison of his over-gelled hair and danced across his forehead as he shook his head. "Whatever. The house is an eyesore and needs to be modernized."

"It's history. And it belongs to my family."

His upper lip twitched. "I own it."

"You tear it down, and the whole town will come after you with pitchforks."

Brett threw his head back and laughed. I wanted to sock him right in the face, but I'd only read about punching and didn't want to hurt my hand. Then, we'd both need medical attention. "As a matter of fact, I've already promised to donate most of the grounds back to the state parks to ensure the Folklore Falls community will accept the building change."

"I haven't heard about it. Is it public knowledge that you're tearing it down?" I asked, tempted to 'accidentally' step on his toes with my heavy boots again.

"The town will like it when they see the new design I have planned. People here don't know what's good for them. They're living two decades behind the times, and Folklore Falls needs an update."

"Maybe we like it quaint."

"Is quaint code for cheap and dilapidated?"

I scoffed. Every time he opened his mouth, my plan withered. If I couldn't manage twenty minutes with him, how would I spend enough time with him to break the curse? Screw it, I'd find someone else. "Right. I forgot that elitist jerkholes like you love to tell everyone else what they do and don't like." I turned but swiveled back before stomping two steps away. I didn't have anywhere to go anyway. "And just because we have less money than the Jensen family," I raised my hands in mock praise, "doesn't mean we need an 'update.'" I bent my fingers into air quotes. "Don't you dare tear down the Villenueve Manor."

The line of his lips ticked up at one corner, and he narrowed his dark eyes. "You mean the Jensen Estate?"

"Villenueve Manor," I mumbled again. "I lived there until I was seven years old."

"And I lived there since I was eight. I've got you beat on the timeline."

My mouth twitched. I wanted to bite back but he wasn't wrong.

The humidity in between the glass doors rose. Brett's hair had gone from smooth and gelled down like a businessman to twisted into thick waves. The heated atmosphere did the opposite to mine, as if the waist-length locks could get any straighter.

"Aren't you running for mayor?" I asked, a new idea formulating.

Brett closed his eyes and sucked in a breath through his nose. "Yes. What does that have to do with anything?"

I smiled. "Good luck with that. If you tear down my family's house, your campaign will be over before it starts."

"Is that a threat?"

I shrugged. Anger and passion for my family's history, the house my mother left behind and my only connection to Grandma V., mani-fested as a confidence I'd never had before. I liked it. I relished the feeling but knew it would be fleeting. Likable, never lovable.

Brett frowned. "Forget it," he mumbled, talking to himself more than me as his eyes searched the small space between our feet. When he lifted his head, all friendliness in his face vanished. He held my gaze. "That crap-house will be gone this afternoon."

I wouldn't back down, though it strained my neck to keep looking up at him. Even with the boots, he dwarfed me by a head. "It's a work of art. And it's not going anywhere unless you get out of here." I twirled my finger around, indicating to the space between sliding doors.

"So, this *was* a prank?" He shouted now, all reason going out the window. Did he really think I'd planned this and trapped his injured body in here with me?

"Maybe it's just my good luck." Or bad luck, considering I had no clue how to stop him from bulldozing my family's architectural history, and time was quickly slipping away.

A maintenance worker threw me a thumbs up as he arrived outside the hospital with a toolbox. With plenty of other exits available, we didn't seem high on the priority list as the hospital grew busier.

"You'll see good luck when you see the plans I have for all the old buildings in Folklore Falls."

"You wouldn't." I furrowed my brows.

He turned his back to me at the sound of the maintenance worker prying the doors open with a crowbar.

"Just wait," Brett said, as he stepped toward the doors. With a bit of manual labor, they pulled open. Crisp autumn air tasted like the first bite into an apple. I lived for this weather, but the taste turned bitter in my mouth when the jerkhole glanced back at me. His face was so smug only the toe of my boot could improve it now.

"By this time next year, you'll be thanking me for what I'll fix in Folklore Falls."

"More like pranking you," I retorted, but he was already outside. If I was the snotty sort of person, I'd wish for infection in his shoddy bandaging. Maybe a fever to top it off.

Instead, I stomped through the doors and pivoted right back for the hospital. Now I had two problems, the curse and the death of my favorite place. Getting Brett to like me, agree with me, maybe even more, would kill two birds with one stone—or rather, save them. Too bad I couldn't stand the sight of his smug mug longer than five seconds now.

So much for my perfect plan.

Six

If nothing else, I learned time management from my mother. She taught me to always arrive early and be prepared. So, when I knew I wouldn't make it back to the estate in time to meet the demolition crew, I broke out in a stress sweat. The argument with Bella didn't help. I'd never fought with her before and while we weren't close in high school, I'd considered her one of the few who didn't dislike me. Why I'd thought that was a mystery to me now.

An old tractor lugged along the highway, blocking a string of cars from going faster than twenty miles per hour. Once I became mayor, I'd enact a ban of tractors on public streets. What my mother once saw in this town, I couldn't imagine.

I rolled down the window and flung my arm out. "Get out of the road!"

The two cars in front of me didn't seem to mind. I swerved my car halfway into the opposite lane to see past the line, then floored it when I saw the coast was clear. The tires screeched as I sped in front of the tractor and yanked the steering wheel to pull back into the lane.

It was then I realized why the tractor was moving so slowly. A deer trotted along the highway, darting back and forth from the road to the weeds on the side, indecisive of whether or not it wanted to cross the street. I cursed and swerved back into the lane that, thankfully, had no oncoming traffic for as far as the eye could see.

The screech coming from the sportscar's tires must have spooked the animal. It bounded toward the hood of my car in a panic. In a second, I was left with two choices; hurt the deer or pull off on the opposite side of the road, scratching the bottom of the low-set car.

I cranked the steering wheel away from the doe and cringed at the scrape of the pavement as my car bumped off the highway and into the gravel. My shoulders relaxed as dust settled around me.

The old man on the tractor lugged by with a friendly wave and a smile.

"Yeah, yeah," I mumbled, offering a curt wave back. "You're welcome, deer."

I dropped my head against the steering wheel and sighed. Maybe this was what Bella meant—this whole town was cursed.

I pulled back onto the road, following the line of cars until it came to my street. At the end of the long driveway was a large truck and construction vehicles. Men stood around waiting for the locked gate to open.

Clammy hands left salt stinging my injured hand, but I ignored it. I didn't have time for the injury with a house to rebuild and a campaign manager to meet. It was only a couple months until the mayoral elections, which meant I was behind before I started. But I never expected Mom's attitude change on her deathbed.

Dirt outside the estate's gate kicked up as the Audi's tires spun. I'd hit the gas a little too hard, spinning in place before launching forward onto the pavement. The stupid city hadn't allowed us to pave the road outside our property. More backwoods thinking, if you asked me.

The demolition crew pulled into the driveway behind me. I glanced at the construction vehicle in the rearview mirror, and Bella's threat popped into my head.

The town didn't care that much about this hideous, old mansion, did it? My phone pinged from the passenger seat.

Chip's picture filled the screen, and the answer button blinked. I let it vibrate, making a mental note to return my campaign manager's call right after I signed the paperwork signaling for the demolition crew to begin.

I slammed the car door and cursed at the dust settling on the RS7's shiny red surface. I hated messy things almost as much as old things, and Folklore Falls was abundant in both. But I'd clean it up. For Mom, I'd clean it up.

I greeted the leader of the crew, exchanging a firm handshake. He handed me a clipboard with plenty of pages attached. I took the pen he offered.

"Autograph here and here, and we'll start ripping into her," he said with a nod toward the Jensen Estate. Or the Villenueve house? I paused with the pen hovering over the signature line.

Everybody knew and liked that insufferable chick for some reason. I'd been aware of the famous stained-glass window. If Falls folks saw the whole estate as her family's home…

"Son of a—" I dropped the pen on the clipboard and handed it back to the man. "I've got to make some calls."

"We have a schedule to keep," he said, as he raised his hands.

I raked my uninjured fingers through my now wavy and unruly hair. "I know, I know," I groaned. "Just let me check on something. I'll pay extra, double, if you let me reschedule without a fuss."

"When it comes to my appointments, I'm gonna fuss. I've got a whole crew waiting—"

"Just don't let this get out," I interrupted. "I'm a prompt and reliable man."

The guy snorted, then spit chewing tobacco too close to my RS7 for comfort. I resisted giving him a glare. Every interaction needed to be positive.

I forced a smile. "Triple. I'll pay triple if you keep this between you and I and come back another time."

He pursed his lips, then shrugged. "We'll get off your property once half the payment hits the account." I bit back a frustrated sigh and swiped away Chip's message to open my bank's app. Moments after I hit send on the amount with too many zeroes, the man tipped his head and sauntered off toward his crew.

"Oh." He stopped and turned around. "I've got a third party bringing more equipment. I'll call 'em, but if they don't get my message, just tell 'em to call Bob about a bulldozer."

I nodded, and he spat again, then continued his uneven walk.

The roar of their engines firing up drowned the rhythmic ring on the other line. I pinned the phone to my ear with my shoulder and turned to face the house. It looked like one giant frown with the espresso-painted eaves and dark green window frames. Ornate curves in the porch's architecture reminded me of a haunted home for Victorian women. Now I saw why Bella liked it—it was her, in house form: dark, outdated, and a problem.

I pictured a sleek contemporary design with a flat roof, and cubicle shapes covered in gray paint.

"Yello?" Chip answered. What made him a good campaign manager was his endlessly upbeat attitude and cutesy sayings, but to me, it came across as juvenile. Why people liked it, I didn't know.

"Camellia," I said.

"Didn't I tell you to call me Chip?" he said. "Camellia reminds me of my mom, and let's just say, she was the H225 of helicopter moms."

I raised my brows, impressed at Chip's knowledge of luxury transportation. He wasn't a poor man from what I could tell, but I didn't suspect he'd ever ridden in a private helicopter before now. And an H225? Even I couldn't afford that.

"Anywho," Chip said, "we have a lot to cover in our meeting today, considering you're months behind on campaigning."

I sucked in a breath through my nose. "But you said it wouldn't be any competition going against the grandpa."

Chip smacked his lips. "Max was the town's sheriff for a long time before inactivity forced him into retirement. He was a friend of the people but generally disrespected for his lack of work ethic. The man never did his paperwork."

"So, that's a good thing, right?" I hoped. I ran my palm over the back of my neck and turned to inspect the damage done to my car. The front bumper suffered scrapes along the bottom from pulling off the highway. That dumb deer better appreciate my effort.

"It's unpredictable is what it is," he said. "People know he's useless, but Folklore Falls is a sentimental town. I'm willing to bet plenty of them will vote with their emotions. Those are the folks we need to turn to—"

"Don't say it," I stopped him.

"The dark side."

"You never listen to me. I can fire you, you know?" I threatened. Maybe Bella had rubbed off on me.

"You won't." He followed the statement with an upbeat whistle. "Speaking of the dark side, I'm ten minutes away from your place. I'm early because I snagged Folklore Fall's photographer last minute. We need to get a friendlier photo of you for the advertisements. Maybe with puppies or something."

"I don't think calling my campaign the dark side will help my case." I appealed to his logic, still stuck on his stupid nickname.

"It's politics, man. It's all on the dark side. See you in ten."

With that, the other line went dead. Left in the silence, I couldn't help but wonder if it symbolized my political career. My first interaction with a Folklore Falls resident in two years resulted in a fight. And all I wanted to do was help—well, help for the sake of publicity. Plus, the fact that it was Bella Villenueve, the one and only classmate I didn't bully or tease or punch in high school might have influenced my desire to *help* a little. She was as infuriating now as she was intoxicating to me then—the girl with the coldest glares but kindest heart. If I made a nerd cry, she'd be there, narrowed eyes at me and shoulder to cry on for the target of my teasing. It drove me insane and made it impossible for me to ignore her.

And here she was again, interrupting the promise I'd made to my mom. Could Bella really tank my political career before it'd even started?

Nah, I had Chip Camellia Potts, the best campaign manager money could buy. Now that I thought of it, maybe he did own a luxury helicopter or two. Chip was infamous for skyrocketing nobodies to popularity faster than my RS7. And my weird crush on the goth girl in high school was years ago, it meant nothing now.

So, why couldn't I stop thinking about Bella? No way could she ruin my campaign, I hoped.

Seven

BELLA

With my head between my knees, the heat in my neck subsided, and my vision returned to normal. Almost. Black spots still lingered on the edges like threatening confetti, ready to turn this argument into an upside-down party, also known as a shouting match. I slowly pulled my ears from between my legs and rested my chin in my hands.

I needed to get out of the hospital but not before getting answers from the oldest living Villenueve woman.

"The curse isn't real!" My mother screeched two octaves too loud. When a baby's cry responded loud and clear, she lowered her voice, realizing the walls of her office weren't thick enough to contain her irritation. "And I won't waste a second of my time on that house, either."

"Grandma V. said there are secrets hidden inside."

"My mother was a superstitious, old spinster with nothing better to do than invent imaginary drama."

"Then, why haven't any of the Villenueve women ever gotten married? Grandma V. loved Elizabeth. She loved Grandpa, too. But they never gave her the time of day." I challenged, sitting straighter now. Posture demanded respect, and I knew the subtle ways to get my mother's attention. She eyed me with pursed lips.

"I told you, she was superstitious and dramatic. Everyone around here hated my mom because she was cold and unfriendly. I don't blame a smart woman like Elizabeth or your grandfather for never falling in love with her."

"What about you?" I folded my arms and crossed my legs, using the gestures to gain power over the conversation. It didn't work.

"I had needs, but I never wanted to deal with the emotions that went along with it."

Okay, that I believed. My mother wasn't an easy woman to love. She was married to her job and the money that came with it. But that was also the reason Folklore Falls suffered seven years of horrible lightning storms, car accidents, and pests destroying crops after she'd turned twenty-five. Grandma V. had proved it with plenty of saved newspapers that I'd yet to relocate after she'd passed away.

"Now." Mom straightened and smoothed her shirt and hair after wagging her finger at me. "Stop wasting my time when I'm clearly swamped. Some of us have real, useful jobs."

Of course my mom couldn't have a conversation without a jab at my job. At least today she was too busy to list all my failures.

Her heels tapped against the tile as she marched for the door. I'd learned the attitude storm-off from her, perfecting the swing in my hips with my head tilted back. But that was where our similarities ended. Oh, and the fact that we were both completely, utterly single—forever. Like Grandma V. and her mother before her, and before her, all the way back to the fake marriage that started it all.

"Isn't it obvious?" I managed, though I knew mentioning the injuries and surgeries and anything else involving blood beyond that door would send my head into another spiral.

"What?" Mom snapped.

"The hospital is busy because of our bad luck."

A little laugh escaped her, and I could have sworn she'd have a successful career as an actress of villains in live-action Disney remakes. She turned just enough to arch an eyebrow at me—okay, I learned two things from her.

"Bad luck for other people is good luck for a hospital."

Before I could process the awful statement, she was through the door and directing her staff.

So much for convincing her to help me save our family's home. Two plans in one day, and they'd both failed. I wondered how Loxley fared in her labor.

After a quick check-in with Gideon, I gave up and headed for the bookstore. Loxley was contracting but not ready to push. The labor could still take a long time, and I was more of a burden at the hospital than help. Gideon thanked me for keeping Lox calm in the car and offered to put a call out for a pickup. I finally relented, because if my mom wouldn't help me save the Villenueve house, I needed to come up with a plan B and fast. Not to mention, I had a few dates to set up. If Brett couldn't be my curse-breaker, I'd need to enlist the help of a few busybodies in town.

Funny that the pickup was an actual pickup truck. Bones and Katrina took up the call Gideon posted on the town's social media page. I squished in between them in the truck's cab and prayed Bones's headache was completely gone when he fired up the engine.

We bumped along in the unsteady truck while Katrina rambled in my ear about the drama at the tavern the night before. Sound of her excitement faded as I tuned her out, and my own drama took over.

Mom's words got under my skin. I didn't have undeniable evidence that the curse was real. Especially since I couldn't find any of Grandma V's old newspapers and journals. If it truly wasn't real, then I'd have wasted precious time trying to find a guy to fall for me when I needed to stop Brett from destroying evidence of my family's history in Folklore Falls. I never really believed it'd stop the curse, that was my job. But Villenueve Manor was my last connection to Grandma V.

So, step 1: save the house.

Step 2: get a boyfriend and break the curse.

Step 3: curl up with a good book, knowing I'd stopped seven years of bad luck from plaguing me and my friends.

Oh, and step 4: let the boyfriend down easy. It wasn't that I didn't want a life partner, someone to share stories and go ghost-hunting with, but I'd seen the men that lived in and visited Folklore Falls and not one of them could live up to the fictional guys I'd fallen for.

I pulled my phone out from my bra and tapped the calendar app. A month and a half until my birthday. But only two hours, or one now, until Brett wrecked the house. Yep, the curse would have to wait a day or two.

The truck rolled along the open highway, slowing as we drew near Sherwood Bed and Breakfast, the tavern, and my bookstore, along with other buildings in town.

"Wait." I pointed a long fingernail down the road. "Do you mind taking me to the Jensen Estate?" The name tasted like bitter coffee. Along with everyone else, Bones and Katrina knew my family once owned the property, but the Jensen family was so famous and had lived in it long enough, that most didn't attribute the place to us anymore.

"Won't you need a ride back?" Bones asked, glancing at me, then back to the road. "You know I'd always help you out, anyone around here would, but the tavern has a lunch menu now. Katrina's got me opening earlier and earlier every day."

Katrina's red hair fell into her face as she bobbed her head, dancing along to the pop song and agreeing with her boss. Though who really ran Knight's Tavern was obvious. Katrina had Bones wrapped around her little finger.

"No." I shook my head. "I'll make the current resident drive me." Or rather, I'd sit on the front porch, blocking a bulldozer from doing its job until Brett gave up. I was nothing if not determined. Except I hated to cancel appointments with my clients. I'd not missed one since I opened Bella's Bookstore years ago.

"I've been thinking we need to update the name, too," Katrina said to draw the conversation back to Knight's Tavern.

"Ugh, don't talk to me about updating or changing anything in town," I said, remembering Brett's threats. No way he'd become mayor, though, right? His only competition was Sheriff Max—or retired Sheriff Max, now that Gideon was elected. Max was a lazy man, but beloved. The perfect mayor for a sleepy town that needed no changes, except for running out elitist pricks like Brett.

"Just hear me out," Katrina continued. "Hop's Hollow." She paused for added affect and raised her palms. Her grin told me she knew Bones would go for it, eventually. "Get it? Because of the hops in IPA beer."

"It sounds like a bunny farm to me," Bones said. But when Katrina's face fell, he quickly changed his tune. "But I like bunnies."

I arched an eyebrow. How did Katrina do it? Bones wasn't the only guy who was head over heels in unrequited love with her, either. She had a handful of regular vacationers eating out of the palm of her hand. Maybe I'd pick her brain later—for the curse, of course.

"I was thinking it sounds like a brewery," I said. "But it's a tavern, not a brewery."

"Oh." Katrina rested against the seat again, her excitement waning. "You're right. But I like Hollow, it sounds spooky yet small-town-y."

"Talk about spooky," Bones said, as we pulled through the open gate of the Jensen Estate. Clouds had moved overhead, casting a shadow over the mansion. The dark eaves and intricate architecture screamed a gothic history.

"She's a beauty, isn't she?" I breathed.

The truck's engine coughed as it climbed the slight incline of the paved driveway. It sputtered again, and Bones let out a string of G-rated swears. Halfway onto the property, the pickup came to a halt. We all twisted around to see the black smoke puffing from below the truck's bed.

"This is Old Faithful!" Bones said. He kicked the door open and leaped out. "My truck has never had an issue."

The curse? If it was only a few vehicle problems, maybe I'd let it slide. We tumbled out of the truck cab after Bones. Katrina continued her rambling about the tavern's name while I tuned her out a second time and stared up at the gorgeous building—my home.

I sighed, then sucked in a long breath. The property always smelled like roses with the bushes that lined the driveway and the front of the house. Except now, it was overwhelmed by the scent of rain. A distant rumble growled and echoed through the sky. A minute later, a flash followed.

"A storm, too?" Bones groaned and slapped his hand against the side of the truck.

"Call Tammy," Katrina offered, naming the only mechanic in town. Though, we all knew Tammy was slower than molasses and wouldn't get to the truck before the storm soaked us all.

"Put a call out on the social page," I suggested. "Apparently, that's the only way to get things done around this sleepy town."

Katrina gasped. "What about Sleepy Hollow?"

"What's a sleepy hollow?" Bones put his hands on his hips but it didn't deter Katrina's bouncing.

"For the tavern," she squealed and hopped from one foot to the other. "It's such a cute name!"

"You're still thinking about a name at a time like this?" Bones laughed. Their flirtation faded from my attention as I marched toward the house with the same rhythm and determination I'd just seen from my mom. There wasn't a car in sight, much less an entire demolition crew. Was Brett just messing with me? Were his schoolboy pranks still part of his behavior even at twenty-five?

Another rumble announced the storm drawing closer.

I climbed the front steps and pounded on the door. A slip of paper fell from the crack between the door and drifted to the ground. I knelt, but a blast of wind carried it away from my reach. I took a step, following the scrap of paper, then snatched it before another gust could steal it from me.

Horrible penmanship covered the scrap of paper, but I made out the words.

Demo cancelled, contact Bob about a bulldozer.

I smiled. Just like in high school, I could still get under Brett's skin and having that nostalgic pull on him would only help if I did decide to use him to break the curse.

But the note's first two words said all I needed to know. Luck had turned back in my favor. And maybe, just maybe Mom was right about the curse. It was all in Grandma V's head.

Thunder roared again, much louder now, and the sky grew too heavy. Huge raindrops splat against the earth. It was the perfect day for reading and meeting with clients in a cozy bookshop.

"Is this you telling me the curse isn't real?" I stepped out from the porch and glanced up at the stained-glass window, Grandma V's favorite part of the Villenueve Manor. A prick sent my heart skipping a beat then doubling to catch up with its normal rhythm again. I swallowed and chewed on my lip. *This is a good thing.* Except the excuse to give the town bully a chance slipped away with the curse. I couldn't date the guy with an anger problem who'd pushed around innocent classmates. Though I wouldn't mind if he pushed me against a wall...

Another roar joined the thunder, but this one was from Bones's pickup.

"It's working!" Bones shouted over the shower of rain pummeling the ground. "We're headed back to town."

"Wait up!" I called. "I changed my mind." *And I might just make it back in time to meet with my clients.* The car worked, the rain fell, and the demo was stopped—it felt like good luck to me. Or just the ups and downs of life as Mom would say, no luck involved.

Rain soaked my hair as I stomped toward the truck. We all piled in, and Bones backed down the driveway.

I shot the Manor one last look for now. Though we were far away now, I could have sworn the window looked different. Something had changed about the cursed rose. I squinted, and my jaw dropped.

One of the petals wasn't rosy. It looked like the paint had shifted to black until I realized it wasn't there at all. The perfect teardrop shape, suspended in an eternal fall, was gone.

The storm raged on into the next morning. I sipped pumpkin spiced coffee from a cauldron mug and stared out the front window of the bookshop. I'd tossed and turned all night with weird, vivid dreams. I was wearing gray sweatpants, which I'd never be caught dead in, and riding a deer around the Villenueve Manor when the house suddenly exploded. But in this unconscious existence, I wasn't sad because inside was a perfect glass rose, untouched and beautiful. Though in real life, not the dream world, I'd never consider a flower a grander beauty than the gothic mansion I'd called home until my seventh birthday.

The steady shower of rain soaked the dry leaves I loved to crunch under my boots. I sighed, hoping the autumn-flavored caffeine would wake me up enough to get through the day.

I leaned my head against the frame of the window and let my eyelids fall. If anybody needed me, I'd cranked my phone too loud, hoping for a call from Gideon. Loxley likely gave birth yesterday afternoon, but she'd requested people didn't bother them for the first twenty-four hours. As her best friend, I barely counted as people, but still respected their privacy and resisted the temptation to call and ask.

I startled as my muscles relaxed a little too much, and I swayed. I took a huge whiff of the coffee and shook my head. Patty Potts had requested a chat with me two weeks ago because she knew she'd take most of my day. Whether the elderly woman would drive in this weather, I didn't know.

Rarely did Patty ever need advice, though. She just wanted a listening ear since her children were spread around the country and never called. Some clients came to me with anxiety about their future, and I'd give them self-help books to organize their thoughts. Others showed up with tears in their eyes, needing an uplifting drama or light-hearted comedy to guide them toward positivity. Though I was notoriously single, folks still trusted me with the details of their love lives, to which I'd recommend a few romance novels to inspire ideas and get that spark back.

I yawned and eased my head against the window frame again.

"No," I said, then startled myself with my own voice in the quiet space. "Time to wake up."

Philip let out a meow in response. I spun around and crouched to scratch behind his ears. In gratitude, he meowed again, then rubbed against my leg, leaving stray black hairs across my purple dotted tights. As soon as I crossed my legs and sat on the floor, Philip leaped into my lap. I set my mug on the floor and stacked the books Gideon had knocked over.

Romance novel after romance novel created a leaning tower of love that I adjusted by stacking a second tower for it to lean against. I thumbed through the pages of a Cinderella retelling.

"I wish you could talk like an animal in a fairy tale," I said. "But you'd probably only say swear words and claims of starvation."

Philip didn't respond. He'd curled in the space between my folded legs and drifted into dreamland. The only thing that could make the day more perfect would be if Heathcliff or Rhysand stepped out between the pages of their books. Or both.

Of course, they'd have to battle my one true love, but Philip would roll over in defeat for a few belly rubs.

"And Erik," I muttered. If the Phantom came alive, too, the sleepy bookshop would need a larger murder mystery section.

"I guess I should be glad fairy tales aren't real since it means curses aren't, either." I let my cat in on my little self-conversation. But was today too perfect to lull me in a sense of security? Why did Brett call off the demolition when he'd sworn to tear it down?

Was this the calm before the storm? Shakespeare's idiom didn't suit my situation, considering the rain was already dumping. And I liked this weather. Life never wrapped up in a nice little bow like this, but I was tired of being suspicious. Yesterday was a long day, and the signs were loud and clear, *here's a little rain to read by*. Or maybe I wanted to believe the curse was Grandma V's imagination because the only eligible bachelor for miles around was a bully from my schoolyard days who wanted to destroy my favorite place in the world.

I wasn't going to let it get to me. If I were a client, I'd recommend myself a reread of *Still Me* by Jojo Moyes because I needed a little reminder that I didn't suck. I was a Villenueve woman but that didn't have to determine my destiny, right? The question went against everything Grandma V. had warned me against when I was growing up. But my mother would be proud of me for setting superstition aside, and I wanted… I shook my head.

"No bad luck here," I said. To that, Philip darted from my lap and disappeared into the storage room. "I know it's a sensitive subject for black cats, but I've never had a reason to believe that superstition!"

An angry yowl came from behind the storage room's door where Philip's water bowl couldn't splash any unsuspecting books when he scooped it out with his paw for a gentlemanly drink.

The bell over the bookshop's door chimed, and I snapped my head up from the Cinderella book. Though she brought in a rush of cool air and wet shoes, Patty Potts's smile warmed the whole store. Her rosy cheeks and wide-set figure reminded me a of a porcelain tea kettle.

And tea was what she often brought, ready to spill the whole town's secrets. Patty knew everyone's business, from Falstaff, the town drunk's choice of alcohol to the retired sheriff's new love interest.

"Cats and dogs," Patty said, giving her umbrella a little shake outside before closing the door. She balanced two paper cups with steam rising out of the opening. Sherwood Bed and Breakfast had branched out to offer to-go pastries, coffee, and tea in the last year. It worked to draw in more business after they'd suffered from Jensen Resort's competition. Plus, Loxley's grandfather brewed a mean cup of chamomile.

Philip yowled again.

"Not real dogs, don't worry," I shouted back. I finished the stack of books and stood to give Patty a hug.

Patty squeezed so tightly I worried the bad luck had returned and I'd suffocate right here. Though, death by hugging while surrounded by books sounded poetic.

"Speaking to one's cats is the mark of a lonely woman," she said with an arch in her eyebrow that rivaled my best looks served cold. After she sank into the squishy, crushed velvet purple chair I called the Throne, Patty snagged a book from the nearest shelf. "See how happy she is?" She wagged the book at me, insisting I acknowledge the smitten woman on the cover, touching foreheads with her beloved. "You deserve this. None of this pretend dating to make Katrina jealous pish posh."

I rolled my eyes. "That was years ago, and I had fun with Bones."

Except kissing him was vomit-inducing, considering I saw him like a brother.

"All I'm saying is that you're a striking young woman and whip smart. You'd keep a man on his toes. And men around here need that. Heaven knows my son does."

"I thought we were here to talk about your needs," I said, pivoting the subject off my love life. The bad luck wasn't real. It wasn't. I'd had Philip for four years and didn't so much as stub my toe around him. So, take *that* curse of the Villeneuve women!

Patty narrowed her eyes and nodded. "That *is* my need. My son needs a break from being a..." she snapped her fingers. "Like a choco-holic but for someone who works?"

"A workaholic?" I offered. I'd turned my back to Patty to search for a book called *Mama's Boy* on the shelf. If this was Patty's drama for the week, the story about a son's mother setting him up on blind dates until the mother unexpectedly finds love with one of the girl's father's would lift her spirits.

"That's the one." She clicked her tongue and sighed. "He's too into his job. And I heard there's a little 'single lady' superstition going on around these parts."

I froze, finger on the spine of the *Mama's Boy*. Of course Patty Potts would know about my family's history. I should be surprised she hadn't brought it up before now. Or at least, she hadn't brought it up to me. The idea of dating Patty's son conjured all kinds of images. Most of them included me yawning and a male version of Patty yammering on about whatever boring job he obsessed over.

I pulled out the book and spun around. "I thought your son never visited."

"He doesn't." She took a sip from paper cup with the tiny logo of a fox and green letters that read Sherwood Bed and Breakfast. "But his work is here right now. I'm assuming you've heard about the last-minute candidate running for mayor?"

Normally, I wouldn't have paid attention to anything political, and Patty would be my first source of knowledge.

"The Beast," I mumbled.

For an older lady, Patty didn't have any trouble hearing. "Isn't it exciting?" She slammed her cup down on the small table beside the Throne. Drops of tea splashed from the small opening. Patty scooted to the edge of the seat and clasped her hands together. "He's so dark and handsome and brooding."

And this was why we were such good friends. Patty appreciated the moody men as much as I did—fictional ones, that is. We'd swoon over Mr. Darcy or Mr. Rochester and avoid real men since they never lived up to the ones in books.

I handed her the book, trading it for my cup of tea. It was transactional but also fostered many friendships. Clients brought me coffee or tea, and I'd recommend a book to help with their problem.

Patty turned it over, then shoved it back toward me. "I'm not interested in dating."

"Neither am I." I swallowed the hot tea, taking a too-large gulp. I knew the question was coming. She'd asked it before, everyone did. *Have you ever been in love?* But I always managed to manipulate the conversation and shift the subject to a new book release or guilt everyone for not finishing their book club story in time. It was an archaic question. Lots of people didn't want a partner, preferring solitude, and there was nothing wrong with that. The issue was, I was never as good at hiding my passion for romance as I was my ability to cry. Eventually, I gave up trying and started stocking the love stories at the front of the store. I wasn't just Folklore Falls's unofficial therapist, I was the girl who knew everything about romance yet never experienced it for herself. And that intrigued people enough to pry. Not that prying was unusual in a little community like the Falls. It was practically a required course to graduate from small-town university.

Today, and knowing Patty's relentlessness, I didn't have the energy to fight it. After she swallowed another sip of tea and opened her mouth, I jumped in.

"I'm not good—"

"Not even to break the single girl's curse?"

We both spoke at the same time, and I quirked my head. The

gesture was uncharacteristic for me, and I suspected I looked as ridiculous as Brett's Doberman expression.

"You're not good at what, dear?" Patty tried again.

I'd never said it aloud. As the one who helped everyone else, I preferred others only see my strong side. So, I didn't cry where people could see me and never ever admitted the mile-long list of my failures.

I cupped my tea closer to me with both hands. The long sleeves of my black sweater reached down over my knuckles and dangled like big gaping flags beneath my wrists. I took a sip and let the fragrant liquid sit on my tongue. It burned, but the pain was a distraction from my mother's list of my failures.

"You can tell me," she said. "I know I'm a bit of a gossip, but your secrets are safe with me. You're always so careful to ask about others and keep everything about yourself inside."

It was a genius plan, really. If people didn't know my failures, they couldn't list them. If I didn't get close to anyone, they wouldn't realize how unpleasant I was.

I tilted my chin up to shake my bangs from sticking to my eyelashes. My gaze trailed to the tops of the shelves that surrounded every inch of the store's walls. Dust collected in faint lines on the highest shelf. I needed to borrow a ladder again, but the metal made it heavy, and it'd sit in the shop looking hideously out of place in the cozy atmosphere for weeks until I dragged it back to Sherwood Bed and Breakfast again.

"You know every detail about me. It just isn't fair. I bet you know Mr. Potts better than I know you, and you never even met him." Patty dug into her purse with an embroidered image of a teapot and teacup, then pulled out a tiny floral mirror in one hand and rouge in the other. The endearing habit warmed my cold, closed-up heart every time. Whenever Patty spoke of her late husband, the man to which not even fictional love interests held a candle to, she dabbed her cheeks with old-fashioned blush. Apparently, mimicking the flushed look of a woman in love was her secret to keeping the fire sparking after decades of marriage.

I leaned against the bookcase and ignored the shelf digging into my spine. "I want what you and Mr. Potts had."

"Well, you'll never find it hiding in the bookshop's storage room," she scolded, then absent-mindedly pulled a western romance off the shelf and flipped through the pages.

I lifted the paper cup to my mouth and chewed on the edge of the top instead of taking a drink. "I'll never find it at all. I'm too sensitive." I coughed, my throat squeezing at the mention of my mother's favorite critique. From there, it was a domino effect. Too sensitive led to too emotional. Too emotional became scatterbrained, and scatterbrained was one of her many nice ways of saying I'd never be as smart as her. She was the CEO of a hospital after all, and I ran around with my head in the clouds and my nose in a book.

"Pish posh." Patty waved her hand as if she didn't even register the full humiliation of my confession.

"I'm just unorganized." I kicked my boot out to direct her gaze to the piles of books that were arranged by favorite tropes rather than the author's last name. My system was nuts compared with most bookstores, but it worked for my messy mind.

"And all I could do was brew a cup of tea," Patty said, lifting her cup to offer a cheer. "Mr. Potts didn't give two licks that I burned every meal I cooked, he still loved me more than Chip loves that dumb job."

"It's different. I've never held a real job, and I never got my degree. I'm not like Katrina or Loxley." Once I started, the floodgates opened. I couldn't stop myself. It felt too good to pour out my fears at her feet, to be the one speaking for once—to be heard. "Katrina is fun and funny and cute, and Lox is passionate about charity and giving back to the community. I like books, my cat, and maybe two people."

"The whole town loves—"

"That's the real curse." I couldn't stop now. "I'm just a mess, and nobody deserves a lifetime of picking up the mess that is Bella Villenueve." I shrugged, bringing the cup to my lips again. I gulped, and my hands shook, either from skipping breakfast or the intensity of the confession.

"You do help—"

I threw up my hands, interrupting Patty again. Thankfully, she didn't seem to mind as she eased back into the Throne and patted her lap for Philip to hop on. I was heating up, and nothing could stop years of listening to everyone else's problems while throwing dirt over mine. I buried it down, but not far enough that the zombie apocalypse rising inside of me couldn't push it back out. The paper cup creased under my squeezed grip.

"Hell, I should be the one nicknamed the Beast because I'm angry. I'm angry that my ancestors were horrible people and that people don't read enough anymore. What's up with that? Who doesn't like the smell of books or getting lost in a new world? And I'm pissed that Katrina and Bones are the perfect couple, but they're wasting time afraid of commitment."

Patty pursed her lips into an apologetic expression but didn't stop me. Not that she could now. It felt too good to admit everything I'd bottled up for years. The 'out of sight, out of mind' technique worked to keep the thoughts at bay, but seeing my mother and the Villenueve Manor triggered me.

"Also, why does Brett think he can come back into Folklore Falls and run for mayor? Does he think he'll buy people's votes? That house was supposed to be mine, and Grandma V. wasn't supposed to die when I was a kid." I swallowed back tears and shifted the emotion to anger, wagging my finger at Patty as if she were my mother. "Mom wanted me to be a doctor, but I faint at the sight of blood." I gasped, stumbling over my words and trying to catch my breath at the same time. "I'm angry and a mess, and that's the truth. I'm the curse."

At that exact moment, I gripped the tea too hard, and the top popped off. The liquid splashed over the edge, soaking Patty's face. Though it wasn't burning hot anymore, it startled Philip, who leaped over her arm. Frantic, he scrambled onto the nearest bookshelf, scrabbling with his claws and knocking a row of hardbacks down like a shower over Patty's head. I lunged forward but only managed to grab two out of the four books before they whacked against her head and neck.

For a moment, I couldn't speak, and the only sound was Patty's knees creaking as she stood.

"I'm so sorry," I said, as I pulled the long sleeve of my shirt down further and used it to wipe the tea from her face. She patted my forearm and gently pushed my help away.

In the chaos, I hadn't heard the front door's bell chime. Patty nodded toward Bones, who was not only soaked from the rain, but from tears as well.

"It was an accident," she said. It was too perfect, or imperfect, to be an accident. I'd confessed my darkest secrets aloud, only to attack Patty with my tea a split second later. "I'll go to the restroom and wash up while you help Mr. Bones."

Before I could protest, she disappeared to the back of the shop. I didn't have a moment to overthink the events as they related to my curse.

At the mention of his name, Bones dragged himself across the room and nearly collapsed on the tea-soaked Throne. Of course, in his soaked clothes, he likely wouldn't even notice. He slumped over and dropped his face into his hands.

"What's wrong?" I crouched beside him.

"After we dropped you off yesterday, the truck broke down again," he sobbed. As someone who cried every time I read *Phantom of the Opera*, I wasn't one to judge his emotional reaction. But a breakdown over a car didn't feel like Bones.

"Let me grab a book about a mechanic." I hopped up, but Bones shook his head.

"Tammy hired a new guy."

"And that's bad?" Usually, I was good at piecing people's sobs together, but this was so uncharacteristic for Bones that I couldn't think straight.

"He asked Katrina on a date!" he groaned.

Uh-oh. This couldn't be another slice of my bad luck pie, could it? My mother had insisted the curse wasn't real, and she'd sworn to heaven and earth she knew leagues more than I ever cared to about life, the universe, and, well, even pie.

Katrina and Bones were soulmates. They dated on and off, and Katrina loved to play hard to get, but she never showed interest or grew close to anyone other than Bones. They were the eternal 'will they, won't they' couple of Folklore Falls, and that was just the way it always was.

Or used to be. Now Bones was heartbroken, Patty had a headache, and… I gasped as the wind pushed the shop's door open.

It all happened so fast, I didn't have time to react. Bones must not have closed the door all the way, and the storm did the rest, shoving it open just wide enough for a skinny, sneaky cat to run through.

A black blur darted out the door.

"Philip!" I shouted, far too close to Bones's ears.

My heart pounded at the thought of losing my baby. I leaped up and ran after him, swinging the door open. Sheets of rain pounded the sidewalk just past the overhang that did little to block the wet when the wind picked up. Philip darted into the parking lot and toward Sherwood Bed and Breakfast. If he made it to the forest beyond, I'd never find him. If only I'd never spoken the curse into existence. My confession came with its own domino effect, one disaster after another in a matter of minutes.

"Philip!" I called again, as my boots splashed in the parking lot's puddles.

What kind of cat ran from a warm, cozy store and into a storm? One whose owner had seven years of bad luck.

Eight

BRETT

Photo-op round four, and I hated every second of the suit Chip had chosen for me. Somewhere, the ghost of my mother was smiling down on me for wearing pinstripes like a gentleman. I thought it looked more like a mob boss's choice of attire, and it didn't match the task at hand. But Chip had insisted raking leaves while looking sharp did double-duty for lifting my reputation.

The photographer gestured for me to face the camera with my other side, but Chip stepped in and stopped her.

"You want the swollen fingers in the picture?" she asked with a skeptical look.

Chip shrugged. "It gives him a sympathetic angle."

I flexed my injured hand, half of it puffed up with a slight pink tint to it, and she wasn't wrong, it looked unbecoming. But I didn't have a second to waste on another trip to the backwoods medical center Folklore Falls considered their local hospital.

I winced as I wrapped my hand around the pole on the rake and dragged it across grass around the playground.

Apparently, appearing as if I were cleaning up the neighborhood playground would grab the attention, and vote, of the local mothers. Mud squelched under the seven-hundred-dollar pair of shoes I'd selected to match the suit. I'd need to get used to suits and tailored outfits all over again just like I did as a boy.

Come to think of it, the photography appointments reminded me of 'portrait day' with our tutors. Mother wanted my brother and me to have yearly pictures taken, just like the children in schools. The only real picture-days I'd ever experienced, one during which I had the pleasure of wearing comfortable ripped jeans and the shirt I'd gotten from woodshop class, was during my years at Folklore Falls elementary.

Chip shot me a double thumbs up as if he was a hired clown trying to make a child smile.

I cracked a tense smile that I didn't have to see to know was awkward. The pinched brow on Chip's face told me I'd messed up another interaction. The photographer was Folklore Falls's one and only professional with a lens so wooing her would win favor with a lot of people. Chip had claimed she gossiped worse than his mother, and with bookings out for a year from newborn pictures to wedding shots, the photographer would no doubt be busy sharing her experience with Brett Jensen.

Think positively. Be friendly. Chip said those phrases like they were as easy as carving a table leg. The thought made me wish I was back in woodworking class, the one and only place I truly loved.

"Maybe we'll try distant shots," the photographer said with a frown.

Chip lifted his arms again but offered a drooping thumbs-down this time from behind her back. We'd had to wait three days after the end of the storm before the photographer agreed to do outdoor photoshoots. While messy leaves and broken tree branches worked for stylistic graduation photos, it didn't suit the professionalism political advertisement shots required.

I shoved the rake out at the photographer's instructions. She focused on light and the aesthetic of the shot while Chip stood behind her and pointed to his biceps. Pointing turned to rolling up his sleeve and flexing, then gesturing wildly at me. I squinted, trying to make out the words he mouthed.

The photographer glanced at him, and he snapped out of it. The confusing behavior returned as soon as she focused on me and the camera again.

"Flex a little!" Chip said with an exasperated show of his hands in the air. He'd surrendered to shouting it instead of remaining discreet.

"I'm wearing a long sleeve." I straightened from the fake raking.

Chip marched up to me, leaves crunching under his pointed loafers. "It took me two hours to convince her to let us use the storm's mess as a photo-op, and you're about to blow it."

"We're losing good light," she said, as she waved for me to return to cleaning.

"This is ridiculous, Chip." I ignored her and let the rake fall against the staircase on the playground.

"No, no, don't give up." He hopped over to me but not without a quick pause to apologize to the professional first. "Hang in there, champ. After this, we'll pop over to the animal rescue in town and adopt you a little terrier. People love a candidate who loves pets."

"How will that help, Chip? How?" I crossed my arms and toned down my irritation for the sake of the photographer's presence. In case she snuck a shot for her gossip tabloids or something, I didn't want to risk photographic evidence of my twisted grimace. "Shouldn't I be assembling a team to make cold calls and preparing for a debate or writing a speech?"

"Right." He nodded and licked his top lip where blonde fuzz decorated his face. "So, those are normal campaign activities for normal places like Boston or San Francisco or even Boise. But this is Folklore Falls, Brett."

"I'm aware. I grew up here." The statement sparked a memory of a particular arched eyebrow and thick, black boots. I'd said the same to Bella less than a week ago.

"Nothing will be normal. We're aiming to capture the hearts of the locals with some *Friday Night Lights* magic." Chip added to the phrase with jazz hands and a wry grin. He tilted his head, nearly resting it on my shoulder. Even with the added height from his loafer's heels, Chip didn't come close to eye-level with my six feet and seven inches.

"I don't know what that means." I glared down my nose at him.

"It means you've already pledged to donate new turf to the Folklore Fall's Foxes football field," he laughed. "Try saying that five times fast. It could be a good warmup for singing the national anthem at the game."

"What the hell are you talking about, Chip?" I barked out his name. None of his yammering made sense, and I almost expected him to break out in song right then and there. I wouldn't put it past him, especially if it drew attention. My mother would have loved him, and I'd be lying if I said that wasn't another reason I'd hired him.

"I'm kidding, unless you can sing. Can you sing? Your voice is so deep—"

"Chip!"

He raised his hands in surrender. "Right. Just keep on keeping on. The goal here is to schmooze the parents by showing them that you care about their facilities. You know, playgrounds, parks, baby-changing stations in all the public bathrooms. But instead of posing next to the urinals, the lovely photographer—" he paused to turn and give her an appreciative wave, "and I decided a park would be more picture-appropriate."

Clouds rolled in overhead, blocking the sun. From the corner of my eye, I caught sight of the photographer shaking her head and shoving the camera into a carrying bag. It was a good thing, too, because clouds meant humidity and humidity would twist my hair into waves—not an ideal image for the clean, well-mannered future mayor of Folklore Falls. It was a title my father never managed to hold and my mother's greatest disappointment, or maybe that was just me.

"Are parks and playgrounds not synonymous?" I asked, focusing my gaze on Chip again.

He sighed and palmed his face in exaggerated impatience. "That's all you got out of that?"

"I get what we're doing, but I've rescheduled for the demolition crew tomorrow, and I want to be prepared for them when they get there. Also, I expected your help on things like building a team, not dragging me to the monkey bars." I pushed past him and shoved my hand into my back pocket. After producing the thick, leather wallet, I flipped it open and peeled crisp hundred-dollar bills from the fold.

"Just trust me," Chip said, as he followed, "gracing a few areas of town with your helpful presence will save hours of cold-calling and begging for votes."

When I offered a roll of Benjamin Franklins to the photographer, her scowl lifted. I wasn't easy to deal with, my mother had made that clear my entire childhood, and sometime in my adolescent years, I'd discovered money helped.

"Wait, did you say the demo crew is coming back?" Chip kicked the rake, and it nearly whacked him in the face as he jumped out of the way just in time.

"I've been meaning to discuss my compromise with you." I tucked the wallet back into my pocket and folded my arms. "I believe I've settled the score. My mother would have hated it, but instead of a modern design, I'll rebuild the Jensen Estate with my own hands."

Chip narrowed his eyes. "You've lost me."

"A log cabin styled home will suit the Folklore Falls aesthetic while still looking new and clean. It'll be a good segue to ease the town into updated buildings, which will bring in new businesses and open up opportunities for the backwoods to become a real city."

He tilted his head side-to-side. "You say you grew up here, but I'm really starting to doubt it, Brett."

Whatever that meant, I didn't care. Chip ran my campaign, not my life, and he wasn't my political advisor, either. The log cabin was my passion project, a piece of myself to hold onto as I fulfilled my mother's dying requests, and the demolition of the Jensen Estate symbolized the start of it. I was eager to make my mother proud, but that didn't squelch the need to be myself, and I couldn't think of a better way to put my love for woodshop to work.

Once the photographer had packed her equipment, she tossed it all over her shoulder and took the short walk to her house in the neighborhood. By now, the clouds blocked all sunlight. I ran my hand over my hair to check for waves, but a cool breeze kept humidity at bay. The wind tossed the small pile of leaves I'd raked around the playground, and I groaned.

"Tell me this wasn't a waste," I said pointing to brown and red flecked leaf that caught against the bottom hem of my pants and flickered with another gust of wind.

Chip pursed his lips and brought his hand to his chin. He stroked the blonde fuzz around his mouth and stared at the leaf as if it had the answers to the universe.

"I'll admit," he started, "this will be trickier than I thought. The weather here is impossibly unpredictable, but the locals seem to understand it. I'd expected the park to be hopping with tykes and their families on a sunny morning, but Folklore Falls thwarted me again. I'll never understand why Ma likes this place and—"

"Chip." I tapped the timepiece on my wrist. "The demo crew. Tomorrow. I've got family pictures to take down and put into storage." This task should have been crossed off my calendar the morning of the first appointment with the crew, but my injury interrupted the plans, then the run-in with Bella set me back even further as I called off the demo.

"Okay, okay," he said, as if trying to calm me down. But I was calm. In fact, that hot rage building up to an uncontrollable temper hadn't resurfaced since I'd agreed to my mother's wishes. *Finish what your father started in the Falls.*

Two women in workout pants pushed jogging strollers along the street. Neighborhoods here didn't worry about sidewalks since the roads were wide and everybody drove slowly. Nothing caused a rush in Folklore Falls, except the occasional freak lightning storms. The women gabbed cheerfully until they noticed us—two grown men wearing dark suits alone at a child's play area.

Chip patted my arm excitedly, clearly oblivious to how creepy we looked. He touched me more often than the situation deemed necessary, but I ignored it. For now.

"That's the head of the school board," he said, giving a slight nod toward the women. "You want her in your court. Time to grab a bat and start swinging."

"You're mixing your sports."

"Good morning, ladies!" Chip ignored me and waved. The brunette reminded me of a chick I'd dated briefly years back, but it was the blonde who glared at me. Their children snacked happily on peanut butter crackers, sharing crumbs as they passed the bag between the strollers.

"I'm Chip, and this is Brett." He turned, and his shoulders slumped when he realized I hadn't followed him. It took no longer than a second for him to regroup and smile at the women. "If you've been around this area for a while you might recognize him as a local."

The brunette snorted. "We know the Jensen family."

Chip clapped his hands together and beamed. "Great! Brett is a committed, lifelong resident of the Falls, and he has a few questions for you on what you'd like to see improved around town. Do you have a moment?"

The women exchanged incredulous looks. Both were conventionally attractive, but they'd look better in dark colors. *Where the hell did that thought come from?* Of course I knew. None of the women I'd dated succeeded in clearing my mind of the girl who glared. Bella was just like me—different and scary—but completely different in that people liked her and it drove me wild that I could never wrap my head around why I did too. Being odd, or weird or the one who didn't fit in made me angry while it somehow made her kinder.

I shook my head of the memory flood and tried to smile, for Chip's sake.

"You're kidding, right?" the blonde laughed.

"Hey, Brett," the brunette chimed in again with a smile that bared her teeth.

"Hello," I said, taking a step forward into the conversation and offering a polite nod.

The brunette wrinkled her nose and angled the stroller away from me as if I'd scare her child. "I see you've branched out from harassing women at the bar to the park now, huh?" she said. At the mention of a bar, it jogged my memory. Her named started with an S... no, maybe an F. I'd hit on her at the casino's bar in the Jensen Resort maybe two years ago that led to a few wild dates between us. "Going for married moms is a new low for you."

"Uh…" I stammered.

Chip glanced between us with bugged eyes, then poked his pointy shoe forward for a tiny step in between us. Good thing, too, the woman looked feral and ready to swipe at me with her fingernails. As far as I recalled, she'd already done so when I publicly dumped her at one of my father's campaign speeches.

"So," he said, "Brett here woke up this morning and decided he wanted to clean all the playgrounds around Folklore Falls because the children's wellbeing is high on his list of priorities. Are regularly landscaped parks something you'd like to see for your neighborhood?"

"That's right." The blonde scowled. "You're running for mayor, aren't you? I saw something about that on the FF's news thread."

The brunette spoke to her friend but didn't take her eyes off me. "Yeah, Stacy, how do you feel about the guy whose bullying is still, to this day, talked about at school board meetings, lingering around the parks your kids play at?"

"Oh my gosh, you're that Brett?" The blonde, Stacy, apparently, shook her head and sucked in her cheeks. She mirrored the brunette by folding her arms.

Chip's eyes rolled to me without turning his head. I could feel the cringe coming off him like steam rising from a boiling cup of tea. For once, I read his mind, and we were on the same page. *This'll be a hell of a lot harder than we thought.*

"Right," the brunette said. Our silence was damning. "Maybe if you can tell me my name after our *year* of dating, I won't tell the entire school board to vote against you."

When I opened my mouth, the blonde's name almost escaped. Perhaps that was why I'd remembered S as the first letter. I knew the school board director, too, though not well. Unless they ran in my circle, or frequented the resort my family had run, I never rubbed elbows with townsfolk.

The brunette clucked her tongue, and her ponytail swayed side-to-side as she shook her head. "Just like I thought."

She shoved the stroller forward, and before I could think of anything to say, the two women were on their way down the street.

"Hmm, that went… differently… than I expected." Chip pulled up the calendar on his phone and tapped the screen. "No worries, we'll refocus and move on. The adoption fair only happens quarterly, which means it'll be packed. Just make an appearance, pick a pup, shake a few hands, and you'll be on your way. We're already running out of time, so you won't be able to change."

"I don't want a dog." I shook my head. At least the conversation distracted me from the terrible interaction with the women and the dull, persistent ache in my hand. The injury wasn't healing as quickly as I'd hoped. I'd have hired people to pack up the family pictures and heirlooms, except that Mom had specifically requested I deal with it all personally. As she aged, she'd gotten more paranoid about theft from hired help—the scandal with that Loxley chick only made matters worse when she'd snuck into my father's office and found my mother's stash of local artifacts.

"More of a cat guy, huh?" Chip asked. "You can return the pooch tomorrow, but today you're going to smile pretty for all the folks at the adoption fair." He grabbed my forearm, pausing for a quick squeeze of my muscle. He smirked and pulled my arms from their folded position. "Come along."

Years ago, when my temper was more unruly, I'd have punched him for invading my personal space. But I needed to play nice. Play nice, win the mayoral election, fix Folklore Falls, and finally, make my mom proud—the list was long enough to spark a headache. And since I needed Chip's expertise, especially with the first order of business, I relented and let him drag me to the car.

Hopefully, a furry flea bag would lighten my reputation around here. At this point, I needed all the help I could get.

Nine

BELLA

Three days without the love of my life. Black cats definitely didn't cause bad luck. When Philip disappeared, my life continued getting worse rather than the opposite. A sick feeling swirled in my stomach as I finally took a moment from the shop and searching for Philip to visit with the new parents. Poor kitty deserved every second of searching I could manage, but there was nowhere else to look and nothing I could do but wait.

With a book tucked under my arm, I walked the short distance from my shop to Sherwood Bed and Breakfast where Loxley and Gideon stayed to get help from her mother. Loxley's family ran the inn for tourists, but it was like a second-home for many of the townsfolks as well. People came for the breakfasts or to hang out in the cozy basement area they'd revamped as a small cafe.

Pumpkins lined the sidewalk in town since everybody decorated for autumn early in Folklore Falls. Unpredictable weather had us celebrating holidays at odds times, but the infamous lightning storms helped to bring in curious tourists in years past. Until the storms grew more dangerous and impossible to track. We'd coined a phrase years ago, *tourists come for the Falls, but they stay for the Folklore magic.* In recent years, tourists came less and less because nobody could hike to the waterfall when lightning and flash floods threatened their plans.

Lack of tourists meant less business, but we all pivoted, helping one another and supporting our individual services. Teachers at the schools assigned reading and sent their students to purchase books at my shop, parents flocked to Sherwood Bed and Breakfast for a caffeine fix from the new cafe, and everybody enjoyed the friendly dart and poker games at Knight's Tavern so they bought plenty of ale to keep Bones in business.

I smiled at the fall decorations everywhere in town, but it quickly turned upside down. Somewhere, out there, was a scared, lonely cat who risked harassment from people who believed he'd be bad luck. Now my mother's judgment made sense, how stupid I was to be superstitious.

Right?

I pulled the book from underneath my arm and studied the cover of the woman and the wolf. *Death of a Fairy Tale* was a modern adventure with a new mother, so it suited Loxley's situation and need for excitement in her life. But it was Grandma V. who'd recommended the book to me. I wasn't a mom, but she'd wanted me to learn the dangers of ignoring the unseen world—the world of fairy tales with witches who cursed families.

"It's dumb. Those aren't real. You're stupid for ever believing it, Bella," I muttered, paraphrasing what my mother had often said to me growing up.

A scream escaped me. One moment, I was running my thumb over the artwork on the book's cover, and the next, my knees slammed into concrete. Thankfully, my hands stopped full impact against my knees and the injury was balanced. Other than a few scrapes on the heel of my palms and skinned legs, I came out without too much pain… physical pain, that is.

"No, no," I said, as I looked at my torn clothes and the bent cover of the book that was in pristine condition only seconds ago.

The rough sidewalk had ripped through the thin mesh of my black-striped tights I'd bought for a Wednesday Addams-inspired look. The book's cover bent back, and the first few pages were left with creases, too.

"You poor baby." I grabbed the book and smoothed the pages before bothering to clean myself off. The minute amounts of blood allowed me to stay clear-headed… or not. Was I thinking clearly if I let myself believe that mention of the curse caused this mini accident? I could have sworn the pumpkins along the sidewalk were out of the way and close to the shop windows, which meant this particular one had jumped out of its own volition. Or maybe I just wasn't paying attention. Leaves clung to the fabric of my tights and jagged-cut skirt. I brushed them off and stood, giving myself a little shake.

Loxley's grandfather and his girlfriend approached me with smiles on their faces. They shared whispers and walked with their arms inter-linked. When they noticed my scratches and tears, they unfolded from one another. Their demeanor tanked with every step they took closer to me. Weren't they just flirting and enjoying a romantic walk together?

"Bella, are you all right?" he asked, concern creasing his forehead as he glanced to my knees. His girlfriend did a double take between him and me and then raised her eyebrow.

I nodded, not wanting to start a long conversation with the lovable but overly talkative couple.

"Lingering a little long there, aren't you?" his girlfriend said, as she folded her arms and faced him. I'd never heard her speak this way to him. They were the most passionate, cheesiest couple I'd ever seen, even after two years of dating.

"I'm asking the young lady if she's okay." He frowned. Loxley's grandpa *never* frowned. "But if we're criticizing one another, how about we talk about the way you always ruin my cups of coffee with too much sugar?"

I'd dodge around them if I could trust myself not to trip over the curb. Their closeness had quickly changed to a wide stance that blocked the entire walkway. Even when I wasn't consciously thinking of the curse, I found myself superstitious of the small things. I couldn't have caused this fight—no. Definitely not. Maybe?

"As I was saying, do you need any help, Miss Bella?" He turned to me, leaving his girlfriend fuming.

"I'm fine." I smiled and took the opportunity to sneak between them, hugging the book to my chest and trying to politely distance myself.

"If you say so." He nodded.

"She says so."

As I backed away, their arguing faded, and I took a breath of relief.

"This is fine," I muttered. If fine meant I'd triggered a hundred-year-old curse and brought seven years of bad luck on myself. What the hell was that all about? I glanced back at them to see the girlfriend storming off, marching back toward Sherwood Bed and Breakfast. She left Loxley's Grandpa in her wake with his hands thrown in the air.

I picked up the pace and hopped off the sidewalk into the inn's parking lot. I took the porch's steps two at a time, letting my boots slam against the wooden planks. After a quick visit to meet Baby-Loxley-Slash-Gideon, I'd take a tenth trip through Sherwood Forest calling for Philip.

The inn's door nearly knocked out my two front teeth as it swung open. I halted to avoid colliding with Gideon and the tiny, blanketed lump in his arms.

Gideon yelped, apparently startled at my presence barreling for the door. I couldn't blame him, I'd had two left feet for the past few days. The quiet bundle wrapped in his arms started to squeak.

"Oh no," Gideon said, as he balanced the baby in one arm while lightly brushing his other palm over the child's head. "Shhh, don't cry. Just sleep. Please…" Gideon's usual grumpy voice had shifted to a softer dad-tone as he begged his baby. If I didn't know better, I'd think the new dad might burst into tears along with the infant. Dark half-moons cupped his lower eyelids, red lines snaked through the whites of his eyes, and his hair was extra-disheveled. It looked like he'd risen from the grave to join the zombie apocalypse.

The bundle split into a dry, newborn cry that left me cringing.

"I'm so sorry," I whispered.

"No point in staying quiet now," he said, gently bouncing his knees to soothe the baby. "We'd just gotten her to sleep."

I gasped. "It's a girl?" I couldn't wait to help her dye her hair black and purple and manicure dark, pointed fingernails thirteen or fourteen years from now. At least the bad luck would be over by then, except that felt like centuries away. Seven years of ruining happy couples, losing my precious pets, and destroying my clothes and knees didn't feel survivable. Especially when it came to wrecking other people's days like my best friend's husband. *Don't think like that.* But how could I not? It was one stumble after another.

"Bella, meet baby Robin." Gideon carefully shifted his arms to angle the bundle toward me. The movement seemed to soothe her, and the wailing blubbered into soft whimpers… until her tiny eyes peeked open and spied me. Robin burst into another round of hyperventilating screams.

Just call me Bella the Horrible. Almost as bad as Henry VIII except I hadn't chopped anyone's head off. Or was it Ivan the Terrible I should compare myself to?

"This will be a while," Gideon said with a sigh. He tilted his head, nodding toward the door. "Lox is inside, taking a pastry break before a nap. I've got this." He shuffled to the wooden rocking chairs. They'd added several extra rocking chairs to the large, wraparound front porch over the years. The chairs offered the visitors a relaxing evening in a small-town gazing at Sherwood Forest on the right and the mountains with the famous waterfall in the distance. It was like a second-home to many of us who'd grown up in Folklore Falls and a quiet tourist attraction for visitors.

As I stepped inside the quaint bed and breakfast, the smell of coffee and cinnamon filled my nose. I personally hated the country-style decor, but I loved this place. Anyone who chose to stay at Sherwood Bed and Breakfast couldn't be too bad and might be the perfect guy to date. Except eligible bachelors never came to Folklore Falls, it was all couples on honeymoons, old retirees, and families.

I smiled at Loxley's mom and gave her a small wave as I passed the kitchen. She tried to return the greeting, but the rolling pin in her hand slipped and landed on her toes with a smash and a yip.

I cringed and dodged into the kitchen to scoop the rolling pin and give it a quick rinse in the sink. She waved me away with a thank you so I ducked toward the stairs that led to the cafe in the basement. I'd apologize for distracting her, but if I stuck around longer, it'd risk burning her hand on the stove or lighting a kitchen fire.

"Okay, a quick hello like I promised and then I'll get out before anyone gets hurt," I whispered the plan to myself, as I hurried down the staircase. The ambient café was illuminated with blinking fairy lights that hung in drapes across the high ceiling. Vintage tin coffee signs decorated the walls, and a large bookcase stood in the back corner with a load of books I'd donated. They were all firsts in long series across multiple genres intended to hook readers and drive them into my shop for the second, third, and fourth books.

Each round table was filled with Folklore Falls residents, and Loxley was slumped at a couch near the bookshelf. I angled through the maze of tables, past the cubbies storing board games, and hopped over the bin of fresh, cozy blankets for cold patrons.

Mrs. Dandy raised her mug and asked the barista for a refill. Poor guy looked busy so I offered to grab it for her. Mrs. Dandy beamed at me and I returned to her table full of the crochet club women with extra napkins and a quick sewing tip.

"Always a delight to see you," Mrs. Dandy said. "Will we get to see the infamous dress at the dance this year?" A twinkle sparkled in her eye. Who better to admit my sewing dilemma to than the crochet club? I'd joined to be around others who loved to create cozy crafts, and had once let my big project slip—the dress I'd designed to wear to my high school homecoming. But it never made it's debut. The dress was proof everything my mom said about me was true, I wasted my time on pointless projects, let my talent slip away, and resorted to an easy life of books and tea.

"Not this time." I said, as I turned and nearly collided with a teacher. He swiped his palm over his bald head and gave me a smile.

"Bella! Just the person I wanted to see, thank you for helping me grade all those English essays. I'd love to have you as a substitute or guest speaker for the advanced placement courses again, but I know you're a busy woman."

"Anytime, Mr. Preston." I smiled, remembering how fun it was to give book recommendations to the high school students. Just last week one of the girls had paid me a visit to return the book I'd lent her and share how much courage reading *Shattered Magic* had given her.

When Mr. Preston bid me farewell, another happy face greeted me. The barista, AKA ex-pawn shop owner Johnny, pulled me in for a quick side-hug while he balanced a coffee pot in his other hand.

"You seriously saved me the other night when I forgot my wallet. I felt so bad when I realized I woke you up just to borrow a twenty. I owe you big." The tattoos on Johnny's face danced as he grinned. "Tell me what to do and I'm there."

"You're busy enough with the cafe and the new guy, I'm good." I leaned in closer to keep his love life private in case it wasn't a good outcome when he'd asked Taylor to make their relationship official. "The date went well right?"

Johnny pressed his lips together in a mischievous smile and nodded, wiggling his eyebrows to add emphasis. I lightly punched him in the shoulder then stepped out of his way so he could get to the table behind me.

A mom and her homeschooled son waved to me and I paused to help him with his math as I often did during a coffee run. His mom claimed I had a patience with him that even she couldn't muster though it took the boy several weeks for him to warm up to my dark exterior. Once he did, I became his unofficial tutor and favorite 'costume lady' as he'd dubbed me. While the nickname was cute and it gave me joy to help him, *costume lady* sounded dangerously close to a cruel jab my mother would throw at me.

After a quick review of multiplication, I finally made it to the back of the cafe where Loxley looked half-asleep. Her foxhead-shaped mug tilted, about to spill tea over her baggy sweater. I stooped to scoop up the mug before something awful happened. At the sight of me, she perked up and straightened.

"I've missed you!" she said, as she took the mug back. "Thanks for that." She lifted it toward me as if cheering with my nonexistent drink. "I know it's only been a few days, but I'm absolutely wiped, and it feels like a whole month has gone by since I went into labor."

Carefully, I sat down next to her and tilted my head to lightly bump against hers as a sort of pseudo-hug. "Honestly, I'm with you on that. I don't have a baby, but it feels like it's been forever since I've seen you. I got to meet Robin, and she's adorable, but how are *you* doing?"

Loxley lazily waved her free hand and took a sip. "I need a break from baby talk. Tell me something new. Oh!" She turned to fully face me. "What about the story you were telling me? I feel bad. I barely remember what you said about the new folklore. With your family, right?"

I shifted on the cushion, crossing and uncrossing my legs. Nothing felt comfortable, and it seemed all eyes were suddenly turned to the back of the room. Except nobody actually paid us any attention. I bit my lip. Loxley didn't need a full run down of the details again, so I gave her the 'too long, didn't read' version.

"So, you know how much I loved my grandma," I started. "I believed this crazy story she told me about how if any of us Villenueve women don't get someone to fall in love with us by our thirty—no, twenty-fifth—birthday, then we'd cause seven years of bad luck. It's a crappy deal."

Loxley nodded. "That's fairies for you. I remembered that part." She smiled. If anyone would believe it, Lox was my girl. She already believed the fantastical Folklore of fairies, Titana and Oberon, and Grayson Baird's whimsical wife from our town's supposed history.

"The whole thing is insane, and I feel like a nutbag for falling for it." I lowered my voice as if that'd tone down the severity of the bad luck. "Except that weird things keep happening around me since I told you about it. And my birthday is a month away."

"So, you have four weeks to find a suitable dude and make him head over heels for you?" she sipped again, raising her brows to keep her gaze locked on me the whole time.

"That's the gist of it." I sighed. "Tell me I've lost my mind and to ignore it."

Loxley pursed her lips, opened her mouth, then closed it again.

"What?" I blinked.

"I mean…" she tilted her head side-to-side, considering what to say. "I'm half-dead and even I noticed your scrapes and bruises. You're literally the most poised person I've ever met."

She had a point. With my shredded tights and scratched palms, I looked like the walking, talking personification of bad luck.

After polishing off the tea with a long gulp, Loxley set the mug on a side-table next to a flickering candle. The pumpkin-spice scent mixed with the natural smell of tea and coffee in the cafe for an autumn ambiance. She clasped her fingers and wiggled on the cushion to settle back.

"Be honest with yourself. You wouldn't hate having a partner to do couples' Halloween costumes with. I've seen you challenging Katrina to a game of darts, then getting mad when she picks Bones to play against instead."

I absent-mindedly traced the bone shape along the sleeve of my skeleton shirt. Once again, she had a point. Would it be so bad to go on a few dates? Yes. Yes, it would. Brett was the only available man around for miles, and with the busiest season for book sales coming up, I wasn't willing to risk my business to travel out of town. Not to mention, I didn't have time to meet a new guy and hope he fell for me in a matter of a few weeks.

"Admit it." Loxley bumped my shoulder with hers. A wry smirk revealed I didn't need to say it aloud. She already knew she was right. "Now's as good a time as any to start taking dating seriously. You've been buried in your books and fake men for a long time. They're great and all, but you can't play a game of darts with them. The way I see it is that you may as well cover your butt in case the curse *is* real."

I glanced around the room. Plenty of bald men and graying women filled the chairs. Others were young married men and women on vacation.

"Who the hell am I going to date?" I said, frustrated with the situation now. The only answer I had was one by the nickname of the Beast. I couldn't date him. Okay, I *could*, but I'd already given up a successful life for the quiet joys of a bookshop, I wouldn't throw my love life down the drain too.

"I heard Bones is a free man now," she joked.

"Our brother?" I rolled my eyes but smiled at the memories. We had plenty of a good times during our pretend dates, but they were always platonic. I'd never get him to fall for me, and wouldn't want to if I could. I wanted a rougher man, one who'd never be intimidated by my looks. Someone who'd challenge me and push me to think differently even if it meant we'd disagree, or fight. My mouth twitched and Brett blocked my mind's eye. Suddenly, I couldn't get our conversation out of my head and how he looked in those stupid, sexy sweatpants.

Reading romance books does things to a girl and a guy like Brett definitely had the guts, and muscles, to challenge me. I sighed.

"Well, he's not actually related to us," she said. As two kids with no siblings, Loxley and I bonded on the school playground almost two decades ago. We'd adopted Bones as a type of brother years later in high school. He took both of us to the prom, a girl in glitter on one arm and a goth in black lace on the other. The photo is still immortalized in a collage on the wall at Folklore Falls High School's hallway.

"Gideon has a brother," she offered. "I've only met him once, and he's married to his job as an accountant, but he's friendly."

"Ew, I hate friendly."

We both laughed. It was the truth, but that wasn't why I rejected her offer.

I sighed. "Seriously, though, I just don't have time to meet someone new or leave town. If I'm going to do this, I need to follow the curse's timeline or else it's all a waste."

"Not if you fall in love." Her eyes sparkled, and she wiggled her brows. It was the most energy she'd exhibited since I'd arrived.

"The only person around is Brett Jensen," I groaned.

"Hmm." She raised her hand and made the shape of a checkmark in the air between us. "A jerk. Single. Hot as hell. He checks all your boxes."

"For fictional men," I finished.

She stood. "True. But you don't have a lot of other options right now. Plus, we've known him for a long time. I swear he had a crush on you in high school and that'd make it easier to get him to fall for you quicker. People are suckers for nostalgia and if he's holding a candle for you, maybe you'd break the curse with time to spare. I don't know how often Brett Jensen tells girls he loves them, but if anyone could make him fall, it would be the girl he had googly eyes for at graduation. I mean, I wouldn't ever recommend the guy, but you know me, I'm a believer in all things fairy tale." The messy bun precariously balancing on the top of her head flopped forward as she nodded. "Speaking of which, you texted that you had a book for me."

A flutter in my chest almost had me coughing. I needed a cup of tea, stat. Loxley's claims about Brett's past feelings for me sparked a flood of thoughts I'd buried. He and I had talked back then, sure, but neither of us ever made a move. He was a rich prick with no hints at evolving like Mr. Darcy or Mr. Rochester, and I was the girl too easily enamored by those fictional men. Brett and I would never work, not really.

"Bella?" Loxley asked.

"Oh, yep." I twisted and pulled *Death of a Fairy Tale* from its place tucked between my leg and the couch's arm. "Mom main character, plenty of folklore, and her husband is about as dorky as Gideon. Checks all *your* boxes."

"Thank the bookish gods! I need something to read while I'm breastfeeding. The nights are long right now."

"I can't even imagine," I said, wrinkling my nose. "I like my sleep."

"So, are you going to try to date to deal with the curse?" Loxley knew me better than I knew myself sometimes. She anticipated I'd change my mind the second I walked out of here. Not because the curse didn't freak me out, but because relationships did. They'd never live up to romance in books—especially not for someone like me. Nobody had yet to fall for the girl with her nose stuck in a book, the girl stupid enough to believe in her grandma's tales, the girl who never learned to love her own mother, much less a man.

Loxley pulled the hair tie from her bun and let the locks cascade down her shoulders. She shook out the tangles and then twisted the hair at the crown of her head again.

"I don't know…" I let my voice trail off as I scanned the shelf next to us. I'd read all the books there, more than once, and in each and every romance was a happy couple—an unrealistic expectation for Bella the Horrible. "Maybe not. Curses aren't—" Before I could deny the existence of my great-great-grandmother's sour fairy deal, Loxley's hair tie snapped apart and shot from her fingers. The thick tie acted like a slingshot as it knocked into the mug. We watched in slow-motion horror as the mug rolled to the side of the table. I leaped to my feet and scrambled to catch up, but I was too late, and two left feet had me tripping. It crashed to the floor with a clatter as I caught myself on the tiny table, elbow banging against the edge. The table tipped and the candle rolled to follow the fate of the mug.

Even in her half-awake state of consciousness, Loxley was quicker than me, the usually poised, never-clumsy girl. Her hand shot out and grabbed the candle right as it slipped over the edge.

Now all eyes were really on us. The cafe employee hurried over with a rag and a broom. The porcelain had cracked into several large pieces. I stood and swallowed, trying to gather my dignity without stepping on the broken mug.

"It's not the curse." I gave Loxley a glare. *Okay, maybe.*

I turned away from her and crouched to help the employee, but she shooed me away and used the broom to sweep the broken bits into a dust pan as I apologized profusely

"Date," Loxley said.

"But Brett—"

"Find somebody else then, but I can see it in your eyes. You believe it."

Dang if she wasn't right. Loxley knew what I couldn't admit to myself, Brett was on my brain and right in my path as a means to an end. That was all this would be, a means to an end, not a relationship.

"It's stupid, and my mom will tell me I'm stupid for even thinking about it." I finally turned to face her again.

Loxley's hair, long and unruly out of the bun, hung down her waist and into the candle in her hand. A bit of smoke wafted up, and my heart skipped a beat.

"Lox!"

"Hmm?" Her low-lidded eyes shifted to follow my gaze.

She squealed, and I grabbed the candle so she could use the bottom of her sweater to tamp out the little bit of flame that singed off her split ends.

It all only took seconds, but I was exhausted when the chaos came to an end.

Loxley slapped her hand to her chest. "Do you believe it now?"

Really, I always did. "Yeah," I muttered.

"Okay, that's enough excitement. It's time for me to have a nap." She stood and took a shaking breath. I matched it. When Loxley laid her hand on my shoulder and met my gaze, I relaxed but only slightly. The gesture was her way of forgiving me for siccing my bad luck on her pretty hair. "And it's time for you to get a boyfriend."

It wouldn't be as easy as she made it sound, but I had to try. Of course, I'd never actually *like* Brett, so I needed a believable reason why I'd date him. To convince him… and maybe myself.

"Okay." I nodded my promise. "I will."

Right after I find Philip.

Ten

BRETT

Even the short drive to the animal rescue left my legs with cramps. The tiny sedan was intended to help me look relatable to whoever spotted me on the road, but I missed my custom-made sportscar since it was designed to fit my unusual height. And the suit looked out of place at the adoption fair.

We climbed from the car and made our way through leaves, leaves, and more leaves. Sherwood Forest shed at this time of year and left its orange, brown, and red mess everywhere.

The small lawn out front had been set up with pens and cages, but the threat of another storm had driven the fair indoors. Stiffly, I forced one foot in front of the other and edged around the bodies packed into the small animal rescue. Townsfolk laughed and chatted while dogs barked. Tension built in my temples.

A woman glared at me for bumping into her as I tried to squeeze into a corner as far away from the puppy pen as possible. The cats in the cages along the wall were quieter, calmer, and more soothing to my inevitable migraine.

A young man at the front desk looked vaguely familiar with his gapped front teeth and bushy brows. The kid, probably only a couple years younger than me, might have been someone's brother or an acquaintance I used to tease on the school playground. I couldn't place him, but he must have recognized me.

The toothy grin on his face dimmed, and he raked judgmental eyes over my suit. With a small shake of his head, he turned to focus on the old woman making her way to the desk. He answered her question about rabies shots with a smile.

Chip jabbed the bottom of my ribcage with his elbow. "You need to mingle. Introduce yourself to the people working the fair and spark conversations with the townsfolk."

I sucked in a breath through my nose. I could do this, none of them looked quite as insufferable as the girl with the black mesh top. Bella's claim to my family's estate, the house *I* grew up in, royally pissed me off.

"I'll get you started," Chip said. He practically skipped to the front desk where he chatted with the young man. Exaggerated gestures in my direction left me scowling, but I tried to flip it around with fake friendliness.

An orange one with faint stripes sauntered to the edge of his cage and reached his paws forward for a huge stretch.

I touched the glass, and he sniffed at my finger. With a white leg, he pawed at the glass, and I noticed it didn't match his other orange paws.

"Brett!" Chip waved me over as he spoke to the desk attendant. "He's looking for a dog that likes to lick people, the happy ones with the yellow fur."

"A golden retriever?" the guy asked, eyebrows smashed together. He glanced between us.

With a snap of his fingers, Chip shot him double finger guns. "That's the one! We'll take one of those."

The guy snorted. As a genius with campaigns and politics, Chip came across as clueless in everything else.

"This is a rescue, not a pet shop," I muttered.

"Doesn't matter," the guy shut Chip down as soon as he opened his mouth. A quick glare to me sent heat raging in my chest. I knew the look, my family received it often from Folklore originals. They hated us for our resort that took customers away from their businesses. But it was more than that, too. They hated me because they weren't me.

Of course, if they stepped into my shoes, they'd find it wasn't all rolling in the dough. We had money, sure, but I'd almost trade it all for one night with one of those families who ate dinner together without the cruel jabs.

The guy had brushed us off as another person approached the desk, and I turned away. I didn't need to convince him to like me.

I froze, one hand on the counter and the other curled in an awkward position in my pants pocket. The injured fingers still ached, and I often caught myself holding my hand in the shapes of witch's claws.

"Where are you going?" Chip skirted around the crowded space to block me from walking away.

"He's made up his mind about me, and I don't need to change it," I said. The tight sleeves of the suit seemed to slowly squeeze the life out of my arms. I wanted to rip the fancy clothes off and yell at Chip to let me go to woodshop class. *Let me be myself, Mom.* I shook my head from the memory and focused on the actual person standing in front of me. This was my manager, not my mother—were the two even different when it came to a Jensen boy's life?

"Uh, yeah, you do." He laughed without humor. "That's exactly what a campaign is."

I flinched. Folklore Falls needed modernizing, but I never wanted the role my dad hoped to have. Still, I owed my mother for the promises I made when she was sick. She'd always seen this town, dingy or not, as a beacon of hope for our family.

"Fine." I grunted and spun around. My fist landed on the table. I was accustomed to demanding attention from service people. "I need a dog."

The guy startled at the sound of my hand against the desk and took a step back. "Excuse you," he scoffed.

"Brett," Chip whispered in a sing-song voice. "Rein it in, buddy."

It was then I noticed familiar midnight-black hair and sparkling pale blue eyes. The brightness in Bella's gaze betrayed her gothic style.

The contrast intrigued me. What made her so comfortable with standing out?

Her arched eyebrow spurred a different kind of heat in my chest.

"Brett," she said my name as if it were a greeting, "interesting to run into you again." My breath caught in my throat at the sound of her voice. She paused with a faraway look in her crystal-shaded gaze, then gave me a weird smile. "So, how's your hand?"

"Hot." Why the hell did I say that? It wasn't untrue. The sight of the injury had warmed over the past couple of days. I'd get it checked eventually—another task on my to-do list.

My odd comment made her smile wider, more genuinely as far as I could tell. I supposed odd suited her.

"Anywho," the guy at the desk started, "as I was saying before we so rudely got interrupted," he shot me a look, "I'm sorry, we still haven't heard anything about Philip."

Bella's shoulders dropped. I hated to see disappointment on someone so… intriguing. Hers didn't last. With a discreet glance my direction, she straightened, arching her back with ballet dancer poise.

"After you," she said more politely than anyone had ever spoken to me.

I took a deep breath and bared my teeth in a forceful smile. "Please, will you let me adopt your friendliest dog?" I'd turned to the nerd behind the desk again. It hurt to squeeze the words out to this guy like he didn't just size me up for being an 'outsider.' I'd lived here most of my life for hell's sake. I felt like a boy again, suffering judgment at the stares of original Folklore Falls families.

"Listen, bud. I wouldn't let you adopt our unfriendliest dog," he said and leaned forward with both elbows on the counter. "You think I don't remember you? You tripped guys like me. One time I had to get stitches from your little pranks. Did you know that?" He pointed to a faint scar on his jawline.

I winced again. Hurting people wasn't me, not anymore. I'd done everything I could to get expelled and sent away from the Jensen Estate and my family. But wedgies, 'kick me' signs, and tripping nerds like this guy never did the trick. At least he wasn't one of the guys I'd gotten into physical altercations with, they'd definitely had to get stitches.

"If you think I'd let someone as aggressive as you adopt an innocent animal, you're out of your mind." With that, he knocked twice on the desktop and straightened.

"I'd never play a prank on an animal," I said. A real smile warmed me from the inside out at the thought of the kitten with the white paw. I glanced at the wall of cat cages.

"While that's probably true," he said, "it doesn't matter because I have the right to refuse service to anyone."

"Won't you let me at least hold a cat?" I asked. "I liked the orange one, the little one with the sock." The smile came back, sudden and startling as I spotted the cat who'd pawed at me earlier. My mother never let us have pets because she'd claimed they were distractions from duties.

When I looked back, the guy had already edged around the desk and shuffled toward the puppy pen. "I have customers," he answered, as he turned away from us.

"Forget this," I spoke to Chip now with a slight turn of my head.

Bella shifted her gaze between the three of us. The sharp peak of her thick, black eyeliner drew my eye from the angular shape of her high cheekbones. Now my gaze lingered where her bangs brushed over her temples as she shook the hair from her eyelashes. It was intriguing, but creepy, like spiders had crawled onto her face and decided to make it a home.

When I turned around this time, I took several large steps to put more distance between me and Mr. Stitches before I lost it and gave him a new set. Thankfully, most of the anger had left when I'd outgrown the teenage angst. Most, but not all. I shouldered my way through the crowd to walk past the cats again. Those, I could deal with. Cats gave you space.

"I-I could help." Bella's voice followed me. I stopped and faced her. She cleared her throat and ran the backs of her long fingernails against one another to create a nervous clicking sound. She paused and narrowed her eyes, considering something—something I'd likely never know. Everything about her was a mystery and yet nothing was. She laid it all out for people to see that she liked black, and from what I could remember, books were a big part of her personality.

"Well, isn't that nice?" Chip said. "Such a friendly lady."

I groaned and realized another sound matched it. Bella and I had both reacted with the same distaste to Chip's words. We shared a lingering gaze before my manager inserted himself again.

"What exactly did you mean?" he asked.

"I'm not sure," she said, eyes searching again. "My cat is missing. Maybe, I don't know." she shrugged. "Maybe if you help me find him, it'd show Lance that you're a responsible pet owner?"

I narrowed my eyes. Why was Bella Villenueve being kind to me after I'd told her I was tearing the house down? We'd left the hospital cold and full of venom for one another. Now she was… nice. What changed? Was I better at Chip's peculiar way of small-town campaigning than I'd thought? It wasn't unusual for women to find themselves drawn to me. But I never expected to attract a girl like Bella, especially considering I'd failed in the past. Maybe it was my preference for cats over dogs or my injury that made me sympathetic as Chip had hoped. Whatever it was, it worked.

If I could win over the town's favorite gothic sweetheart this easily, and after we'd spouted angry words at one another, I'd have the rest of Folklore Falls in the palm of my hand.

I probably wasn't in a place to adopt the orange kitty, but maybe an afternoon spent with Bella wouldn't be a total waste. I'd be a generous, helpful citizen, and I wouldn't have to rake one leaf.

I smiled, real again, and offered my elbow to her as a gentleman should. "I like your proposition, Bella."

The surprise on her face was evident by the peaked brows that disappeared into her dark bangs. After the initial shock wore off, she licked her purple painted lips and accepted my arm, though awkwardly at first.

"Good, it's a deal then. Help me find my cat, and I'll change Lance's opinion of you." Though the look on her face was unreadable, I believed her. If anybody could win over a Folklore Fall's resident, it was Bella. Or so the town's social media forums said. It'd just seemed like good research to peruse the posts and comments.

We were an odd pair as we marched from the animal rescue with Chip in our wake. The two of us together garnered more than a few glances, and I grew more confident in my plan with every step we took, crunching over leaves.

We didn't fit—the bully and the sweetheart. But fit or not, this was exactly the key to changing my reputation from 'the Beast' to 'the Best.'

Eleven

BELLA

Brett was the perfect choice for a Philip scavenger hunt in the forest. His height allowed him to reach into the tree branches and push the stubborn leaves that had yet to fall out of the way. While he inspected the trees, I checked behind bushes.

The afternoon stayed clear of clouds and sudden stormy weather. Sunlight streamed in through the skeletal branches, casting bright pockets of light on the forest floor. The crunch of a small animal scurrying into a hiding place triggered a leap in my heart.

"Philip?" I called out.

"No, his name is Chip," Brett said. When I turned around, I caught a glimpse of the slice of skin between his hips and ribcage where his shirt lifted. He grunted as he stretched and shoved a thin branch aside to peek in the tree.

"What?"

Neither of us had spoken much on the short walk from the town to Sherwood Forest, but his little buddy chatted enough for the both of us until a phone call. We left him pacing on the edge of the tree line as he shouted at someone on the other line.

He huffed as he leaped onto a rock, adding to his monstrous height.

Dark eyes shifted over the forest floor, and the flex in his jaw had me staring. "My campaign manager."

"Right." I rolled my eyes. *Not everything is about you, dude.* "My cat's name is Philip."

His eyes narrowed as he glanced at me. "I never understood calling a pet a human's name. They're animals."

"Ah," I said, crouching and brushing a blanket of leaves away from some small creature's hole they called home. "And here I thought you liked cats. Or was your interest in the tabby mix all for show?" I bit my lip before my voice garnered more venom. If I continued with the cold shoulder, I'd never give the curse-breaking a real chance. It wasn't so much the bad luck in my life that I minded, but the guilt of bringing others pain would kill me.

Brett grunted. Maybe he should have been named after an animal.

"Shockingly, no," he mumbled. After hopping off the rock, he marched toward the echo of his manager's voice and whipped out his phone, flicking his thumb over the screen, lost in the technology.

So much for helping me find Philip. His animal aid lasted less than fifteen minutes and we'd barely made it past the edge of the forest.

"You're giving up?" It came out more curt than I'd intended. The thought of getting this jerk to like me twisted my insides. Pretending to date Bones was survivable because we were close friends and Bones was a decent man. But Brett was rude and selfish, not to mention as boring as the rock he'd just kicked off the path.

Without affording me the respect of a glance back, he responded. "I never give up."

Okay, what the heck was that supposed to mean? I frowned at the sight of his confident gait walking away from me. On the one hand, I liked the distance between us and admiring his rear-end. On the other, I wanted to throw my boot at the back of his head for flaking on our little deal so easily. Apparently, he didn't want to adopt the tabby as much as he'd portrayed. Brett picked his way through the bed of leaves that blanketed the entire forest floor.

"Fine, don't help me," I whispered in a mocking voice.

A creature's rustle startled me. I gasped and hurried toward evidence of an animal. My boots crunched across the forest floor, but I eased up on the stomping and carefully approached the bush.

"Philip, I have treats for you." If I were smart, I'd have brought a can and a can opener on the search with me. Under normal circumstances, he'd come running at the first crack. But Philip wouldn't run out the door under normal circumstances, either. Even in a storm, he never acted so erratic. Instead, he always hid under my desk at the bookshop where he used to snack on the cash register's power cord before I coated it with bitter, anti-chew spray.

I crouched and used both hands to separate the dense brush. My heart jumped to my throat as a gray blur blasted out of leaves. A squirrel nearly collided with my knee, but it darted sideways and scurried up the closest tree. It chittered nervously from the lowest branch.

"Okay, okay, okay."

I caught the drift of Chip's upbeat voice through the trees. He matched the squirrel in repetition until Brett approached. I stood, debating whether I should stop Brett. With only a little over a month until my birthday, I knew I should go after him. He was my only option, and if Grandma V. was right, the closer I got to real love, the better the luck would get. *That's how you'll know the curse is breaking.*

"Bye, Mom," Chip said, interrupting me from the memory. "Hey, there's the brilliant man himself." He shoved his phone into his pocket and clapped his hands. "This was genius, really."

"Helpful," Brett agreed, "but inefficient, and I need to pack those pictures. If you hadn't booked every second of my time, I'd have it done already."

Chip slapped his hand on Brett's bicep. I swore he gave the muscle a little squeeze, but I was squinting through the trees.

"That's what you pay me the big bucks for. Every second counts when you start a campaign this late. Can't you hire people to pack things nowadays? Heaven knows you have the money for it."

Brett shook his head, but didn't look up from scrolling on his phone. "My mom had a paranoia about theft, so I promised I'd do it myself."

I stifled a snort. Just a few short years ago, Loxley and I had scouted all the wealthy snobs' vacation homes on the outskirts of Folklore Falls. Though the Jensens lived here, they weren't immune to our righteous trade of property. Loxley had snagged excess items like hideous, overpriced art from jerks like the Jensens and had pawned it for cash to give to the struggling locals. I'd served as her lookout since I knew everyone and everything in town. But who'd want some stuffy, creepy old pictures and paintings of the Jensen family? The frames must be worth a fortune, I figured.

"How about this?" Chip took the phone from his client and clicked the screen to black. "You help the nice lady, and I'll pack the pictures with my own hands. You trust me, right?"

"Phone," Brett said, holding his palm out. The breeze picked up and rushed between the trees, tossing my hair into my face. I regretted not taking the time to style it into two braids to keep it from sticking to my lipstick. After picking the locks from my lips and eyelashes, I squinted at the guys.

Chip sighed and slapped the phone back in Brett's hand. "Help me help you. You have to take every positive opportunity you can get. The Halloween Harvest is in three weeks, and I've scheduled for you to give a little speech. It'd be great if you'd gain at least one person's favor before then."

Another gust of wind sent the leaves clapping like the roar of an ocean. The breeze muffled Brett's response. Why did he need to gain Lance's favor? It seemed a lost cause since Brett had bullied him so heavily in high school. Why waste time focusing on one person's vote when he had a whole town to convince? And it didn't seem adopting the tabby would make Lance happy. Though giving a pet a home wasn't a bad plan when it came to winning over the local animal rescuer.

In any case, it worked out in my favor, too. Lance and his girlfriend loved me, so it was the perfect reason to convince Brett to hang around me. I just needed to figure out how to trick him into believing I was lovable.

I continued the search for Philip, pathing through the trees in a zigzag. If I kept going this direction, I'd pop out on the residential side of Sherwood Forest, which made sense for a wimpy cat like mine. With any sense, he'd avoid predators in the forest and make for the neighborhood.

Of course, I'd already knocked on doors and scanned the park and people's front yards to no avail.

My mind wandered as I kept my eyes focused for sight of a black cat with a candy-corn-colored collar. What type of woman would Brett the Beast Jensen find attractive? I wasn't about to swap my boots for heels, but I could feign interest in foreign cars or golf or boating, or whatever rich pricks did with their time, for a few weeks. All I needed was to hear those three little words before I turned twenty-five and capiche! the curse would break. But nobody told me they loved me— not beyond the bond of friendship anyway, so the thought of hearing Brett say it left the taste of bile in my mouth. Hopefully, I wouldn't projectile vomit in his face if I managed to win him over.

Footsteps followed me. Speaking of vomit-inducing faces, I turned to see Brett's scowl. Okay, it wasn't that bad. My gaze trailed his jawline where stubble dotted his otherwise smooth skin. He stomped behind me, not so much as picking up the pace to a slight jog to catch-up. With his tree-trunk legs, his slow march was really five of my steps.

"Bella," he said, clearing his throat. "Let's try the neighborhood."

I ducked under a branch and pointed toward the light streaming from the edge of the forest on the opposite side where we'd left Chip. "That's where I'm going. Great minds think alike." I laughed, knowing the true meaning behind the phrase, though I assumed he'd take it as a compliment.

"Though fools seldom differ," he said, eyeing me from the side. My lips parted as I looked up at him. "Odd to put yourself down like that." A smirk snuck onto his face.

I shook my head. "I didn't expect you to know the full phrase." Heat burned my cheeks, though neither of us were bleeding. This wasn't a faint, light-headed feeling, though. It matched the embarrassment twisting in my stomach. I liked to pretend I didn't care what people thought of me. I was good a pretending. Usually too good.

People never picked up on my nuanced self-deprecation. I couldn't let anyone in on my flaws, but speaking them aloud in the form of misunderstood idioms at least felt like I was being honest.

"I'm familiar with Shakespeare's idioms," he said. "There's nothing like seeing *Macbeth* performed at his original theater."

Embarrassment shifted to the heat of envy. The idea of Brett knowing anything about Shakespeare surprised me. I knew he had the money to travel the world but figured he chose to visit topless beaches rather than historical monuments or museums. I'd kill to see a play at The Globe, or even better, an opera at the Palais Garnier in Paris.

"Actually, the source of that idiom is unknown," I said, confident that I'd one-upped him and regained power in the conversation—at least the feeling of power.

"Is it?" The scratch of skin against stubble drew my attention to him. He scrubbed his palm over his chin thoughtfully. "I actually didn't know that." He caught up with me and nodded ahead. "According to the town's posts, a kid named Andy lost his cat a few years ago, and the whole neighborhood agreed to set out food to lure him out of hiding."

"You scrolled years back?" I raised an eyebrow.

"You're a favorite of the townsfolk, aren't you?" He met my gaze. Bold, considering he'd straight-up ignored my question. "I'm sure they'd be happy to help."

"I already posted a few times. Everybody knows to keep an eye out for him."

"If we turn back, I'll drive us," he said.

I shrugged. "We're already almost through. You're hell-bent on giving me a ride in your car, huh?" This was how people flirted, right? Teasing with a bit of truth behind it? But without cutting too deep, of course. I recalled his offer to give me a lift from the hospital. He likely just wanted to show off his overpriced, impossibly inconvenient convertible, whatever. Maybe that was how he'd gotten women before —a joyride in a sportscar. Though, that'd suggest he actually liked me, rather than wanted to use me to gain Lance's favor.

"Only in the interest of efficiency and time management," he said.

"So, what's so important about getting the vote of the guy who runs the animal shelter?" I asked, as we drew closer to the edge of the forest. I figured politics filled the role of interesting topics for guys like Brett, and maybe it'd give me a little insight on what he actually planned to do to my beloved town.

Light streamed in through the half-naked branches. The trees were spaced farther apart now, and if I squinted, I could see the white-picket fences and rose bushes that decorated the yards of most homes in Folklore Falls.

"It's not. I know I came across gruff before." He glanced at his feet. Was this a confession from the great town bully, Mr. Brett Jensen? It couldn't be, though he likely had a lot of apologies and confessions coming, maybe prodded by his campaign manager, if he wanted to win over more people like Lance. "But I do plan on helping Folklore Falls, for the better."

"That's debatable." It slipped out before I could stop myself. I wanted this guy to like me. Well, I wanted to break the curse, that was all.

"It can be modernized—"

Okay, nope. Before I could spew what I really thought of that idea, I swallowed and considered my words. "You enjoyed The Globe, right? I mean, seeing Shakespeare's play in its original theater must be magical."

He nodded, wavy hair falling into his face. "You cannot compare ratty buildings like Sherwood Bed and Breakfast to Shakespeare's Globe."

"I can, and I will," I said it in the voice my mother hated. She called it my 'stubborn talk,' and apparently, I'd been doing it since I was a child. I was stubborn, disagreeable, and downright obnoxious. Hopefully, I could hide those qualities well enough to get Brett to like me. Though, he wasn't free of those faults himself. "Never mind," I quickly said and shook my head.

"Have you ever been to The Globe?" He pushed a branch out of my way and held his palm out as if to say 'ladies first.'

"Me? No. I have a shop to run. I don't have the luxury of travel time." Shoot. Travel and flying in fancy jets were his choice of topic, and it wouldn't be a lie to say I wished for a visit to London or Paris. "But I've always dreamed of seeing *Phantom of the Opera* in Opera Garnier." That was the whole truth, and nothing but the truth, so help me, Erik. This was a perfect balance, something I enjoyed but still relative to the hobbies of a wealthy playboy.

"Did you know box number five is still reserved for the phantom? They always keep it vacant for performances, but you can see it during touring hours."

I froze. My heart leaped into my throat again, but it wasn't a squirrel's fault this time. I swallowed it down and stared up at Brett, temporarily halting our hike. "Don't tell me you've been there."

Brett nodded, and for the first time, he grinned. Never had I seen the dimples that dipped into his cheeks at the edges of his slightly crooked smile. Rows of perfect, pearly white teeth looked like they belonged on a movie star, but this wasn't acting. We hadn't found Philip yet, but a sighting of the Beast's genuine smile was almost worth the dirt on my tights and disheveled hair from the relentless wind.

"It's amazing," he said, dark eyes glittering at the memory. I could almost see Opera Garnier in his expression, and my heart skipped a beat. "You have to see it someday."

"I can't believe you like Gaston Leroux," I mentioned *Phantom of the Opera*'s original author before it had become a musical.

A smile turned into a scrunched expression on his face. Though the dimples vanished, his wrinkled nose was no less charming. It was like I'd seen the Beast for so long, I'd never noticed Brett.

"I hate the book," he said.

Was I holding my breath? I gasped for air. Suddenly, everything turned to normal, and I was standing next to the town's infamous bully and wealthy playboy again.

He shook his head and continued walking, facing his broad back to me. "It's so dry and emotionless compared to the play. And it's missing the music."

"I like originals," I said, remaining firm in place. *Fight the stubbornness, you knew who he was.* And that made him the perfect pawn to use to break the curse. I sighed and followed him, but I couldn't hold back my one last comment. "Like the original buildings and layout of our town."

"It needs an update," he said, matching my hard-headed words. If we continued on like this, we'd be two goats with our horns locked in place, neither person getting what we wanted out of the deal. Brett needed me to get Lance's vote apparently, and I needed him to tell me he loved me. Oof, that felt unbalanced.

Last comment, I swear. I glanced up, as if Grandma V. could hear me. And maybe she responded. The clouds moved to block the sun.

"This is Folklore Falls's history," I said.

We emerged from the trees at just the right time. The old cottages and quaint houses drove my point home. Each building was unique, and though some had renovations added like extra floors or air conditioning systems, they all held on to a piece of originality with carved overhangs inspired by the fairy lore behind our small town's legends.

I wanted to return to the subject of the Villenueve Manor, to thank him for keeping it standing, but he walked ahead of me now, picking up to a pace I couldn't match.

"Brett?" I hurried to catch up with him.

"Shh!" He shot his arm out, nearly clotheslining me. Hair fell to the other side of his head as he tilted it toward an oak tree in Patty Potts's backyard.

Easily, he hopped the picket fence and approached the tree. The wind sent another roar through the forest, but when it quieted, I heard it, too. A tiny, pathetic mewl echoed from high up in the branches of Patty's tree.

"Philip!" I shouted. A desperate meow responded.

Brett scanned the tree. "The branches are too thin. I'll break them if I try to climb it. But he's way up there."

"I can do it," I said, as I tried to hop the fence. The hem of my skirt snagged on the pointed picket's tips and tore. I landed in the yard with a huff as I tripped. Thankfully, this fall was cushioned with soft grass unlike the accident I'd suffered outside the inn. I groaned as I lifted the edge of my skirt and inspected the damage. Two favorite articles of clothing torn in two days.

Brett offered his hand. "Will you accept my lift this time?"

I rolled my eyes. It was a natural response for me, though I might need to tamp it down for the next few weeks.

Except Brett didn't frown or accuse me of attitude. In fact, he smirked. Had I successfully flirted back?

I returned his smile, and for the first time, my ridiculous plan to end the curse of the Villenueve women felt possible.

Twelve

BRETT

I promised not to look up her skirt when I lifted her, but she opted to sit instead of stand. She didn't trust me, and I couldn't blame her. That was why I was here—to gain her trust, and through her, everyone else's.

The muscle in her thighs flexed as she used her legs to grip my neck. I straightened from the crouched position where she'd climbed onto me and I lifted her toward the tree.

I huffed and tried to hide my struggle to move without tilting forward. "Wow. Do those boots weigh thirty pounds each?"

"Hey!" She gripped my hair in a handful as I failed at not tilting. I couldn't say I hated the feeling, even when the hair pulled away from my scalp. Bella adjusted her legs, and I held tighter to her as we took another step closer to the trunk.

"It's strictly a comment on the shoes," I said, voice straining. "Your heels are digging into my ribs."

I caught the irritated little scoff she released before a forced apology. The boots unlodged from my ribcage, and she squeezed her legs against my neck again. I resisted the urge to run my hands over the mesh of her tights and forced myself to keep them firmly in place. The wind had picked up and dropped several degrees with the cloud cover. It whipped the pleats of her skirt around my face.

"Come on, baby," Bella cooed. Her thighs pressed tighter as she stretched and reached a cupped hand out toward the cat.

Philip, as she called him, meowed and flicked his tail. Huge yellow eyes glared at me, and it seemed the animal was judging me for enjoying this. Bella's interest in Opera Garnier pleasantly surprised me. I knew she enjoyed books, and *The Phantom of the Opera* was a book, but to favorite such a cultured piece of literature didn't match my description of her. I'd previously suspected she read moody teen novels or modern horrors with their reliance on jump scares and lack of class.

The cat's angry meow pulled me from my thoughts.

"I can't reach him." Frustration in Bella's words matched that of her pet's voice.

"I told you that you'd need to stand."

"Then, fall and kill myself? Great plan." She spoke in curt, cold sentences. It was a facade clearly. I knew the townspeople went to her for a listening ear, and she had more friends than even Chip could claim. Somewhere beneath the spider-like eyelashes, mesh, and tattoos, she was a cozy, sweet, small-town girl.

"Philip, it's Mama. Come on," she said.

The screen door to the house swung open. An older woman emerged with a hammer raised in one hand and a kitchen knife in the other. She glared at me with as much venom as the cat's yellow gaze. It wasn't until her eyes trailed up to the chick on my shoulders that she squealed and hurried down the porch's steps. Sight of Bella must have eased her because she abandoned the makeshift weapons on the porch's steps and bustled toward us.

She looked familiar, too, but not in the way that I knew her, more like I'd seen her doppelganger somewhere—maybe on my last trip abroad.

The grandmotherly woman gasped more dramatically than the situation called for and slapped her hands to her large bosom. "Bella, my goodness, what in the heavens?"

"Hi, Patty," she said. "Philip seems to have sniffed you out."

The woman inched closer, eyeing me as if I'd bite her, then peered up the tree. "Oh, what a smart kitty. Yes, you are." She seemed to carry a full conversation with Bella's pet as the cat meowed back, opening its flexible jaw and baring sharp, white teeth. Yellow eyes flicked back to me, and for a second, I wondered if they were conversing about me, as if animals could talk.

"We should have made a request before entering your yard," I said, ready to apologize.

"Heavens no." She stopped spinning the many rings on her finger to wave off my comment. "We're all family around here. It makes me finally feel like a local that people welcome themselves in."

"You're new to Folklore Falls?" I asked.

"Just about two years," she said, nodding. "That's considered fresh out of the womb for this town. And—oh!" she stopped, hand slapping her chest again for a flair of the dramatics. "I will call the fire department. And the police. Look at me standing here gabbing while the poor kitty is trapped in my tree. Isn't Esmeralda filling in while Gideon is on paternity leave?"

"You know better than I do, Patty," Bella said, "But you don't need to do all that. We'll get Philip down."

"Heaven knows this young man is tall enough. What are you, seven and a half feet?" she eyed me, clearly impressed. Would she have felt the same way if I'd met her without Bella on my shoulders? Most people shied away from me, intimidated by my height and, before Chip's insistence on smiling, my resting angry face. Patty seemed a warm, kind woman but also flighty and easily anxious. She'd come out here armed and ready to defend herself against the intruder in her yard.

It was comparative to my life here. The Jensen family were always seen as intruders in Folklore Falls. My father was supposed to change that, and since he failed, the responsibility fell on me to fulfill my mother's dreams. *This place will save our family.*

"Brett!"

I startled, but it wasn't my mother who shouted at me. Bella repeated my name.

"Let me down to take off my shoes, and I'll try standing."

Patty pulled out her phone. The click of the faux camera sound rapid-fired as if we were celebrities and she the paparazzi.

"I'm going to post on the lost pet forum right away to let everyone know we found Philip," she said, tapping away on her phone with more ease than I'd ever seen anyone her age use technology. It was a comment I might have once said aloud until Chip had scolded it out of me. Such observations were considered rude and offensive and, as he claimed, 'made me appear judgmental.' But judgment was how I was taught to separate myself from those beneath our family's status. It was meant to protect us from people who wanted to use us for our money.

Patty squealed again as she admired the picture she'd taken. "I'll add a caption about how you are a local hero, Bella."

"For saving my own cat?" she laughed, as she unlaced her boot and tugged it off her foot. She repeated it on the next shoe and shook her head. "Don't you think that's a little overboard?"

"Not if it'll attract some eligible gentleman," she said with a cluck of her tongue. Patty winked, then glanced at me as if she'd forgotten I was standing there, too.

Bella rolled her eyes, a statement of expression she relied on often. "Nobody outside of Folklore Falls looks at those forums." She rolled her tights down and slipped them off her feet. I swallowed and looked away before I came across as a creep. My gaze swept over the fence then beyond to the street where the leaves scattered. Cloud cover left the whole neighborhood in a shadow.

"Sally does," she said.

This woman was making my life a hundred times easier. If townsfolk saw the pictures of us together, especially with me helping Bella, it'd speed the process along. And time was of the essence. Between this and Chip's promise to pack my family's portraits, I'd save a whole day's worth of work. Before I knew it, I'd have most of the items on my mother's list crossed off.

I crouched again, allowing Bella to climb onto my shoulders. This time, I gripped her ankles.

"Don't look up, or I'll scalp you," she whispered the demand into my ear. That cold-hearted, empty threat of violence was the Bella I remembered from elementary school and my two years of public high school. And if I were honest with myself, it might have sparked my schoolboy crush on the Addams family girl. In my mind, the two were interchangeable, Bella and Wednesday, except the character on TV couldn't hurt me. Bella was the only kid in class I never pranked because I worried it'd come back tenfold. Had she ever noticed?

The decades-old memory came back in a rush. The chilling looks she gave me across the schoolyard were the only good moments I could conjure from my short-lived childhood at Folklore Falls Elementary. They'd gotten lost among the many bad memories that I shoved down. Another thought resurfaced—prom, senior year of high school. I knew Bella better then, she was the girl in black at the back of the classroom, the girl I fantasized about taking to the dance. She went with the man that owned Knight's Tavern now. A real shining armor moment for a guy who let everyone call him Bones.

I stood slowly, letting Bella use the tree as her balance. Patty watched with huge, bulging eyes. I shifted my gaze from her to the trunk, making my stare at the tree bark obvious enough that not even this dramatic grandmotherly figure could accuse me of sneaking a peek up Bella's skirt.

"If you're not careful, you'll end up with a bump on your head to match mine," Patty said.

"I'm really sorry about that," Bella apologized.

"Oh, it wasn't your fault. Things happen."

A little grunt escaped Bella, and I smirked. As different as we were, her the town's favorite and me the scapegoat they loved to hate, we shared more than a few mannerisms, and interests apparently.

"That's a good Lip-Lip," Bella said. "Okay, I've got him." She used one hand to balance against the tree as she slowly crouched. When her free hand gripped my hair again, I winced but bore the pain until she was safely in the seated position.

Patty seethed and nearly released a whimper as she watched. Wind threatened to topple us, but I braced against it. It succeeded in stripping the tree of a few more leaves that floated down around us like orange and brown snowflakes.

I took one careful step back, then eased to my knees. Collectively, we breathed a sigh of relief as she returned to solid ground.

"You two must stay for dinner and tea. I have a roast in the slow cooker and son in town whose too busy to visit." Patty clasped her hands together.

Bella and I exchanged a glance, and for a moment, it seemed we understood one another. I spoke first, letting the old woman down easy.

"We couldn't intrude," I said.

"I was thinking we could get dinner, just the two of us?" Bella looked at me, but with her tight hold on Philip, I couldn't tell whether she meant me or the cat. This morning, I would have said hell no. But with everything coming together, I had a couple of hours to spare. Plus, I wanted to know what else I'd misjudged about her. I was normally spot-on with my assessment of others.

In the silence, another faux camera click sounded. We both snapped our attention to Patty who beamed and tapped the screen on her phone again. When the flash blinded us, I realized how dark it had gotten.

"We'd better get back," I said with a nod toward the sky. "I'd like to continue our conversation about Shakespeare, if possible."

Patty's head moved like a metronome, rhythmically ticking from me to Bella and back again.

"As long as you get your idioms correct, I suppose I could handle a conversation over burgers at Fryer Tuck's." The small smirk on her face told me it was a date.

And the best part was, a public appearance with her at the town's most popular, and only, restaurant would solidify my soon-to-be good standing as approved by Folklore Falls's sweetheart.

Thirteen

BELLA

I hated to turn Patty's offer down, but she'd understand when I explained it to her later. In fact, the suggestion of my sort-of date with Brett was likely reason enough for her. Patty was a gossip, but she still loved everybody, and it seemed he'd made a good first impression.

It was a miracle we'd found Philip, then safely retrieved him from the tree without an accident. I couldn't even walk down the street a couple of days ago or drink tea standing next to Patty without injury. This had to be the luck shifting back in my favor, which meant snagging Brett's attention was easier than I'd anticipated. But how long could I keep the crappy parts of myself hidden? How long before he figured out the real me and the whole illusion shattered, bringing down my entire plan? Or better yet, when would I realize it was all a dream and this was the jerk Jensen I remembered?

Nope, that part didn't matter. Never did Grandma V. mention I needed to love the person back. This was about the horrid Villenueve women and their distasteful personalities. I didn't need to like Brett, I only needed him to break the curse. So why did a spark ignite in my arm when our hands bumped? I shifted Philip to the arm on the same side of me where Brett walked so we wouldn't have another hand-to-hand collision, though I couldn't help but wonder how warm it would be to sidle up next to him. Despite my cold appearance, I loved a good cuddle and I'd fit right into the crook of Brett's neck.

No, he's a jerk! What am I thinking? At least the pretend-dating would be fun while I tried to break the curse. I couldn't actually like a guy that used to make my friends cry, but I'd allow myself to enjoy the fantasy of the angry, brooding man.

The long walk back to town turned into a run. Brett held his million-dollar, or whatever, coat over my head while I cradled Philip, and we made a break for the overhang that the shops shared. Once under the shelter on the small strip of building past the inn, we caught our breath. Thankfully, lightning illuminated the sky miles from us, and the storm wasn't dangerous yet.

Philip yowled angrily as Brett shook out his coat and the water splashed a few droplets on the feline king's fur.

We trailed the shops, stepping over pumpkins and door mats to keep close to the building and out of the rain until stopping at the bookstore's front. Fairy lights sporadically flickered in the front window, decorating the display of hardcover classics.

Brett stared at the old copy of *A Christmas Carol*.

"You like Dickens?" A cough cut the last word short, and Brett snapped his gaze to me. "Charles Dickens," I said, again.

"Uh," he scraped his hand over the back of his neck and sighed. "Yeah, I read all kinds of classics when I was a kid. My brother tried to ruin this one by convincing me that the Manor had the ghost of past, present, and future haunting it. He told me that they'd come out every Christmas and show me all the ways I'd ruined our family."

I jiggled the sticky handle and pushed the door open. The stupid bell chimed at the wrong moment, echoing its cheerful jingle right at the end of Brett's depressing childhood story.

"That's awful," I said, doing the 'ladies first' signal for him this time.

Brett shrugged as he stepped inside the bookstore. "Where do you think all those ghost rumors came from about the place?"

I laughed. "Those existed long before your family came." Though not lit, the scent of my pumpkin muffin candles filled the room and mixed with the smell of fresh rain. Evenings like this delighted me, though the rain was a little heavy.

He cleared his throat and picked up a copy of *Oliver Twist*, changing the subject. "My mother forbid me from reading this. She claimed it was a cruel depiction of successful people."

Another laugh escaped me, but by the look on Brett's face, the subject wasn't a funny one. I cringed and decided not to dive too deeply on a discourse in Dickens's work. If I insulted his mother's intelligence, it wouldn't look good on my dating resume.

I popped open a can of tuna from the small cabinet in the storage room, then fluffed the blankets in Philip's downstairs bed.

"Do you have any old hardbound copies of *Othello*?" he asked. Brett held a damaged, but rare version of *Frankenstein*.

I leaned on the small desk and paused to think. "Hmm, all of the early print copies of Shakespeare's work are combined. If you want an older one, it wouldn't just be *Othello*. I have one from the late eighteen hundreds that's hardcover but it also has *Romeo and Juliet* and *The Comedy of Errors*."

"How much?"

"What?"

"I'd love to buy it off you. I've read books on my phone for the past decade since I travel so much. Now that I'm settling here, I'd like to build a library."

I raised my brows. Talk about impressive and unexpected. Maybe he was sexy for more reasons than the gray sweatpants and gruff voice. A Brett who liked to read was a who new Brett in my eyes. Of course, anyone who enjoyed books often learned empathy so I wasn't convinced the towering man in front of me was the bookworm he claimed to be.

"It's around here somewhere." I shrugged and waved toward the staircase. "We can look for it later. Or I'll let you know when I find it, I store books under my bed sometimes."

"I'd love that. Do you live here?" Brett asked, pointing to the mini fridge beside unopened boxes of books.

"Upstairs," I said. Suddenly feeling the need to defend myself against Folklore Falls's richest man, my words stumbled over one another. "But it's nice. A big loft area, and I prefer being close to my shop because, you know, the commute." I nodded toward the spiraling staircase beside which were the only fully-dusted and organized shelves. Without a ladder, it was the only spot I could reach to the top shelf.

Brett twisted his lips and nodded. "Nice." He echoed my description of it.

Ugh. The stupid curse required me to care about his opinion, otherwise I'd never notice. I would not care about Brett Jensen's idea of me. Absolutely not. Who would? The man was a jerk. A jerk who'd never read *Oliver Twist*. Though, I'd never have guessed he read any of the classics until getting to know him. A Jensen was someone I assumed read nautical magazines or dry books on stock trading. Not that those were less-than, just not *my* style.

The growl of his stomach broke the silence, and Philip meowed back. The exchange broke the tension created by our opposite lifestyles. I lived above a bookstore in an apartment that was so tiny I had to buy one of those beds that folds against the wall during the day, and he lived a life of luxury probably with a house in the city that had a garage twice the size of my shop and home combined.

"Food?" I pointed to the door, and he nodded. "Let's go before I get hangry. You don't want to see me on an empty stomach." *Shut up, Bella! You're not supposed to tell the only eligible curse breaker for miles around that you're a grouch without a heaping plate of carbs.*

Speaking of which, why were fictional men considered sexy when grouchy but never the women? Not that I didn't love those fictional men, but still.

I said goodbye to Philip and closed the door.

"Won't you lock it?" Brett asked. "You know theft was rampant here recently?"

I stifled a smile. Know it? I organized the crimes, but he'd never know that. Only Loxley was ever exposed. I insisted on outing myself, too, but she wouldn't allow it. Eventually, it all blew over, and we made a pact never to do anything like that again, not unlike the protagonist of Dickens's story.

"If someone wants to steal *Oliver Twist* and read it, they can be my guest," I said. "They'll learn real fast that dishonesty gets a bullet in the arm."

Brett cocked his head, the confused Doberman expression returning as we walked. The diner's lights lit up the town, and the echoes of laughter and cheers drifted from beyond where Knight's Tavern sat on the edge of town.

"Never mind."

The smell of fried potatoes and cheese stirred my stomach to rival Brett's in an angry growl. He opened the door like a perfect gentlemen. All eyes turned to stare at us, not because we could wring out a whole pond from our soaked clothes, but because of who we were—together.

Bella and Brett. I helped people, he hurt them. At least, in the past, when he'd pulled all those pranks. I tried not to think about what kinds of plans he had for the town. They couldn't be that bad. Not as bad as the luck I'd bring on the people I loved, that was.

Fryer Tuck nodded at us from his place in the kitchen. He'd hired more help recently since the diner was always busy, but he still greeted every customer that walked in the door. After wiping more grease stains onto his apron, Tuck raised his hand in a single wave, then returned to shaking the bubbling basket of oil and fries. A high school girl skated up to us in rollerblades and grabbed two sticky menus.

Every eye watched as she guided us to a table. A weird smirk hinted at Brett's lips. I could tell by the dimple forming at one corner of his mouth. I wanted to brush my finger over the indent in his skin then feel the shape of his jaw on my hand. If the curse ever required me to kiss him to inspire that necessary 'I love you,' moment, I'd enjoy every second of holding his face and feeling his breath on mine.

I shook my head before the thought descended to second-base and took a seat.

After turning up his nose at every item on the menu, I convinced Brett to try the black bean burger. I didn't eat meat, or any animal product, so that burger was one of the only plates I could order from

Fryer Tuck's, but I never got tired of it as long as it came with three thick slices of tomato.

"I know it's not charcuterie or fish eggs, but it's amazing."

"I eat steak," he said, "and lobster."

"Okay, well, that's worse. Let's pretend you never said that." I raised my hand to stop him. "I don't need your daily menu."

"I meant when I go out dining." He slapped the menu down and waved for the server.

"Don't do that." I grabbed his hand and pulled it down. The lightning didn't catch us in the storm, but I certainly felt something when we touched. My hold lingered, relishing the feeling of his hand, large enough to cover mine completely. I'd read plenty of scenes where a guy like Brett quickly went from hand-holding to hip-gripping and the visual left me sucking in a gasp.

"Why?" he asked, narrowed eyes trailing down my neck and torso like he was thinking about my hips too.

I rolled my eyes. Yes, my eyes would get stuck that way eventually, and I'd cosplay a possessed person or a ghost. Honestly, it'd suit my style just fine. *Take that, mother.*

"Because they're busy, and she'll come back when she gets a chance."

"Hmm," he grunted and settled back against the booth, then thought better of it when a child in the booth behind flung chili into the air. The mother apologized, but the kid did it again, and Brett frowned, sitting pin-straight in the bench seat. "Is there anything else I do that's rude?"

How was I supposed to answer that? A million things? He was the kid who bullied everyone until he grew into the guy who only acknowledged townsfolks' existences at the annual archery competition. He was killer at hitting the target, but his temper had definitely showed when Loxley ultimately beat him.

"Um, I don't know."

"No, be honest." He leaned closer, and the scent of mint and fresh rain filled my nose. "You said people called me the Beast."

"I mean, you were Mister Prankster." I laughed. Now was not the time to dig into our personal flaws. This needed to be a Hallmark Channel movie where he visits town, falls for me, and, well, breaks my curse. Okay, I guess that didn't fit the sweet Christmas romances, especially since I was using the guy. I still hoped it'd be that simple, that cookie-cutter to get from point A, Bad Luck Bella, to point B, 'I love you, Bella.'

Saved by the server. She skated back to our table and took our easy order of extra-tomato black bean burgers, but Brett had her hold the tomatoes. Gross.

"Just add his to mine," I said. When she rolled away, I took the opportunity to change the subject. "What other classics have you read?"

Before I knew it, our burgers were devoured, the diner cleared out, and the girl in rollerblades was counting tips. We kept the subject to literature, carefully avoiding any mention of Villenueve Manor. Though I appreciated he cancelled the demolition, it was a sore subject for us both. My childhood spent there was stolen from me, and he'd hated growing up at the place I loved. Or so he'd claimed before I quickly jumped back to authors and playwrights.

We argued over Shakespeare's best play. Of course, I liked the tragedies, and he chose the plays with the most betrayals, per character. I'd almost coughed up my last tomato slice when he'd brought up *Pride and Prejudice*. Brett the Beast Jensen read Jane Austen, though he didn't get the point at all, considering he'd defended Mr. Darcy's prejudice against Elizabeth. Who did that?

I didn't have time to dwell on it. Our conversation moved from one famous author to another, spanning centuries and genres.

"I still can't believe you've seen *Macbeth* at The Globe, and an Opera Garnier tour? Ugh." I slapped my hand to my heart, a gesture I'd picked up from spending too much time with Patty Potts. I spied Brett's discreet dip of his gaze to where my hand landed. "Why not see the musical while you were there?"

"Didn't have time." He shrugged, pushing the leftover lettuce around on his plate with a dull fork. "I cut my trip short when my mother got sick."

I opened my mouth to offer some sort of consolation, but he continued before I could speak. "But I have plans to go back. I could take you. Seems a shame you've never seen the story of the phantom as it should be experienced. Trust me, the musical far surpasses the book or movie."

"Oh, a movie is blasphemy when you're talking to a bookseller," I joked, getting the ease of flirting now. Okay, that wasn't a joke, though. Did he just promise to take me to Paris? Did I have some sort of spell on me to make this man fall for me, or what? This was easier than a Hallmark movie plot. If my grandmother's ghost floated through the diner's doors and told me she'd cast a love spell on us, I'd believe it. I actually *liked* talking to Brett, and he seemed as equally intrigued by me.

Was this real life?

He laughed. "Noted."

After he insisted on paying for dinner, Brett walked me home. Of course, it was only a short route back to the bookshop, but I appreciated it, nonetheless.

The rain had stopped, leaving the ground sparkling with puddles and soaked leaves that caught the glint of the rising moon. He pushed a pumpkin that sat too far out in the middle of the sidewalk back against the wall with the side of his foot. Before I'd concocted the Brett Jensen Plan, I'd have face-planted after tripping over that pumpkin. Now, I was walking home enjoying a friendly debate about whether Jane Eyre should have married Mr. Rochester or not.

"Thanks for dinner and finding Philip."

"Thanks for a nice evening."

"Let's do it again?" I asked, turning my back to the bookshop's door and meeting his gaze.

"I suppose I should get to know you better if I'm going to take you to Paris." The dimples almost made an appearance. Almost. The shadow of the overhang blocking the moon's light made it hard to see. The fairy lights only gave off enough light to see the books in the window they decorated. It didn't matter, I preferred him like this, more like the fictional men—out of reach, right here in front of me but without feeling his body close to mine. If only he'd take one step closer I could feel the heat of him, remember that he's real, flesh and muscle and lips that'd probably look as good kissing me as they did in a smirk.

Brett leaned over me. When he reached for my waist, my breath caught in my throat as I waited to see where his touch would land. I tensed wondering if he'd be bold enough to use my hips to pull me toward him or simply slip his palm between the dimples of my lower back.

All of the breath and pent-up energy inside me flopped when I heard the chime of the bookshop's door. He'd twisted the knob and opened it for me like the gentleman I never expected, all while I was hoping he'd end the night with a demanding kiss.

My face must have betrayed me because Brett pulled back and pinched his brow. "I'll look for the book another time." I opened my mouth but no words came out since I was still breathless, anticipating a moment of shared touch that never came. Hair fell into his face as he gave me a curt nod. "Goodnight, Bella."

"Night," I managed. I'd completely forgotten my promise to look for the old copy of Shakespeare's works and inadvertently turned him down. I gnawed the inside of lower lip as I watched him stalk off into the parking lot. He walked with a swagger I'd once chalked-up to the pretentious elitism of rich men. But I couldn't say I hated the way he looked from behind.

I shook my head. This was a means to an end, not the start of anything real.

I'd never actually date Brett Jensen, so why did the absence of an date-ending kiss leave me so disappointed?

Fourteen

BRETT

After two days of questioning myself, I finally put the mistake aside. Based on her flushed skin and startled reaction, Bella had wanted something more from me and I hadn't realized it until it was too late. With the election coming up fast, I didn't have time to deal with anyone's emotions. Not even my own.

Black boots and bookish arguments distracted my thoughts from the campaign but Chip pulled me back to focus. He had insisted I make another public appearance with Bella, so I planned to ask her to attend the Halloween Harvest with me when I saw her again. *Don't let her slip through your fingers. Keep this going until after the election, and we're golden, buddy. Everybody is talking about you two at the diner together. She's the key to your approval rate.*

I hated being used for my money, so it felt wrong to do the same to Bella. But if I actually enjoyed her presence, it was honest. I wouldn't fall prey to lies like my mother had and when we bumped into one another at the coffee shop yesterday, I found myself wanting more and more time with her. We'd chatted about books over my black coffee and her steaming tea but it wasn't enough.

I swiped Chip's text away and pulled up the calendar app on my phone. Today, I'd meet with the demo crew, move my luggage to Sherwood Bed and Breakfast, then meet with Chip to brainstorm ideas for more public appearances. Somewhere in there, I'd make an effort to stop by Bella's Bookstore and see her again, maybe hear her laugh at me for my choice of favorite plays.

I trudged through the empty house and scrubbed my palm over my face. The morning sun peeked in through the skylight in the massive kitchen. The only thing I'd dug out of the cabinets was a coffee maker, which I flicked on after preparing the water and grounds the night before. My brother had claimed it made the coffee ground stale to remove it from the package and leave it in the filter all night, but I was all about efficiency since Mom was diagnosed. I'd had years of wasted time, sleeping in late, and disappointments to make up for.

The coffee maker whirred to life as I bounced from foot to foot. Productivity cycles say to stretch in the morning. An orange slice wakes better than caffeine, and yoga or running gets the blood flowing. I took a bite of a mandarin, peel and all, then took a short jog through the hallways in my sweatpants that doubled as my pajamas. The echoes of my footsteps bounced off the empty walls. It was spooky—no, lonely—without our portraits decorating the halls.

I stopped for a quick breath at the front door and inspected the water damage.

The rain left a long dripline down the inside of the entryway where the rose petal had broken from the window. None of that mattered now, the house would be gone today, and I'd return the window itself to Bella. She'd thank me, maybe the old gal would be there to take pictures, it'd hit the forums, and boom, my ratings would skyrocket. Of course, ratings and political statistics in Folklore Falls were based more on rumors and social media posts than actual facts.

I sighed and turned from the damage. The old house, with its ghost rumors, bad family memories, and ugly architecture would haunt me no more.

A faint knock came from the other side of the door, and I nearly jumped out of my skin. The demo crew wasn't scheduled to arrive for another hour. Though I appreciated promptness, I'd rather they follow the schedule, seeing as I wasn't dressed. I unlocked the bolt at the top of the door and twisted the knob.

The leathery, sun-beaten face I expected to see was replaced by ghostly white cheeks framed in midnight black. The morning sun after a storm shone brighter than usual and streamed through the perfectly straight hair. She wore it styled simply, flowing over her shoulders like the Falls themselves had turned to ink.

The peak of her eyebrows hooked me. I liked a woman who could challenge me, and that arched look said she had endless tricks up her lacy sleeves.

"Bella?" I asked, like an idiot. Clearly, it was her. When I tried to make eye contact, I realized her gaze was pouring over my chest. Wearing nothing but sweatpants suddenly felt akin to being bare naked.

Her thick, spider-like lashes ticked up and met my eyes for a moment before falling to the book in her hand.

"I found it." She held out a brown book with gold lettering on the spine that read *The Incomplete Works of Shakespeare*.

I patted my empty pockets. "I don't have my wallet on me." It was a stupid thing to say. Something about seeing her in the daylight, on my front porch, threw me off balance. I should be excited to see her except her showing up here brought me back to plenty of other failed dates and relationships where the chicks found an excuse to routinely appear in my path with hopes of gaining something. The other night was fun, but women never came back for more unless they wanted my money, or for me to buy them expensive crap.

The book was still in her grip, waiting for me to take it.

"I'm giving it to you," she said, as she lifted it an inch higher. "I've never met anyone else as well-versed in Shakespeare, so I think it belongs in your library."

I accepted the offer, but it took a moment for my brain to catch up. Didn't she want money for it? People always wanted payment of some sort. My mother may have been wrong about Folklore Falls fixing our broken family, but she wasn't wrong about that. I moved out of the doorway and hoped she'd step inside.

Thank you didn't feel appropriate. What response would suffice?

The last person I'd shared my interests in the classics with was my brother. He'd teased and pranked and wrestled it out of me until I'd stopped mentioning it. Of course, wrestling with Bella wouldn't be unpleasant, if she removed the heavy boots first.

"Would you like a cup of coffee?" It was the only thing I could think to say. Normally smooth, something about Bella's unexpected behaviors and unpredictable nature captured my attention and left my brain stuttering.

She stepped inside, taller now with a different pair of boots. These had thicker soles and high tops that reached all the way to the middle of her calves. Bare skin poked out between her black skirt and the orange-tinted thigh-high tights.

I silently thanked the heavens that my morning jog gave my sweat an excuse for shining on my hairline. Apparently, I'd spent too much time around Chip lately if I resorted to thanking the heavens or stars or planets or whatever. When Bella walked past me, heading for the kitchen with a swing in her hips, I snuck a wipe of my arm over the sweat.

I hurried to jog up beside her and finally managed to thank her for the book. Counters encircled us as soon as we pushed through the swinging side-door and entered the kitchen. Countless cabinets filled the room, and large counters were left bare except for the coffee maker.

"I enjoyed our conversations last night," I said, rinsing out one of only two cups I'd brought—a coffee mug and a water bottle. The rest were gone—packed in the shed with everything else or thrown away. The water bottle I normally used when out on a run didn't suit the coffee, but it worked. I handed her the mug from beneath the single-serve coffee maker and started on another cup.

"Sugar? Cream?"

"Bitter as my heart is what I always say." She laughed. Bella Villenueve was comfortable with me. People were never comfortable with me. Either, they knew my past or my family, or they tripped over themselves trying to impress the wealthy guy. But Bella, she exuded confidence as she cupped the mug with both hands, long fingernails clicking against the ceramic.

I pressed my back against the counter, then hopped up to take a seat on the tile. "So, I wanted to ask you…" Usually, I flaunted my car or designer clothes at the casino to garner a girl's interest for a night of kissing and fun, but I couldn't do that with Bella. I got the feeling, even if she hadn't grown up knowing my family, she wouldn't be impressed by the cost of my sportscar or the suggestion of my bank account numbers based on the brands I wore.

"That's the only hardbound Shakespeare I have," she said before taking another sip of the steaming coffee.

"No, no." I shook my head. "The Halloween Harvest. We could go together?" The way I'd worded it came out more presumptuous than I'd intended. Unlike me, Bella had friends who she'd likely already made plans with.

"I've never seen you at a Folklore Falls event." She kept her eyes on me as she sipped. "Didn't you try to sabotage the Homecoming dance our senior year?"

I winced. If only her memory wasn't so clear. That was me. By then, I wasn't trying to get expelled anymore. I was almost eighteen and more mature about not running from my family. But I still didn't fit in, and pranks were the only way I knew how to interact with my Folklore Falls classmates. I was just so mad. Everyone had treated me like an outsider my whole life. I couldn't contain my anger.

Bella smirked. "It was epic, honestly. I mean, you were a jerk, but it made the dance memorable. I only went to be ironic. Loxley dragged me from my annual reread of *Phantom of the Opera,* and I thought I was going to gag at the endless pop songs but then you came in with that clown mask on. Where did you get all the snakes anyway?"

I laughed. I shouldn't be surprised by her enjoyment of it. The more we spoke, the more Bella and I seemed mirrors of one another. I had to admit, I wouldn't mind seeing her topless, wearing nothing but my sweatpants. The crude thought was quickly overshadowed by the other ways we matched each other. If I could, I'd spend an entire day listening to her laugh at me and tease me for my basic literary opinions. I loved a girl who could put me in my place and Bella had no trouble doing that with as little as one look.

"Money can buy stupid things, like the reptiles at all the pet stores within two hundred miles of here."

"Why snakes?"

I shrugged. "They're scary but harmless. Those types anyway. It felt right." Scary but harmless, I'd staked my entire personality on that phrase, though not everyone agreed—take the animal rescuer and the women at the park for example. Mostly, anyone in Folklore Falls. What made Bella different? She wasn't afraid of anything, which meant she had the guts to stand up to me. Once again, the thought of her challenging me sent a shiver down my bare spine.

"I have to go open the shop," she said, setting the mug down on the counter next to my leg. "I'll think about the Harvest." A small smile betrayed her potential rejection. "I don't see how that will help you gain Lance's vote."

I wasn't sure what that meant. Lance didn't matter to me, though I did need majority approval in town. I didn't specifically need his.

"Let me walk you out." I hopped off the counter and followed in her wake.

"I know this house," she said over her shoulder. As soon as she stepped in the entry, Bella looked up. "But I don't know what happened to the window. Do you?"

"It's how I hurt myself." I lifted my free hand. It was still swollen, but it didn't ache as much anymore. "It kept swinging open so I tried to latch it, and it all went downhill from there."

Bella brushed the bangs from her eyelashes and squinted. "It's odd that only the petal fell out, right? Or does it just seem odd to me?" It was almost as though she spoke to herself. Her eyes never left the stained-glass, though it'd leave us with a crick in our necks if we stared up that high for too long.

I sucked in a breath. "I was actually going to bring the window to you later today. My schedule is packed but—"

"What?" She spun around. Her long hair swayed with the movement and cascaded over her bare left shoulder. The shirt's sleeves started beneath her shoulder but reached past her wrists. I realized I was staring and snapped my attention to her eyes.

"The window." I lifted my chin. "I'm keeping it intact and saving it before the house gets torn down."

Her jaw dropped, and the angles of her eyebrows sharpened. The trust and curiosity in her eyes darkened to something I recognized all too well—deep, intense anger. Initial shock shifted to a grimace, frightening, even for Bella.

"I thought you changed your mind."

I tilted my head. "I postponed it to speak with my manager but—"

"No." The hair above her brows quivered as she shook her head. "No, I thought you cancelled it. You can't do this."

My lip twitched. Wasn't this what I fantasized about, Bella challenging me? I would have liked it if the argument was over anything other than the house. This house, the house my mother had dragged our family to to 'save us' after my existence had ruined everything. Secrets had slipped out, and our family had cracked into two with me at the center. Folklore Falls I could change, but this house and the memories it bore inside the walls had to go.

A flood of moments rushed my mind from my mother's tears and my father's screams. My brother prayed for me to die so our parents would love each other again. We'd moved far, far away from the painful truth of my mother's mistakes—but they couldn't rid themselves of me, a constant reminder of a broken home.

"Brett!" Bella snapped. "Did you hear me? You will leave this house alone." She stepped in inch away from me, jabbing a finger in my face that I instinctively stepped back from. I wanted her close to me, but not like this.

"I have to—" I straightened and towered over her but it only ignited the flame in her eyes.

She splayed her hand and shoved her palm into the center of my chest, as if pushing me back, telling me she'd block my plan. "Don't you dare."

"It's already scheduled," I said before I could stop the words. Anger won out of the desire to keep Bella close to me. Not just physically either. Apparently, my decision on the house would cut all ties our long conversations and short dates had created. But I'd made a promise to my mother and I'd never survive around these memories long enough to carry it out. The house had to go.

She shook her head, and a strange smile full of anger spread across her face. "No." The smile flickered. Something stopped her before she could pour boiling hot hatred all over me in the form of curated words. The expression didn't match her behavior. Her shoulders dropped in defeat.

"Look, I'm saving the window, but the rest of the estate is outdated and needs to go."

Bella shoved past me and yanked the door open. The scent of her hair faded and I immediately missed the heat of her hand on me and the fire that burned between our arguments. This disagreement felt more like an end to what I'd wanted all those years ago—the girl with the glare.

"How about this?" She smirked and I couldn't help but wonder how much it'd piss her off if I kissed that look right off her face. I hated myself for missing the opportunity before everything came crashing down. Her iciness and my heated temper would be electric. "You don't hurt my house, and I won't hurt your career in politics. People take my advice."

The venom in her voice told me I'd failed Chip. *Don't let her slip through your fingers*. I needed Bella. Plus, our friendship, or whatever it was, couldn't end this way—not right in the middle of my campaign.

I wanted her, that was obvious, but I needed her too. And didn't she need me? Or at least my promise that I'd leave the Jensen Estate standing?

BELLA

The Villenueve Manor was Grandma V's home. I couldn't let Brett destroy it, so I promised to destroy his chance of beating Max in the election. I'd talk up the retired sheriff with every one of my clients and remind folks of Brett's pranks one-by-one.

Unfortunately, the Beast was as stubborn as me, and my threat didn't sway him so easily. Of course not, he probably thought he could buy people's votes with his excessive load of cash. His frown, wide stance, and folded arms told me I'd hit a brick wall, no amount of threats would change his mind now. And the pressure of my hand on his chest barely moved him an inch.

This time I didn't touch him except with the force of my shoulder. I shoved past Brett with a promise.

I grabbed the doorknob and paused on the threshold, anger burning on my tongue and clouding my mind. "The second the demolition starts, I'll be the number one cheerleader for Max's campaign."

Before Brett could respond, a piece of glass shattered on the floor in front of us. I gasped and blinked, focusing on the tiny bit of sparkling shards that caught the glint of the sun through the open door.

We both looked up to see another missing petal. The perfect shape of one of the drooped petals was now an open spot in the glass.

The curse. How could I forget the curse and my plan with Brett? My stomach twisted as anger and reason argued.

I needed time to think about this. Maybe I wouldn't destroy his career. Which was worth more? The house? Or breaking the curse on the women in my family? I couldn't choose. My brain stalled between the two, and I needed time.

I backed away, but Brett grabbed me. I nearly gagged at the bruises and scabs on his hand.

"Let go." I yanked, irritated by his need for control, but I was no match for the strength of a nearly seven-foot sized man.

"Wait, let's talk about this," he said, more a demand, though he should be begging. He didn't know I needed him.

"Too late." Anger won over, for now. I pulled from his grip, loosened now, likely due to the pain in his untreated injury. Freed, I turned, ready to run down the front steps.

"Bella, stop!" He grabbed me, using his good hand this time. I was forced to spin back around so my shoulder didn't pull from its socket. His anger mirrored mine, and I almost saw myself in him.

Gravel crunched as a car pulled into the driveway. I glanced over my shoulder, following Brett's gaze to the sight of Chip in the front seat with a phone to his ear and one hand on the steering wheel.

Brett cursed and dragged me inside before slamming the front door. Glass crushed beneath my feet, and he leaned over me as I pressed my back against the door. His other hand splayed on the door, and he hunched to meet my gaze.

My chest heaved with fire. This time I didn't want him to kiss me. Maybe. Breath caught in my throat as I felt his on me, hot and bitter. He'd taste like coffee, slightly sweet with a hint of salt from his exercise if I'd dare to close the tense distance between us.

"Stay here," he demanded.

I frowned. *House or curse? House or curse?* At least with the curse I'd still get to talk to him, show him books at the shop, see his library one day, maybe finally get to kiss him. But the house was a dream I'd held since we left when I was seven years old. How could I deny the child version of me the joy of living here again someday?

Once again, anger won temporarily. "What are you going to do, kidnap me?"

His nostrils flared and jaw flexed. "How about we strike a deal?"

"How about I knee you in the nards?" A boot would be better, but he was standing too close to me.

The peak of his lip twitched. "Bella. Listen to me." He sighed and shook his head. "I'll leave the house, but you must swear to me that you'll help my reputation. It's a trade."

House or curse? Then, it hit me. I didn't need to choose. I had the answer to both right in front of me. If we raised the level of the trade, I'd get a chance to win him over, for the curse of course, while saving the house, and he'd get his reputation boosted.

I arched an eyebrow, and it stirred something in him because he mirrored it.

"Why don't we raise the stakes?" I said. "You already have a campaign manager, but you don't have a girlfriend."

His brow furrowed but interest was evident as his eyes narrowed. "What are you proposing?"

"Wow, don't plan the wedding yet," I joked. I was getting good at this flirting thing. Was this flirting? I finally felt like I had a real plan, and guilt wasn't a part of it. We both needed something from each other. "I mean, folks already saw us on what looked like a date last night. Let's keep this going, take it to the next level. With me by your side, as your girlfriend, people will trust you. Like I said, everyone around here takes my advice."

He released his grip on my wrist to scrub his palm over the scratchy stubble that was more than a shadow on his chin and jaw now. The smirk wasn't one of joy, but it looked promising. "You'll really do that? You'll pretend to date me, the whole nine yards?"

"I'm not a football fan."

For a moment, his stoic expression blinked to confusion, then back again. "That's not—it's a World War II reference. I thought you knew history."

"I know books."

The subject shifted back to the situation at hand. "If you do this, you have to really sell it. I don't like dishonesty."

"Then, you shouldn't be in politics."

Brett grunted. He knew I was right, but his response surprised me. "It's not my choice." His gaze wandered down the hall where studs lined the walls but nothing hung on them.

"I'll sell it. We can keep our conversations on books, and maybe people will really believe we're in love." That was all I needed from him. I had to stick it out long enough to get those three little words.

He sniffed, wrinkling his nose, and then nodded. "Okay." Brett pushed off the wall and straightened. "You're my girlfriend for the whole campaign, which means appearances at the Halloween Harvest and the Homecoming game."

I nodded along. "And the townhall meetings, and you have to come to my big book sale."

"Right." His Adam's Apple bobbed with a swallow. "You must agree to always be prompt and available for any event between now and the election. And if this'll work, we need to be open with one another. As a politician, people will be looking for me to slip up, and I need to prove that we're committed. Can you do that? I respect people who honor their commitments."

"Done."

A car door slammed outside.

Brett swore again. "We're starting right now." He pulled me away from the door and slipped his hand around my waist.

"What?"

"Now." He nodded toward the door. Footsteps came from the other side followed by a knock.

I grabbed his hand and shoved it higher around my stomach rather than where it had landed near my butt.

"Fine. It's a deal."

Brett leaned forward and opened the door. "Hey, Chip."

The campaign manager stared at us, gaze shifting from me to Brett, then Brett to me, and rinse, repeat.

"I take it your cat-hunting venture went well," he finally spoke. A wry smile snuck onto his lips as he surveyed Brett's shirtless body and the arm around me. This looked far more intimate than I'd intended. We wanted people to believe we were falling for each other, not a fling.

"Hunting would mean we killed the cat," Brett corrected.

Chip waved the comment away. "Whatever it was, this is good news."

Another car pulled into the driveway, this one a large truck towing a trailer. I glanced at the stained-glass window, then jabbed Brett at the bottom of his ribcage.

"Call off your dogs," I whispered.

"Huh?" Chip turned around. "Still doing that?"

"Actually, I need to cancel with them again," Brett said, unlacing his hand from my waist. He dropped his voice and mumbled so only I could hear. "Jensen Estate lives to see another day."

Before he could pull away entirely, I jabbed him again, enjoying the feel of his muscle beneath his shirt. I'd made the right choice. "And call it by the real name."

He frowned, and I folded my arms. Our silent standoff took place behind Chip while he squinted at the demolition crew.

"Boyfriends are nice like that," I added.

Brett sighed. "The Villenueve Manor, I mean." He dodged around Chip and marched down the steps.

His broad shoulders shined in the sun while his dark hair soaked up the morning light. It was either the flutter of excitement or too much caffeine on an empty stomach, but my heart skipped a beat as I watched him. The deal solved all my problems, *and* it gave me an excuse to spend time at my favorite place. What could go wrong?

I smiled up at the stained-glass window. Sunlight cast rose and green tints from the colors of the art against the low-hanging wall opposite of it. I squinted and twisted my head. I know the manor well, but that wall never got much light, and I'd never noticed the tiny divot across from the window.

Maybe Brett knew what it was. I'd ask later because somewhere inside the house Grandma V. had sworn she'd hidden her grandmother's journals when she was a child.

I dropped my gaze back to my new boyfriend at the sound of shouts. The worker threw up his hands in frustration.

Chip shook his head, and I realized we both stood in the exact same pose, one foot out, arms crossed, eyes on the reason we were here—my fake lover and Chip's client. Brett matched the guy's volume and shouted back. That was the Brett I remembered, short-tempered, condescending. Maybe pretending to love him would be harder than I'd thought when I made the deal. When I'd discussed it with Loxley, Brett felt like the only option, but it was going to be a private relationship where I'd, hopefully, woo him into breaking my curse, then I'd get out of dodge. That would only require enough faking to convince Brett, not all of Folklore Falls. And with his ego, I'd assumed it'd be a breeze.

"So," Chip said, leaning his head toward me but never moving his gaze, "I heard you met my mom before ya'll enjoyed a date at the diner. Tell me, what's Brett like romantically? Does he actually enunciate, or is it all growls and groans?"

Why would Brett's campaign manager admit his client was gruff and off-putting like that? *Right. He doesn't know our dating is fake.* Chip expected I already knew and accepted Brett's flaws.

Time to turn on the tricks. Good thing Brett was the king of pranks. I just needed to learn how to lie, except the words that came out first weren't dishonest.

"He… surprised me."

Sixteen

BRETT

The book sale happened first. Though the two weeks that went by in between weren't without plenty of Bella moments. She attended a Farmer's Market appearance with me where we argued about what constitutes good food and forced fake smiles to everyone we passed.

The book sale was the first big event where most of the town was expected to see us together, not just diner patrons and moms out for a walk with their kids at the market. It'd give us plenty to talk about that wasn't food, at least.

As I approached the bookstore from the crowded parking lot, it became apparent I'd arrived late. I hated arriving late. Had Bella told me the wrong time? Was she already dropping the ball on our deal? I hated when people couldn't follow through on their commitments.

People milled about, checking tables spread around the front of the shop, most were already empty. I squeezed through the doorway and spotted Bella at the desk. The bookshelves lining every wall were sparse now, nearly sold out in some sections. She beamed as she gripped a copy of collected Greek mythologies and discussed Medusa's story.

It irritated me more that we'd had this specific conversation already, and she'd broken the first rule of commitment.

"Hi." I nodded and walked around behind the desk. "Did you lie to me about what time this event started?" I kept my voice low, aware of the wandering eyes and eavesdropping ears.

Maybe I shouldn't have come in with flames blazing because she matched it with her own fire. Bella straightened and looked me up and down. "What are you doing back here? This is for employees only."

"Employee."

She forced a smile to the woman buying the Greek mythology book. "One second." She lowered her voice. "What's your deal?"

"My deal is that we have a deal, and I expect you to be up front with me. I respect promptness, and I'll expect you to be on time to my events."

"We had a nice time at the diner. Can't we just keep that going for a few weeks? No need for the Beast to come out." She patted my arm, and though I didn't hate the touch, the condescending gesture irritated me.

I pursed my lips before saying something I'd regret. The deal required me to behave, too. I couldn't be grouchy to my girlfriend in front of half the town. After a cleansing breath, I evened my tone. "The public appearance side of the deal is crucial for me. If you can't hold that up, the deal is off." I thought I'd spoken in a matter-of-fact voice, but Bella frowned.

"Keep it down," she whispered, glancing at the woman and around the shop. "I told you to come later because I was busy, that's all."

"That's all?" I echoed.

"Yes, now, if you'll constantly look for mistakes or issues, maybe I don't want the deal, either." She turned back to the customer and bagged the book in a small cloth pouch with a stack of romances the woman also purchased.

I snorted at the covers of women in Victorian dresses with their cleavage obvious and the men rugged in the countryside but somehow spotlessly clean. After the woman walked away, I pulled one of the historical romances off a nearby shelf and fanned through the pages.

I shook my head at one of the passages. This kind of junk didn't deserve to share space with Dickens's books or Herman Melville's work.

"Do you have a comment?" Bella asked.

I looked up and shoved the fallen hair from my eyes to see her in a defensive stance. With her arms crossed and boot tapping, Bella looked the picture of irritation. I smirked.

"This." I slapped the book shut and held it up. "This is the kind of crap I thought you read."

"Excuse me?" She snatched the book from my hands and held it close to her chest as if protecting it from me.

"Nothing." I shrugged. "I was happy to find out you read the real books by Austen and Shelley and Morrison."

Bella scoffed and slammed the book onto the desktop. A black blur darted out from beneath. Philip dodged through the open door to the small closet behind me.

"That's a sexist thing to say," she said.

"I just mentioned all female authors. I'm not—"

"You know these books are marketed to women." She jabbed the Victorian romance, then redirected her poke and pressed her fingertip into the center of my chest. "Now's not the time." Bella moved me out of the way, but I stopped her, stepping in front again and blocking her way out from behind the desk. I couldn't turn down the challenge. Hell, maybe we'd look like a real couple if we had a disagreement in front of folks. Of course, we'd only been on one date, and most people only knew about our interactions from the diner or the pictures Patty Potts had posted.

"No, I want to know how you can possibly read the classics, then defend mindless junk like that?"

"You need to stop before I do more than poke you with my finger-nails." She flexed her hand, showing me the shape of her long acrylics like a claw. Speaking of which, Philip re-emerged from the back room and snaked his skinny body through our legs.

"Fine. Whatever." I shook my head, disappointed to discover she was just the person I'd judged—a backwoods chick like all the rest of these folks. "At least they'll train you to be a good girlfriend."

She froze. The thick liner flattened as she narrowed her eyes. "You did not just say that to me."

Our disagreement had garnered more gazes than I'd thought. Nearly every customer paused their browsing to sneak peeks our direction. Their conversations fell to murmurs so they could hear ours. I needed to rein it in before I offended anyone else with my opinion of romances.

Bella's eyes shifted from me to the couple standing closest to the desk. Understanding dawned, evident by her smile. I'd forgotten all about the people watching us, the very people I needed votes from. Bella had that air about her, she could suck every bit of oxygen from me and force me to look at her and only her. It was as intoxicating as it was enraging.

"What did you think about this book?" She lifted the Victorian romance and raised her voice several volumes.

If I wasn't careful, she'd get her end of the bargain, and I'd still lose the election due to my own big mouth. The bully side of me needed to stay hidden, or I'd never cross the last item off my mother's checklist. But it wasn't just about her anymore. I wanted to change my memories here, too.

I cleared my throat and swallowed. "I hope to read it someday," I lied.

"Great!" Bella smirked. "We'll plan a book club for it, right, Patty?"

A familiar voice chimed in from the other side of the small shop. "Count me in, dear!" Patty pushed through the tight spaces and winked at us. "I was just delighted when I heard you two had made it official."

"Are you guys dating?" The woman near the desk inserted herself into the conversation. Though her husband didn't speak, he looked as equally interested in the answer.

Bella glanced at me, spider-lashes flicking up. "Yes, but—" She held up her palm toward Patty. "If it were at first sight, we'd have dated in elementary school. So, more like at first date."

"Oh, that's right. Of course." Patty nodded as she patted down her thick gray hair, cut in a style that curled under her chin.

The other woman gasped. "I never would have put you two together. I mean, I saw the photo of you on his shoulders, of course."

Of course. Gossip was for small minds, but it worked in my favor. In fact, my campaign relied on it.

"Me neither," Bella said. "I mean, he's changed?"

How was it that she lied so easily to me about the time of the book sale but couldn't manage to tell them I was a decent man.

I cleared my throat. "We discovered we both love books. The rest is history." I glanced at her as I emphasized the last word. Those were the two topics we could stick to, nixing romance books apparently.

"Yep." She forced a smile.

"Were you just having a fight?" Patty seemed attempting to whisper, but it came out loud enough for the whole shop to hear, and she knew it. She reached across the desktop and swatted at my arm. "Oh, go ahead and kiss and make up. Just pretend I'm not here." The old woman feigned interest in the books stacked on the edge of the desktop, likely piles that people had selected, then changed their minds about at the last moment. I was remiss to see someone had left *The Odyssey* behind.

The woman in the couple wiggled her eyebrows at her husband, then pretended not to look at us.

Bella and I exchanged uncomfortable glances. This was part of the deal, and I was attracted to her, but the situation felt wrong. She was pissed, and I suffered second-hand embarrassment at her choice of entertainment.

When she tilted her chin up in an awkward, jerky movement, I realized the responsibility to take the next step was on me.

"The ball is in your court," she whispered.

"I thought you didn't know football?"

"Football isn't played on a court," her voice was as flat as her brow now, unamused at my joke.

I licked my lips and leaned down so she could reach me. "Just a little pop quiz to test you're still in your right mind after that choice of genre." I faintly tilted my head toward the book with the woman in the Victorian dress.

Bella took my hand in hers and squeezed a bit too tightly. "Kiss me before I kill you."

I winced. She knew which hand had suffered the injury, and she chose violence. *And they call me the Beast.*

With all eyes on us, exactly as I'd thought I wanted, I pressed my lips to hers. Did her purple lipstick taste like tart berries, or was that just the trick of the color playing with my brain? If dozens of eyes didn't bore through us, I'd pull her closer, take a breath, and return to the feel of her soft lips on mine where we could linger, tasting one another.

Except, didn't I want them to watch us? That was the whole point, a point that quickly faded to the back of my mind as I used my free hand to lightly trail up her bare arm until my palm landed in the base of her hairline.

When she pulled away, I decided it ended early, way too early. The flavor of her lingered on my tongue, and I wanted to do it again, but the romance book haunted me. The Victorian woman seemed to mock me with her pointed look at the viewer.

Another buried memory stirred. Long before the deal with Bella, back when I was a boy with a broken family, I swore I'd never let myself love any woman other than the one who'd raised me. Dating, marriage, it was all transactional, and books like that were full of lies. Romance was nothing but a facade, just like mine and Bella's relationship.

Plus, I'd hoped Bella was smart enough not to waste her time with fluffy books.

The heat of her body close to mine dissipated as she squeezed past me and stepped out from behind the desk but not without a passing comment whispered below her breath.

"You're lucky I'm trapped in this deal."

Nope, she was just the Bella I'd recalled—threatening, attractive, but not a fit for my world. I could never take her to The Globe if she'd embarrass me with a romance book in her bag.

It was time to leave. We'd try again at the next event. As I stepped forward, my foot bumped into something. I'd forgotten Philip was wedged between my legs. The cat got the boot, accidentally, as I stumbled and caught myself against the desktop.

Philip screeched and yowled as he scrambled and landed on his feet next to Bella. She scooped him up and shot me a scowl.

This was going to be a long month and a half until the election ended.

Seventeen

BELLA

S*tupid, stupid, stupid.* I lightly bumped my head against a box of a books while I sat crisscross applesauce on the floor. My behavior still haunted me two days later.

I was trapped in the deal more than Brett. Though he didn't know about the curse, of course, his feelings for me needed to be real for it to work. How did I let myself fight with him and threaten him? And worse, how did I miss our kiss? It felt like it happened so fast that I blinked and it'd ended. Would we get a chance to share another moment like that? Would it always be in front of others.

Of course it would. This was a deal, a plan, not a relationship. Lightning pain bolted through my heart, disappearing as fast as it came, a quick, unpleasant reminder that I wanted a kiss that I shouldn't.

It was all too confusing. Brett and I were together, but not *together* and it twisted my emotions into a dozen tangles worse than my hair after I thicken it by back-brushing.

I shoved a heavy box toward the front of the store, one step at a time. I'd flicked off the 'open' sign but didn't bother to lock the door since Folklore Falls didn't have a lot of tourism in the early fall when schools started and people returned to work full-time after the summer rush. Plus, my offer still stood to any thief who wanted a book.

I huffed and turned around to use my back. I slid down the box and sat on the floor, pressing with my boots to inch the box forward. Maybe I should have unloaded armfuls of books and carried them to the front shelf in batches, but I didn't have time to waste.

Our first public appearance as a fake couple was a dumpster fire. Brett called me unintelligent, insulted my beloved books, and I threatened to murder him. A small smile tugged at my lips. At least our pretend relationship was exciting.

And that kiss. It popped into my head again, refusing to let go of me. I let out a puff of breath as I gave the box one last shove forward, then let myself go limp for a break.

"It was terrible," I told Philip, as he slinked over to me, pausing to rub his chin on the bottom of the Throne. He took a seat and stared at me with his tail flicking from side-to-side. "Okay, not terrible, maybe not bad at all. But not good, either!" The thought of it twisted my stomach, and my gaze drifted to where we'd stood only two days earlier, sharing an act of intimacy reserved for people who loved each other. Or at least didn't hate each other.

Philip meowed and sauntered up to me.

"Fine." I sighed and lifted my tired arm to give him scratches behind the ear. "I don't hate him." Philip hopped into my lap, and the bell on his collar jingled cheerfully. "But I would if he didn't mention he wanted to build a library. It's his one redeeming quality." Okay, two if you counted his wavy hair.

A gentle humming stirred in my lap. Philip's purrs continued as long as I scratched in the spot he liked—until he didn't like it. He whipped his head around and chomped my fingers, carefully, so as not to hurt me, but just enough to send me a warning.

"Yep." I nodded. "That's the perfect example of how it feels."

Brett and I were two cats. His presence was nice, sometimes, and only when we talked Shakespeare or authors in history. Plus, he was easy on the eyes considering how well the stoic, permanently pissed-off vibe looked on him. I appreciated him from a distance. A far distance.

And I supposed he felt the same about me. Most people did. They came to me to be heard but never wanted to listen. Everyone loved me, but that was the version of me I allowed them to see, the curated one who didn't hate herself.

Stupid. Stupid. Stupid. My mom's words replayed in my mind every year like clockwork around my birthday. She'd first said it when I was twelve, and I told her I hated math. *Then, how will you pass medical school?* Two years later, I'd confessed I didn't want to go to medical school but take art classes in college someday. That had sparked the name-calling, so I'd run away into Grandma V's arms until she passed the year after. From then on, every time Mom said I was stupid for choosing my own path in life, I'd visit my grandma's grave where I'd laid a rose on her headstone.

Her last words always haunted me because I never made sense of them. *Love changes everything, even curses.*

The door's chime rang out and startled me from my cozy spot on the floor behind the box. Philip leaped from my lap and darted behind the Throne. I twisted to see a bright smile decorated with a scraggly blond mustache.

"Oh." Chip halted and laid a hand over his chest. "Oh dear, did I interrupt?"

I stood, my brow furrowed until understanding dawned. My nose was stuffed and eyes stung. I wiped the wetness from my cheeks.

"Is it Brett?" he asked. "Do I need to have a talk with my client? He really lives up to that nickname sometimes, doesn't he?"

I shook my head, feeling foolish for crying on the floor of my shop. And letting Brett's campaign manager witness my little breakdown was the sour cherry on top. "I, uh, no. My grandma passed away years ago, and it's always painful this time of year to know she's gone."

Chip hurried around the box and insisted I hug him. It was a little much for me. I preferred my personal space, but he meant well, it seemed.

"Have you told Brett this?" he asked, releasing and letting me breathe again. "I know he's rough around the edges, but you're his girl-friend. I'm sure he'd be happy to provide a nice, muscular shoulder to cry on."

Not much made Brett happy, as far as I could tell. And I doubted a trip to Folklore Falls's Cemetery was his idea of a good time. If he hated old buildings like Villenueve Manor, he'd cringe at the sight of the weather-beaten headstones with dates as far back as three hundred years.

I, on the other hand, felt peace among the passed. They never invaded my personal space, for one. And two, they listened to me. I could talk as much as I wanted without worrying about hiding the ugly parts of myself, the stupid parts.

"Well, if it's not too much trouble, I came to ask if you'd like to have dinner with me and Brett in the city tonight?"

In the city? That sounded like a lot of unnecessary pretending for no gain on Brett's part. Nobody in the town's voting pool would see us there.

"Why?" I wrinkled my nose.

"You're Brett's girl!" He floated past me as he spoke to steal a few pets. Philip enjoyed the attention, the traitor.

"No, I think I'm going to visit my grandma tonight."

Chip stuck his lips out like a duck and then comically glanced between the cat and me as if Philip understood our conversation. "A live one, right?"

"What? No, I take a rose to her grave at Folkore Cemetery every year around—never mind." I waved my hand.

"We've got a private plane, so you'll be back in plenty of time. But I don't want to intrude. It's no skin off my nose if you say no, but Brett insisted." Chip raised palms in surrender, then stretched his neck to peer into the box of books. "Ah, *The Glass Coffin* is a great little book. Mari's husband is my favorite. Have you read the series?"

Why did Brett want me to have dinner with him and his manager? It'd be a public appearance, but in the wrong public, and Chip already seemed keen on Brett, so it wasn't my job to help tame the Beast there. If nothing else, I wanted to say yes out of sheer curiosity.

Philip meowed, and I arched a brow at him.

It might kill me. You're right. If only my cat could read my brain. Surviving an intimate dinner with just the three of us wasn't likely. Not after Brett had hit a soft spot. The hints to my lack of intelligence went right for the jugular, leaving me choking and breathless. Only my mom was allowed to call me stupid and live, and that was only because I had no other living relatives left.

Philip meowed again.

Of course I wouldn't murder anyone! I shot him a pointed look. Okay, maybe I needed to get out of the bookshop and my head before I totally lost my mind. I'd spent the last two days stocking shelves, shoving boxes, and balancing the checkbook after the big sale. It was exhausting to say the least.

The dinner would give me a chance to reconcile with Brett. I'd threatened his life when I needed to charm him. This curse would be a lot easier to deal with if I were a siren instead of a bookseller.

"Yes," I finally said, cutting Chip's rambling short.

"The series is over?" Tragedy must have struck based on the gaping, heartbroken expression on Chip's face.

"What? No, I mean, yes. I'll go to dinner."

He slapped his chest, the gesture all too familiar, though I didn't know Chip very well. "Thank heavens, I thought you were answering my question. The *Mari Fable Mysteries* must not end before the author addresses The Little Cloak Girl fairy tale."

"I—wait, yeah, I actually agree with that. You like fairy tale retellings?" I followed Chip to the door.

"I don't have time to read, so it's all audiobooks for me. Retellings keep a little magic in my life between the political books and cut-throat campaigns." He scanned me up and down. "Do you want to grab a purse first? Or a coffin?"

I frowned.

"Sorry, tasteless joke. You remind me of a vampire, and that's a compliment. Trust me." Chip swung the door open and exited before I could respond.

The drive into the nearest city was a welcome break. Chip talked enough for the three of us, which allowed Brett and I plenty of space to sit and glare at one another. I did my best to tone down my cold stare. *Think of the curse, Bella.*

The reminder encouraged me to select the seat beside Brett in the booth at the fancy restaurant. I slid in next to him, scooping my skirt underneath my butt, and I tried not to grab the steak knife and stab his arm when it bumped mine. In a flash, my brain registered the electricity between us as our arms brushed. The flipping back and forth confused and twisted my emotions. Brett fired me up in every way, anger, interest, desire…

As soon as the hostess left us with our menus, Chip excused himself to make a call. The classical music couldn't break the awkward silence between us. The heat from his skin reminded me how close we sat. If I moved a centimeter to the right, we'd be touching.

I needed to be the first to speak, considering I needed him to love me. His affection had to be real, while my half of the relationship could remain fake and still fulfill the deal. The problem was, it wasn't fake and I scolded myself for enjoying Brett's presence after the rude crap he'd said about my beloved books.

"Was there a reason for this?" I asked. Not a good start, but it physically hurt to act as though I forgave him for insulting me.

Brett shifted in the booth, too small for a guy his size. Though he wore the right clothes and styled his hair like any other pretentious playboy, he didn't fit in the fancy five-star restaurant. The other wealthy vacationers who visited Folklore Falls mostly kept their judgments under wraps with smiles plastered on plastic faces. But Brett wore it all on his sleeve, his anger—I wasn't sure if he had a heart, yet.

"We failed the mission," he spoke out of the side of his mouth.

"Is that another World War II reference?"

He turned to face me now. "We bombed the book sale appearance."

"On that, we agree." I unrolled the cloth napkin and smoothed out the wrinkles to keep my hands busy. My brain still argued whether to stab him or scoot closer to him.

"So, I wanted our next date to be out of town."

"With your campaign manager?" I wrinkled my brow and finally shifted to meet his gaze though I avoided looking at his mouth.

"It'll give us good practice." Brett straightened to check the exit where Chip had excused himself. "He doesn't know about our agreement. If we can convince Chip we're a real couple, townsfolk will be a breeze."

"I'm surprised you didn't choose a Shakespeare metaphor, considering he's the only approved author according to Jensen snobbery."

Shut it, Bella! My mouth had a mind of its own, yes I was pissed at him but I still had a curse to break. Also, why shouldn't I expect an apology? Maybe Brett would like me more if I demanded respect.

"Do you like to fight or what?" He raised his eyebrow though his eyes held the hint of a smile. If it dared to make it to his mouth, I'd smack him. It'd be like the old movies where women slap the guy then kiss them.

No, no kissing right now. Why was everything an argument? My fake boyfriend and I disagreed on books. My head fought with my heart and my heart's sidekick, AKA the desire the grab Brett's sharp jaw and yank his face toward me. For a moment, my mind wandered as I pictured myself kicking one leg out and climbing on top of him, either to choke him or kiss him, it wasn't clear in the fantasy.

The server walked by and dropped off a basket of warm bread and butter in a ramekin. I gasped, startled back to the reality of the restaurant. *Get it together, Bell.* Straddling Brett any time, much less during a fancy dining experience, was out of the question. The server opened her mouth, then clamped it shut again, her eyes wide after noticing our expressions.

"I can't say I hate irritating you," I mumbled. If I didn't whip my runaway mouth into gear before Brett stormed away, I'd be stuck with seven years of screwing up the lives of the people I loved. The other option involved self-isolation. Even Philip couldn't come since I'd worry he'd step on his tail or suffer endless hairballs. "You could've at least prepared me for this. What are your hobbies? What's your favorite food?"

Brett leaned his head on his fist and gave me a bored expression though I could see right through it. Was he thinking what I was thinking? *No. Straddling!*

"I doubt Chip will give you a pop quiz," he said, a mischievous spark in his dark eyes.

I resisted the urge to knock his arm out of the way and watch his head bang into the table. Of course, he couldn't kiss me if he was unconscious. He'd sprung this on me on purpose. Revenge for lying to him about the book sale? I was clearly committed. I rode all the way to the city in his luxury sedan that stunk of excess cologne.

"Play along, and we'll be fine. I'm here because it's your turn to show a little effort."

My neck burned, and I curled my fingers, nails digging into my palms. If the server didn't stop by to deliver three glasses of water, I might have wiped Brett's smug expression with my fist. Instead, I nodded, lips pursed. "So, this was on purpose."

His lips twitched into a faint side-smile. "Payback's a—"

"Beast," I interrupted, proud of the slight to his reputation.

It did the trick, making the smirk vanish. Brett returned to the picture of stoicism, a pissed-off Greek god carved in cold stone. Instead of a comeback, he reached for the loaf of bread and tore off a piece.

"What if Chip asks how we met?" I asked.

Brett slopped the slice into a curved plate of oil and swirled it around. He didn't pause to answer my question but tossed it into his mouth and made me wait until he fully chewed and swallowed before eyeing me. "Tell him the truth."

When he reached for the loaf again, I intercepted with a poke of my acrylic nail into his forearm. I not-so-gently pushed it out of reach of the appetizer. "Excuse me? Would you like to share an explanation with the class?"

He licked his lips, then met my gaze. "Exactly. We were classmates, and that's the truth. You tried to murder me with your death stare across the school, and I impressed you with snakes years later."

"Right. As if the snakes were for me." I laughed, but it faded. He glanced at me with the absence of a smirk this time. More than a decade had passed since I'd met Brett, and while I remembered him as the boy who teased other kids, he never did it to me. I was intimidating like that. I'd assumed nobody would mess with me. Though Loxley was no easy target, either, and Brett pranked her plenty of times. Was I the only classmate he hadn't bullied? The thought had never occurred to me before.

Why did he act like meeting in elementary school was the start of our relationship? He'd called it *the truth*. For a guy lying to the whole town about his personal life, he sure did throw that word around a lot.

Brett lived a different truth than the rest of us—one full of judgment, condescending comments, excess money, and a general disregard for the important aspects of life like friendships, generosity, and love.

When he tore off another slice, he offered it to me, then slid the plate of oil in front of me. "For you."

I almost thanked him until Chip appeared like a fairy godmother poofing into existence. The thoughtful sharing was all for show. Of course. Like the rest of Brett's life, showy cars, showy campaign, blah, blah, blah. Nothing about *us* was real and I needed to get that through my thick skull.

"Thank you," I decided to say it anyway. I needed him to like me, after all. And didn't the unknown 'they' claim that fake smiling tricks your body into feeling happy? Maybe it worked the same for love. If I pretended to care about him, he'd return the favor, and I'd have tricked him into falling for me. I reached out and brush my hand over his forearm. "You're so sweet, honey."

An awkward grin followed the flash of his raised eyebrow. "Anytime, baby."

He selected the same word I'd told him I reserved only for my cat. So, he knew I hated the term of endearment and he did it anyway, the game was *on*. Before I could think of a comeback, Brett turned to Chip, who plopped down across from us.

"Their bread is delicious." Chip kissed his fingertips for emphasis. "I've had too much politics. Let's talk fun." He opened the menu but kept his eyes peering over the top at us. "Oh!" Menu went down. "Tell me how you met."

I swung my foot to the side to whack Brett with the heel of my boot under the table. He grunted but didn't take the bait. Instead, he fired the question right back into my face.

"Well, the truth is," he upped the volume on his favorite overused word, "Bella's better at telling the story." His dark eyes dropped to slits, holding my gaze. "Right, baby?"

You want commitment? What about the truth? Buckle up, Beast.

I grabbed the whole rest of the loaf and plopped it onto my mini plate. The butter was next. I cupped the ramekin and flipped it over until the warm butter slid off and dropped onto the loaf where it spilled down the sides in a gooey, yellow mess. It was meant to irritate Brett on his cheating day, or whatever gym rats called their carb binges, but guilt struck me when Chip's jaw dropped. He was too good at acting heartbroken, Hollywood needed to hire him for a tragic romance ASAP.

I slid the bread over to Brett, and he furrowed his brow.

"It's for you," I said. "I don't eat butter."

The server appeared before I could dive into our elementary escapades, which included, and was limited to, evil glares. Also, maybe a few conversations when we were the only two kids sitting on the bleachers during dodgeball. I'd concocted reasons why I couldn't play since I hated sports, and Brett always threw too hard, smashing kids' glasses right off their faces. Since he'd been banned and I'd been bored, we might have shared words more than once.

"Another round of bread, please," Chip said with a swirl of his finger. The server nodded and disappeared.

"You wouldn't know it with his gym obsession now, but Brett sucked at sports," I started. It was true, throwing too hard in dodgeball got him banned, in flag football, he tackled so the teacher pulled him out, and during the swing-dancing circuit, I was pretty sure he flung his partner across the basketball court and was, once again, banned. "And me, well, I despise anything to do with a ball and net, so I was the queen of cutting P.E. That's where we first found each other." I tilted my head and beamed at him.

The recognition in his eyes said he remembered. He nodded slowly. "I forgot, you were the little class liar."

I pursed my lips. Not only did he interrupt my story, but he tried to hit where it hurts. Unfortunately for him, I'd been lying my whole life about who I really was. I built a personality where I'd pretend to be smart by I packing my brain full of facts from books to prove to my mother I hadn't failed. Lying didn't bother me like it did him.

"What'd you tell our gym teacher?" Brett prodded. He squinted, and I could almost see the wheels turning as he tried to conjure the memories. "Something about surgeon's hands?"

I laughed. He'd found the one reason that wasn't a lie. "You're absolutely right." I turned to Chip to explain. "My mother wanted me to be a surgeon when I grew up, so she wrote me a note to get out of dodgeball. She thought it risked smashing my fingers and permanently damaging my dexterity."

Brett cocked his head. Big, rude Doberman. *Come at me.* I was finally ready to fully embrace the fake dating and he could see it.

"That's when I knew," he said, with the tick of his eyebrows to emphasize the double meaning in his words. "Bella was the girl for me."

I offered him a wink that told him the game had officially begun, and thankfully this one didn't involved a net.

"Let's get a bottle of champagne," Brett said, as he raised his hand to flag the server down. I shot him a glare that pinned him in place. His dark eyes darted to me in realization. I was here to help him become, or at least appear, better, right? He dropped his arm. "We'll wait to order when she comes back around."

My lips curled into a smile and I looped my arm around his. Somewhere between my hand landing on his forearm, and when he leaned into me, our communication twisted and he reached for my hand. Brett slid his fingers between mine and I looked up at him. Instead of meeting my gaze, he gave my hand a slight squeeze.

When the server arrived and spoke with Chip, Brett dipped his head and leaned into my ear where his breath sent shivers down my neck. "I'm not going to threaten to kill you, but I'd love it if you'd kiss me. Again."

The play on my threat to him left me breathless. It told me he thought about our botched moment at the bookstore too. And if we was whispering it, that meant this wasn't for Chip's sake. I chewed my lip and considered the possibility that fake could slip into real at lightning speed if he kept talking into my ear with a low, growling voice like that. All I needed was another mention of books or the opera house and I might throw caution to the wind and straddle him anyway. Of course, I'd have to ignore the awful things he'd said about romances and that might prove impossible.

Three flute glasses clinked together in the server's hand as she returned with a massive bottle of champagne. The cork popped and bubbles spilled into the clear cups. When Chip insisted we lift our glasses into a cheer, I felt Brett's questioning eyes on me.

I arched a brow, and when Chip went to down his champagne, I met Brett's gaze and gave him a slight nod. *I'll kiss you again.*

His lips curved just enough to expose the dimples.

I lightly pressed my chin into his shoulder and breathed into his ear, returning the intimate favor. "Let's see if you can handle a girl who reads romance."

That sparked a brief look of shock that melted into the competitive spirit I'd seen on a frustrated young Brett back in gym class when he'd wanted to win at dodgeball but threw the balls so hard he injured people.

The rest of the evening surprised me as much as the pasta. Folklore Falls's one diner didn't offer many alternative options, so I delighted in the expensive restaurant's vegan meatballs with my spaghetti. Chip admitted he'd heard the story of our first fight in the bookstore. When Brett and I exchanged worried looks, Chip only laughed and shared a few anecdotes of his own dating blunders.

Even the drive back went smoothly until Chip insisted on dropping us off at the cemetery.

Eighteen

BRETT

No matter how many daggers I threw with my eyes, Chip didn't get the message. I couldn't argue when he continually claimed I was 'a good guy.' Apparently, good guys go to graveyards with their girlfriends. Someone shoot me. Though the thought of being alone with Bella again intrigued me. Still, I didn't know what her challenge meant. Would she kiss me again or was it an underhanded threat resulting from leftover anger about the romance books?

I skulked after her as she marched toward the black iron gate. The style reminded me of her beloved Manor—my family's house.

"You can leave if you want," she said with a wave of her hand. "I really don't need company."

"That's not what Chip said," I muttered. Dinner was a dream between the bubbles, the teasing, and Bella's body pressed to my side. But in the dark of the night, among the dead, all sensuality flattened and her mood changed. I couldn't blame her, I barely managed to think of my mother's passing much less visit her grave.

"Chip doesn't know me."

Dang. The woman could hear a pin drop. Actually, anyone would here. The dead silence soaked all outside sounds. Even the echo of crickets from the Falls didn't reach to the edge of town.

Moonlight cast odd shadows through the leafless trees that hung over the iron fence. Bella unhooked the latch and stepped inside, her boots squelching in the damp grass. A pair of jack o' lanterns decorated either side of the small gate, carved too early in the season to survive until Halloween.

Folklore Falls always followed its own calendar as if it lived separately from the rest of the world. That was another thing I'd fix, no pumpkins allowed out until October. The Harvest Festival was only a few days away, which was still too early for Halloween parties.

I swung my leg over the short fence and followed her through the maze of headstones and angel statues frozen in eternal prayer.

A crow's squawk broke the silence and drew my eyes to its perch on the scraggly branches above us. Bella stopped, and I almost ran over her. She brushed her fingertips over the clean headstone, clearly much newer than some of the crumbling ones.

When she eased to her knees, I looked away. The moment felt too personal for me to intrude, though Chip had insisted. I wanted to wring his neck.

"You look like you've never been in a graveyard before," she said, a cruel smile on her lips. The blue lipstick remained intact, or maybe she'd reapplied it after dinner. What did blue taste like? Or was it Bella who reminded me of the flavor of unripe berries, tart with hints of sweetness?

"What?" I scoffed. "I've visited Sleepy Hollow Cemetery and Pere La Chais where Oscar Wilde was buried."

"Okay, but you look so uncomfortable."

I scrubbed the back of my neck, unsure what to do with my hands. The imaginary itch behind my ears provided a good distraction. But Bella's quiet stare dug under my skin and seemed to control my neck as I turned to meet her eyes. Something about her hushed patience demanded I speak.

"My mother died recently," I admitted.

When she swallowed, the choker necklace around her throat shifted slightly, and the black jewel dangling from the center caught the moonlight. "I'm so sorry, Brett."

I coughed and cleared my throat. "We're here for you." I pointed to the grave in front of her, then shoved my hands into my pockets. "You were close?"

She tucked hair behind her ears as she nodded. "Yeah, my mom is…" she snorted. "Well, she's unpleasant to say the least, so I preferred my grandma."

I folded my arms, then unfolded and left them dangling at my sides. "I never thought someone like you and someone like me would have so much in common."

Bella's brow furrowed, creating a flat line beneath her bangs. "Someone like me?"

"Hey, you're not judgment-free." Anger, arguments, throwing stones—those I could manage. It was a safe zone, so much more comfortable than addressing death and family and the fact that I enjoyed another evening with the odd girl who lived above a bookstore. Women I dated partied on cruises in their free time, not quoted Shakespeare.

"Really?" She crossed her arms over her ribs.

"Can you tell me you haven't called me the Beast since we graduated?"

"What?"

"Can you?" I prodded.

"No, everyone calls you—"

"They don't know me. Not anymore. Maybe this campaign wouldn't be so hard if someone hadn't started that nickname."

"Me?"

"All your little stories at dinner about P.E. class and school activities brought back a memory. You called me the Beast first because I was a head taller than everyone else in our class." The wind picked up and forced tree branches to scratch against the iron fence for an eerie, squealing sound.

"So?" She scrunched her face and shrugged. "People were supposed to be afraid of me, not the new kid. Plus, that was a decade ago, and you were bully."

"I was, but I'm not anymore, so if you've called me the nickname anytime in the past few years, you're just as guilty of judgment as I am."

"All right." She stuck out her hand. "We're the same."

"I don't know about that." I shook my head. "But if we're talking about dealing with death, maybe." After I nodded toward the headstone, Bella followed my train of thought.

A little smile, if the curved edges of her blue lips could be classified as that, betrayed her harsh style. "Chip said you were a good shoulder to cry on, is that true?" She jabbed her finger toward me before I could answer. "You have to tell the truth."

I surrendered, hands up. "You've got me. Probably not, but I can try if you need it." I mirrored her slight smile and patted my opposite shoulder with an overly aggressive smack of my palm. The injury ached, but now wasn't the time.

"Thanks." With that, she spun around

The cracked grave markers only depressed me. My mother was laid to rest in a golden urn that we'd stored inside a mausoleum on my father's new property in New York. We never took her to a cemetery because she'd said she deserved better.

But did it matter? She couldn't take her wealth or manners with her. Now she was as isolated in death as she was in life because she didn't want to associate with those beneath her. Except they were all underground or locked away in an urn now, equals in death. The thought had never crossed my mind before, and it left me gritting my teeth. Maybe Bella was right, we weren't so different. We both approached others with a careful coldness.

I sighed and surveyed the overgrown grass that blocked some of the flat stones etched with names and dates. My mother chose demands on her deathbed rather than peace, and I'd received the brunt of it.

Would I have come back to Folklore Falls if she didn't push me into it? I was never as judgmental as my mother. Our careful assessment of others kept us safe from falling prey to those who wanted to use us or pull us down to their level. The truth was, I felt a pull to this small town that I couldn't explain, not until I saw Bella again, anyway. She wasn't the girl that got away, because I'd never had her, but the one that haunted the back of my mind whenever I tried to date another woman. I'd carried a torch for Bella all the time and the flame burned even brighter now that I'd gotten to know her as an adult.

A matching sigh came from Bella as she reached out and touched the cold stone. My eyes trailed her fingers in the divots of her grandmother's name.

Isabelle Villenueve. Where did I know that name?

A lump gathered in my throat. I hadn't spent much of my adult life in Folklore Falls, only returning from travels at my family's demand. So much of the town I'd shoved away, intentionally forgetting the memories and moments and unimportant things…

Like Belle V.

A breath escaped me. Everybody knew Belle V., and if anyone deserved my beastly nickname, it was her.

"She's your grandmother?" The words came out in a shout. The crow startled and flapped its wings, carrying itself away from us.

Bella twisted to look up at me. "You didn't know?"

"What? How would I?" I shook my head. Thoughts jumbled together. I didn't want to be like my mother. I never really said other people were beneath me like she blatantly would, but this was too far. This situation called for a judge of character. "Do you even care about the house?"

She stood now with arms folded and one foot jutting out. "What's that supposed to mean?"

"Why didn't you tell me you're related to Belle V.?" I threw up my hands and paced between headstones. "Did you concoct this to mess with my career? I can't date the granddaughter of Belle V., even if it is fake!"

Moonlight struck Bella's high cheekbones and the angle of her gaping mouth.

"Listen to yourself, Brett." She tapped her temples. "Think about it. People appreciate me, I'm helping your reputation. You had to have known she was my grandmother, you live in her house." In the wake of my accusation, Bella was surprisingly calm. Didn't it light a fire under her to suggest she was anything other than perfect? That was sure how it seemed at the book sale.

Before she could respond, I continued. "Belle V. was the most hated woman in Folklore Falls history." It was the truth but I was also wrong. I knew, somewhere in the back of my mind that the two were related. How could I not when the witchy woman's reputation stemmed from the very house Bella claimed as her family's? I'd ignored it because I *wanted* this excuse to be with her. Whether she could really help my campaign or not, I'd probably have agreed to this fake-dating bit because it meant I could talk to her about literature and listen to her laugh and taste her wildly-colored lipsticks.

"Says the most hated man in Folklore Falls." Her voice was even, intense, spooky. I couldn't get enough of it. I'd push for a fight just to hear her put me in my place again.

I kicked a rock out of my way and watched as it knocked into a particularly damaged headstone. "Nice. Real nice." Though I wanted to close the distance between us, my brain and mouth suffered a miscommunication called a *hot temper*.

"Do you even know why she had that reputation? Ask me, Brett." Bella toyed with the key on her earring. "People never ask, they only want me to listen." The wind almost carried her whispered words away.

I stopped pacing, shoved the hair from my face and stared at her. The request was a quiet piece of honesty and I respected her for ability to be calm and demanding simultaneously. Unexplained anger burned in my chest, I wanted Bella but our dating wasn't real. I wanted to win the election but that was for my mother. The anger was misplaced as I slung Bella irritated looks but I couldn't help it. I needed everything to work, the fake relationship, the fulfillment of the promise to my deceased mother after years of disappointing her when I couldn't lie on her behalf. *I'm sick of pretending.*

Large, dark, intoxicating eyes stared up at with thick lashes I no longer equated to spiders. Or maybe I liked spiders. Either way, she'd sucked me in with quiet patience—my opposite, yet the mirror to many of my behaviors and interests.

I released a breath and raked my fingers through my hair. "I'll bite."

"I'm sure you will," she muttered. *Dangit.* The innuendo tormented me and by the gleam in her eye, she knew it. I resisted the urge to storm across the cemetery and shove her against the tree where I could taste blackberries and feel her long, pointed nails dig into my back.

With my legs wide and arms crossed, I usually intimidated people. Not Bella. She folded her arms too then curved her neck as if intentionally exposing more of her skin to me.

I coughed to clear my throat. "Why did people hate your grandmother?"

Bella's gaze shifted to the edge of the cemetery, then trailed the fence line. She paused to stare at the ornate iron gate and rub her thumb and forefinger over the key earring before looking at me.

"My grandma pretended to be cruel. Not unlike what we're doing with the fake relationships." She laughed without joy. "She was a big believer in the fairy lore around here but also the darker side of paranormalities, like curses and bad luck." After she swallowed, the story continued. "So, she was mean, or acted like it, to push people away. It's a long story, but basically, she said she was cursed and anyone she'd interacted with suffered seven years of misery. By the time that was up, people wanted nothing to do with her. And that's the *truth.* Do you believe me?"

The whole wild tale sounded like a load of crock to me, but if anything matched Bella Villenueve, it was that story. Maybe I'd say the same and come out to the public with the claim that I was pretending to be a bully way back when. Once again, Bella and her oddities, including her infamous grandma, mirrored me more than I wanted to believe.

"I do. That sounds on-par with Folklore Falls."

"Anyway," she started, folding her arms again. "Thanks for asking." She marched past me, boots sinking into the squishy soil. The noise faded, and I didn't turn to see if she'd left me alone among the dead.

Somehow, Bella had successfully twisted her family's reputation around. If nothing else, I could learn from her.

The creak of the iron gate announced she was still here.

The sharp clarity of her enunciated voice cut through the heavy atmosphere around the graves. "If you'll still be my fake boyfriend, then walk me home. Otherwise, I'll see you in the crowd at the Halloween Harvest."

The lump in my throat hurt as I pushed down the pride and turned around.

"Honesty from here on out?" I asked. "No sabotage, no scheming your way out of your half of the deal, and no lies to make me look bad, like arriving late to the book event."

Bella ran the back of her fingernails against one another. The rhythmic clicking drowned out the thick silence. Finally, she lifted the pointed tips and made the signal of the letter X over her chest. "Cross my heart."

That was it, one simple little phrase like a pinky promise among school children. I'd never experienced that, only seen it on TV.

"Isn't there more to that?" I asked.

Bella twirled on her heel and started a slow march back into the heart of Folklore Falls. "You won't catch me saying the rest in a grave-yard. Superstitions and all." The tips of her long, shining hair brushed her lower back as she walked. "Did you know the phrase comes from a play?" When she tossed the bait over her shoulder, I had no choice but to follow.

I couldn't let my girlfriend walk home alone in the dark, fake or not. I jogged to catch up with her, swinging the gate shut behind me.

Nineteen

BELLA

The blow of my breath mimicked a distant, cheering crowd. It left a foggy circle on the floor length mirror. I reached out and traced the shape of a skull and bones before it faded.

A week and a half later, I still couldn't get over our graveyard conversation. Brett had actually listened to me, and I hoped he'd do the same at the Halloween Harvest tonight. We'd shared a few more dinners at the diner and a game of darts at the tavern that were more fun than I'd ever expected to have with the Beast, but the conversations stayed fairly shallow on books, food, and childhood memories of old classmates.

"Don't look at me like that," I scolded Philip for his endless, yellow stare. At the sound of my voice, he stood and his front paws crossed like a model on a runway as he came to sniff at the bottom of my mascara tube.

I'd paused mid-application to argue with my cat, just business as usual. I sat crisscross applesauce style on the floor in front of the mirror. The small container designed to slide under my bed was pulled out from beneath the low frame like a drawer. The compartments housed every shade of black eyeliner from midnight to raven.

Philip meowed his disagreement with my celebration.

"What? It's a swing and a hit." I leaned forward and swiped another layer of crow's feather black mascara over my lashes. "Listen to me, with the sports cliches and all."

His tail tickled my arm as he showed me his butt. The cat had more attitude in one toe bean than all the angsty characters I'd ever read about. My gaze trailed from furry feline to the old dress hanging in my closet. The red fabric peeked out, reminding me it existed. I'd spent months and months perfecting Christine Daae's dress, sewing, ripping seams, and re-sewing until it was perfect. The hours took me away from studying and I eventually dropped out of physics since I'd already decided I didn't want to pursue a medical degree when I graduated.

The pinched seam that gathered the skirt in the perfect angle seemed to scream at me. I sucked in a breath and turned back to the mirror only to see a face that looked too much like my mother's. My imagination ran wild, as my reflection morphed into her and I recalled the biggest fight we'd ever had. It wasn't the first time she'd called me stupid, not by a long shot, but it was the first time I believed it. I'd chosen wasting my time recreating fashion from books when I could have prepared myself for a medical degree that'd lead me to saving lives in her hospital.

Philip's meow disintegrated the memory before me and I swallowed the lump in my throat. Poor kitty was lonely and not used to me leaving in the evenings as often as I had been lately so I'd tossed around the idea of getting another cat.

The tabby with the white paws came to mind because it'd drive Brett wild. And if I loved to do anything, it was that.

"I know." I capped the mascara, secured it back in the organizer bin, and selected a shade of matte, burgundy lipstick. I chose to shove the memories away and focus on tonight, starting with a positive attitude. "It was risky to put it all out there like that. He doesn't know I'm cursed, and he never will, everything is fine. Besides, he's not the only one who can pop a quiz. And guess what? He passed with flying colors." With my lips in a pout, I carefully pressed down the smooth lipstick and buried my natural shade with the red tint. I'd forgotten Brett wasn't around much the past couple of years when I made it clear I was Belle V.'s granddaughter after years of my mom's attempts to severe our relation from her. Only the older residents remembered, and after her passing, nobody cared to think about it anymore. It made sense Brett didn't know, but I never intended to keep it a secret.

The flicker of Philip's tail caught the corner of my eye as he dipped his back and stretched. A moment later, the rip of claws in carpet forced my hand. I spun the lipstick back into its tube and swatted at him.

"Stop that!"

Philip darted away, too quick for me. I sighed and shoved the makeup drawer back under my bed. The tacks jammed into the mirror's wooden frame stored dozens of choker necklaces and longer chains with charms of bats or a woman's skeletal silhouette. I selected the one with a silver chain designed to look like a long snake curled around my neck. Brett would get a kick out of it.

We'd shared another date at the diner where we'd agreed to strictly speak books. Thankfully, it'd passed uneventfully—just two adults sharing a meal where townsfolk could witness it. I'd wanted to dig deeper and offer consolation for his mother's passing, but I'd stuck to the rules of the evening: no politics talk and no mentioning any genres other than the classics. It kept us in check without any risk of a fight where curious eyes and eavesdropping ears had pointed in our direction. Unfortunately, it also restricted my ability to connect with him, even on a fake level, and try to pique his interest in me.

I stood and swung open the pantry door. The loft was small, even for one person, but I made do using the kitchen cabinet for my folded clothes and the counter as storage for half-empty pasta boxes and pumpkin-spice flavored oatmeal packets.

The weather dipped into cooler temperatures, so I slid the shorter skirts aside and reached in the back of the pantry for the ankle-length lace skirt.

I slipped my legs between the lace and paired it with a hooded, black sweater. Finally, I topped the outfit off with a matching corset around my midsection to tighten the look. After checking my reflection across the room, twisting my torso to see my back and ensure all the hooks were connected on the corset, I descended the spiral staircase.

If it didn't make me feel like a heroine in a gothic romance, I'd have the staircase redesigned to save space in the shop.

"Bye, Philip!" I dodged around stacks of books and darted out the door.

Apple cinnamon scent filled the air from the homemade bread Loxley's mom always provided at the Harvest. Tables, hay bales, and a small stage packed the parking lot and spilled into Sherwood Forest where Katrina had designed an adult scavenger hunt among the trees. Booths offered pumpkin carving contests for kids and bowls of candy sat out ready to award the cleverest children who offered small tricks and jokes.

I spied Loxley sitting on a bale of hay in front of the makeshift stage. She cradled Robin and nursed. The dark rings under her eyes had lightened since I'd last seen her.

"It's a shame your built-in Halloween mask is gone," I said, as I took a seat next to her.

Loxley groaned. "Robin hates it when I feed her with the tent thing on."

"Tear it off. If people are offended by a hungry baby, then I have a boot ready for their butt."

After a quick laugh, Loxley changed the subject. "I need to talk about something other than motherhood. How's the, you know, deal going?" She raised her free hand and twitched her fingers in air quotes.

"Honestly, not bad if I pretend he's isn't a jerk who hates my favorite books."

"Your text said he's a Phantom fan. A fan-tom. Ha! Get it?" Loxley snorted at her own joke, then trailed off and her shoulders slumped. "Oh man, I'm tired. What's on the agenda tonight?"

I sucked in a delicious sniff of apple bread when Bones walked past with a paper plate heaped three steaming slices high. Loxley's mom always saved a loaf made with her vegan recipe for me.

"Well." I exhaled. "I swear he likes it when I argue with him, so I was thinking about drinking him under the table at the adult scavenger hunt, then bringing up his nickname. It's his favorite subject to hate."

"Doesn't he know you're a fan of beastly men?"

"Fictional beastly men," I corrected. "If I didn't know better, I'd think you wanted me to like him."

Loxley shrugged and finally yanked the breastfeeding blanket off her shoulder. She crumpled it into a ball and set it on the bale of hay next to her thigh. "Call it motherhood intuition, but I'm sensing you'd be a good couple."

I lifted my brows, exaggerating my bugged-out eyes. "Do tell."

Another shrug followed a yawn and a shake of her head. "He's quiet, lives in the house you love, you both hate your moms, and I swear he was checking you out in the picture Patty posted."

I'd admitted too much. Loxley couldn't possibly be getting attached to the idea of me and my fake boyfriend. "I was sitting on his shoulders," I said, voice flat.

The wrinkles in her shirt remained as she tugged it back down over her torso and shifted Robin into prime baby-burping position. "It was the look in his eyes. Gideon gets the same hungry expression whenever I touch him, much less cup his neck with my thighs."

I shook my head. The Great Cat Rescue of September felt like months ago. Fake dating takes a toll on a girl's schedule. Everything I planned revolved around public appearances and moments stolen where I forced myself to flirt. It fell flat most of the time. I wanted real. I wanted to tell him how much I hated him for insulting my choice of romance reads. I wanted to piss him off enough to slam the door and pin me against the wall at Villenueve Manor with his stare again.

But wants took a backseat to needs, and I *needed* him to like me enough to break the curse. That required a private burial of flaws that included, but was not limited to, laziness, college dropout, failed family relationships, and an unhealthy belief in the unexplained.

The stiff straw poked through the thin lace and wispy slip underneath my skirt. I shifted to lean on one butt cheek, but nothing made a hay bale comfortable. As much as I wanted to sit and chat with the exhausted new mother, I couldn't stand her choice of seating for much longer.

"Bella!" A deep, demanding voice cut through the laughter of kids trading jokes for candy at the treat booths.

Saved by the Brett.

I stood and whirled around, enjoying the flow of my long skirt. His hulking figure stuck out like the tree in the cemetery where the next tallest object was the short, iron fence.

"Walk with me," he said with a sharp nod of his head. I said goodbye to Loxley, who clucked her tongue at me, and followed him past the rows of pumpkins waiting to be gutted.

Brett stalked to the edge of the kid-friendly festival where Katrina sat on a stool near the forest.

"Chip just called me." He spoke in a hushed tone, and I enjoyed the intimacy of our proximity. His hunched frame hung over me like the curve of tree branches. Apparently, my brain thought Brett was part of Sherwood Forest tonight.

"It's bad," he continued.

"What is?" My heart skipped a beat. Did he find out about the curse? I wouldn't put it past Chip to do his background research on me, though small-town superstitions stayed clear of the internet thanks to my mom's cutoff of any mention years ago. Talk of the curse died with Grandma V., before social media pages existed, and I'd kept the family's fatal flaw close, only daring to share with safe friends.

"My ratings." He raked his fingers through his hair. I appreciated that it tugged loose the flattened style and allowed the waves to pull free from the gel prison. "Sheriff Gideon took a poll, and Max is still more popular."

The other candidate was the town's retired Sheriff—good guy, but unimpressive otherwise. Still, Folklore Falls favored good over anything else. Now Brett's insistence on honesty made sense.

"I..." He paused, and his Adam's Apple bobbed with a hard swallow. "I need help here. Any ideas? People know we're dating, don't they? Have we not been obvious enough?"

"Let's take it to the next level." At my suggestion, Brett froze his nervous movements. "I mean kissing. We haven't since the book sale, and we both know how that went." Yes, it was a sly way to get what I wanted but it'd satisfy both of us to share another kiss.

Katrina looked up from her phone, and I lowered my voice. "Can you do something romantic? Maybe if people see you being sweet to me, they'll feel like you're trustworthy."

"I am trustworthy. It needs to be bigger than that." Brett paced again, small steps back and forth across the dirt before whacking a low hanging branch to the side. It wasn't even in his way. When he paused, his scowl turned upside down. Was this Halloween or Christmas, because I swore I just saw the Grinch's grin? "What if people overhear us having a discussion about moving in together?"

"Ew, no. Way too much. We've only been pretending to date for a few weeks." I glanced at Katrina to make sure she hadn't heard my little outburst. *Note to self: just call it dating next time.* "Except you do live in my family's house, so it almost makes sense…"

Brett shot me glare that said 'not now.' With every second passing, the stress doubled on his face. His lips twisted down again and creases formed on his forehead. He wiped imaginary sweat from his brow and shook nothing off his hand.

"You're really stressed about this," I observed. "It's an unofficial survey."

"I'm competitive." With both hands behind his head, I enjoyed full view of his biceps. Except I found myself holding his gaze instead. Did I care that he was upset about this? I didn't want him to win and ruin Folklore Falls. My brain argued while my heart skipped a beat.

"It's more than that, isn't it?" I asked.

The flex of his jaw told me not to pry, but it relaxed as quickly as it had appeared. "I made a promise. It's a story for another time."

I nodded. I was the last person to blame him for keeping personal information to himself. "What about the Homecoming dance?" Folklore Falls celebrated the high school football game with a town-wide Homecoming dance hosted at the school. We'd even donated to rebuild the gym twice the size to fit everyone. Kids as young as seven attended while their parents shared slow dances and stole kisses. Brett probably thought it was childish for the adults to crash the high schoolers' dance every year, but it was quickly becoming a town tradition and a fun excuse for everyone to dress up. One of these years, I'd wear my Christine Daae dress as the crochet club encouraged, but I was still a long way from feeling ready to face that memory. Besides, it'd like need some alterations since then.

Brett exhaled, and his mouth curled into another smile, genuine this time. "That's perfect, Bella." He stopped pacing and faced me. "I'll do a prom proposal. It's perfect." The giddy laugh that came from him was almost cute. Gross and not my type, but also cute.

Before I could say 'ew,' he was on me, hand at the back of my head and mouth against mine. Instinctively, or maybe because I'd been dreaming about holding him for a while now, I wrapped my arms around his torso. The intensity of it sucked every bit of oxygen from my lungs and I soaked in the warmth of his hands cupping my head. But the kiss was so sudden and unexpected, even he was shocked and it ended too quickly, leaving us both breathless. When he pulled away, his lips were parted and his eyes scanned my face.

"Good," he said with a nod. "Okay. Got that out of the way." With that, he marched away, back toward the small stage. I awkwardly smiled at Katrina, then turned to follow.

Chip had arranged a little speech where Brett would make empty promises, but Max had already taken the microphone.

"A vote for the former sheriff is a safe vote!" Max announced.

Loxley's mom took the microphone after he finished and directed everyone twelve years old and under to meet her by the pumpkins. I almost followed, in a daze after the kiss that held more passion than I had the breath for. People could accuse Brett of a lot of things, but lacking in passion wasn't one of them.

I scanned the festival for Brett, but he'd vanished. Not even the tents over the booths could hide him.

After chatting with Patty, taking two hundred pictures of Gideon and his daughter at his insistence, and grabbing a slice of vegan apple bread, I checked the time. According to my phone, an hour had passed since Brett left. Why didn't he borrow the microphone and ask me before people split off into the scavenger hunt?

The simple suggestion suddenly left me feeling antsy. What could he possibly plan on the spot? And for his fake girlfriend? Was it still truly fake after a kiss as real as that? I brushed my thumb over my lips as if that could seal the memory of his mouth on mine.

After a breath, I straightened and headed for the pumpkin carving to vote on the kids' designs. The cat face won my checkmark. Next, I found Bones mixing drinks at his booth.

He poured my order without me saying a word. The neat whiskey burned my throat, but I relished another sip.

"So, you and the Beast?" he said, as he shook a mixer bottle. The ice clattered around inside. I leaned close so I didn't need to shout for him to hear me.

"Maybe don't call him that," I said.

Bones laughed. "Right. What's the catch?"

Uh oh. "There's no catch."

"You don't date anyone, much less pricks like him." He handed the margarita to a mom who'd sent her kids off to the candy tables. To show appreciation, she dropped a few dollars into the plastic pumpkin at the edge of his table.

"Nice tip jar."

"Don't change the subject," he said, tossing an empty bottle of red wine into a plastic bin behind the table. He leaned on the table with both elbows and locked on my gaze. "You've hated Brett for as long as I've been in love with Katrina. What gives?"

I shook my head and stole a sip of the spiced alcohol. "He's more like me than I thought." It wasn't a lie, Brett would be proud. "I heard Katrina dumped the mechanic."

Bones nodded, beaming. *You're welcome for keeping the curse at bay.* He glanced at Sherwood Forest and dropped his voice to a hoarse whisper. "I think I'm going to do it. I'm going to ask her out. Officially this time."

I rolled my eyes. I'd believe it when I saw it. At least it got his brain off Brett and the relationship I didn't want to lie about.

A loud announcement drowned out Bones's next words. Brett's voice boomed over the microphone, drawing all eyes and ears to the stage other than the kids busy counting the candy in their baskets.

"I had a quick speech planned for tonight," he said. Someone booed, and I swore I saw him wince. A fire lit within me, and I wanted to throw my cup at whoever'd dared to be so rude. Brett took a moment to breathe—the only sound was the kids' conversation now. Brett didn't enunciate or address the crowd with his eyes sweeping over everyone. Good thing he'd opted out of the speech because he sucked at it. "Instead of shouting at you to vote for me," he paused to let that sink in. It was exactly the strategy Max had employed only a couple hours earlier. "I decided to speak from the heart."

So, he *did* have a heart.

"Bella," he said.

If blood could freeze, mine turned to ice. *Terrible timing, don't think about blood.* I knew he planned to do this, so why did embarrassment suddenly arrest me? My heart thudded in response, but it was my brain that knew the truth. I wasn't embarrassed, I was nervous.

At some point between the deal and tonight, I'd subconsciously, and without my permission, decided I *wanted* to do real couple things like stupid prom proposals with Brett Jensen. Or was it before that? I'd never let myself consider a date with him when we were teenagers. I'd needed people to like me, and that was an impossible feat for anyone dating the Beast at the time.

"She remembers, as well as everyone else I'm sure, how I pranked the Homecoming dance during our graduating year."

A few groans scattered across the crowd. Where was he going with this? I half-expected Chip to launch onto the stage like a sideways torpedo and take Brett to the ground, microphone and all. Why remind people about his past?

"I know, I regret it now. But not as much as I regret missing my chance to do this seven years ago." He produced a limp looking flower from behind his back. "Will you be my date, Bella?"

Clapping echoed from the back, and I guessed it was Katrina. I couldn't move, couldn't breathe. Brett paralyzed me with his gaze. He didn't lie. Did that mean his little confession was the truth?

"What's the catch?" Bones whispered from behind me.

It was then I realized the silence came from everyone waiting for my answer.

I forced myself to walk to the stage. Closer now, I could see it wasn't a flower at all—not a real one. Pages of a book were folded into the shape of a rose, but it was flattened on one side, and the plastic stem was creased in several places.

I furrowed my brow and looked up at him. Brett stepped off the stage, and for the first time, we shared a kiss that wasn't forced or sudden. I leaned into him as much as was appropriate for a family-friendly event, but I wanted to soak up the warmth of his body and pull him back when the kiss ended.

People didn't exactly cheer, but a few ladies clapped before everyone returned to their activities.

"Where did you get this?" I held up the origami flower.

"Uh," he stuttered and looked around, suddenly interested in every-thing else. "Where's Chip? I need to make sure he doesn't have my head for skipping the speech."

"Brett. The flower?"

He waved his hand, brushing the question off. "I've had it a long time."

Was the story in your speech true? I meant to ask the question out loud, but when I opened my mouth Chip interrupted me.

The guys discussed the public display of affection for a few seconds before shifting gears to prepare for next week's townhall meeting.

A million thoughts clouded my attention from their conversation. I rolled the crumpled stem between my thumb and forefinger and watched the rose spin side-to-side.

Could I have dated Brett in high school and broken the curse long before it threatened me with bad luck? And more importantly, did he have feelings for me then… and now?

Twenty

BRETT

Before a dance could take place, the townspeople had to prepare which meant a lot of cleaning, decorating, and plenty of heavy lifting at Folklore Falls's High School. On my morning run, I pushed myself to make it out to town which had me passing the campus. The crochet club full of older ladies carried tablecloths, and handsewn napkins to the school's gymnasium, likely a quick decorating run before school started for the day. I raised my hand to wave as I jogged by but they either didn't hear me or didn't like me.

I should have worried considering my political career hung in the balance. Despite the ladies' cold shoulder, everything felt right. I'd finally gotten the guts to do what I couldn't all those years ago: I'd asked Bella Villenueve to accompany me to the dance.

The crisp air helped me clear my head after the big promposal, so I resorted to outdoor runs every day since the Halloween Harvest. A breeze tossed my hair and the smell of cinnamon wafted from Sherwood Bed and Breakfast as I rounded the corner and made my way into town. My calves burned from the workout and I loved the energy it ignited in me.

I took a breath and jogged right up to the front door at Bella's Bookstore. The bell chimed its friendly greeting as I pushed through.

The cheerful sound provided the perfect contrast from Bella's glare as she looked up, peering through a curtain of black bangs.

"Brett, hey," she said, straightening on the stool. The glow from her phone brightened the dark corner of her desk, shadowed by a large stack of boxes with new books. "I was just about to text you."

"Oh yeah?" I caught my breath and wiped the sweat from my brow. For now, I kept distance between us in case the exercise left me smelling unpleasant.

Maroon lips twisted into a grimace, like a bloody half-moon on her face. No matter what Bella did I couldn't keep my eyes from her. Apparently, I hadn't been capable of keeping my hands and mouth to myself before the promposal at the harvest either. The sudden kiss plagued me because it was too fast, too public, and too passionate on my side since I couldn't confirm if she'd felt the same.

A candle flickered beside her on the desktop, emanating the scent of bourbon and apples. The dancing light highlighted her frown but before I could worry, she filled me in.

"Has Chip told you that people aren't impressed by the grand gesture?" she asked. "You know?" When she tilted her head, my gaze followed, landing to the paper rose I'd made her all those years ago, but only given her recently. With her silky, thick hair falling to the side I could have sworn I was looking at a black waterfall.

Again, I expected to be worried, disappointed, upset, maybe angry. But nothing came. Instead, I wondered only one thing. Was *she* impressed by it? If I wasn't so sweaty, I'd step up to the desk and lean across, pulling her face toward mine. I'd kiss her in the privacy of the empty, just-opened bookshop surrounded by many of our favorite authors. I'd dig my fingers in her smooth hair while she'd snaked her arms around my neck. I'd…

I'd do that if we were in a relationship. Which we weren't. I swallowed and shook my head, finally answering her question. "I noticed the crochet club ignored me this morning. How—" I cleared my throat. "How did you know?"

"Patty," she confirmed my suspicions. "She came into the shop yesterday after having lunch with Chip. I guess the women liked it, which means their husbands will think you're making them look bad. I don't know, it was a whole thing she rambled on about. I bet Chip could explain it better and without Patty's opinions tacked on. Basically, you look less trustworthy as a candidate to the husbands in town than you did before."

I laughed. "Huh, maybe I should be the one writing those romances."

Bella's eyes rolled back so far into her head I thought they'd stick there. And she'd still be intoxicatingly gorgeous.

"I'm kidding," I said, daring to take a step closer to the desk. "I'm not—" I shook my head. How could I have dissed on those books so hard when I'd just pulled a romantic stunt, one I'd fantasized about for years for the girl I couldn't get off my mind? I was a massive hypocrite, but now wasn't the time to talk genres. "I'll call Chip." I said so she'd know I heard, and believed her.

"Actually." She swung her hip around the edge of the desk and squeezed between the boxes. "I have an idea." Pumpkin and vanilla scents filled my nose as the smell drifted from her hair. She pointed to a post on the town's social media page. "The PTA put out a call for help about the dance. I'm going to close up early this afternoon and decorate with them. If you join me, do some heavy lifting, and make yourself seem charitable, I think it could really turn things around."

As much as I wanted to spend the afternoon with her, and at the site of the dance I'd wanted to take her to all those years ago, I couldn't see her point. "Won't the husbands hate me more if I go above and beyond to help their wives?"

"You'd think." Bella poked her fingernail into the air. A silver gem sat at the tip of the crescent moon painting on the acrylic nail and caught the light from the candle. "But they hate decorating for this thing every year. Trust me, if you did most of their work, they'll be thanking you."

"I'm in." I nodded.

"It's a date," she said with a half-smile and I wondered what kind of date she meant. Real or fake?

I mulled over the question as I paced around back at the house.

After killing time with two showers, lunch, and a call to let Chip know my plans, I was left emptyhanded. For the next hour, my life had slowed, forcing me to pay attention to the house I hated.

My footsteps echoed through the long halls. I paused at the door to the ballroom and twisted the handle. The giant room came with a musty, unused smell where it was once filled with life—though just as stuffy. The political parties my parents threw always had multiple ulterior motives rather than simply sharing a good time. The ballroom came with dozens of moments I'd rather forget. If I didn't tear down this house, this room had to change.

After years of boisterous voices and speeches and stuffy music, it deserved a quiet atmosphere. I closed the door and blew out a breath, cleansing my lungs of the dust and antique smell. What memories did Bella have here, if any? What would she change the ballroom into?

I knew the answer but led the thought slip away. Before I knew it, my phone was buzzing with a timer reminder to arrive as soon as school released and the gym would open for volunteers to get to work.

I silenced the reminder and headed for my car. Never had I thought I'd get the chance to drive to Folklore Falls High School for a date with Bella Villenueve again. I'd blown it years ago, by never getting the guts to try. Maybe my mother deserved thanks for inadvertently pushing me back here.

I whistled a ballroom dancing song since the only lyrics I remembered were about a tale and something as old as time. With a skip in my step I marched to the new building designed for the townwide dance and swung the door opening, expecting to see the crochet club, the PTA, and definitely a girl in black boots.

After scanning the room, I spotted Bella with the group of older women. They looked to be in a serious discussion about lacy doilies. Once I drew closer, I realized the sewing debate centered around a dress rather than decorative linens.

"Bella," I greeted her with a nod and tried to smile for the crochet club. They snubbed me with their wrinkled noses in the air.

One woman reached out and gripped Bella's forearm. "I want to see that dress this year. You can't keep it hidden anymore. It's famous in our circle now."

Bella forced a laugh and shook her head as they disbanded, distracted by some new dilemma relating to the dance this time.

"You're early," I said.

"I'm learning from the best," she joked, jabbing me in the ribs with her elbow. It felt like we were a couple for the first time—at ease, casual, teasing without venom. A tension tightened in my chest as I waited for the other shoe to drop. She wasn't my girlfriend, not really, and, as far as I knew, every bit of this was fake.

"What's this infamous dress I heard about?" I nodded toward the crochet club as they squabbled about the font on a banner that said *Third Annual Folklore Falls Homecoming Dance*. The high school had been around much longer, but the townwide dance was new.

"Oh, it's nothing."

"Doesn't sound like it." I prodded, wanting Bella to know she could talk to me. Plus, I was curious about her life. What else did she like besides cats, vegan burgers, and books? If she'd let me dig deeper, I would take the opportunity. Of course, I'd been rash before, grabbing her and kissing her at the Halloween Harvest. It was smarter to take things slowly so I could linger in the moments and relish this non-relationship longer. I flinched at the phrase.

"I used to sew literature-inspired dresses a long time ago but I stopped. It's dumb." She shook her head and I wanted to tell her that the only dumb thing around here was our fake dating when it could be real. But I still had a campaign to run and a promise to keep. If I didn't do everything I could to win the election, I'd never forgive myself for letting my mother down even beyond the grave.

I couldn't risk our deal by letting something as trivial as feelings interfere with the agreement. If Bella didn't feel the same, it could drive her away and now, I didn't know if I had the venom in me to hold the house as a threat over her head.

"Anyway." She whipped around and pointed to a stack of folding tables against the wall. "We need to line those up on the back wall and clean each one. Then—"

"What is *he* doing here?" Blonde hair caught the corner of my eye. Both Bella and I looked in the direction of the irritated voice.

Stacy and the brunette I'd dated stood with their arms crossed and each jutted out a hip in a dangerously Desperate Housewives stance—a show I only knew because a college buddy of mine had claimed he had a one night stand with one of the actresses.

"Oh, hell no," the brunette said. They marched up to us, heels clicking from one and the tap of tennis-shoes from the other. "Bella, please tell me you were dared into this or lost a bet?"

Bella glanced between us, likely gathering the information that these ladies definitely didn't plan to vote for me along with the husbands I'd annoyed at the Halloween Harvest.

"We're dating," she clarified. The crochet club had abandoned their disagreement about the banner and shifted their interest toward us.

"Everybody knows after that sickening display of attention at the festival," Stacy spoke now, loud enough for the whole room to hear. Teachers who stayed after classes to help set up, some I even remembered from my high school days, looked up from their jobs. A few men, likely the husbands who were sick of decorating every year also paused at the shrill sound of the school board director's voice.

"Seriously," the brunette agreed. "Were you not getting enough attention, Brett? You had to make up a ridiculous, sappy proposal so all eyes were on you again, huh?"

"Look, I'm here to help." I raised my hand and though I wanted to shove the women out of my way and storm out, I resisted, instead holding it up in a surrendering gesture.

"We don't need your help," Stacy said. "You're not taking my baby and turning it into the Brett Jensen Show. This dance is my favorite time of year and I take pride in how much joy it gives everyone in town."

A member of the crochet club scoffed then piped up. "All I know is that Little Boy Brett used to tear up my garden with his bike tires."

Instead of the normal burn of anger in my chest, my temper took a backseat to fear. The truth only stripped my chances of making this thing with Bella real and, really, it was a joke to ever think I could.

I cringed and hung my head, refusing to meet her gaze. From the corner of my eye, I saw her looking from the accusers back to me. If nothing else, their words would serve as the most blatant reminder why this relationship was still fake—Bella loved this town and its people, and they didn't like me.

"He crashed his car into my fence years ago and didn't bother to fix it much less say he's sorry!" Another older woman chimed in.

"Well, of course, Pearl." the brunette turned to nod at the older woman. "Brett only does whatever serves Brett."

"I don't need your sullied name attached to my event." Stacy pointed to the double doors behind me where an exit sign glowed green. "You can see yourself out. Now."

"Wait." Bella stepped forward as if the angry mob was ready with their pitchforks. I'd say the words hurt like pitchforks, except they were true and I deserved to bear the pain of embarrassment in front of her. "He's telling the truth. Brett wants to help. And look he can do all the heavy lifting." She tried to lighten the mood by grabbing my bicep with one hand and pointing to it with the other.

It only made the men in the back grumble.

"The Homecoming isn't an event Brett can take over with his political aspirations," Stacy said. "The only thing he's welcome to do is leave."

Bella paused for a moment, the quiet patience holding everyone's attention. I fiercely admired her ability to stay calm.

"Okay," she said. "You're right."

My chest stung as if Bella had unsheathed a knife and stabbed it right between my ribcage. Could I blame her? Did I deserve her? I couldn't answer that. I'd insulted her books, used her for political gain, and fought with her over and over.

"Brett does a lot of events and appearances to advance his career. But isn't that what this event does for you, Stacy? It paints you in the best light so all the parents appreciate the work you do at the school."

Stacy's jaw dropped but Bella kept going, interrupting whatever the school board director had ready to fire back at us.

"We're all a little selfish with our jobs and aspirations but Brett isn't the bully he used to be." When she glanced at me this time, I met her gaze. She offered a half-smile, rarely ever fully grinning, it just wasn't her style. Or mine. "He's actually…" Her gaze trailed my face as her expression softened. "He's kind. I never would have believed it from the guy who set snakes loose at our Homecoming dance, but it's true."

Bella's eyes narrowed as she read me. Something between relief and warmth flooded me. She didn't hate me like they did. In fact, she didn't even believe them.

"Snakes?" A crochet club woman squealed.

Stacy shook her head. "Nope. Nuh-uh, that's it." She waved her hand toward the door again. "You're out."

"Stacy—" Bella started.

"We'd love to have your help, Bell, but Brett doesn't have the track record we're looking for." She held Bella's hands as she said this but Bella pulled away.

I'd heard enough. I turned and stalked toward the door, only pausing for a moment at the sound of her voice.

"He's my boyfriend, couldn't he be a plus-one on the volunteer list?"

But the setup mob had already made up their minds with Stacy at the helm of the ship. She denied Bella's request once again and the next thing I heard was heavy boots stomping after me before the door swung shut.

"I'm sorry," Bella said, voice echoing from behind me.

I didn't stop in the center quad by the flagpole and instead, made my way to the edge of campus where the older buildings were. I recognized the Main Hall, where cases stored school trophies and displayed pictures.

Black hair caught the sunlight, shiny and smooth as it cascaded around her. Bella dodged in front of me, holding up her hands.

"I swear I had no idea they were going to do that."

Normally, I'd fold my arms but I didn't want to put more distance between Bella and I.

"They really don't like your *boyfriend*," I emphasized the title to see how she'd react. Did she see me as her partner? Her other half? If I squinted, I could see the pictures displayed in the glass case in the Main Hall, one with Bella, Loxley, and Bones at the dance before I had overrun it with reptiles. Loxley beamed a perfect grin while Bella glared at the camera and Bones looked goofy with a sideways smile.

I refocused to the Bella that stood before me, here and now. Did I have a chance to change what I'd ruined? Her bangs had overgrown lately, catching in her eyelashes now. I reached out to brush the hair from her eyes but, confused, she waved my hand away.

"Well, yeah, that's the deal."

The deal. Not a relationship, a deal, and nothing more. Who the hell was I kidding? I'd punched the guy who actually took Bella to the Homecoming dance for parking too close to my car. Bones had lost a tooth because of my fist, forever ruining Bella's Homecoming pictures. The guy looked like a seven-year-old wishing for his two front teeth for Christmas.

"Thanks for trying." I meant it. She'd called me kind and I could have sworn the hint of a smile on her face was proof she meant it, too. Right now, I wanted to get home, change into sweats, and go for for an evening run before it got dark. The clear air and movement would help me focus on the promise and campaign instead of wishful thoughts about Bella and our stupid, fake relationship. Besides, the more time I spent around her, the most I wanted to kiss her and cross the line from pretend boyfriend to real.

"Where are you going?" she asked, as I clicked the unlock button on my car. It beeped, signaling my time of departure.

"Home," I said. "I can't stay here."

"This is as much your Alma Mater as it is Stacy's." Bella tilted her head toward the Main Hall. "Come on, your snakes are immortalized here. Wanna see?"

I groaned. *Not really.* But Bella slipped her fingers through mine and gently squeezed my hand to pull me along. I couldn't resist.

As with everything else in this town, it wasn't locked. She opened the door to the Main Hall and tugged me inside. The glass cases held hundreds of memories. Many faces I didn't recognize until we made our way down to the spot I'd spied through the window, our graduating class.

"Right there." Bella pointed to a picture of her holding a snake coiled around her neck. She wore the reptile like a live necklace, fearless and statuesque, an icon among the hundreds of pictures pasted against the poster boards of guys in suits and girls in colorful dresses. I'd never seen this version of Bella's night at the Homecoming dance. "I wanted to adopt him but animal control wouldn't let me. Not to mention my mom didn't—" Bella stopped short with a gasp. "Shoot! I was supposed to call my mom today and cancel our dinner."

She danced around, digging her phone out of the skull-shaped purse that hung from her shoulder. After furiously tapping, she put the phone to her ear and paced half the length of the hall. The stress-marching was another behavior we shared and I didn't mind the view of watching her hips swing back and forth as she stomped along in the thick-soled boots, though I didn't like the worried expression on her face. Moments ago, Bella comforted me, now I wanted to return the favor but didn't have a clue how to help.

"Yes," she said, pinching the ear that didn't have a phone against it. "I know I'm late. I was helping—" she sighed. "Never mind. I'll be there in twenty."

Once she tapped the screen and shoved the phone into her purse, Bella met my gaze. "I have to go."

"What's wrong?"

She waved her hand dismissing me at first, then paused to eye me. I hoped the sincerity shown through. I hadn't cared for a lot of other people before and lacked practice in helping others, but I wanted to try —to change that.

For a moment, I thought she'd reach for my hand again where I'd feel her fingers intertwine with mine but she only nodded. The view of her hair slipping over her bare shoulders not covered by the black tank top distracted. I should run my fingertips up her arms until I cup her chin and pull her in.

I blinked. *A deal, not a relationship.* I shouldn't kiss her.

"My mom isn't my biggest fan," she said, shuffling with her purse.

I'd never seen Bella rattled before. Her calm, icy, intense demeanor always enchanted me, but I didn't dismiss her worry either. This only made me want to help her get back to herself. "And I'm not a fan of having dinner with her. These *dinner* meetups always have an ulterior motive." She curled her fingers into air quotes and rolled her eyes.

"Want me to come with you?" I'd said it before I could stop myself. It was the offer of a true boyfriend, not the fake, and I didn't want her to feel pressured or get the wrong idea. If I showed my feelings now and she rejected me, before the deal was done, it'd wreck everything. I raked my fingers through my hair, unsure of what to do until she responded.

"My mom is the worst. Are you sure?"

"Shoulder to cry on?" I offered, patting my shoulder with less force than I had in the cemetery. I could be that guy for her. If Bella could stand up for me in the face of the PTA mob, I could learn how to comfort.

To my surprise, she nodded. "Why not?"

If our deal, was just that, nothing more, than dinner with her mom had to count as above and beyond.

"Consider me your personal shoulder guy."

Corny. I cringed but her eyebrow peaked, a signature expression I'd learned as Bella's version of a grin. Seeing Folklore Falls alongside Bella had the town seeping under my skin with cheesy phrases like that. And maybe if she liked the corny line, she wouldn't mind a sappy kiss either, but I didn't dare take advantage of her stress. I wasn't that guy. Not anymore.

Instead of waiting, I grabbed her hand this time. The evening plans gave me all the excuses I needed to play up the boyfriend card—hopefully removing *fake* from the title.

Twenty-One

BELLA

Why did he offer to come with me? And when did I start thinking he was kind? Everything about the evening threw me off kilter. Brett held my hand in the car, where not a single soul could see us.

A million thoughts swirled in my head and with every minute that passed the fight or flight response built. My heart raced faster as I directed him to my mom's house just outside of town. I wanted to squeeze his fingers and tell him to whip the car around. We go to Fryer Tuck's or enjoy a drink at Knight's Tavern, anything but dinner with my mom.

I watched his eyes scan the road as he drove in the dusk. The sun had dipped below the horizon and my favorite time of day began. Brett's five o' clock shadow darkened his jawline. I wanted to feel the sandpaper roughness against my skin but to touch it meant I'd have to unlink our hands.

We pulled into my mom's driveway and the house, though not a mansion like Villenueve Manor, was big, modern, and sleek. It was exactly the hideous architecture style Brett had wanted to modernize Folklore Falls with. I observed the slight raise of his brow as we drove closer.

"Fancy, right?" I said what we were both thinking.

Instead of agreeing, Brett pulled the car into park and looked at me with a quiet gaze. After a few moments of thought, he narrowed his eyes. "You think it's hideous, don't you?"

I laughed. "You know me."

Did he? Know me, that was? We'd been dating—faking—for several weeks now. How well did Brett Jensen really know me? He'd agreed to this deal because I'd achieved one thing in my life, a persona. I'd led everyone in town, including him, into believing I was a worthwhile person, friend, and confidante. And maybe I helped a few people here and there, but I'd never outrun my failures.

A shiver stole down my back and I immediately blamed the fear that he'd find out the truth about me. Instead, I realized it came from his touch. Brett reached across the center divider and brushed away the hair caught in my eyelashes.

It was tender, proof of his kindness that I'd defended in front of Stacy and the crew at the high school. I couldn't blame them, it was hard to see Brett inside the Beast without time and patience. And if I had anything, it was patience.

When I didn't pull away, he let his fingertip fall from my temple and trace down the side of my face. A question hung in the air between us. *Will you kiss me?* Or was it, *is this real?*

I swallowed and chewed the inside of my lip. It took everything I had not to lean into him, to return the passion he'd kissed me with after the promposal. I wanted to feel the angle of his jaw in my hand and the pressure of his palm against the back of my neck.

He leaned closer.

But a kiss in the privacy of my mom's driveway didn't fit with our deal. And if the curse was still out there, hovering, waiting to drag me down into the bad luck ditches, I couldn't risk letting my feelings twist the relationship.

The heat of his breath warmed my neck.

I needed him to love me, but if I loved him it'd complicate everything.

His hand slipped behind my head and gently pulled me toward him.

Still, that didn't mean we couldn't kiss.

My eyelids fell and lips parted.

It only meant Loxley would have to pick up the pieces once the fake relationship inevitably ended, because guys like Brett didn't like Folklore Falls bookstore owners like me, right?

I angled my head back and melted into him. But the kiss lasted seconds, if it could be called that. The brush of his lips yanked back when the porchlight flooded us.

We both snapped back to our respective seats to see my mom standing before us. She squinted at the brightness, not able to fully see us.

"Bella?"

I forced a weird smile at Brett in a silent apology as I felt like a teenager again. The sound of her tone sent me right back to childhood where I inwardly recoiled, ready to curl up with a book as a defense mechanism against my mom's judmental jabs.

We emerged from the car.

"Interesting." Mom placed her hands on her hips and nodded. "Just the man I wanted to talk about. Come inside. You look bony, Bella, time to put meat on that skeleton."

"I don't eat meat, Mom." I groaned.

"You will tonight, I don't care for pickiness." She ignored my wishes, as always.

I shot Brett another apologetic look then trailed after my mom. The winding maze of the hall was filled with frames holding her certificates, accomplishments, and pictures of her at charitable events run by the hospital. Not a single frame displayed a photo of her daughter and it seemed Brett noticed. He furrowed his brow, taking in his surroundings then met my gaze.

As usual, my mom overdid the dinner with too much gourmet food, and none of it vegan, even the vegetables were covered in butter. That was something she did enjoy displaying, her wealth.

"Be my guest," mom said, as she pointed for Brett to sit in an empty chair far away from her end of the long table. But Brett wasn't one to be bossed around, so he took the seat beside me and sparked a frown from my mother.

"So." Mom clasped her fingers and rested them on the table like a true villain. "This is awkward."

Brett and I exchanged looks. "Nice to meet you, Mrs. Villenueve."

Mom pursed her lips together and gave me an annoyed, wide-eyed expression before directing her attention back to him. "It's Dr. Villenueve and that is what you may call me. As I was saying." She reached for a large knife and I wouldn't be surprised if she stabbed Brett with it. I couldn't deny she was where I'd gotten my moment of fire from in between the cold calmness. Instead, she dug the blade into a Cornish game hen on a silver platter in front of her. "This is awkward." She lifted a slice and dropped it on my plate. I frowned. "Not for me, of course. I don't care if Brett Jensen hears what I have to say." She curled her tongue around his name as if disgusted to say it.

"I'm not here for a lecture," I managed. I'd stand up to the bully of Folklore Falls, of course, he wasn't that anymore. But the point remained, nobody intimidated me, except the woman who birthed me. Our resemblance was the only proof I had that we were related, in every other way I couldn't see myself as Dr. Villenueve's daughter.

"That's fine." She dropped a slice of the poultry on Brett's plate too, a power move in my mother's language. "When one spends a full day at a real job, one rarely has the energy to lecture another."

I hated it when she spoke in 'ones'. If any time was the right time to grab Brett's hand, it was now. We'd run like hell and return to the missed kiss that I wanted but feared. The kiss my mom had ruined, like she everything else in my life from the dress to my love of cats. When would we get the chance to be alone again? I wanted to get there where Brett touched my cheek again and held my gaze, where I couldn't resist the part between his lips.

After serving herself, my mom scraped a second knife against her ceramic plate with a screech. I cringed at the sound but she continued, careless of how anyone else felt.

"You've wasted enough of your life with the cute, little bookstore, haven't you?"

Brett's head snapped up and he looked between us. I kept my gaze forward, not meeting either of their eyes. If I stared ahead, emotionless, I wouldn't give my mom the satisfaction of rattling me. And Brett, he didn't deserved to be dragged into this.

My mom was in a crueler mood than I'd anticipated when Brett'd made the offer to join me. I reached for the glass of water and tipped it to my lips.

"Anyway," she continued after slaughtering the slice of hen on her plate with another screeching drag of her knife. "I must implore you not to throw your personal life away as you have your professional one."

At that, I blinked and turned my head, meeting her glare-for-glare. "What does that mean?"

Mom raised her knife and jabbed it toward Brett. "Mr. Jensen here is a playboy. I'm aware you know this, yet you've seemed to misplace your better judgment. Honestly." She wagged the knife around, gesturing wildly as she chewed. If my mother didn't follow manners, it was a sure sign she'd lost her temper. "I didn't think you could waste any more of your life but I'd forgotten the personal side of it. Good thing I've hired a new doctor at the hospital whose single and success-ful. Great with diagnostics too." She took another bite, chewing long enough for me to cut in.

"You don't know anything about Brett." I glanced at him but before I could speak again, my mom had swallowed and cut me off.

"I'm hopeful that dating a doctor will remind you what you've sacrificed by choosing the easy life. It isn't too late to go back to college and get the degree you need to apply for medical school."

"I love my life!" I said with the whole truth and nothing but the truth so help me Grandma V. Lying didn't freak me out the way it did for Brett, but I didn't need to do it now, not anymore. "I didn't sacrifice anything."

Mom popped another cutlet of poultry in her cheek, but that didn't stop her from speaking over me. She wagged the fork back and forth. "Let's see, financial security, a decent living space, a true education, intelligence."

"Bella is one of the smartest people I've met," Brett said.

We both startled, looking at him speechless. I could only imagine how it felt to be the one stared at by two nearly-identical Villenueve women. Though, of course my mom dressed in pantsuits and minimal, plain makeup that she claimed as professional. We blinked at him, stunned for different reasons. I almost smiled and he returned it.

My heart warmed but the loud laugh that came from my mom snapped me back to reality.

"Did you know she spent half her life sewing dressed to match book characters?" She nodded as if confirming her own words and then took a sip of red wine. It looked like blood swirling in her glass and black spots dotted my vision. I snapped my eyes away from her cup and shifted my thoughts before I fainted face-first into the Cornish game hen.

"We're leaving." I shoved the chair back and stood. Brett followed, dropping the napkin onto his plate.

On our heels, my mom's heels clicked through the halls.

"I'm sick of watching you waste your life away, Isabelle!"

I clutched Brett's forearm and dragged him with me, eager to put as much distance between my mom and me as possible. When I looked back to reach for him, I didn't doubt he saw the tears in my eyes but it was too late to care. He was my shoulder guy, right? Could I allow myself to think that way about him?

I grabbed the doorknob and twisted, shoving through with the force of my body.

"Talk with me like a civil woman."

I scoffed and paused in front of Brett's car. His shadow cast over me as he stopped behind me. "Is she talking about the dress you mentioned earlier?"

I nodded but didn't turn around. Instead, I chewed my lip to keep from acting like a screaming teenager in front of Brett. Only my mom could reduce me to this level of immaturity.

"I've never seen you anything but confident before. Why do you let her get to you?" Brett's breath blew on the back of my neck as he spoke in low tones meant only for me to hear. I heard the tap of my mother's foot from the porch. "You stand up to me. Hell, you threatened to kill me if I didn't kiss you."

I brought my fist to my mouth covered my lips with my fingers. It wasn't appropriate to laugh right now. But the 'correct' behavior, dress, and manners were only constructs I worried about when around my mom.

As if reading my mind, Brett spoke again. "This isn't you. I know because we're the same, remember?"

I laughed, allowing the pent-up emotion to release a little. "I don't know why I still come here."

"Let the Beast out." His voice was gruffer now, tempting me to do as he'd said. But I'd never stood up to my mother, not directly. How long had I let her talk down to me? The dress in my closet haunted me, an unworn, missed memory of me being myself all because of her. And I was killer at sewing, the Christine Daae dress deserved to see the light of day.

I spun around and stepped from Brett's protective block between us. I didn't stop there. Marching up the steps in my heavy boots was as good as a shot of liquid courage. My mom didn't move, and I met her eye-for-eye.

"You can't stand that I love my life because you hate yours. You don't want me to love myself because you hate yourself." Her jaw dropped but I kept going, undeterred by the twist in her shocked scowl. "You claim that you save lives but I know why you really became a doctor. You're no different than your gold-digging great grandmother, and that's the real curse." I turned on my heel and plopping down the steps one-by-one, no longer in a hurry to hide from her.

Shock left her silent until I'd almost reached Brett again.

"Break up with him, Isabelle. This relationship is embarrassing."

"Good thing it's fake!" I shouted without giving her the satisfaction of turning around.

"What's that supposed to mean?" My mom stomped down the steps, voice shaking with anger.

I continued to the passenger door, but paused as I met Brett's gaze across the top of the car. Hurt riddled his expression as evident by his wrinkled brow. I didn't say anything other than the truth, but somehow it felt different between us when we got into the car.

A tense silence hunge between us as he revved the engine. Before we could drive off, my mom disappeared into the house, refusing to let me have the last word.

I reached for his hand to hold across the center console again. He didn't pull away and allowed me to slip my fingers between his but something felt different.

I tried to push the worry away and enjoy the moment of courage I'd had after facing my mother for the first time. For now, I'd revel in the woman Brett inspired me to be—which was really just myself.

Twenty-Two

BRETT

Rapid heartbeat and the nausea that accompanied nerves felt foreign to me. The townhall meeting gave both candidates the opportunity for an informal debate and to answer voters' questions. Still, the tension knotting my muscles and tricking my heart into skipping beats didn't steam from the upcoming campaign speech.

Bella's declaration messed with my head. I wanted all of her, but the relationship was nothing but a ruse from her side and I didn't have the energy to hash it out until after the debate. The more I thought about it, the more faking felt like lying, and lying prickled my skin.

I flicked the blinker on and pulled off the highway toward the town. A drive cleared my head and allowed me to consider possible questions. *How will you address the pot holes on the neighborhood roads? If crime worsens again, do you have a plan to attack it?*

Dirt kicked up and settled on my windshield as I pulled into park. These questions didn't drive my nerves, but the unexpected deviation from my plan did.

I raked my fingers over my scalp, then snapped the visor down to check my hair in the mirror. Bella was a wild card. I never expected to think twice about her after I graduated and left Folklore Falls, much less feel matched with her.

The fact that we both enjoyed classic books was surface level, and I'd thought our similarities ended there. In the privacy and silence of my own car, I allowed myself to think it again: I was wrong.

I flipped the visor back into place and gripped the steering wheel. The solid, smooth surface beneath my fingers grounded me. My mother had requested I finish what we'd started when we'd moved to Folklore Falls all those years ago. *Build a place that suits us.*

Nothing fit the Jensen family. She'd wanted the family-oriented aspect of a small-town but the luxuries of a big city. Still, she'd obsessed over this place as the answer to our broken family.

Movement caught my eye in the window at Bella's Bookstore. A hand grabbed a paperback from the display, then the silhouette disappeared deeper into the shop and out of view. I ran my hands back and forth on the steering wheel and sucked in a cleansing breath.

I didn't want to wait for the next scheduled public appearance to see her again. I stepped out of the car and wiped the sweat from my palms to my pants.

The bell on the front door chimed as I pushed through. Bella clung to the bookshelf next to the giant, velvet chair. It appeared she'd climbed the shelves to reach the top but some of the books were still too far back and out of her grasp. When she tried to twist to greet me, her foot slipped, but she regained balance quickly.

"Do you need help?"

"Nope." She stretched and brushed the books' spines with her fingertips. The arches of her bare feet straightened to push her higher. She successfully knocked the row of books to the edge, scooped them into her arms, then hopped backwards, landing in the chair's cushion. The determination in everything she did sparked a smile on her face. Bella was nothing if not herself. I'd been envious of it as a kid, but coming back here, seeing her choose exactly the job and style and life she wanted, shifted my feelings from envy to admiration.

She hopped off the chair and dropped the books where she'd stood. Dust fell from her hands as she wiped them together.

"I thought I wasn't going to see you until tonight."

"How about lunch?" I didn't know what else to say. We only had two events left, then our deal would end. If I threatened to knock the house down again, it'd force her to stay with me, but it'd still be fake.

"Sure. Are you still worried people don't know we're together?"

I'm worried you don't know we're together. We could be. And maybe that'd be enough for my mom if one member of our family found happiness in Folklore Falls. I shoved my to-do list of promises aside and cleared my throat. "Maybe you could tell me what I'm missing in those." I lifted my chin toward the romance section on the shelf behind her.

The peak of her brow told me I'd surprised her again. Pleasantly, I hoped. "You want to talk about historical romance?"

I shrugged and stepped past her to pull down a book that faced out. The cover showed a whip wrapped around a dagger in a dimmed spotlight.

"Or any. Is this historical?" I held it up, and she suppressed a laugh.

"Dark romantasy."

"I don't even—is that a word?"

The smile faded, and she glanced at the desk. I followed her gaze and spotted the origami rose I'd made years ago. A candle labeled 'apple orchard' flickered beside it.

"I'm looking forward to the, uh, Homecoming dance," I said, as I returned the book to its place.

Bella busied herself with the stack she'd pulled off the top shelf. One-by-one, she wiped dust from the covers and lined them up on the small table beside the chair. "Yeah, I'll be sure to crank up the effort on faking it. I know the dance is right before the election."

I clapped my hands together. "Sounds good."

"Good. And you won't pull something sneaky and take out the manor after you win your votes?"

I licked my lips and folded my arms. The familiar heat of irritation and impatience returned to my head, but she didn't have a reason to trust me. The question was fair. "I'm not going to hurt the house."

"What about your modern library?" She hopped on the chair again and began her dangerous stunt to reach the rest of the books at the top.

"I mostly read ebooks anyway. Will you let me help you?"

With the next row of books secured under one arm, she stepped down. "I've got it." She shook the bangs from her eyelashes and met my gaze. "Lunch?"

Listening to her talk about love story tropes was the perfect pre-townhall meeting activity. The passion in her words and excitement in her voice left me inspired. I didn't know what half the tropes meant, but she happily explained them and even related them back to classic novels. We'd left only when Chip called and reminded me of our quick get-together before the event.

Before I said goodbye, Bella reached for my face, indicating for me to lean forward. Just like on the shelf, she arched her feet and closed the gap between our heights to leave me with a kiss.

The warm feeling lingered hours later as I stood in front of the entire town in the auditorium at Folkore Falls High School. Max defended his position with plenty of promises about lowering the speed limit on the highway to prevent people speeding through the town and something about a community garden to combat rising produce prices.

I offered my suggestions regarding modernized buildings to draw more tourism, but Chip had insisted I tone that down, and I'd agreed. I added promises to put more tax money into the fire department to protect Sherwood Forest and a plan to ensure the waterfalls stayed clean.

Bella sat in the second row, and I found myself continually glancing her direction. Did she agree with these ideas? Would she prefer Max win?

Sheriff Gideon monitored questions and started calling on raised hands.

A blonde woman stood. "Brett, you have a bad past here."

I rubbed the back of my neck but nodded to agree with her.

She continued. "How can we trust that you'll have Folklore Falls's best interest in mind?"

Murmurs spread throughout the rest of the crowd. I coughed and spoke into the microphone.

"Sometimes people portray themselves as someone they're not." I glanced at Bella. Did she know it was a reference to her grandmother?

Did she have any clue she'd showed me people could change? "My past behavior was a mistake. I'm not that guy anymore. I've finally decided to make Folklore Falls the home my mother had always wanted it to be for my family."

Seemingly satisfied, the woman sat back down. The sheriff called on another hand beside the first, and a brunette raised her voice.

"I'd like to know if Brett is actually dating Bella. Or is it just a fling? I know you're the king of flings—"

Sheriff Gideon waved his hand to shut her down. I glanced at Chip, and he nodded, meaning I needed to address the question.

"It's… not fake." My gaze found Bella again but was pulled away when the brunette shouted.

"I didn't ask if it was fake!"

"I heard you were going to tear down the Manor. Is that true? Is that what you'll do to all the buildings?" another audience member chimed in.

The questions continued, out of the Sheriff's control now.

"If you and Bella break-up, will you leave town?"

"If you break Bella's heart, I'll have two friends ready to meet you," Falstaff, the owner of the local apple orchard, balled his hands into fists and shook them in the air.

"Did your old man put you up to this since he failed when he ran for mayor?"

"Your family have all left, why did you choose to come back now?"

The last question struck me harder than the rest. I'd only shared about my mother's death with Bella. They didn't know I needed to fulfill a woman's dying wish. Was that what her demand was? Or did she just want me to fix everything she'd ruined in our family?

I answered to the best of my ability and stepped off the stage. Max received a few mild questions that faded as I shoved through the doors and let the chilly evening breeze wash over me. The autumn weather cooled the heat in my neck.

I scrubbed my palm over my face and let my head fall back. The stars shined clearer in Folklore Falls than in many of the places I'd visited. Their quiet presence calmed me the way I felt around Bella's patient listening. The thought of breaking her heart never crossed my mind. This was transactional, as all relationships were. I'd never seen myself with anyone long term after watching my parent's marriage crumble.

I didn't need to cause any more pain.

A door swung shut behind me, and I spun around to see her walking toward me. Her boots slammed against the cement in the middle of the school's campus until she stopped beside me.

"I guess we can't break up now." She laughed.

"No." I shook my head. "I don't expect you to keep this up just for my career. I'm tired of pretending. It isn't fair to either of us, and I need to start my term as Mayor from a place of honesty."

I didn't mean for it to be rude, just honest, blunt, and quick. Bella's eyes shifted from place to place, refusing to meet mine. Disappointment creased her brow, and she released a breath before placing both hands on her hips.

"What about the dance?"

"We'll go to Homecoming together, then quietly call it quits. Since it was all fake to begin with, people will see we're amicable, and it shouldn't be a big deal."

"No." She shook her head, sending the dark hair of her bangs quivering. "I don't accept that. We made a deal, and you're going to stick it out until the election at least."

"Look, the house is fine. I swear I won't lay a finger on Villenueve Manor."

At that, she straightened. Her posture stretched, and she glanced at her hands. "Good."

"Okay." I liked that we could talk like this. Short, simple words reached our point quickly. Neither Bella nor I were ever big on rambling or wanting to be the center of attention. I wasn't fond of most people, but I enjoyed her presence. It was a shame it needed to end, but the deal was like a prank we'd played on ourselves. Pretending helped nobody, and if I spent more time around her, I'd forget it was all supposed to be fake. Someone was bound to get hurt, and I'd hurt too many people in my life already.

"Thank you for everything." I turned, but her hand shot out and gripped my wrist.

She tugged me toward her. "Wait."

The twist of her lips. I'd promised to protect her precious house, so the expression didn't make sense. Was she worried about losing me?

"I'll still be around. I just think we've fought a lot and faked a lot, and this isn't what a relationship is supposed to look like," I said. Thoughts of my parents fake marriage after the affair flooded me.

"We can't break up."

"We're not even dating," I corrected.

"Brett, please."

When she stepped closer to me, a berry scent drifted from her hair. I wondered if she tasted the same, but kissing was out of the question. Wrinkles scrunched on her brow, and she squeezed my arm a little too tightly until her pointed fingernail broke the soft skin of my wrist.

I turned my arm over to see blood bead to the surface. Bella gasped and let go.

She swore and pressed her palm to her forehead. "It's back." When she leaned over and dropped her hands to her knees, I bent to try to meet her gaze.

"Are you going to pass out?"

Black hair spilled over her shoulders and curtained her face. Her head dipped lower as she shook it. "No… maybe. But it's the curse."

"The what?"

"Brett, just date me until the election. Just that long, okay?" She straightened and wiped at her temples with both hands. "Do you care about me?"

"I—what? Yeah, I guess." I did, but why did any of that matter now? It was all a ruse for those watching us, and she'd faked it well.

"Do you…" she waved her hands as if coaxing a scared animal toward her. "You know?"

I shook my head. "I'm lost."

The wind tossed hair into her face, but she ignored it and raised her hands in surrender. "It's okay. This is fine. Look, my birthday is next week, and I want to come look for something my grandma said she'd hid at the manor. Can I do that? Maybe we can together? And then dinner?"

"For your birthday?"

"Before."

Her eyes trailed back to the bit of red on my wrist, and she swore again. A distant, glazed look overcame her, throwing worry aside. Even in the dim moonlight, the crimson in her cheeks was evident. When her eyes rolled back into her head, I expected a joke to follow.

Instead, she leaned closer to me.

"Bella?"

Just like that, her body went limp, and I crouched to catch her.

Twenty-Three

BELLA

I blamed the blood for my unconscious collapse into Brett's arms, but I was left wondering if the threat of the curse closing in had caused me to faint. Or was it more than that? I assumed the accident with my fingernail was a warning of bad luck. Except… if Brett had successfully faked it the whole time, why wasn't the curse constant? Only real love cut curses.

I slapped the pages of *Phantom of the Opera* shut and rubbed the key I'd designed into an earring between my thumb and forefinger. With only a chapter left of my annual reread, I couldn't focus. Now wasn't the time to bury my nose in my comfort book and hide from the inevitable march of time…or my feelings.

I hopped off the stool and stepped out of the storage room. The bookstore was quiet while everyone was at home preparing for the Homecoming dance. Moms like Loxley loved the excuse to get out and dress fancy while the men enjoyed watching how it delighted their wives to feel young again. Of course, the high school students had their own parties and sections of the basketball court where they'd convene and ignore the annoying adults.

As much as I wanted to look forward to wearing my most expensive, handcrafted corset, I didn't know if the dance would get my mind off everything. Actually, it'd make it worse, considering I had to hold Brett's hand and feel his on my waist.

Fur brushed against my legs as Philip twisted between them like a snake. I picked up the paper rose off the desk and gently ran my thumb over the flattened petals.

"I needed him to say it, but it's too fast." I sighed and leaned my elbows to rest against the desktop. Philip meowed. "I mean, I don't love him or anything, and it'd be weird as heck if he already loved me, but my birthday is in five days!"

Another meow but angrier and muffled this time. Philip had disappeared into the storage room to circle his empty food bowl.

I dropped the rose and let my head fall into my palms. "It gets weirder." The pressure of the heel of my hands felt good on my temples. "I don't want to break up. Not even after my birthday and the election because I really like spending time with him."

Pissed now that I'd ignored him and let him wither away into nothingness, Philip meowed louder.

"That's right, I *actually* like the Beast of Folklore Falls. I'm Christine Daae. Do I choose what I've known since my childhood or the guy who haunts my dreams?"

Nothing now. My cat had given up on me, irritated that I'd failed him as an owner and allowed his food bowl to remain empty for approximately one hour.

"Fine, the comparison is a stretch. You're right." At least I could dress up as Christine Daae, even if Brett wasn't Erik, though I'd shock the whole town if I showed up to the dance in white. I dragged myself into the storage room and dug around for a bag of cat kibble.

As my birthday closed in, the curse felt farther and farther away. But Brett didn't love me, so why'd it go quiet?

Where did the bad luck go when we were at the Halloween Harvest? Wouldn't he have fallen off the stage for pretending to care about me during the romantic promposal?

When I sighed, Philip meowed louder and bared his white fangs in frustration at me. I located the bag of kibble behind a box of mysteries and stooped to snag it.

Why hadn't I tripped on my skirt and broken my nose when I'd walked up to accept his fake offer? The questions inundated me. I'd thought we were headed in the right direction and that maybe Brett had feelings for me. Then, it was all assumptions about those feelings keeping the bad luck at bay. Everything changed with his attempted break-up. It shattered the illusion and all I thought I knew.

We'd said we were pretending, and 'we' included him. I knew I wasn't the most lovable person, my mom had made that clear.

Philip circled the bowl excitedly, and I came back to the present to see a mountain of cat kibble spilling out of his bowl and over my boots. Lost in my mind, I'd dumped out the whole bag. The pile reached higher than Philip's head, and he looked absolutely delighted about that. Since I didn't want to come back to a cat I'd have to roll to his litter box, I sighed and unburied my feet.

"Better get this cleaned up, so I won't be late."

I scrolled through the text thread to double-check the time Brett expected me. He'd rescheduled my visit to the Manor twice, pushing it back to the day of the dance. Most of his recent texts came in one word answers, and it'd sent my heart to my stomach.

I squinted at the stained-glass before stomping up the steps. The rest of the rose remained intact while the broken petals left two holes in the window.

Brett opened the door wearing jeans and a T-shirt. I never saw him dress casually except for gym clothes, but it fit him nicely. If nicely meant I wanted to put my hands all over him.

"Hey, Bella. Come in." He stepped out of the way and waited.

"Thanks." I smoothed an imaginary wrinkle on the front of my cropped black turtleneck and adjusted the purple crystal to the center of the silver chain on my necklace. "So, you said you might know where my grandma's stuff is?"

Brett nodded. "I haven't had time to get up there again." Without moving out of the entryway, he pointed above us. "There's a keyhole on the wall across from the window where it appears there's a false ceiling. I've got the ladder out, but I don't have a key."

I reached for the earring and pulled the pin from my lobe. The key had lost its shine over the years of bumping against my neck and picking up oil from my hair and fingers.

"It's a stretch, so I don't think you'll be tall enough to reach, may I?" he asked, palm out. I pressed the key into his hand and nodded. When did I learn to trust the Beast? The shift had slipped by so subtly but not without plenty of fantasies about straddling him or feeling the weight of his hand on the back of my neck.

"So, I have a question." I followed him to the ladder. The fabric of his T-shirt stretched tightly over his broad shoulders. To match the casual style, he'd left his hair untouched of gel and product, and I wanted to feel it between my fingers.

"Yeah?" The metal ladder scraped against the floor as he checked the stability of its placement, then stepped on the lowest rung.

"Were you lying at the diner?" I asked.

Brett craned his neck to glance down at me. "I'm all about honesty."

"Okay, but you said you wanted to give reading romance a try after I told you all the tropes and about my favorite books." I fiddled with the crystal on my neck, pulling it side-to-side to try to get it to lay straight in the middle of my chest.

"That's the truth. I told you, people can find new interests. I had no idea those books were read by anyone other than old, lonely ladies."

I scoffed. "There's nothing wrong with people like that."

"You're right, I'm sorry. I still have a long way to go to break from what my mother taught me." *Ugh, don't mention mothers.* The memory of Brett's breath on my neck, encouraging me to stand up to my mom sparked a flood of appreciation for him. I wanted to pull him off the ladder and thank him with my lips on his. Our kisses burned with enough passion to convince the whole country we were dating, but we hadn't enough opportunities and ever since the night at my mother's I couldn't read him.

"What do you mean?" The thick braid down my spine pulled against my scalp as I looked up. Brett almost made it to the top when he paused and sighed.

"Basically, she wanted me to be someone I never could be. I guess I became the Beast instead." The confession left me momentarily speechless. Like me, Brett wasn't one to open up about his thoughts and feelings, so the casual way he shared this piece made me realize what had changed. Over the past weeks, we'd become friends, not just fake boyfriend and girlfriend, not businesspeople in a transactional relationship, but real, true friends.

"Oh." I knew the feeling all too well. I imagined Mrs. Jensen hoped her son would grow up to be the desperate, judgmental person she was. She'd taken a historical artifact from the town a couple years ago, believing she deserved it simply for being rich. I already knew the details on that, and I didn't care to rehash it. I wanted to know more about Brett and his feelings for me, not his mother.

"And what about when you asked me to Homecoming?"

"What about it?"

Rolling my eyes caused my lashes to catch the tips of my bangs. Talk about pretending… he knew what I meant but I also didn't have the guts to spell it out for him. *Did you want me then? And what about now?* If he did, I'd lean into him.

"The whole bit about regret and not asking me years ago." I glanced at my hands, still fidgeting with the crystal.

When he didn't answer, I looked up. He'd reached the keyhole and twisted the key in the lock. It stuck, so he tugged and jiggled the key a few times to see if it was fully unlocked.

Finally, the false ceiling popped open and papers slipped out as it seemed they'd been haphazardly shoved inside. He tried to catch a few, but they spilled out and floated to the floor like dozens of giant snowflakes. I hurried to collect them. If Brett knew I needed him to say that he loved me to break a curse, would he ever say it? And if he did, how would I know if it was real?

I was so sick of trying to clarify the blurred line between reality and fiction.

"Wow, this goes way back," he said. He'd stretched to his full height to see inside. "It's a giant, creepy crawlspace. You could film a horror movie in here." He reached and pulled out a porcelain doll. "See what I mean?"

"That was probably my grandma's." I smiled at the thought of a horror movie set in my favorite place.

"This, too." Brett tucked a small book under his arm and descended rung-by-rung. Once he reached the bottom, he handed me the journal and the doll. I took it, letting my hand linger against his for a moment. The awkwardness between us was an invisible barrier, holding me back from the scene my imagination played out. I wanted to ball his shirt into my fist and pull him down to me where I could taste him. We'd lost the fire of our hate and the spark of our passion. All teasing was put to the side as the election closed in. Was he wondering if the relationship would come to an end after all votes were in?

I directed my attention to the journal, carefully turning the pages and scanning the cursive handwriting. It matched the letters my grandma wrote to my mom after Mom had stopped visiting. A word caught my eye, and I trailed the sentence with my finger.

"She wrote out the whole curse."

"Curse?" Brett asked.

I nodded. "Remember? I told you about it in the cemetery." Though I'd strategically didn't give him enough details to realize I was using him to break said curse.

"Right. Well, I hope this helps. I'm going to get showered and changed for tonight." His voice was flat, devoid of the passion we'd shared just days before. I knew Brett wanted me then, what had changed?

I'd called our relationship fake. But wasn't that the truth? And didn't Brett appreciate the whole truth and nothing but the truth?

The air left in his wake smelled of sawdust and sweat, and I immediately missed the scent when he walked away.

Just ask him. "Hey, Brett." I spun around. If my brain wasn't shouting at my heart, I'd be able to gather my thoughts and ask him on a real date. No more faking. "Thanks." I held up both the doll and journal. Courage waned at the sight of my grandmother's handwriting in my grasp. I was so close to my birthday, our relationship talk could wait just a few more days.

I had a lot of reading to do before I turned twenty-five, and I planned to cram as much as I could before the dance tonight. If Grandma V. had remembered the details wrong, maybe I didn't need Brett to love me to break the curse.

Maybe I just wanted him to.

Love changes everything, even curses. I write this as I know my days are limited. Getting old isn't for the faint of heart and I can't help but wonder. What if I'd only loved the woman I'd become? Perhaps, that is the key the the curse. I'll pass this knowledge on to Bella, she'll know what to do.

Belle V.

Twenty-Four

BRETT

The past few days without talking to Bella sucked. When Chip convinced the animal rescuer to let me adopt the tabby, I wanted to call her. I flopped on the little cot I'd been using as a bed. Maybe it was time to unpack the sheets and rebuild the bed frames since the house would remain intact.

I dug my phone out of my pocket and hovered over Bella's name in my contacts before swiping up and tapping the internet icon. I searched for romantasy novels on Amazon, but several on the list came up in foreign languages, and I needed her help sifting through the thousands of other choices. I gave up, swiped out of the search, and accidentally opened the Notes app on my phone.

> *Mother's Requests:*
> *Run for mayor.*
> *Clean up Folklore Falls.*
> *Make us proud.*

The last words she'd spoken about this town came with a demand that I find happiness here. When I'd first arrived, that felt impossible until I bumped into Bella, literally. She was annoying and insufferable and incredibly intriguing. Not talking to her made Folklore Falls depressing and boring again.

I switched over to text messages, tapped her name, and shot her a quick text to meet me at the Manor early tonight. It was our final date, and I wanted it to last.

The second time I opened the door that day to Bella's knock, I almost fainted. Earlier it was low blood sugar to blame, but now my brain worked to catch up with the sight in front of me. If I passed out, I didn't think she'd be able to catch me. Thankfully, those roles were reversed when we'd first ran into each other. That day at the hospital felt like half a year into the past rather than a month ago.

I blinked and rubbed my eyes, struggling to accept the person who stood on my doorstep was Bella Villenueve. Instead of all black, spiked nails, and heavy boots, she wore a burgundy corset over a golden skirt. Delicate, white lace sleeves clung to the edges of her shoulders and her hair, even the bangs, was pinned back from her face and lifted at the side with a large, red rose.

It was beautiful, but she looked like someone else.

"I thought I'd asked Bella Villenueve to the dance," I joked and scrubbed my hand over the back of my neck. It was dumb, but I didn't know how to act after the break-up. The relationship wasn't real, but the end of it left me lonelier than any other break-up I'd experienced before.

Bella brushed her hand over the front of the corset. "This is what I wanted to wear to Homecoming when I was a teenager." The side of her hair that wasn't pinned with the rose fell into her face like a curtain.

I cocked my head. "Is this the dress?"

She only shrugged and nodded, but the hint of a smile on her lips told me it was more than just a dress. Whatever the story was, it'd have to wait. Huge raindrops dotted the ground around her so I offered my hand to have her step inside.

"I thought you wanted to arrive early?" A crease pressed between her brows.

I glanced behind me into the dim space where the chandelier wasn't lit. It sucked too much power to turn on the lights when I needed to save the generator for morning coffee. Eventually, I'd get around to starting electricity service to the house again, but it was the last step before accepting I would stay here. Selling the whole property felt wrong. At least with rebuilding, I'd keep the estate my mother had poured her hopes into, but that wasn't an option anymore with Bella's attachment.

"Come inside." I beckoned with my fingers.

The timing was impeccable as the pace of the rainfall picked up. As she followed me into the halls and the large entry with the expanding staircase and crystal chandelier, the sound of rain grew louder. Every drop pelted the ceiling in a constant, white noise only cracked by distant thunder.

"It's so dark," she said, pulling her phone from the pocket in her skirt. The flashlight brightened the staircase, then sparkled off the crystals.

"I've been overusing the generator," I admitted.

Admiration shined in her dark eyes as she took in the room. When she sighed, a small smile brightened her face. "I love this place."

"Yeah." I marched for the ballroom and shoved the double doors open. "That's actually what I wanted your help with."

The flicker of her phone's light followed the echo of her footsteps. The sound was gentle, not heavy and solid the way she walked in her boots. It didn't suit her. The Bella I'd always admired from a short distance was nothing if not herself.

She followed me into the empty room—where the town's dance should be held. Villenueve Manor was old and full of lonely and empty memories for me, but maybe I'd find some beauty in it if I looked through Bella's eyes.

"If I'm not going to tear it down, you need to help me like it."

The peak of her eyebrows sparked a smile on my face. It'd only been a few days without her while I focused on my campaign and gave myself space. I was only kidding myself that a Folklore Falls girl would ever see me as anything beyond the Beast. Right?

"I mean, we're friends, right?" I hoped, but I wasn't sure. How much of our conversations and shared experiences were fake? I'd held her to the deal for this long. It was likely she wouldn't trust me.

"Sure, yeah." She nodded, but the corners of her lips tugged down.

"So, starting here, show me what you like." I turned my palms up and looked around the room. Other than storing a few packed boxes, the room was empty, an open space for dancing a time long ago. I stepped beside the mini bar and put my hand on the counter, leaning to one side.

Bella's eyelashes ticked up as her gaze trailed the space. The light from her phone faded and didn't illuminate the other end of the room. Rain pattered the roof in the entry, mocking me for not turning the generator back on before the storm hit.

"Well, other than that it's a piece of my family and reminds me of my grandma, it's also spooky and gothic and…" her voice petered off into a little laugh. "Don't make fun." She stepped up to me and poked her finger into my chest.

"What?" I feigned ignorance but predicted what she said.

"It's romantic." Bella shrugged, and the delicate lace sleeve, if it could be called that, slipped off her shoulder. A lump in my throat made it hard to swallow. I'd told her I broke up with her in the honor of honesty, and if I wanted to live up to that, I needed to be honest with myself.

And one question still gnawed at me.

She brushed past me, flashing the light into the empty shelves behind the bar. The familiar scent of pumpkin and vanilla pushed me to come out with it.

"Bella." I spun around. "I can't help but wonder…" I swallowed and scratched at the stubble on my jaw. Her huge eyes stared up at me with the quiet patience that encouraged me to speak, but my courage waned. "Why didn't you wear what you wanted to the dance?" Confusion angled her brows. "In high school, I mean. The, uh, dress."

Understanding dawned, and she adjusted the fallen sleeve. "It's stupid."

If anything was stupid, it was me. I should have asked her what I wanted, but she was already deep into her answer.

"This is a Christine Daae imitation outfit. I sewed it back then to wear, but my mom said it was a perfect visual example of how I planned to waste my life away." Her lips twisted into an unhappy smile before she laughed and looked at her hands. "I'm sure you heard, everyone in town know she wanted me to be a doctor, and I didn't even try."

I nodded along, listening but also lost in my own disappointment. The light from her phone shined up from where it sat on the counter, creating a disturbing affect that matched her story.

"It looks amazing," I said. "You should do whatever you want."

Ironic, coming from me.

She laughed. "Tell that to my mom next time you see her."

"No, I'm serious. I hate it when people try to tell me to change. You've always been so good at being yourself."

Bella pointed to the open doors. "We both hate being late, so we should probably go?"

I nodded and followed her into the entry. The way she moved in the gown reminded me of a ghost floating beneath the chandelier. Maybe the house, spooky or not, wasn't so bad. This was the first beauty I'd seen in it.

"I know I talk like Villenueve Manor is perfect, but it's not," she said with a laugh, as she tossed a look over her shoulder at me.

"Yeah?"

"It needs a library. Who doesn't put a library in a gorgeous mansion like this?" With the mood lightened, she spun around under the chandelier, but she didn't look comfortable. I missed seeing her in her usual style, and her sense of self that came with it.

Her style was nothing like mine, in house and clothing, but that's where our differences ended.

When I looked at most relationships, I'd believed in the phrase that opposites attract. But in Bella, I saw many familiarities reflected back at me from the determination to go after what you want, to family loyalty, and even the little things like an affinity for cats over dogs and other pets.

Though the house wasn't actually haunted, I heard my mother's voice clearly in my head. *We lie to protect others.* Screw that.

Cold wind rushed in as Bella opened the front door. Sheets of rain blasted sideways, splashing the steps and porch and even reaching inside the entry. Before she could step outside, I grabbed her arm, not wanting to have this conversation in the storm.

"Bella, I actually meant to ask something else."

She had already clicked off her phone's flashlight, and darkness fell around us. As my eyes adjusted, I could make out her silhouette but not her expression. Even with the door open, night had fallen quickly, and the clouds blocked the glow of the moon.

Instead of pushing me, she waited in silence, inviting me to be open.

"Why did you want to keep dating when I promised to protect the house?" In the second that followed, I got antsy and hurried to add to it. "Are you worried I wouldn't keep my word?" *No, total truth.* I rubbed my palm over my face and released a breath. "I missed talking to you the past few days, and I'm wondering if you felt the same way."

For a moment, I swore her entire face lit up until I realized she'd received a text and her phone's screen temporarily brightened. But the dim glow revealed a small smile at the edges of her mouth. "I did. I mean, you're a good listener, and most people don't do that for me."

I could have left it at that and then made a break for the car in the rain, but I'd wonder all night if this dance couldn't be more.

"Okay, then would you accompany me to the dance for our first real date?" It sounded stupid, and I could barely see her reaction or hear her answer over another roll of grumbling thunder. The sky lit up with one of Folklore Falls's famous lightning storms. The strike hit the ground beyond the tree line of Sherwood Forest.

"Yes, definitely."

"And you actually want it to be a real date? Be honest with me, no more games or pretending, right?" I asked, ready for the faking to end. If we were going to try this, I wanted to go all in.

"Right." She motioned an 'X' with her fingers over her chest. "Cross my heart."

It was official, no more faking.

When she grabbed my hand, she pulled me from the safety of inside, and we made a break for the car. Our first date rushed by in a whirlwind of townspeople. Many people wanted to continue questions from the townhall meeting until they noticed Bella getting annoyed.

The gym at Folklore Falls High School looked nothing as it had during our Homecoming dance. The space had been doubled in size and elegantly decorated in a theme they lovingly called Fall meets Ball. I definitely had to bite back a few choice words about it, but the people looked happy. What had my mother insisted I fix?

Smiling faces danced and laughed and traded gossip. It matched the joy I witnessed during the book sale and Halloween Harvest, and even in everyday moments like a stop at the Sherwood Bed and Breakfast cafe. If the townspeople liked their way of life, who was I to change it? Wasn't that exactly what my mother thought she could do to me?

I cupped Bella's hand in mine, and we moved together to a slower song that I didn't recognize. She hummed the tune and ignored the stares at her unusual dress, instead leaning into me.

The scent drifting from her hair matched perfectly with the ambiance around us. Bella meant more than the other girls I'd kissed easily on first dates, but was this really our first? I'd meant it when I'd asked her to the dance, even if she thought it was all staged.

I pulled her closer to me and felt the heat of her body pressed against mine. Though I'd wanted this many years ago, the dance and to feel like a part of Folklore Falls, it all faded. The feel of Bella's arms wrapped around my neck was all I could focus on.

"I've really enjoyed this past month," I said, hoping the feeling was mutual.

She pulled away to look up at me. "Honestly, I did not expect to have so much fun with you."

"Did I tell you I tried to order a romantasy?" I asked.

Hair fell back off her shoulders as she threw her head back and laughed. "You did not. You're too good for those, remember?"

I shook my head. "I'm sure I've been missing out on a lot of things I was blind to."

"You know," she started, "when we walked in here, I realized how much nicer it is since this building was redone. Maybe you were right about needing to update some areas of town. I bet if you approach it the right way, people will see your side of it."

"I can fire Chip now, right?" I joked.

Her laugh rippled, and it reminded me of a villain's, dark, different, irresistible. I ran my hand up her back, feeling the ties on the corset and leaned closer so our conversation stayed between the two of us. Instead of showing off, we could enjoy the luxury of privacy now.

"What does your tattoo say?"

Bella's head rolled back to meet my gaze. Red lined lips curved into a smirk that told me she'd continue challenging me, even in a real relationship.

"Sir, it's only our first date." She winked and pulled away when the slow song concluded.

The music switched to a bubbly beat, and people cheered. Bella disappeared in the crowd as she marched for the table where Bones mixed drinks for the adults.

One corny song blared over the sound system after another like every tired playlist from weddings and dances. It didn't stop people from enjoying it. I stood and sipped an autumn-flavored drink that's color matched the reddish brown garland of fake leaves strung across the ceiling. Fall decorations mixed with blinking fairy lights for a disjointed but ethereal affect only passable in a quaint place like Folklore Falls.

When Sheriff Gideon disappeared to break up an argument between two teen boys, Loxley stole Bella away. The two chatted, and I caught a piece of Loxley's praise for the outfit Bella had sewed.

After Bella excused herself, Loxley drifted to the table for a drink. She shouted over the music, but the song had switched to something even more obnoxious, and I tapped my ear to signal I couldn't hear her.

She refilled her cup before stepping closer to me. "Real date, huh?"

"She told you?"

When she nodded, her motherly haircut bobbed. Loxley had cut her reddish hair to her chin after having a child and looked nearly unrecognizable to me, but I knew well enough to remember her and Bella's friendship had begun all the way back on the playground.

Loxley and I had never addressed the tension between us after she called my family out for theft, and it seemed we both liked it that way. It was another memory I refused to give energy to.

"Yeah, she loves that house." I shook my head and brought my drink to my lips. Maybe the awkwardness between us would fade someday, but Loxley had been accused of a crime my mother had committed. I couldn't think of that now, so I filled the silence. "If you ask me, the manor is haunted or cursed, like her grandma or whatever."

"She told you about the curse?" Loxley lowered her cup, and her mouth gaped.

"Yeah, we even found old newspapers and journals about it hidden in a crawlspace."

She shook her head. "Wow, she really does trust you. I'm glad you guys aren't faking it anymore, though. She wanted to break that curse on her so badly, but I knew the guilt of possibly breaking your heart killed her."

I swallowed the last of the cinnamon-flavored drink and set the cup on the table. "What?"

"I mean, if you told her you love her, none of it even matters now, right? It all worked out."

My gaze trailed to Bella's figure as she pushed past a group of older ladies. Loxley was still talking, but I left her behind, closing the distance between Bella and me.

"Can you be honest with me?" I hunched over her and caught a whiff of vanilla pumpkin. "We agreed to that, right? I thought we agreed to that."

The red rose had been removed from her hair. She let the locks flow freely over her bare shoulders, but I kept my focus on her face. I refused to let my baser instincts forget the real deal we'd made.

"What's wrong?" She pinched her brows and looked me up and down. When I realized I towered over her with muscles tensed and a frown, I tried to relax for the sake of the people watching.

"Is there another reason you didn't want to break up?" I lowered my voice.

"I—"

"Is this a real date or not?" I interrupted.

The moment of hesitation brought me back to the first time my mother had told me to lie. *You must answer quickly. Don't let them know you're thinking of a response. Don't let anyone know about your real father. Well-behaved boys are not bastards.*

Rage burned in my chest and threatened to spill over in a shouting match.

Bella nodded. "Yes, why wouldn't it be?"

"Do you want to tell me more about this curse you're trying to break then?" The words came out evenly, and I took pride in the calmness I exhibited while the storm raged inside of me. The whole deal was wrong and stupid and beneath me. Why did we ever agree to fake a relationship and lie to everyone? It'd felt right at the time in my desperation, but I hated myself for making the decision as much as I wanted to hate her for lying.

Even in the dim light, I could see Bella's face shift to a brighter shade of pale. Her bottom lip curled under as she gnawed on it, and her hands busied with a loose thread on the pocket of the skirt.

"I told you about my grandma, remember?"

"I'm talking about a curse on you."

She was a ghost now, transparent in her fear and shock. "Brett, it's just a superstition."

"I don't care about that." I ran my fingers through my hair and sighed. "I just want to know one thing, and I want you to be honest. Is there an ulterior motive to this date or not?"

Thick lashes ticked down as she closed her eyes. Bella wiped her hand over her forehead, snagging hairs and ruffling the smooth style. "Yes, kind of—"

I shook my head. Why did I trust anyone? My mother had taught me that people would always want to use me, and she was right. I hated that she was right.

I shoved past Bella and the group of older women as I headed for the doors under the glowing green exit sign. The door swung open from a push harder than I meant to give. It whacked into the wall behind it, then fell shut again, blocking out the ridiculous music. Bella might have called after me or followed, but I didn't look back, and she'd never keep up with my long strides. It didn't matter. I'd opened up and risked vulnerability for once, and it bit me in the face.

Thankfully, arriving late meant the long walk to my car gave me time to cool down before anger convinced me to speed unnecessarily.

Dirt kicked up as I pulled into the driveway at Jensen Estate and shifted into park. I marched into the house and slammed the door. The frame rattled, and a tiny piece of glass shattered on the floor behind me.

I grunted and glanced at the stupid stained-glass window. Another petal had broken free from the artwork. I stalked down the hall and headed for the wine cellar. Knowing I'd drive home, I avoided Bones's table and now needed a strong drink now to help me forget.

The stairs creaked as I stomped down each step into the cooler and dimmer underground room. I snagged a bottle opener from the shelf at the bottom of the steps and found an old red blend. The pointed tip dug into the cork as I twisted.

With the election one week away, Chip would have my head for storming out of a public event, but I didn't care. I'd accomplished the first part of my mother's list. I ran for mayor, but I'd have to accept that the last three demands she'd given me from cleaning up Folklore Falls to making them proud and finally finding happiness here were impossible.

I was done with lying to myself. Chasing impossible feats would drive me to my grave. I'd never be the son my family wanted, and I'd never find a woman who didn't want to use me.

I popped the cork out and drank straight from the bottle.

Twenty-Five

BELLA

Glass crunched beneath my heels. I tapped my phone's screen to see shattered pieces sparkling across the floor, then directed the light to the window. It didn't reach high enough, but I knew another petal had fallen. Grandma V's journals confirmed it, though in her theory, the rose was a real flower enchanted by the witch who cursed our ancestors.

Wind blasted through the open door, sprinkling my bare ankles with rainwater. One question still plagued me: what did her last words mean?

Love changes everything, even curses. But the last sentence written in her journal differed from the phrase she loved to repeat. *You are the key.*

The door creaked as I pushed it shut against the force of the storm. Brett's voice echoed from down the hall, but his words were blocked by another roll of thunder.

I followed the sound, knowing exactly where it'd come from. The time I got to spend here was short-lived but I explored it to its fullest as a child.

From the top of the cellar's staircase, I heard Brett's sigh and something clatter. I assumed he dropped his phone after hanging up a call.

The floorboards creaked under my feet as I descended the steps. "Brett?"

Light from his phone illuminated the large underground room with a faint glow of white. He sat hunched against the far wall with a bottle of whiskey in one hand and fingers raking through his waves with the other. He let his head fall back against the stone wall and sighed again.

"I'm not in the mood, Bella," he said. "I heard about your superstitions and guess what—" When he lifted his head, hair fell into his eyes. "I'm tired of being used, and I'm tired of lies."

I slowly approached him, careful not to trip after a night of dancing in heels. My feet were not used to the arch and ached for the comfort of my cushioned, cozy boots.

Brett pointed at me with the top of the bottle. "Fake dating was a terrible idea, Bella." He said my name with emphasis.

"Are you drunk?" I eyed the bottle, but it didn't look like more than a sip was missing.

When he shook his head, more hair fell into his face. "Unfortunately, not yet. I had a few gulps of wine and switched to something that wouldn't give me a hangover."

I crouched and tried to cross my legs, but the tight skirt wouldn't allow for flexibility. It didn't matter because Brett waved me away.

"I'm not open to discussing anything with you."

"Brett, just let me explain." The damp smell of the cellar masked the delicious scent of his cologne.

He scoffed and took another sip of the brown liquid. It sloshed a drop out of the top as he slammed the bottle against the floor. "You know, I get that we were lying to everyone else, but I could have sworn we agreed to be honest with each other."

It pricked my heart that he cared so much. If I wasn't careful, I'd drive him away for good when all I wanted to do was sit beside him and put my head on his shoulder. I wanted to drink red wine with him and argue about which was Shakespeare's best work.

My stomach twisted as he met my gaze with a frown and venom in his eyes.

"It's embarrassing."

"Is it? Try taking the person you care about on a date only to find out they're using you. Try that for embarrassing. Try being lied to." He grunted and pushed to his feet, towering over me now. He shoved the bottle into my arms and pushed past me. "In fact, I think we owe this town an apology, don't you? Let's tell them our little deal. Let's share with all of Folklore Falls about how you were cursed, even though I'm the one nicknamed the Beast."

"Brett—"

Stomping footsteps drowned me out. He stormed up the staircase and disappeared past the shelves before my brain could catch up that I was left in the darkness and he was headed to ruin his career and humiliate us both.

"Wait!" I scrambled after him. Thankfully, the desperation in my voice caused him to pause. I squeezed past him on the staircase and blocked the last step to freedom from the damp smell. Jumbled ideas clouded my mind, but I didn't want to lie anymore. He was right about that. I was cursed, *I* was the Beast. But if I gave up now, everyone I cared for, including him, would suffer. Bad luck definitely ensured he'd lose the election, maybe baby Robin would get sick, and if Philip got lost again, I'd have a breakdown.

"Move," he demanded, voice low and growling.

I rubbed the key on my earring and took a deep breath. "This is going to sound insane, but just tell me you love me, and I'll explain everything."

Shock lasted only moments before his raised brows melted into angular lines, and his whole face fell in a grimace. "And here I thought you'd used me enough."

"Brett—"

"No!" He gently pressed my bare shoulder with his palm to move me aside. I stood my ground, but it wouldn't last, he was too strong. It broke my heart that he thought I'd lied about everything. Didn't he know I wanted to see The Globe with him? And Philip needed a feline friend. He'd love the little tabby Brett had adopted. And what about the kiss after the promposal? He must have felt that I cared about him then.

"Just say it."

"I said move!"

Before he could force himself past me, I skipped backward on the last step and scrambled to slam the door shut. For the first time that night, I was thankful I'd worn heels. The extra height helped me reach the lock at the top of the door that I quickly slid into place.

Brett rattled the door handle, then shook the entire thing in its frame. "Bella!" He banged several times. "What the hell? Open the door."

"Just say it, please." Did it hurt to confess the curse? He at least cared for me, maybe it was enough if he'd only admit that aloud.

"You locked me in here?"

"Listen…" my voice trailed off. Brett was good at listening. In fact, he was the first person to really hear me. Loxley tried, but her brain was always in ten places at once, and it didn't feel the same as his singular, intense focus on my words. "Here's the thing." I sighed and paused to hear if he was still on the other side of the door. "I don't even know if there's a curse. It's probably stupid of me to believe." I laughed without joy. "My mom tells me I'm stupid all the time."

I swore Brett grunted at that. Did he understand? His mother had passed, and she was an interesting woman, to say the least, but I didn't fully understand their relationship and why he struggled to love her.

"Anyway." I looked at the key in my hands. I'd removed it from the earring to nervously fiddle with it while I spoke. "The curse says Villenueve women are so unlovable that they'll bring years of bad luck to everyone around them. Honestly, whether it's real or not, I know I fit the description. I'm too emotional, and I waste time on books. I'm lazy, my shop is unorganized, and it barely passes as a job."

The floodgates opened now, and years of my mom's rude words and beliefs I'd built about myself came rushing to the surface in the form of stinging tears. Flashes from the lightning occasionally lit up the hall as the glow shined in through the windows. "Really, I'm shocked you even gave me the time of day. I mean, I've never seen you date anyone who wasn't a rich heiress. When you asked me on a real date tonight, I thought maybe I'd actually accomplish the far-fetched goal of someone telling me they loved me. I got caught up in the curse because it excused all of that. If I could just get someone to say it and mean it, I could ignore all the terrible parts of myself. And then I started to like you. Everything was fun." I laughed and wiped tears from my cheeks. The wetness smeared across the back of my wrist. "It's even fun to fight with you. After everything, I got the courage to finally wear this dress I made, and it finally felt like I wasn't the world's crappiest person. I don't expect you to understand. I know you're confident and sure of yourself—"

A scoff interrupted my confession.

"What?"

"Unlock the dungeon, and I'll tell you." His voice was distant now. Another roll of thunder seemed to say I'd be safer underground.

The curse still scared me, and I hated the thought of bringing everyone bad luck, but I did have one other option—I could follow in my grandma's footsteps and isolate myself so that nobody other than me had to suffer. The Brett I knew now didn't deserve this.

I unhooked the lock, pulled the door open, and shined the light from my phone down the stairs. Brett was gone from the steps.

I found him in the same spot with the bottle beside him again. Instead of drinking it, the top was corked, and he had the flame of a lighter tapping a candle's wick on a half-empty candelabra likely left here by my ancestors.

"My phone died," he said, as an explanation for the two candles he'd ignited. Their flames flickered and danced along the mostly empty wine racks as he placed the candelabra on the floor next to him. The trick of the light made the racks appear to be moving, as if they'd come alive.

"So, why did you laugh at me?" As I approached this time, he didn't wave me away. I sat beside him and leaned my back against the cold, stone wall. It really was like a dungeon down here.

Brett shook his head, the waves unruly now from the storm and the cellar's humidity. "I've always seen you as the one person who was exactly herself." He uncorked the bottle of wine this time and handed it to me.

The warm liquid soothed the squeeze in my throat. Though sobbing left me dehydrated, and wine certainly wouldn't help, I took an extra sip before handing it back to him.

"You're always unique in everything you do and say and wear. It's hard for me to believe that confession of yours." He glanced at me, eyes narrowed, then sighed and raked the hair from his face. "But I do understand."

His head fell against the wall, and his eyes followed the flickers from the flames on the ceiling. I kept my gaze on his, noticing the flex in his jaw had relaxed. When I stayed quiet, he continued. The chill in the air sent goosebumps up my bare arms and over my collarbone.

"My family moved here, into this house and Folklore Falls, to recreate me, but I couldn't be anyone other than myself. They hated that, and I spent most of my life hating myself until recently."

I kept silent and waited as he swallowed a sip. His chest rose and fell with a deep breath. "My mother had an affair, and I was the result. That's why I hate lies now. I found out when I was seven when my real dad came by our house, and I'd answered the door. She asked me to lie to my father and brother, but I was terrible at it." He cleared his throat and glanced at me. "I figured we were trading confessions. We're all cursed in our own ways."

"It's stupid that I kind of believe it, isn't it?" I reached for the bottle, but he tightened his grip and didn't let me take it. It forced me to meet his gaze.

"No."

Tears pressed to the surface again, slowly filling my eyes. Brett listened, and he took in every word I said without judgment. This definitely wasn't the man I once believed he was. And maybe he'd changed, as he'd said he changed.

"You know what is stupid?" He took a swig from the bottle and waited for me to ask.

I only arched an eyebrow at him. With arms balanced on his raised knees, the comfortable position exuded confidence—something I needed a slice of.

He smirked. "Fake dating. Oh, and nicknames."

I returned the smile with a shove, and he laughed.

"Seriously, it was a terrible idea."

The cellar blocked most of the noise of the storm, but a door or window rattled from somewhere upstairs. The shaking echoed throughout the house, and the wind must have caught through a small opening as it howled.

"And this house?" Brett stretched his arm out, indicating at the steps. The candles gave us the light we needed, but I wished for more to see the smile on his face clearer. "How can you like this place? Tell me that's not creepy." He rolled his head to the side and met my gaze, pointing toward the staircase and the general direction of the rattling echo.

"It's charming," I said, "in a Halloween, spooky, historic type of way."

The grin only deepened on his face. "You're not any of those things you believe about yourself, but sometimes you scare the hell out of me. I'm not the only Beast in this room."

I rolled my eyes. "How can I hate you and need you at the same time?"

"Because you're just like me. And being a Beast isn't so bad, is it?"

Similarities were the last thing either of us expected to have. Though the shared lies, painful upbringings, and cold childhoods made sense, we were connected on so much more. But he was one step ahead of me. Brett still let his mother's words control him too much, but he'd accepted himself while I was left in purgatory between hating who I believed I was and wanting to move forward.

"I'm not going to say it." His voice was barely audible. He'd caught on to my suggestion with the word 'need.' But I meant more than that. I needed him to tell me this wasn't the end. How could our first real date be the end of our relationship?

A shiver rippled through me. The cellar dropped another temperature or two as the draft from the open door and window reached us.

I forced myself to meet his gaze again. It was intense, like the way I pictured the fictional men I fell so hard for, but honest and open, too.

"It wouldn't mean anything. It takes me a long time to get there and a lot of trust," he explained.

I swallowed a lump in my throat and nodded. I could do without the words, but I wanted his arm around me. The small space between our legs separated us too far, and I longed to close the gap, to feel him hold me and kiss me.

Instead, he whispered an apology and fell silent for several painfully long moments. When he spoke, it was the opposite of the words I'd hoped for. "I need some space. I'll take you home when the storm clears."

My heart cracked, and suddenly, the curse didn't scare me anymore. Isolation, plus a few falls and scraped knees, couldn't hold a candle to the emptiness I felt now. Seven years of bad luck felt like nothing when I realized I'd missed the chance of a potential lifetime with the one person who matched me. And was it even real? Fake dating's a beast, but jumping through hoops all for a fake curse was worse.

With the key still tucked inside my fist, a thought came to me in Grandma V's voice. The house wasn't haunted or enchanted, but I definitely felt her spirit as her last written words echoed in my mind.

You are the key. Suddenly, the last entry in her journal made sense. It was why I hadn't broken my neck after Brett rejected me tonight. I didn't need his love, I needed my own.

I hid the ugly parts of myself for so long, right up until tonight when I put on the dress that symbolized my failures in my mom's eyes and confessed everything to Brett. I'd showed him the hideous side I always buried away.

The icy air sparked a shudder through me. Brett wrapped his arm around me and pulled me into his side, but he wouldn't look me in the eyes. Instead, he used his free arm to pat his shoulder.

He didn't tell me he loved me, and even ended our relationship, but warmth spread through me, and it wasn't from his body heat. Brett let me lean on his shoulder, and though I didn't think he knew I cried, it fulfilled his promise.

I didn't need his love, but I definitely wanted it.

Twenty-Six

BRETT

The dating ended, the election was over, and I had only one thing left to do before leaving the house: feed my unnamed cat. The tabby tried to dart into the pantry every time I opened it that I almost decided to call him Dart.

It didn't suit him, and Socks felt too cliche.

I opened a can of wet food and set it on the floor near the counter. The cat scurried to the can, almost colliding with the kitchen cabinets, and started gobbling the food. I leaned against the counter and opened a text message from Chip.

It was good getting to know you, man. Better luck next time!

I swiped away and hovered over Bella's name. The text thread had remained unchanged since before the Homecoming dance. She'd granted me the space I'd requested, and I respected her for that, but was it too long?

I tapped the calendar app on my phone and counted two and a half weeks since her birthday. If I'd had the guts, I would have at least texted her, but I used the time build and perfect my woodshop skills. The calendar said I still had the rest of the year, six weeks, to wait until I called her again. If she still wanted to date me after the time passed, I'd be ready to trust her again. I'd set the rule to protect myself.

Sawdust and sweat lingered on my black shirt. It was a poor choice of color for woodworking.

The tabby licked his lips and meowed.

"I know, you need a name." If my mother could see me talking to my cat, she'd tell me that well-behaved boys didn't concern themselves with pets. Good thing I wasn't well-behaved.

"Screw the rule," I muttered. Everyone associated trouble with the name Brett Jensen, may as well give them what they want.

I grabbed the keys off the counter, gave the tabby a quick pat, and headed for the office I'd transformed into a workshop.

Though it was two and a half weeks too late, and I hated being late, I'd call it a present for Bella's birthday.

BELLA

The bell on the door chimed, but I had only one page left in *Phantom of the Opera* to finish my reread. After the breakup, I'd put the annual read on hold and opted for lighter, fluffier books full of comedy. Though I enjoyed rereading it, it'd become a chore to finish it before my birthday every year, and I'd already set too many rules on myself.

When I turned twenty-five, my suspicions were confirmed. *I was the key.* And apparently, loving yourself is as powerful as when someone else loves you. If only I'd known that a month and a half ago, I wouldn't have found myself wrapped up with Brett Jensen and left heartbroken now. I could have avoided it all.

I turned the page to the final few words of the book. A black tail brushed against my leg as Philip sauntered out from behind the desk to greet the person at the door.

I soaked up the last of my favorite story, then set the book down.

Devoid of all hair product and gel, Brett stood in front of my desk with hair hanging in his eyes. I hadn't realized how long it was since he often wore it slicked back or tamed in a businessman style. He looked like the Winter Soldier from the Marvel movies Gideon and

Loxley had forced me to watch. Instead of a shield or weapon, Brett held a ladder under his arm.

The casual black T-shirt fit his arms tightly, and though his jeans were worn, he always looked put together. Half a month had passed since I'd last seen or spoken to him, and now nothing came to mind. I sat speechless across from him.

Tradition held up. He didn't fill the silence, either, and made for the bookshelves. The ladder looked handcrafted, simple but strong, and in the same finish as the shelves in my shop. When he rested it against the shelf, it lined up to the exact height of the top.

"Perfect fit," he said.

Finally, I got myself off the stool and edged around the desk. "Did you make that?"

Brett turned and nodded. "Happy birthday. Uh, belated." He ran his hand through his hair to pull it away from his face. It fell right back to framing his jawline.

"I'm sorry about the election." Why did I say that? Why not simply thank him for the gift? My brain didn't catch up with him here in front of me. Two weeks had felt like months after all the time we'd spent together for the campaign.

He shook his head. "I'm not."

"The ladder is beautiful." I tried to force my feet forward, but I was frozen in place, pinned by his intense gaze.

"I've gotten pretty skilled with woodworking. I figure I can fix up the buildings without being mayor."

I nodded, a simple gesture to hide the millions of thoughts swirling around in my head. What did the gift mean? Was it just an offer of kindness between friends? He hadn't reached out to me, and I left him alone like he'd wanted, so why was he standing in my shop?

"You know what's stupid?" He broke the silence, his fist curling and uncurling at his side.

I only managed a confused look.

"Space," he answered. "Fake dating was a stupid idea, but having space was worse."

I didn't hide parts of myself anymore, so I didn't even try to stop the smile that snuck onto my face. Before I could speak, Brett closed the distance between us and buried his hand in the hair at the back of my head.

I tilted my chin up as he pulled me into him and pressed his lips against mine. Like the ladder to the shelf, the curve of his mouth on mine was the perfect fit, and nothing about the kiss was fake.

BELLA

HALLOWEEN: ONE YEAR LATER

Both cats meowed in unison like a miniature feline choir singing songs of lamentation for the absence of food in their bowls. Philip circled his bowl the way I'd seen dogs do while Beast ran between my legs and left orange hairs across my black tights. If I didn't know any better, I'd think they conspired to bring me to my demise with Beast tripping me after Philip's circles made me dizzy.

I dumped kibble in their separate bowls, but Beast could not be tamed. He followed at my heels as I headed for the front door to turn the Open sign to Closed.

Beast's desperate, frustrated meows were endless.

"I'm sad, too." I sighed and stooped to scratch behind his ears. "I don't know why Brett's been MIA lately or why he dumped you off here." I lowered my voice to a whisper. "And I'm sorry Philip doesn't share his beds."

After almost a year of real dating, Brett and I spent all our free time together, but that'd faded lately. He'd become secretive and distant and too busy, even on the weekends.

But Brett was nothing if not honest so I didn't let my imagination wander into Worry World or What If Land.

Beast trotted away, satisfied with the scratches, and returned to his food bowl. This time, I followed him to grab my phone off the desk and double-check the time Brett asked me to meet him at the Manor before my birthday dinner. It was weird he didn't want to pick me up at the shop as usual, but I tried not to overthink it.

When I swiped the text app closed, the picture of us in Paris came up. The memory filled me with warmth and love for him all over again. On a tour of the Opera Garnier, Brett told me he loved me for the first time, and it was a thousand times better than a fake confession for a curse that'd changed over time.

I clicked off my phone and headed upstairs to give myself enough time to get ready and in my new dress before our date. I'd taken to sewing again when I was in a reading slump. Brett even shared a corner of his workshop with my sewing supplies, and I crafted while he worked on shelves, window frames, and other items people in town ordered from him to update their old homes. Though, the frequency of that had waned lately and he rarely invited me over.

I pulled on my favorite design, a recreation of Anna Karenina's dress as described by Leo Tolstoy. It was too much for Fryer Tuck's, but Brett promised we'd have my favorite food for dinner, so it had to be the black bean burger from the diner in town.

The dress barely fit into my car as I squished into the front seat and drove to the manor. When I pulled into the driveway, I was disappointed to see Brett still hadn't gotten to repairing the stained-glass window.

I hiked up the skirt to keep it from picking up dirt and headed for the steps. The sun had already set, and nobody would notice a thin line of dust on the dress in the dark, but I'd know it was there.

When I knocked on the door, Brett didn't answer. I twisted the knob to find it unlocked.

"Hello?" I poked my head in.

The entry was shadowed in darkness. The door creaked as I pushed it open. Once inside, the flicker of a faint glow caught my eye in front of the ballroom.

I followed the source of the light to find the candelabra from the cellar on the floor outside the door.

"Brett?" I opened the door.

Hundreds of candles filled a room I didn't recognize. Where there was once open space for dancing and smooth wooden floor was a huge shaggy rug with two leather chairs. Tall bookshelves encircled the room, covering every inch of the walls. Even the window was framed by shelves full of old books.

A gasp died in my throat as awe and excitement and a million questions flooded me. I couldn't speak. Brett stood from his place in one of the chairs and met me at the threshold. He pulled me further into the room.

"I know I've been busy lately." He scrubbed the back of his neck the way he used to when he was nervous. "It was hard hiding this from you. Oh, did you see the copy of *Othello*? Top shelf." He pointed at the shelves by the window. "And the ladders slide so you never have to worry about them tipping over. Not that you're clumsy."

His rambling hinted at a change. Brett didn't overtalk unless nerves pushed him into it.

"And here's the best part." He laced his fingers between mine and gently pulled me to the far corner. "This is the romance section, the whole wall."

My gaze followed where he pointed to a copy of the fantasy romance with the dagger and whip on the cover. Since it was on the highest shelf, I had to tilt my head back. I stepped on the first rung of the ladder to see what else he'd filled the shelves with, but a noise stopped me.

Brett cleared his throat, and I looked down to see him on one knee in front of me. My heart skipped a beat, and my hands flew to my mouth. A tiny black box was perched in his palm with a silver ring that had a snake on top. A ruby sparkled as the snake's eye, and I bubbled something between a laugh and a sob at the callback to Brett's prank that I'd loved. Before he asked the question, I knew my answer.

"I love you, Bella Villenueve. Will you marry me?"

THANK YOU FOR READING!

PLEASE CONSIDER LEAVING A REVIEW AT YOUR FAVORITE PLACE TO PURCHASE BOOKS IF YOU ENJOYED THIS STORY! ALSO, A SHARE WITH YOUR FRIENDS WHO LOVE CLEAN, SWEET, SMALL-TOWN ROMANCES WOULD BE GREATLY APPRECIATED. MY QUEST AS AN AUTHOR IS TO MAKE OTHERS FEEL SEEN THROUGH THE ADVENTURE OF FICTION. PLEASE REACH OUT TO ME AND LET ME KNOW IF MY STORIES HAVE TOUCHED YOU. YOU, DEAR READER, ARE WHO THIS BOOK WAS WRITTEN FOR.

I CAN'T WAIT TO SHARE ANOTHER ESCAPE INTO THE IDYLLIC TOWN OF FOLKLORE FALLS WITH YOU! JOIN ME IN CELEBRATING THE HAPPILY EVER AFTER RETELLING OF A CERTAIN HEADLESS HORSEMAN IN A SLEEPY HOLLOW.

RELEASE DATE TO BE DETERMINED, STAY TUNED!

About the Author

Congenital Heart Defect survivor, Emily Fluke, finds joy and peace through the expression of writing. She is a firm believer that all stories need a little magic and a lot of excitement. Emily and her husband spend their free time wrangling two children and playing video games in their busy California lifestyle. Otherwise, you'll find Emily solving an escape room, running, or writing Magic the Gathering-based poetry.

To stay up to date on new releases and connect with me, visit my website at Emilyfluke.com or follow me on social media under Author Emily Fluke, or @emilyflukefairytales